ELIZABETH HEITER

ISBN-13: 978-0-7783-1738-8

Vanished

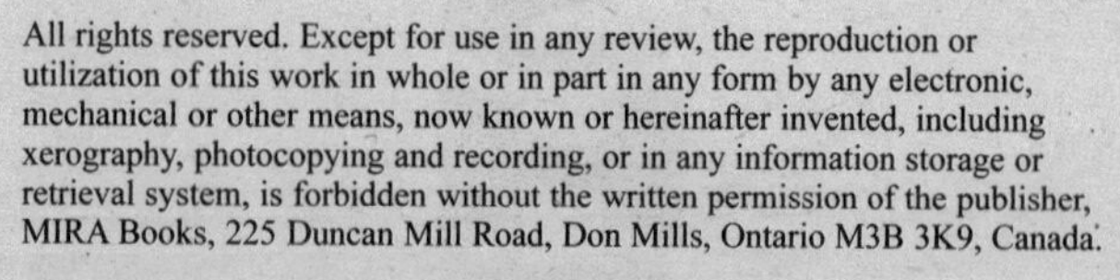

For questions and comments about the quality of this book, please contact us at CustomerService@Harlequin.com.

www.MIRABooks.com

Printed in U.S.A.

Praise for Elizabeth Heiter's *Hunted*

"This is a really excellent thriller—fast-paced and exciting, with a memorable cast of characters. Well done!"
—*New York Times* bestselling author Suzanne Brockmann

"*Hunted* is a terrific, gripping, page-turning debut by a talented new voice in suspense. A great read!"
—*New York Times* bestselling author Allison Brennan

"When you pick up *Hunted*, get ready for a roller coaster ride that will twist, turn and spin you around until the very last page! I loved this book! Evelyn Baine is one of the most amazing characters created in print that I've ever had the pleasure to get to know.... If you love a book that grabs you by the throat and holds you there until the very end of a breathless journey, *Hunted* must be added to your wish list of books."
—*Fresh Fiction*

"Elizabeth Heiter has written a thriller that grabs readers from the first page.... *Hunted* is a fast read because the pages fly by as the narrative gets more and more exciting and suspenseful. For a debut, Heiter has hit a high note right at the start of her writing career."
—*BookReporter*

"Heiter...provides a fascinating insight into the minds of killers.... Author Heiter has created well-developed characters and a gripping story. I look forward to reading what happens next in The Profiler series."
—*Suspense Magazine*

"Heiter's *Hunted* is intriguing and tightly plotted. A strong debut!"
—*New York Times* bestselling author Laura Griffin

"A gripping, powerful read.... I love psychological suspense. Unlike many books where I can pick out the guilty party, this book is set up so that there is no possible way. I loved that! I learned things as Evelyn did, which is a real treat in a suspense or mystery novel. From start to finish, I was on the edge of my seat."
—*Roundtable Reviews*

Also by Elizabeth Heiter

HUNTED

Look for Elizabeth Heiter's next novel
in **The Profiler** series,
available soon from MIRA Books

This book is dedicated to the memory
of my grandparents. Thank you for always believing.

I love you. I miss you.

Dear Reader,

Thank you for taking this journey to Evelyn's hometown as she digs into the case that has haunted her since she was twelve years old. If you haven't had the chance to read it, Evelyn's story began in *Hunted*. In that first book in The Profiler series she learns a key piece of information about Cassie's disappearance that her grandparents had hidden from her for seventeen years.

As much as *Vanished* is Evelyn's story, it's also Cassie's. I loved creating Evelyn's strong, brave, outgoing best friend, who shaped her life so much. I also wanted to address the topic of child abduction. With all cases, those first hours are crucial, and the FBI (as well as organizations like the NCMEC) bring a lot of specialized resources to the search. I hope *Vanished* provides a small glimpse into the world of these dedicated professionals.

In February, I hope you'll look for *Disarming Detective*. It's the first book in The Lawmen, my new romantic suspense series with Harlequin Intrigue. It follows three friends who made a pact ten years ago to join the FBI and what happens when the case that brought them there returns. After *Disarming Detective*, *Seduced by the Sniper* releases in March and *SWAT Secret Admirer* comes out in April.

Then, later in 2015, watch for Evelyn to return! She'll be handling what looks like a routine investigation—until it lands her on the wrong side of a hostage situation and in the middle of an emerging terrorist threat.

If you'd like more information about upcoming releases, events and extras, please visit me at www.elizabethheiter.com. (You can also sign up for my newsletter for release reminders.)

A heartfelt thank-you for reading *Vanished*—I hope you enjoy it!

Elizabeth Heiter

VANISHED

Prologue

The girls raced through the backyard, holding hands and giggling, oblivious to any danger. They kept running, faster and faster, until they reached the far end of the property. It was a solid two hundred feet from the house. Too far for anyone inside to see them.

Anger burned, intense enough to light sparks of pain along his nerve endings. If he wasn't here, anything could happen to them.

He hunkered deeper in his dugout in a clump of huge, blooming lilac bushes, drew a deep breath of South Carolina's humid summer air and waited. Watched.

He'd been watching for weeks, so he knew exactly how much time he had before they'd be called inside for dinner.

It was the little blonde girl's yard. Cassie. He'd noticed her first, the bouncing ringlets, eyes the color of the sky on a perfect summer day. She was too innocent, too trusting. Cassie had no clue what the world had in store for her.

He never wanted her to have to find out. He'd picked her before he'd seen her friend.

Cassie's friend was different. Small for twelve, skin the shade of coffee with a generous helping of cream and moss-green eyes that were way too perceptive, way too wary. Evelyn.

Evelyn wasn't the kind of girl he'd been searching for, but considering how everyone treated her, she'd be better off with him. Which was why he was watching them both, why he was still trying to decide which one to save. They both needed him. But which one *could* he save? Which one?

Pain punched up his back, vertebra by vertebra, until it ricocheted around in his head. Another migraine. Probably the stress of having to choose.

He didn't want to leave either one behind. But he had no choice. He was already taking a big risk by doing this in Rose Bay. He'd never dared to scout so close to home before.

Cassie laughed, the sound loud and ringing. The vibrations seemed to skim along his skin, even though she was twenty feet away.

"Let's play hide-and-seek," Cassie said, closing her eyes and counting.

Evelyn pivoted too fast and let out a yelp as she almost pitched herself onto the dirt. He thought she was going to dash past him, but she stopped, running tiny hands over the purple flowers, as though testing whether she could crawl inside and hide there.

You can, he wanted to whisper.

She leaned closer, peering through the branches, and he hunched lower in his hiding spot. She tilted her head and he tensed, ready to grab her if she spotted him.

"Girls!" Cassie's mother called. "Lemonade's ready!"

Evelyn turned away from him, waiting for Cassie to

race over before the two of them hurried back to the house, hand in hand.

Once they were out of sight, he left the bushes, the scent of lilac clinging. He wove through the hundred-year-old live oaks at the back of the property and out to the street behind, where his van waited. The migraine receded as peace swelled inside him. He'd made his decision.

He'd take this same route late tonight, when the whole town was sleeping, careless with their children, ignorant of what could happen in one unguarded moment. After tonight, none of them would be so neglectful again.

Because tonight, everything was going to change. Maybe he only needed one of them, but he couldn't leave either behind. Tonight, they were both coming with him.

One

Eighteen years later

Evelyn Baine knew how to think like a killer.

In fact, she was damn good at it. Serial killers, arsonists, bomb-makers, child abductors, terrorists—she'd crawled around in all of their twisted minds. She'd learned their fantasies, figured out their next moves and chased them down.

But no matter how many she found, there were always more.

Even before she stepped inside the unmarked building in Aquia, Virginia, where the FBI hid its Behavioral Analysis Unit, Evelyn knew the requests for profiles on her desk had grown overnight. It was inevitable.

She strode through the entrance and a blast of air-conditioning chased away the mid-June heat, raising goose bumps on her arms. As she headed toward the drab gray bull pen packed with cubicles, the scent of old coffee filled her nostrils. The whiteboard near the front of the bull pen was covered in her boss's distinctive scrawl—notes on a case. They hadn't been there when she'd left last night.

The handful of criminal investigative analysts who'd arrived before her—or hadn't gone home—gazed at her with bloodshot eyes and quizzical expressions. But it had been a full two weeks since she'd been cleared to come back to work. A full two weeks for them to get used to her *not* being the first agent through the door in the morning and the last to leave at night.

A full two weeks for her to get used to it, too. But it still felt unnatural.

Slipping into the comfort of her cubicle, she set her briefcase on the floor, hung her suit jacket over the back of her chair and slid her SIG Sauer P228 off her hip and into a drawer. Then she looked at the case files stacked on her desk. Yep, the pile had definitely grown. And the message light on her phone blinked frantically.

Guilt swirled through her, rising up like a sandstorm. If she'd stayed an extra few hours yesterday evening, an extra few hours the evening before, she might've gotten through another couple of files. But she knew from a year of ten-hour days, seven days a week, that cloistering herself in her cubicle wouldn't stop the cases from coming.

It would only stop her from having a life outside the office. And after she'd almost been killed by the serial killer she'd been profiling a month ago, that had become important.

So, she shoved the guilt back, dropped into her chair and dialed her voice mail. There were three requests for follow-up on cases she'd profiled, a pretty typical way to start her morning. She jotted them down and kept going.

The next call was from the FBI's Employee Assistance Program, reminding her that the Bureau had psychologists she could talk to about the case that had nearly killed her, and had claimed another agent's life. Evelyn ground her teeth and deleted it. She had her own psychology degree, and her professional opinion was that she was doing just fine. She was about to hang up when she realized there was one more message.

"I'm looking for Evelyn Baine." The voice was vaguely familiar and every word vibrated with tension. "The Evelyn Baine from Rose Bay. This is Julie Byers. Cassie's mom."

Whatever she said next was drowned out under a sudden ringing in Evelyn's ears, under a bittersweet flood of memories. Cassie, the little girl next door who'd come over the day Evelyn had moved in with her grandparents and announced they were going to be best friends. The girl who hadn't given a damn that Evelyn was the only person in town—including Evelyn's grandparents—who wasn't white, at least not entirely white. And eighteen years ago, in Rose Bay, that had mattered.

Cassie had been Evelyn's first real friend, a symbol of everything that was supposed to change in her life when she came to stay with her grandparents.

For two years, she and Cassie had been inseparable. And then one night, Cassie had disappeared from her bed. In her place, her abductor had left his calling card, a macabre nursery rhyme.

Cassie had never come home. Julie Byers calling now, eighteen years later, could only mean one thing. They'd found her.

Pressure tightened around her heart. Evelyn had worked enough child abduction cases in her year at BAU to know the statistics. After eighteen years, Cassie wasn't going to be found alive. But she didn't want to snuff out the flicker of hope that just wouldn't die.

With unsteady hands, Evelyn called her voice mail again and skipped through to the last message, to hear what she knew Julie Byers was going to say. Cassie was dead.

She clutched her hands tightly together as the message replayed. "I'm looking for Evelyn Baine. The Evelyn Baine from Rose Bay. This is Julie Byers. Cassie's mom."

In the pause that followed, tears clouded her vision. Her whole body tensed as she waited for Julie Byers to destroy the dream she'd had for eighteen years. The dream of one day seeing Cassie again.

"Please call me, Evelyn."

Her body deflated and she dropped her head to the desk.

"Evelyn?"

Willing her pain not to show on her face, she turned around. "Greg," she croaked.

Greg Ibsen was the closest thing she had to a partner at BAU. Even if she'd sounded normal, he was the only one in the office who might have seen through it. As he stepped into her cubicle, worry brimmed in his soft brown eyes.

"What happened? Are you okay?"

She stared up at him, trying to get control of herself. But her eyes kept losing focus, and her heart still tripped erratically.

"Come on." Greg set his briefcase next to hers and took her arm, pulling her out of her seat.

"Hang on," she croaked, jotting down the number from her voice mail.

She spun back, her eyes on the loud plaid tie someone—probably his daughter, Lucy—had paired with his somber blue suit. Then Greg was propelling her into an empty interagency coordination room.

He guided her into a chair, then shut the door and leaned against it. "What's wrong?"

Everything was wrong. She'd joined the FBI, joined BAU, to find Cassie, but she'd never told anyone at the Bureau about her past. Except Kyle McKenzie.

Kyle was an operator with the FBI's Hostage Rescue Team. Since HRT and BAU worked closely together, she'd met him the day she joined BAU. And for a whole year, she'd managed to resist his incessant flirting, assuming it was all a joke. Until last month.

Last month, she'd acted on the attraction. And everything between them had changed. Despite the fact that he'd been called away on a case too soon for them to figure out where their relationship was going, she wished he was here. Wished she could lean into his strong arms while she called Cassie's mom.

But Kyle wasn't here. He was somewhere not far from where she'd grown up, on a mission she didn't "need to know" anything about. And the nature of his job meant she had no idea when he'd be back.

Greg had trained her and he'd become a good friend. Hell, he was her emergency contact, because she didn't have any real family left except her grandma, and these days, Evelyn took care of her.

A month ago, Evelyn would have pretended to be fine. She would have brushed off Greg's concern and gone back to work. But she was trying to make a change in her life. So, she told him, "When I was twelve, my best friend, Cassie, disappeared. She was never found." It had been the driving force in her life for eighteen years, the one thing she'd been willing to sacrifice everything else for. "And now..."

She squeezed her eyes shut. She'd always wanted closure, always needed to know what had happened. But if Cassie was dead, she suddenly, desperately, wanted to stay ignorant.

Greg's hand rested on her arm, and when she opened her eyes he was kneeling next to her, his gaze steady and compassionate. The gaze of someone who'd sat beside too many victims and always known the right thing to say.

And maybe, more than anyone, he'd know what she should do now. He was practiced at comforting survivors—his son, Josh, had watched his birth father kill his mother before Josh had been adopted by Greg and his wife.

"Cassie's mom wants me to call her." The next words didn't want to come, but she forced them out. "It must be because they finally found her body." Saying it out loud felt like ripping a bandage from a wound it had covered so long it had grown into the skin.

Sorrow folded into the creases beside Greg's fawn-colored eyes. "I'm so sorry, Evelyn." He squeezed her hand, those gentle eyes searching hers. "Eighteen years is a long time. Too long for there to be any good outcome."

He was right, of course. If Cassie *had* still been alive, what hell might she have endured for the past eighteen years?

A rush of images stampeded through her head from a child abduction case she'd profiled in her first month at BAU. She'd gone to the scene to advise HRT when they went into the suspect's house. She'd watched Kyle kick the door in. She could still smell the cordite from the flash-bang, still feel the tension, the restrained hope that maybe, just maybe, they'd find the boy alive.

She'd waited and waited until finally they'd come out. First, two HRT agents leading the suspect, naked, handcuffed and swearing. Then Kyle carrying the boy, miraculously still breathing. Someone had wrapped an FBI jacket around his violated body, but the anguish in his eyes—seven hundred days past terror—had burrowed deep into her soul and she'd known. He hadn't really come out alive.

Greg's voice brought her back to the present. "You were too young to have saved Cassie, Evelyn. But she brought you to us. And to all the victims you *did* bring home."

"I don't want to hear there's no more hope," she admitted.

"I know."

Greg didn't let go of her hand as she pulled out her phone and stared at it, not wanting to dial.

"You need to get it over with. It's not going to get any easier, and waiting won't change anything. You can do this."

Evelyn nodded, tried to prepare herself. She dialed the number fast, before she could change her mind. Some cowardly part of her hoped Julie wouldn't pick up, but before the first ring ended, she did.

"Mrs. Byers? It's Evelyn Baine." Her voice sounded strange, too high-pitched and winded, as if she'd just run the Marine training course over at Quantico.

"Evelyn." Julie's voice betrayed that she'd been crying.

Dread intensified, and slivers of ice raced along Evelyn's spine.

"I'm so glad I found you." Julie's voice evened out. "I heard you joined the FBI."

She had? Evelyn had left Rose Bay at seventeen, after her grandma had gotten sick and her mom had suddenly shown up again. She'd never gone back and she hadn't talked to anyone from Rose Bay in more than a decade.

"Yes," Evelyn managed. *Get on with it,* she wanted to say. *Just tell me Cassie's dead.*

A sob welled up in her throat and Evelyn clamped her jaw tight, holding it back.

"You probably figured after all this time I'd only be calling… Well, it's about Cassie."

Evelyn's fingers started to tingle and she realized she'd squeezed Greg's hand so tight both of their knuckles had gone bloodless. But she couldn't seem to loosen her grip.

"You found her?"

"No. But the person who took Cassie is back."

Two

The Nursery Rhyme Killer was back.

The words repeated themselves in her head the way gunfire echoed after the shooting stopped, but she couldn't make sense of them. Eighteen years of silence and then another abduction? It wasn't completely unprecedented, but it was really rare.

Eighteen years ago, before kidnapping Cassie, her abductor had taken two other girls, from two other communities in South Carolina. No bodies had ever been found, but the press had called their abductor the Nursery Rhyme Killer.

After Cassie went missing, all of Rose Bay had been terrified, expecting him to strike again. But he never did. The trail had been cold ever since.

And Evelyn had waited eighteen years for the chance to investigate. Determination put speed in her steps as she strode through the bull pen toward her boss's office.

"Attitude incoming," Kendall White singsonged as she marched past his cubicle. "I knew that laid-back thing you had going for the past two weeks was just a ruse," he called after her.

She ignored him, but something uncomfortable wormed around in her gut. In her year at BAU, her work ethic had been intense and nonstop. The past two weeks had probably seemed like an anomaly to her colleagues, but she'd intended to make a real change.

It wasn't going to happen now. Not with the Nursery Rhyme Killer grabbing new victims. She pushed open her boss's door without knocking. "Dan, I need to go to Rose Bay, South Carolina."

Dan Moore, the assistant special agent in charge who ran BAU, lifted his frustrated gaze to hers and sighed. "Damn it." Then he said into the phone at his ear, "I think I know who has it. I'm going to have to call you back."

He hung up the phone and then barked, "Shut the door."

Shit. She should have knocked. But Dan wasn't exactly her biggest fan on the best day, so she tried not to let his reaction worry her.

When she'd closed the door and turned back to him, Dan said, "That was Chief Lamar from Rose Bay."

Relief swept through her. If Rose Bay was formally requesting a profiler, it would be a lot easier to get herself assigned. "I already know the case. I—"

"Because you requested the case file under false pretenses?" Dan interrupted, his cheeks darkening to an angry, mottled red. "Chief Lamar was calling to find out if the FBI had come up with anything on the abductor since we'd asked for a copy of the file a month ago. I was in the process of telling him we'd never requested that file when you barged in."

He slapped the desk hard, making her jerk backward. "What the hell are you doing, Evelyn? Assigning yourself cases without the Bureau's knowledge or approval? Are you *trying* to get yourself investigated by OPR again?"

Evelyn stood a little straighter and prepared for a fight. The Office of Professional Responsibility hadn't really investigated her, but they *had* reviewed the case she'd profiled last month that had cost another agent his life and almost took hers, too. She'd never been in trouble before that case. It hadn't occurred to her that requesting Cassie's case file could put a stain on her FBI personnel file.

When her grandma had let slip after seventeen years of silence that the note left by Cassie's abductor had said he'd taken her, too, she'd needed to know. And the case file had told her it hadn't been her grandma's dementia talking.

Eighteen years ago, she'd somehow escaped dying alongside Cassie.

Evelyn reached a hand up to smooth hair she knew was tucked neatly into its usual bun. "I had to find out what really happened. This is why I joined the Bureau in the first place."

Dan rubbed his hands over his temples, sending the hair on the sides of his head—the only place it grew—shooting outward. "This is *that* case?"

He hadn't realized? She knew he was aware of her past. Having been best friends with a kidnap victim and being so intensely invested in the case had almost prevented her from being accepted into BAU. But apparently Dan either hadn't looked into the case too closely or had forgotten the details. He'd been a lawyer before joining the Bureau, and since he could easily spout court case details from thirty years ago, she suspected it was the former.

She'd nearly lost a spot in BAU and Dan hadn't even known the facts of the case. She pushed her annoyance aside. It didn't matter now.

"Yes, this is the same case. If the perp is back, I'm in the best position to profile him. I know the case and I know the people involved."

Dan shook his head. "Or you're the worst possible choice, because you're too personally involved to be objective."

"I'm the only one who can—"

"A CARD team is there now," Dan interrupted, his tone hard and final.

The FBI had Child Abduction Rapid Deployment teams throughout the country that could respond quickly to child abduction cases and bring specialized resources. Usually a BAU agent coordinated with the team, either from Aquia or, more often, on-site.

Evelyn tried to put on her most professional voice, but it vibrated with emotion she couldn't hide. "We don't have one of our agents on-site yet?"

Dan's jaw jutted out and she sensed that he was debating whether or not to share something. Finally he said, "Vince is in Florida. He was supposed to be on his way, but his current case just had a major turn."

Before Dan could tell her who he planned to send instead, Evelyn interrupted. "I'm already up to speed. I can leave now."

Dan made a noise that might have been laughter, except instead of amusement it was filled with frustration. "I have to choose the agent best suited for the case, Evelyn. And we have agents who've worked many, many more child abductions than you. Agents without a conflict of interest."

Evelyn stepped closer, rested her palms on Dan's desk. She had to convince him. Nothing was keeping her off this case. "There is no one—*no one*—who cares about this more than I do. Okay, you're right. It *is* a conflict of interest. But maybe that's *exactly* what will solve this case after eighteen years."

She stared at him, unblinking, certain the passion in her tone and the truth in her argument would convince him.

But he frowned, emphasizing the deep lines bracketing his mouth as he reached into his desk drawer and popped a handful of antacids into his mouth. "Evelyn, I'm sorry. I can't assign you."

"I'm going, anyway." The words burst from her mouth without thought, then her heart started pounding a rapid, almost painful tempo. Her job was everything to her.

Dan's lips compressed into a thin line that hooked up at the corners with disapproval. When he spoke, his voice was quietly intense. "You're willing to throw away your career for this? Because if I don't send you and you go, anyway, any OPR investigation will be for show. You'll be out of the Bureau."

Pain pierced her eyes. She'd given up everything to be in the Bureau. But she'd joined for Cassie.

"I have to." Her voice quavered, but she pressed on. "Whatever the consequences, I can't turn my back on this. She was my closest friend." Evelyn clenched her fists. "I have to do this for her."

Dan jolted to his feet, his face a mask of fury. "You are the biggest pain in the ass I have ever supervised."

"What?" Hope pushed through her dread.

"If you fuck this up, do you know how much heat *I'll* be in for sending you? Damn it, Evelyn! You're a good profiler. I don't want to lose you. And I don't appreciate being put in this position."

He didn't give her a chance to respond, just pointed at the door. "Get the paperwork in order now. And when this case is over and you come back here, you are going to be the most obedient employee in the whole damn office—do you understand me?"

"Yes," she choked out, suddenly wanting to run around the desk and hug Dan. Instead, she croaked, "Thank you," and hurried out the door.

After thirteen years, she was finally going home to Rose Bay. And this time, she wasn't leaving without knowing what had happened to Cassie.

"You've got to send her home."

Police chief Tomas Lamar looked up from the information about the Nursery Rhyme Killer covering his desk. "What?"

Jack Bullock, longtime police officer, son of the previous police chief of Rose Bay and general pain in Tomas's ass, stood in the doorway of his office. Jack was scowling as he let the chaotic noise of the station blast in.

"Evelyn Baine," Jack snapped, a tic quivering near his eye and a vein throbbing on his forehead.

Tomas jerked to his feet. "The FBI profiler is here?"

"You've got to be kidding me." Jack gaped at him. "You don't know who she is?"

It figured Jack would have some kind of problem with the profiler. The head of the FBI's Behavioral Analysis Unit had told Tomas that Evelyn was originally from Rose Bay, but he'd gotten the impression she'd left town at seventeen.

"What now, Jack?"

"Wow. Really? Did you even read the case file?" Jack made an ugly sound through his nose. "She was named in one of the damn notes!"

Tomas leveled a warning look at him. "Lose the attitude." Then he frowned. Jack had a decade less experience than he did but knew the town better. And Jack had been a rookie during the original investigation eighteen years ago. "What are you talking about?"

Jack's nostrils flared as he made an obvious attempt to rein in his temper. "Evelyn Baine. She was best friends with Cassie Byers. The note said the perp had also taken Evelyn. We don't know why he didn't, but Evelyn is way too connected to this case. She shouldn't be here."

Frustration bubbled up, amplifying nerves already frayed to the breaking point. As if he didn't have enough problems. A police force he'd inherited from Jack's father, too many of whom distrusted him because of the color of his skin or where he'd grown up. A child abductor hunting for victims. And a terrified town looking to him to stop a predator who'd gotten away with it for eighteen years. "Damn it."

Jack nodded, the vein in his forehead disappearing. "You're going to send her home, right? We have plenty of FBI crawling around. We don't need an intended victim mucking around in the investigation."

Tomas's shoulders slumped. He'd spent nineteen hours at the station, running on adrenaline and caffeine, but he suddenly felt bone tired. "Tell her to come in."

"Chief…"

"Just tell her to get in here, Jack."

Resentment sizzling in his eyes, Jack nodded curtly and left the office.

When the door opened again, Tomas wasn't sure who

was more shocked, him or the woman standing there in her prim, boxy suit and tidy bun.

Her surprise must've been because the top law enforcement official was black in a town she would've remembered as almost entirely white and intent on keeping it that way.

His was because when Jack said she'd been an intended victim, he'd assumed she was white. And she was. Partly. But she was partly black, too.

When he was a boy, Rose Bay had been a town stuck in the past. North of Hilton Head and south of Charleston, nestled in a small bay, it was mostly old money. The town had relegated its poor and unwanted to the outskirts of town, near the marsh. Rose Bay had been almost totally segregated.

Tomas had spent his childhood in the marshes, but he'd been long gone by the time the Nursery Rhyme Killer struck. Still, he knew attitudes hadn't been vastly different then.

He studied Evelyn curiously, her light brown skin so different from that of the girls in the pictures he'd spent the past few hours reviewing. All the Nursery Rhyme Killer's victims had been white. But if Evelyn had been an intended victim…

Dread rushed over him like a tidal wave. He'd already drilled it into each of his three boys that his youngest—his only daughter, who was in the age range of the perp's victims—wasn't to go anywhere alone. As soon as he talked to the profiler, he was calling home to make certain they were following orders.

Shaking himself out of his stupor, Tomas held out a hand. "Agent Baine. I'm Police Chief Tomas Lamar. Thanks for coming."

She put a tiny hand in his and he shook it briefly, carefully. "When I spoke with Dan Moore, he didn't discuss your personal connection to the case."

Evelyn dropped the FBI blue duffel bag that was about as big as she was from her shoulder to the ground. Then she placed her briefcase on the floor, settling back in her seat and unbuttoning her suit jacket, which made the gun on her hip visible.

He didn't need to be a profiler to read *that* move. She was telling him she wasn't leaving, no matter what he thought of her personal connection. "Relax, Agent Baine. I'm not thrilled that I had to find out from my officers, but I'll take all the help I can get. And I'll assume the fact that you requested this case file a month ago means you're committed to it and you're going to help us nail this son of a bitch."

Her shoulders relaxed a fraction of an inch and so did the tight line of her mouth. But the intensity in her eyes didn't diminish as she said, "He's not getting away with it this time."

He hoped to God she was right. Brittany Douglas had been missing for thirteen hours. And to his mind, catching the Nursery Rhyme Killer wasn't a success unless they could also bring Brittany home alive.

He sank into his seat, couldn't keep his shoulders from slumping as he took a gulp of coffee that had gone cold an hour ago. "Give it to me straight, Agent Baine. Are we already too late?"

She leaned forward and locked sea-green eyes on him. "I can't tell you that. Not yet, not even when I've reviewed the case—not with one hundred percent certainty. Which is what you'd need in order to call off all the searchers I saw when I arrived. But I do have to see

Brittany's file. Everything you've got. And the ones from eighteen years ago, as well. Then I'll give you a profile of who you're looking for. Sometimes, if you can't trace the victim's movements, you get inside the abductor's head. Because if you can find *him*, you'll find Brittany."

Tomas nodded quickly, the sliver of hope that had refused to vanish even as the hours ticked by beginning to grow again. "I talked to the Child Abduction Rapid Deployment team the FBI sent. They said they knew you were coming." The FBI's CARD team had shown up fast, set up a command post in his conference room at the back of the station and gotten to work immediately. But so far, they still didn't know where Brittany was. Maybe a profiler would change that.

"The CARD team has a desk for you in their command post. They have everything you need. But let me give you the basics right now."

"Great." She pulled out a pen and notepad.

"Brittany Douglas disappeared last night from her front yard. Her mother was inside when it happened. She didn't see the abduction, but she said she'd been checking out the window periodically, so there's a pretty small time span when he must've grabbed her. Around 9:30 p.m., Brittany hadn't come in yet, so her mom went outside—and found a nursery rhyme." As soon as they'd seen it, all the veteran cops on the force had gone pale.

"Just a nursery rhyme?" Evelyn's voice was steady, but the tension in her body betrayed her.

The media had gotten hold of the fact that the abductor left nursery rhymes at the abduction scenes eighteen years ago—that was how he'd gotten his moniker. But what the media didn't know was how the Nursery Rhyme

Killer had changed the rhymes. "A twisted version of a nursery rhyme."

Evelyn released a loud breath. "Just like before."

"It's the same person from eighteen years ago, isn't it?"

"I don't know yet. I need to study all the notes first. I've read part of the original case file, but to be honest with you, I haven't read the whole thing." She looked at her lap, obviously struggling with something, then finally added, "I only read the note they found at Cassie's house."

The note that had mentioned her. Tomas didn't like it, but he understood. "Okay. So, now you can read them all. And after you go through the files, you'll be able to tell me if this is a copycat?"

Please, please, let it be a copycat, Tomas silently prayed. Having a child abduction was bad enough. But the Nursery Rhyme Killer hadn't left a single piece of useful forensic evidence eighteen years ago. Tomas had reviewed the old file enough to know they'd never caught one promising lead on the perp. He'd been like a ghost.

If he was back, Tomas was terrified this time wouldn't be any different. No matter how many FBI agents with their databases and manpower and specialized experience showed up in Rose Bay.

"Yes," Evelyn promised. "Give me a couple of hours and I should be able to tell you if it's the same person."

A few more hours. The weight pressing on Tomas's chest seemed to double. It made him wish he hadn't asked the lead agent from the FBI CARD team earlier in the day what Brittany's odds were. Made him wish she hadn't told him that most abducted children who were later found dead had been killed in the first three hours.

Were they already too late?

* * *

The FBI CARD team's command post at the back of the station was the size of Evelyn's study. Tables had been crammed into the room and covered in laptops, files and photographs. Briefcases and FBI duffel bags were shoved under tables and littered the small aisles. There was even a bloodhound asleep in the corner—from the FBI's Forensic Canine Unit, Evelyn assumed.

At one point, the room must have been crowded with agents and officers, but now it was mostly abandoned. Only one agent remained, trying to ignore the frantic buzz from the front of the station. She spun her chair around and jumped up as Evelyn stepped into the room. Everything from the lines on her forehead to her no-nonsense stride as she met Evelyn in the center of the room, hand already out, screamed *in charge*.

Evelyn put her hand in the agent's, who shook it vigorously, her mass of curls bouncing in a high ponytail. Words burst from her mouth in an overcaffeinated frenzy. "I'm Carly Sanchez, the lead agent here. We got the call about ten hours ago and we've been on-site for seven."

"I'm Evelyn Baine. Tomas told you I was on my way?"

"Yep. We'll need the help."

"How far have you gotten?" Evelyn asked, feeling overheated in the tiny room. Despite the air-conditioning pumping through the vents on the ceiling, between the South Carolina early-summer heat and the number of computers running, the room was stifling.

"We've taken statements from the parents. Gotten our basics on Brittany's routine, possible grudges against the family, that kind of thing. Most of my team's out canvassing and conducting interviews. We'll reconvene here as soon as you're ready to present your profile."

"Okay."

"In the corner there is Cody." She pointed to the bloodhound. "He arrived just before you. His handler will be back in a minute and they'll be heading over to Brittany Douglas's house. They're from the Human Scent Team."

Well, Evelyn would hope so, since the other Canine Unit was for victim recovery and trained to scent on human decomposition. "Any promising leads?" Evelyn shifted her heavy bag on her shoulder as she looked up at Carly, who had a solid eight inches on her own five foot two.

Carly's lips twisted and Evelyn read frustration there, but not defeat. There were ten Bureau CARD teams, spread across the country, ready to leave at a moment's notice to assist local law enforcement whenever a child went missing. If it was a parental abduction, chances of recovering the child were good. But for nonparental abductions, the statistics were a lot grimmer. Anyone who chose to work on a CARD team had to be either unrealistically optimistic or impossibly hardened.

Probably the same could be said about BAU. And Evelyn knew on which end of the spectrum she fell.

"We don't have much," Carly answered. "Brittany lived on High Street. You remember it?"

Evelyn nodded. It was a few blocks over from where she'd lived with her grandparents from the time she was ten until she was seventeen. If it was like it had been thirteen years ago, the houses were big and far apart, neighbors were cordial but not close, and landscaping was designed for privacy.

"Then it probably won't surprise you that we had no witnesses. I've got a team of seven here and they're all paired up with officers. One of my agents is running down the nearby sex offenders and five are conducting interviews with neighbors. We're hoping to get lucky on a vehicle description, but so far, nothing."

"What about forensics?"

Carly shrugged, shoving back the sleeves on her pin-striped blazer. "Unlikely. The note was taped to Brittany's bike, and we dusted it, but we only got Brittany's mom's prints on the note. We're running the prints from the bike, but I doubt we'll get a hit."

Evelyn tried not to feel disappointed. She'd expected that. She'd been too young eighteen years ago to be told much about the investigation, but she'd understood what was going on from her grandparents' expressions. Evidence had been slim. And as the days turned into years, hope had become even slimmer.

She vowed that this time would be different. "Where's my spot?" She raised her voice to be heard over the chatter that had picked up in volume at the front of the station. When a child went missing, people often assumed that a police station would be empty, but it was usually packed. With officers manning tip lines and coordinating with specialized resources. With civilians reporting suspicions, demanding answers and volunteering to join search parties. "I'd like to get to work."

Carly pointed to a place at the end of one of the tables, stacked with boxes. "Right over there. Brittany's file is on top. And the boxes contain copies of the evidence from eighteen years ago. You've seen those already?" Carly asked, eyebrows raised, telling Evelyn she knew her history here.

Evelyn shook her head, then walked toward the case

files. A sharp whistle brought her up short, made her spin around.

The bloodhound shot to his feet and followed his handler out of the room as a pair of cops pushed their way in to give Carly updates.

Dumping her FBI bag on the floor, Evelyn squeezed around the table to get a better look inside the boxes. She tried to ignore the increasing level of noise as officers walked in and out of the room, but it was a sharp contrast to the morgue-like quiet that usually pervaded the BAU office.

Folding back the cardboard top, Evelyn looked inside one of the boxes and saw a stack of photographs. The first photo showed a well-loved and dirt-caked doll lying on the grass, an evidence marker next to it.

Matilda. The name of Cassie's doll came back to her as soon as she saw it.

Evelyn slapped the lid shut. She felt Carly looking at her, but didn't lift her gaze. She could do this. Dan *wasn't* right about her being too close to the case to properly profile it.

She just hadn't expected to see Cassie's toy. She'd gotten a copy of the case file two months earlier, but she'd mainly wanted to read the note left on Cassie's bed. She hadn't read through the list of cataloged evidence. She didn't know they'd found Cassie's doll. She'd only known they hadn't found Cassie.

Fortifying herself, she tried to open the box again, but her hands trembled. She needed to do this in private, not surrounded by the chaos of the station.

Hefting the boxes in her arms, she went back the way she'd come. She tried to make her voice sound normal as she told Carly, "I'm going to find a quiet corner to work."

She glanced at her watch and frowned. "I'll be back in three hours with a profile." It wasn't enough time, not really, but Brittany had already been missing for thirteen hours, and after twenty-four her chances decreased even more. They all had to hurry.

Three

Evelyn clutched three boxes of case details, carrying them as low as she could to see over the top. Her duffel bag swung toward them with every step and her briefcase dangled precariously from her right hand. Her thighs bumped the boxes as she hurried toward the hotel.

Normally, the files wouldn't have left the station, since it was no longer a cold case. But they were only copies and she'd promised Tomas she wouldn't let them out of her sight until she got them back to the station in three hours.

The chain hotel was a few miles from the police station, on the outskirts of town. It was well back from the road, hidden by a canopy of live oaks draped with clumps of Spanish moss. A hundred and fifty years ago, a plantation had claimed this spot. When she'd lived in Rose Bay, it'd been the location of a little bed-and-breakfast. But the town had grown, both the permanent and tourist populations booming in the past decade. The results of that, at least the ones she'd seen so far, were more bars, restaurants and hotels.

It felt surreal to be back. She kept expecting to turn a corner and see her grandparents. To see Cassie.

But her grandpa had been gone for fifteen years and her grandma now lived in Virginia, in an old-age home near Evelyn. And Cassie… Whether Cassie was dead or alive, maybe Evelyn would finally learn where she'd been all these years.

Greg had booked the hotel for her. He'd made all her reservations while she'd rushed straight to the airport and hopped on the first flight to South Carolina. The nature of her job meant her FBI "Go Bag," currently weighing down her left shoulder, had already been in the trunk of her car.

As she held the boxes higher, blocking her sight, then grabbed the door and pushed through, the bag slipped off her shoulder. The strap dropped to her elbow with enough force to jar her hand from the boxes. "Shit!"

Evelyn yanked her hand back up, bag swinging, trying to catch the boxes before confidential case information spilled all over the hotel floor.

A pair of hands grasped the boxes from the other side. "Got them!"

She knew that deep, drawling voice. As the boxes were lifted away from her, Evelyn stuttered, "M-Mac. What are you doing here?"

Heat rushed up her face as Kyle McKenzie's eyes locked on hers. "I figured you'd be staying on-site." She'd known HRT was in the area, but they were working a case a few towns over, so she'd assumed they would have set up a command post there.

She'd thought about calling him and telling him she was going to be nearby. The idea of having Kyle to lean on while she looked into Cassie's case had been too tempting. She'd resisted because he had his own job to do, and she didn't really know where things stood between them.

Kyle gave her a big grin, complete with dimples, and despite the fact that he had heavy circles under his deep-blue eyes and his hair stuck up in odd directions, Evelyn's entire body went clammy.

"The activity we're monitoring is happening at night, so that's when we're surveilling. During the day, we're here. The people we're investigating live in a small town, and if we stayed too close, they'd definitely notice us. We're telling the people at this hotel that we're engineers, in town on a company-sponsored trip."

Evelyn raised an eyebrow. Did they really expect anyone to believe that? HRT agents were the most fit group in the Bureau; their regular routine included physical training, helicopter rappelling and mock terrorist takedowns. HRT agents tended to either look like Olympic-level long-distance runners or military special-operations guys. Definitely not engineers.

"Don't blow our cover, okay?" he added with a wink, shifting the boxes with annoying ease. "Where am I taking these?"

Evelyn held out her hands. "I can carry them. I just got here, so I need to go to my room and work on my profile." She ran a hand over her hair, tied neatly back in a bun, aware that she was talking abnormally fast.

In an average social situation, she was shy and uncomfortable. Throw Kyle McKenzie into the mix and she was instantly self-conscious. Especially in the past month, since she'd opened up to him about her past, about Cassie. Since she'd kissed him, and considered jeopardizing her place at BAU for him.

Technically, they weren't on the same squad, which was usually when dating a colleague meant risking reassignment. But the Critical Incident Response Group was unique, an overarching group made up of BAU, HRT and other essential units that responded to crises around the country. At any given time, she might be called to travel or to work intensely stressful situations with the other CIRG units. She didn't know quite what the protocol was for dating another agent in CIRG, but her boss had made it abundantly clear that it wasn't happening on his watch. And for years now, her job had been her whole life.

Still, after Kyle had helped her face down a serial killer, she'd shocked them both by acting on their attraction. She'd thought they would sort out what it all meant while she was on medical leave, but he'd been called out of town three weeks ago.

And now that her immediate emotional vulnerability from that case had faded, and the most important investigation of her career had surfaced, she couldn't make any mistakes. Not even for Kyle.

As she shuffled her feet, Kyle's expression got serious. "Greg called. He told me you were on your way."

Unspoken was that Greg had asked Kyle to watch out for her, but Evelyn heard it in Kyle's voice.

He stepped closer, seeing far too much as he studied her. "I know you're working on your friend's case, Evelyn. If you need anything, I'm here for you."

She nodded silently, unable to meet his gaze, unable to talk about it yet.

He must have sensed that, because he told her, "I've got the boxes. Go check in and I'll carry them up for you."

Letting Kyle anywhere near her room? Bad idea. Her

mind might've been made up, but her hormones didn't seem to have gotten the message. "You don't need to do that."

Amusement sparkled in his eyes, as if he could guess exactly what she was thinking. "Sure I do."

Instead of wasting time arguing, she checked in and let him follow her up to her room. After he'd set the boxes inside, she shooed him out by telling him she had to be back at the station in three hours with a profile.

And when the door closed behind him, she breathed a nervous sigh of relief. She'd worry about Kyle later. Right now, she had to figure out if Cassie's abductor really was back, or if Rose Bay had a copycat.

Turkey vultures soared overhead in wobbly circles, their wings spread in a wide V. They were scavenging, and Kyle knew what that meant. They'd found a fresh carcass.

Kyle looked at the sky, out in the distance, over the high grass that led to the marsh. In his line of work, he'd seen way too much of what one human being could do to another. But the kids always hit him the hardest.

Knowing how important the case in Rose Bay was to Evelyn made it even worse. He hadn't been able to get her out of his head since he'd seen her at the hotel. How the hell was she profiling this?

He prayed she'd get the answers she'd been searching for all these years, but even if she did, they were unlikely to be good. And there wasn't much he could do besides join the search for the girl who'd gone missing yesterday.

Behind him, police officers and civilian volunteers from the search parties were heading in the opposite direction, toward the overgrown field beside the cemetery. Overhead, a helicopter buzzed, on its fifth hour of an aerial search.

Officially, despite his training, Kyle wasn't supposed to be involved at all. He wasn't here for this case. But his current mission only claimed his nighttime hours, so he and his Bureau partner, Gabe Fontaine, had volunteered with the civilian search parties looking for Brittany Douglas this morning.

Gabe wasn't aware of Evelyn's connection to the case, but Kyle didn't need to tell him about it for Gabe to want to help. In HRT, they were often a last resort—an overwhelming tactical solution when all else failed—so they'd seen a lot of screwed-up situations. But the ones where kids were in danger tended to piss off the guys the most. The rest of his team would probably take a shift later in the afternoon.

When he and Gabe had arrived, he'd pulled aside Noreen Abbott, one of the administrative assistants from the Rose Bay PD who was coordinating the search parties. He'd quietly told her their full names and shown her their badges, knowing they'd be checked out otherwise. All volunteers were, because sometimes the perpetrator joined the searches. He didn't want anyone wasting time doing background checks on him and Gabe.

Exhaustion weighed down his steps. He'd managed a three-hour nap after his team came in from their mission around 8:00 a.m. But he and Gabe had vowed to help as soon as they were marginally functional. Sleep was overrated, anyway.

Except that now, as the turkey vultures narrowed in on something they wanted down below, sleep sounded like a damn fine idea.

"Shit," Gabe muttered next to him. He swiped a hand

over his forehead and Kyle knew it wasn't the ninety-degree heat, but fear of what they might find that was making his normally unflappable teammate sweat.

"Not a good sign, turkey vultures," a man said.

Kyle turned around, surprised someone had come up behind them without him or Gabe noticing.

And the man was big, considering his stealth. He wasn't tall—he was actually a solid four inches shorter than Kyle's six feet. But he was wide. And none of his girth was fat. He appeared to be in his sixties, although Kyle's gut said he was younger, and the deep lines on his face were from hard living.

Kyle held out his hand. "I'm Kyle. This is my friend Gabe. We're here on a company trip, so we figured we'd help with the search."

The man's dark gray eyes narrowed in his craggy face, then he put his hand in Kyle's and shook forcefully, before pulling his hand free. "Frank Abbott."

Gabe gestured back toward the sign-up table for the search parties. "Are you related to the girl handling the sign-in?"

"My niece," Frank replied. "She works at the station. And I didn't have any jobs today I couldn't reschedule, so here I am." He heaved out a heavy sigh. "This again."

"You lived here during the original abductions?" Gabe asked.

"I've lived here all my life. Can't believe this shit has started up again." He shook his head, suddenly looking tired, and headed toward the marsh, glancing back to call, "You want to check this out with me?"

Hell, no. Instead of saying it, Kyle nodded tightly and fell into step beside Frank. The older man walked fast, with purpose, his jaw set in a grim line.

The sounds of the search party faded as they walked, replaced by the strange clapping sounds someone had told him were made by Clapper Rail birds. It would've been peaceful had the circumstances been different.

Beside him, Gabe and Frank were silent, too. Gabe had the same training he did, the same ability to force back fear and get the job done, but a civilian wouldn't. To Frank's credit, he didn't slow as the low, nasal whine of the vultures reached their ears.

Kyle tried to prepare himself as they continued walking, as the marsh grasses got taller and thicker, as his feet began to get stuck in the muddy ground.

"Watch your step," Frank warned, trudging ahead without looking back. "The marsh is low now, but to get to the vultures, we have to go in."

"If there's a body out here, wouldn't the alligators have gone after it by now?" Gabe spoke up, shoving back blond hair in need of a cut.

Frank snorted and kept going. "No gators. Not in these marshes. Down the coast, maybe. But not here. Come on."

Kyle followed, his shoes sinking deeper until it was difficult to pull them free. The marsh grasses crept up around his knees as they got closer to the water. High enough to hide a body. And definitely deserted enough. The sound of the other searchers had become nothing more than a low murmur.

Kyle knew that as soon as Evelyn gave her profile, she'd be out there among them, just like she'd probably insisted on doing eighteen years ago. It was easy to imagine her as a young girl. Her best friend torn from her life, abducted only hours after Evelyn had seen her.

Even at twelve years old, Evelyn wouldn't have sat

home hoping everything would turn out okay. He could picture her, green eyes too big for her face, long hair in pigtails, wearing the determined look that seemed to be her default expression. There was no way she would've tolerated being left behind.

And he knew there was no way she'd leave Rose Bay now until she uncovered the truth. No matter how horrible it was, no matter what it cost her.

The image of Evelyn faded as the smell of something rotting wafted up. *Please, God, don't let it be Brittany Douglas.*

He tried not to inhale too deeply as Frank splashed into the low marsh waters, startling three turkey vultures. They gave deep, guttural hisses, then took off into the sky, revealing a carcass along the edge of the marsh.

The breath stalled in his lungs. It was the remains left by some hunter, but it wasn't human. Just a deer. He shut his eyes and allowed himself a moment of relief.

Beside him, Gabe sighed. "Thank God."

Frank stared down at the carcass, then off into the distance, where the marsh wound through tall grasses and eventually disappeared from sight. "Let's keep looking."

Far behind them, the search was continuing.

Each time Evelyn read the note that had been taped to Brittany Douglas's bike, goose bumps rose on her skin.

It wasn't so hard,
I went to the yard,
Where you'd left the poor child alone.
When I got there,
It felt like a dare.
I thought to myself, Take her and run.

It matched the notes from eighteen years ago...and yet, it didn't. Back then, just like now, the nursery rhymes focused on two ideas. First, that the child was being neglected in some way by the parents. And second, that the abductor was rescuing her from that.

But eighteen years ago, the abductor hadn't displayed such obvious joy at the abduction. That idea dominated the new note, a macabre revision of "Old Mother Hubbard."

Unlike the notes eighteen years ago, which had talked to the victim, this one was directed at the parents. In context, the change made sense, given the increased focus on the abduction stage.

But was it because the abductor had developed a taste for the actual abduction? Or because it was a new predator entirely? She'd pored over the case details from the three old abductions and the new one for more than an hour, but still wasn't positive.

And that was the most important part of the profile she'd promised to deliver to the cops in less than two hours.

So far, what she knew were the statistics. She knew the chances of a child abductor going dormant for eighteen years and then starting up again were slim. She knew Brittany Douglas, at eleven years old, was the average age of child abduction and murder victims. Statistics said Brittany had first met her abductor within a quarter mile of her home. Statistics also said she'd been dead before Evelyn had even arrived in town.

But it didn't matter how slim Brittany's chances were; if there was any hope at all, Evelyn had to try.

A rush of cold swept over her in the too-warm hotel

room, leaving behind an intense fear. The fear that she might fail.

Evelyn tried to ignore it as she picked up the photograph of Brittany Douglas. With her long, dark brown hair, hazel eyes and shy smile, Brittany looked nothing like Cassie. In fact, none of the victims looked alike. The only similarity was age and gender. And the fact that the killer either believed—or wanted police to think he believed—that their parents were neglecting them.

"Damn it!" Evelyn sprang to her feet, raking her hands through her bun so violently she'd have to fix it before she went back to the station. The most important case of her life and she was blowing it.

Was Dan right? Was she too inexperienced in child abduction cases to spot the important details? Too personally invested to see the case clearly?

Evelyn blew out a heavy breath. No, she could do this. She'd been training all her life for this case. She was going to put everything she had into it. She couldn't consider the profile from eighteen years ago, couldn't review the original suspects, because it might taint her analysis. Especially if this was a new abductor.

She had to rely on her training and the case evidence to tell her about the perpetrator. And even though Brittany's abductor hadn't left much behind, he'd left *something* of himself. They always did.

Dropping back onto the hotel bed where she'd spread out the case files, Evelyn lined up the four notes. Direct communication from the abductor could tell her a lot or it could lead her totally off track.

A smart perp, knowing the police were going to analyze the notes, would use them to misdirect the investigation. And everything about this case, from the lack of forensic details to the high-risk abduction right out of the child's front yard, screamed that this was an intelligent perp who planned carefully.

But the notes also had an odd intensity about them. He was taunting, yes, but there was more to it. The abductor had left clues to his identity in the words. And Evelyn vowed that would be his undoing.

She glanced at her watch again. Ninety-eight minutes and counting. Somehow, in that time, she needed to figure out whether the original Nursery Rhyme Killer was back or if they had a copycat.

The Rose Bay Police Station's briefing room was jammed full. Cops, both in uniform and in street clothes, watched her, all with exhaustion slouching their shoulders and fear lurking in their eyes. FBI CARD agents stood stiffly among them, trying to look confident. The smell of sweat and dirt, of too many bodies packed too closely together, overwhelmed the inefficient air-conditioning. The buzz of voices came to an instant halt as Evelyn stepped up to the front of the room.

She gripped the podium with slick hands. She'd given hundreds of profiles in her year's tenure with BAU, but she suddenly felt all of twelve again.

She had an instant flashback to the last time she'd been at the Rose Bay Police Station. She remembered sitting on a plastic chair, her feet dangling. She'd held tight to her grandpa's hand on one side and her grandma's on the other while the cops asked unending questions. Did she remember anything unusual from the day Cassie had gone missing? Had she ever seen Cassie talk to a stranger? Did she know anything that could help them bring Cassie home?

Now, just like then, those answers seemed elusive.

Someone in the audience coughed loudly, bringing Evelyn back to the present. She looked over the sea of law enforcement officers, and jerked backward at the animosity she saw in one cop's eyes.

Jack Bullock. It had to be. He was in his midforties now, not the rookie who'd questioned her until she'd cried so many years ago. But there was no mistaking the too-sharp planes of his face, the deep-set brown eyes, the thick shoulders stacked on a stocky body. The thin streaks of silver through his brown hair and the lines etched deep into his forehead were new, but not the intimidating glare.

Evelyn redirected her gaze. "I'm Evelyn Baine, from the FBI's Behavioral Analysis Unit. My job is to review the evidence in your case to give you a new perspective—a behavioral portrait of your perpetrator. I'm here to tell you how he thinks, why he's choosing his victims and what he'll do next."

The officers seemed to lean forward as one, glancing at one another as if to gauge their colleagues' reactions to her. At the front of the crowd, Tomas was listening carefully, his deep-brown eyes filled with too much hope, too much expectation.

She prayed she could provide him and his officers with what they needed to find Brittany. Looking down at the profile she'd furiously finished minutes before racing back to the station, Evelyn began. "Your perpetrator is a male in his late forties or fifties. He's almost certainly white."

"Why?" someone from the back of the room called.

"Why do I say he's white? Frankly, because High Street is still all white. Someone who's not would be noticed, even now."

"*Even* now? Does that mean he's been here before? Is it the same guy from eighteen years ago?" Tomas's voice vibrated with dread.

Nervous whispering rippled through the room.

"I'll get back to that." She knew discussing those details first would distract everyone. And she didn't want them to miss anything that could help them find Brittany.

"First, let's talk about how the abductor fits in. He lives close by, either here or in a nearby community, and has for a long time. It's possible he moved away and came back, but he's recognized here. He's accepted as belonging, which gives him a plausible reason to be in the vicinity of the crime scene."

"Hold on," Jack demanded. "You think the asshole we're looking for *belongs here*? He's well liked?"

"Probably. It's unlikely he has a lot of close friends, but he is socially competent. He doesn't stand out. If asked about him, people would probably describe him as being decent, and if not likable, at least not unlikable. And he's intelligent. He doesn't act inappropriate around children, although a closer look into his background may reveal a suspicious incident. I'll get into that later, when we talk about motivation."

"This guy is grabbing *kids*," the officer beside Jack argued. "How can he be decent?"

"I didn't say he *was* decent," Evelyn clarified. "Just that people *view* him that way. We're not talking about the usual suspects here, because this guy is too smart to attract attention to himself. When we find him, people aren't going to say they always thought something was off about him. Quite the opposite. Everyone will be shocked, because he's been living among you."

Officers shuffled, looking down at their feet, frowning. When they looked back up at her, their faces showed a mixture of trepidation, wariness and disbelief.

"The offender drives a vehicle that doesn't stand out, and it is conducive to hiding someone inside. It could be a van with tinted windows or a sedan with ample trunk room. He also has a job with flexible hours. He works for himself, has hours that change, or a job that would require him to be away from the office for periods of time. The kind of thing where people wouldn't notice unusual absences."

"But Brittany was taken at night," an officer near the podium pointed out. "Why would he need to miss work during the day?"

"Because he stalked her first. This offender is a planner. He knew Brittany's routine and her family's schedules. He wrote this note *in advance* and it fit the situation when she was abducted. She was in the yard alone at that time. And he knew she would be, because he'd watched it happen before. So he waited for the right time to grab her."

Evelyn glanced around at the attentive officers and added, "He's probably developed a ruse to approach children. He may have used it when he abducted Brittany, so she wouldn't be concerned when he approached her in the yard, or he may have used it beforehand, to test her response. A lot of serial criminals do this, especially those who target strangers."

"I thought you said this guy was known in the community?" Carly Sanchez spoke up, her voice clear and loud.

"Yes, but not necessarily to the children he's abducting. So, he may try to test them. A child who's eager to please or naive about strangers is a more likely candidate than one who's street-savvy. Of course, this is also dependent on his motivation."

"Which is what?" Carly pressed.

Evelyn wished she had one absolute answer for them. "There are two possibilities," she began. "The first is that his motivation is exactly what he's telling us in the notes—that he believes the child is being neglected. If that's the case, he sees himself as her savior. And he has a tragedy in his own past involving an important young female. It could be a daughter, a sister or someone else he cared for deeply. He's using that loss to justify his actions now."

Jack jumped in. "What's the other possibility?"

"Well, as I said, this offender is intelligent. He may be leaving the notes to throw us off track. And if that's the case, then his true motivation is molestation."

"Damn it," Jack burst out. "We've got to go talk to Wiggins again."

Before Evelyn could ask who Wiggins was, Carly demanded loudly, "Which do you think it is?"

"I don't know." It galled her, but pretending to have the answer when there wasn't enough behavioral evidence to conclusively support either option would do more damage than admitting the truth.

Except perhaps to the stock these officers put in her profile, Evelyn thought ruefully as Jack shouted, "Isn't it your job to know?"

The room went quiet, and Evelyn tried to pretend it didn't bother her. "When I know more, so will you. But it's possible both motivations are right. If the abductions are driven by molestation, the offender might have tried to convince *himself* as well as us that he's saving his victims. An excuse he tries to believe to make himself feel better."

Jack just scowled at her, but Tomas cut in. "What about the connection to the earlier abductions? You said you'd tell us if this was the same abductor." He rubbed a hand across his temple and asked, "Is it?" as though he was afraid to hear the answer.

"Yes."

Evelyn had expected an eruption of voices, but instead Tomas's voice, barely above a whisper, seemed to echo as he asked, "Are you sure this isn't a copycat?"

"Yes." She'd gone over it again and again in her hotel room and it was the only way to explain the similarities. "Take the notes, to start. I know there've been a few false confessions over the years, and those people always knew nursery rhymes were left at the scene, because that was in the papers. But the station has done a good job of keeping exactly how the nursery rhymes were changed out of the press. And these notes are too similar—in tone, content, style, everything—to be from a copycat."

"Damn it," she heard Tomas muttering, new stress in his voice.

"I'd like to have an expert in handwriting from the FBI give a second opinion, but the notes are our best indicator. And this perpetrator just knew too much to be a copycat."

She frowned down at her profile, not really seeing the words, not really needing them. "The abductions are also much too similar to be a coincidence. The lack of forensic evidence and the pattern of abducting the child from her own property late in the evening or at night after stalking her first suggest a patient, determined predator."

She surveyed the room, wanting everyone to understand why she'd concluded that they were looking for the same person. "I reviewed all the evidence from this case first, separately from the older cases. And everything about this abduction points to someone who's done it before. It was way too savvy for a first abduction, and way too close in the details from the older cases that were never released to the public."

"And he's either molesting these girls or trying to 'save' them, whatever that means?" an officer asked.

"That's right. Although, this time around, his motivation has definitely shifted. With this latest abduction, he's enjoying the actual act of kidnapping more. He's fantasizing about it beforehand and it's part of the thrill, maybe as much as his ultimate motivation of molestation or his idea of saving them."

"Then why did he stop for so long?" Tomas asked, his voice even wearier than it had been a few minutes earlier.

"There are a number of possibilities." Evelyn ticked them off on her fingers. "He was jailed for another crime and recently released. He's had an illness that prevented him from carrying out the abductions and he's since gotten well. Or he was otherwise prevented from carrying them out for a period of time—because, for example, someone in his life would have noticed."

It looked like Jack was going to interrupt, so she said quickly, "It's also possible he didn't really stop. If it's molestation he's after, he might have had an available victim in his life, like a family member. Or he obtained a position in the community that gave him easy access to children. He could have moved away for a while and still been abducting children without leaving the notes, so the cases weren't connected. Or he was abducting children who wouldn't be missed at all."

"What, like runaways?" Tomas asked.

"Yes," Evelyn said. "Another possibility, although unlikely, is that this offender's precipitating stressors—whatever set him off in the first place and made him act on his fantasies—stopped and didn't start again for eighteen years. Or that he relied on trophies to relive the experience and those satisfied him until recently."

"Are we talking body parts here?" Carly asked tiredly.

The officers around her looked disgusted.

"No," Evelyn said. "But this offender would keep *something.* A necklace or hair bow or other item the victim was wearing. The abductor keeps it as a symbol of what he's done." Evelyn took a deep breath and tried not to put faces to the names from the case files, tried not to think about Cassie and what could have been done to her. "Which is kidnapping and most likely killing his victims."

The room went silent again, but everyone was staring at her tensely.

She knew what they wanted but were afraid to ask. So she just told them. "Whatever his motivation, whatever his reason for stopping and starting up again, time is crucial. I don't know how long Brittany has. And it *is* possible that he's hanging on to these girls long-term. But either way, he's not finished. Unless we stop him, he *will* abduct another girl."

Four

"So that's Evelyn Baine," an unfamiliar voice was saying as Evelyn finally broke free of cops' questions after presenting her profile.

Evelyn's steps slowed as she headed toward the CARD command post. Whoever was talking was around the bend in the hallway of the station.

"The way you were ranting about her, I was expecting a total disaster at the profile briefing. But she seems smart."

"Smart?"

Evelyn didn't recognize the first voice, but she knew who the snarling response belonged to: Jack Bullock. What she didn't know was why he felt so much animosity toward her. The last time they'd spoken at any length, she'd been twelve years old.

"She's a liability," Jack said dismissively. "But if her profile matches my suspect, then why the hell can't I go harass him? Give me a few hours with him and I guarantee you I can get this bastard to confess."

"Evelyn?"

Evelyn jumped at the voice behind her, and Jack and

whoever he was talking to were instantly silent. She spun around.

Tomas stood behind her, exhaustion hanging off him like an oversize coat. "What are you doing?"

"Spying, apparently," Jack drawled, coming around the corner, animosity in his eyes.

Next to him was a man about his age, with rapidly receding blond hair, broad shoulders and a gut that strained his uniform. A flush spread out from beneath his neatly trimmed beard, but he held out his hand politely. "I'm T. J. Sutton, ma'am. I joined the force about ten years ago, after you were gone." His gaze whipped to Jack, then back to her. "Sorry about what you just overheard. We're glad you're here."

Evelyn shook T.J.'s hand, then, ignoring Jack's frown, asked him, "Who's your suspect?"

Before he could reply, Tomas sighed. "Not Wiggins again."

"Yeah, Wiggins. Are you honestly going to tell me he's not a suspect?"

"Of course he's a suspect," Tomas snapped. "But you already questioned him with that CARD agent. You're not going back. Not now. Not unless we have some new evidence."

Evelyn's head moved back and forth between them. With only three hours to review the case evidence and create a profile, she hadn't had time to look at any suspects—and it was BAU practice not to, until the profile was complete. Knowing the suspects beforehand could taint the profile. She'd hoped to investigate the most promising suspects next.

"Who's Wiggins? How does he match the profile?"

The name sounded vaguely familiar, but she couldn't place it until Tomas clarified, "Walter Wiggins."

And then a hazy memory of a young man with light brown hair flopping over his forehead and big ears flashed through her mind. "Wasn't he a teenager eighteen years ago?"

"He'd have been twenty then," Jack said.

"That's a little young. How does he match the profile?"

"He's a weenie wagger," Jack spat.

Surprised, Evelyn asked, "He exposed himself? To children?"

Jack released a disgusted sigh. "Probably. But he was convicted of child molestation."

Queasiness rolled in her gut. She'd known this would be part of the investigation. She'd expected it. She'd even profiled it. These days, the majority of nonparental abductions were by sexual offenders. But somehow, talking about a potential suspect with a specific criminal history made her feel sick.

Don't think about Cassie, she warned herself. But it was too late.

She'd realized for years that Cassie was probably dead. But she'd tried so hard not to imagine what had come before that, after she'd been abducted.

The cops were staring at her expectantly, so Evelyn said, "Tell me about his conviction."

"It was after he finished college," Tomas said. "He'd moved out to DC for some lobbyist job. According to the trial notes, he volunteered at his local church, babysat all the neighbors' kids and was generally well liked until he was arrested for child molestation."

"And then he came back here?"

"Yeah. Apparently his neighbors in DC started taking baseball bats to his car windows on a regular basis, so Wiggins thought he'd be safer in Rose Bay. He moved back in with his parents, and he's lived there ever since. Well, just his dad now. His mom died last year and his dad's in bad health himself. There's been a lot of pressure over the years to run Walter out of town."

"They should've done it," Jack said. "Everyone would have been better off."

Tomas frowned. "Walter's parents always maintained his innocence."

"But you said he was convicted, right?" Evelyn asked.

"Oh, yeah," Tomas replied. "His parents couldn't stand to believe it, but I read all the trial notes. There's no question Wiggins was guilty, and he went to jail. Not as long as he should have, if you ask me, but then, I'd lock these guys up for life. Anyway, that's why the CARD team wanted to talk to him—he's on the registered sex offender list."

"Is he a preferential molester?" If he was, it meant he had a specific age and gender he targeted, instead of preying on any easy target.

"He is," Jack said. "His victims in DC were girls between six and twelve. The sick bastard."

Cassie's age. "What does he do now? Something that gives him time to stalk potential victims?"

"Something with computers," Jack said, looking at Tomas, who shrugged. "I think he works from home, contract stuff."

"So, no scheduled hours at an office, where he'd be missed," Evelyn concluded. "Girlfriend?"

Jack snorted. "Hell, no. Far as I know, he's never had one."

"Who's got the notes from today's interview with Wiggins?"

"The FBI agent," Jack said. "But we should just go back there. Hell, you can come if you want to. Let me do the talking, though. I can get under this guy's skin."

Evelyn shook her head. "No. If he's a strong suspect, we need to monitor him carefully. If we make him too nervous, if he feels like we're paying him special attention and he *does* have Brittany, he might kill her."

"If she's still alive," T.J. contributed softly.

"If she's still alive," Evelyn agreed. "But we have to proceed as if she is."

"Well, what if we *don't* do anything and that gives Wiggins time to kill her?" Jack argued.

Tomas and T.J. turned to look at her.

Tension knotted in her neck. "Where was this guy eighteen years ago?"

"College," Jack replied. "About an hour north of here. He spent his summers there, taking extra classes so he could graduate early. But he came home on weekends often enough. After he moved back home and word got out about what happened in DC, people started wondering if he could've snuck in and out of the towns back then. Only one of those original abductions was in Rose Bay..."

Jack broke off, because of course she knew that. Only Cassie had been taken here. The other girls were from small towns up the coast.

Jack cleared his throat and continued. "Once a molester, always a molester, right?"

Evelyn felt her shoulders slump and forced herself to stand straighter. "Not necessarily, but once a pedophile..."

"Always a pedophile," Jack finished. "See?" He looked at Tomas. "We've got to act on this before it's too late!"

"Was he ever investigated in connection with the original abductions?" Evelyn asked.

"He was," T.J. answered. "Once he moved back here from DC. I was part of the force then and we pulled the Nursery Rhyme Killer as a cold case to revisit. It was… what?" He glanced at Jack, creases forming around his eyes. "Nine years ago?"

"He was arrested nine years ago?" Evelyn asked.

"No. He was arrested when he was twenty-five. But he finally got sick of the harassment nine years ago and came back here."

"Like *we* wanted him," Jack put in.

"So? Did you find any connection to the Nursery Rhyme cases?"

T.J. shook his head. "Jack and I were part of the team working on it, but we couldn't come up with anything."

"That doesn't mean he's not guilty," Jack insisted. "I have a bad feeling about this guy."

So did she. But experience told her he was far from the only sex offender in the area who preyed on children. And it didn't mean he was the Nursery Rhyme Killer.

"I'll go through the interview notes and come up with a strategy for you," she promised Tomas. "I'd like to do that with any promising suspects you have."

Jack leaned forward and opened his mouth, but Tomas silenced him with a long, hard look. "Okay, but hurry. And start with Wiggins, if you think he's probable. Brittany's been missing for…" He checked his watch. "Almost seventeen hours now. And damn it, I want to bring her home alive."

* * *

"Let's hear it. What's the strategy on Wiggins?" Jack demanded an hour later.

He was sitting too close to her in the CARD command post, his wide shoulders invading her personal space as he read the notes from Walter Wiggins's interview over her shoulder. Why he needed to read them again when he'd been part of the interview team, she didn't understand. It was probably to piss her off.

Evelyn shifted subtly away. "Walter talks repeatedly in this interview about how people in town follow him around wherever he goes."

"Can you blame them?" Jack asked. "Everyone knows what he did. No one wants him here. But if we can't get rid of him, we're going to watch his every move."

Evelyn raised her eyebrows pointedly, but Jack just stared back at her until she sighed. "If people are constantly watching him, could he really have stalked and then abducted Brittany without being noticed?"

"It's not like we have some kind of schedule. The Nelsons follow him around from two to six, then the Grants take over, then…"

"Yeah, I get it," Evelyn broke in. "But if people tend to be aware of him, could he actually pull this off? Think about it, okay? I know you don't like him and I don't blame you, but let's not waste time on him if he's not a viable suspect."

Jack scowled, but he was silent for a minute before admitting, "He'd have to be really sneaky. If people saw him on High Street, they would've taken notice, you're right. It's not like, I don't know, say if T.J. was walking down the street. Most people wouldn't remember it, because he belongs. But Wiggins? Yeah, people would chase him off with sticks. And they'd definitely remember if they saw him around Brittany's house close to when she was grabbed."

"Okay, so..."

"But I'm not counting him out. I've been a cop a long time and experience tells me that coincidences like this are rare. I mean, we have one sex offender who likes girls the same age as Brittany and one man abducting them. What are the chances it's not the same person?"

"Experience must also tell you that if you check the database, you probably have a couple more registered sex offenders in the area who also fit."

Jack nodded. "Yeah, well, I got partnered with the CARD agent interviewing those particular scumbags, so believe me, I know. There's a guy one town over who's nonpreferential—he'll screw anyone or anything and he's been arrested for all of it and keeps getting out. And there are two more in the town where the first girl was abducted eighteen years ago who could fit, too. But all three of those assholes have pretty solid alibis for Brittany's abduction."

"Are you sure? Because the ones from the town where the first girl was abducted..."

"I'm positive," Jack interrupted. "The alibis are airtight. So, let's focus on Wiggins. I see your point, but this guy is slimy."

Evelyn held in a sigh. Walter Wiggins seemed like a dead end to her, but if she dismissed him and turned out to be wrong, she'd hate herself for it later. "Okay. What might Walter do with Brittany if he abducted her? You said he lives with his father?"

Jack tapped his thick knuckles against the table, his brow furrowed. "Yeah, he does. But hell, who knows if he kept her at all, right?" His anger suddenly seemed to deflate, leaving him looking older than he was, and very tired. "If he just…you know, raped the girl and then buried her…" His voice broke.

Evelyn nodded, staring down at the interview notes again. "I'll talk to Tomas about putting an officer on him. We might try interviewing his father, but if Brittany is still alive, we can't spook him. If Walter is the perp and he feels too much pressure, he could kill her out of fear."

"It doesn't matter what we do. Wiggins is feeling pressure right now. The whole town knows what he is. His dad's house has already been vandalized. Someone spray painted the words *child killer* and *pervert* all over the front door. No one was outside when we went to talk to Wiggins, but I could see the curtains moving on the neighbors' houses. They're all watching him."

Evelyn tried to think positive. "Well, in some ways, that's good. If he does have Brittany, that makes it harder for him to move her."

"I guess." Jack looked around the room.

The CARD command post was empty except for the two of them. Even Carly had gone, to meet with Noreen Abbott, the Rose Bay PD administrative assistant coordinating the search parties.

In fact, most of the station was empty. The cops who'd come in to hear her profile had cleared out. Those who hadn't been on shift had headed home. Most of the others had gone back to canvassing neighborhoods.

She'd never get a better chance to clear the air with Jack. "So, Jack, why the animosity? I haven't seen you since I left for college."

Jack's gaze shifted back to her, anger flickering in his deep brown eyes. "I don't care what you do for the

FBI, Evelyn. You don't belong here and you know it. You never did."

Evelyn instinctively leaned away from him, then stiffened her spine. "This is a *race* thing? Is that why you questioned me so hard eighteen years ago? Were you *trying* to make me cry?"

"No, it's not about race," Jack snarled, but the expression in his eyes said otherwise. "I don't give a shit whatever mix you are. I questioned you hard because you were one of the last people to see her alive. It wasn't about your precious little feelings. It was about bringing that girl home."

He got to his feet, jabbing a finger at her. "And it's the same now. Can you really tell me you're impartial? Can you honestly profile this case? Or are you so jammed up with hatred and anger that you're going to overlook something? So focused on Cassie Byers that you're going to miss seeing what's going on with Brittany Douglas?"

A vein started throbbing in the center of his forehead. "You're here for Cassie, but she's been dead for eighteen years and you damn well know it. You feel guilty because you were supposed to be a victim, too. But we need someone impartial. We need a real profiler here, not an intended victim coming home to play hero."

He pounded a fist down on the table. "We need to *catch* this asshole!"

She swallowed hard, unable to form a reply, and then just watched him as he shook his head in disgust, and strode from the room.

She wasn't trying to play hero. Finding Cassie meant finding Brittany, too. But damn, as nasty as Jack's words were, he was half right. She could try to use the original abductions to tell her about the perp, but her focus needed to be on the girl missing now, not Cassie.

And for her, it was always going to come back to Cassie.

She pressed a hand to her temple. Maybe Jack had a point. Maybe she didn't belong here.

Eighteen years ago, she sure as hell hadn't. Eighteen years ago, everyone had stared at her as though she were some kind of curiosity with her light brown skin in a world of white. At the time, she'd been the only one living in town who didn't fit.

Some people—like Cassie—hadn't cared. But a lot of them had. Most were too well-mannered to be rude to her face, but even at ten, she'd heard the whispers. She hadn't always known what they meant, but she'd known they were about her.

It had been twenty years since she'd first set foot in Rose Bay. The town had changed. But maybe not as much as she'd thought.

She was trying to rein in her emotions when Tomas raced into the room. "Where's Jack?"

"He left a few minutes ago. Why?"

Tomas's eyes narrowed, as if he could tell something was off with her, then he said, "I need him to get over to the hospital and talk to his favorite suspect."

Evelyn stood. "Walter is at the hospital? Why?"

"Brittany Douglas's dad just beat him up."

"Why?" Had she screwed up, rejecting Walter as a viable suspect? "Did he have a specific reason to suspect Walter?"

"I don't know," Tomas replied. "Two of my officers are bringing Mark Douglas in."

When Evelyn started to follow him to the front of the

station, Tomas warned, "I'd stay where you are. We just arrested the victim's father. No one's happy with us." Instead of returning to the CARD command post, Evelyn picked up her pace to match Tomas's stride.

He glanced at her, looking surprised, then warned, "Everyone was terrified already. Now we've pissed them off. Things are volatile out there."

As she walked to the front of the station with him, she saw that *volatile* was an understatement. Angry residents swarmed the parking lot, held at bay by a pair of cops. The crowd was mostly men, between twenty and sixty. They wore everything from shorts and T-shirts to suits and ties. Evelyn guessed there were thirty of them, but with only three cops who hadn't been expecting this kind of trouble, it was too many.

The crowd was pushing and screaming and the cops, even though they were obvious veterans, looked overwhelmed. Evelyn had never seen her hometown like this, even eighteen years ago. Despite what she'd seen in the Bureau, it was actually a little scary.

Especially as a police car pulled up as close to the station door as it could get and two officers dragged a man out of the backseat who had to be Mark Douglas. His eyes were bloodshot, his face ragged with grief, his hands raw and bloodied.

The cops were young, clearly rookies. One held tight to Mark's arm. The other's hand lingered near his sidearm, his gaze darting nervously around the crowd as it rushed in on him.

"Pigs!" someone shouted. "We do your job for you and get arrested for it?"

"Let him go!" someone else yelled.

"Shit," Tomas said. "Jack! T.J.! Get out here! Grab your batons!"

"Maybe..." Evelyn began.

"Stay inside the station," Tomas told her, heading for the front door. "Most of our officers are out running down leads, and this could get ugly."

Evelyn grabbed his arm. "Do you have a bullhorn?"

Tomas gave her an incredulous look. "In my office," he said, pulling free and opening the front door.

The yelling roared several decibels louder. The pair of cops trying to manage the crowd was being pushed back toward the station. The cops trying to bring Mark inside were trapped against their patrol car. One of them pulled his weapon, and just like that, two residents had him slammed into the car.

Evelyn saw the weapon drop to the ground and Tomas raced into the crowd as she spun for his office. She wasn't a negotiator, but she'd worked with the best the FBI had. And she knew calming the crowd down fast was the best chance to avoid getting someone hurt.

As she sprinted into Tomas's office and found the bullhorn, Jack and T.J. hurried past, carrying heavy shields she hadn't expected a small town like Rose Bay would have.

Jack and T.J. shoved their way through the crowd with their shields, trying to get to the rookies by the car.

Evelyn spotted Tomas in the middle, his hands out in a calming gesture. A broad-shouldered man with silver-streaked hair who seemed to be the closest thing the mob had to an instigator yelled back at him, slapping Tomas's hands away.

The two cops who'd been holding back the crowd were yelling, too. It sounded as if they were agreeing with their neighbors that Brittany's dad shouldn't have been arrested, and promising to let him go if the crowd went home.

The rookies who'd brought in Mark Douglas were down near their patrol car. One had crawled half-underneath it to avoid getting trampled, while the other struggled to get back to his feet, his hand pressed to his bleeding head.

Mark, still in cuffs, was being dragged through the crowd. He kept looking backward, and seemed to be arguing with the crowd to let him get arrested, which was only making them angrier.

Evelyn opened the door, stepped to the edge of the crowd and lifted the bullhorn. She pressed the button to broadcast, knowing she needed to return their focus to what really mattered. "This isn't helping Brittany. You need to leave the investigation to the police!"

The crowd quieted, seeming to still almost instantly. But that only lasted a fraction of a second. Then the man talking to Tomas yelled, "Was it your idea to arrest the victim's father?" And the crowd surged forward, shifting direction, toward the front of the station, toward her.

Evelyn took a quick step back, pressing the button on the bullhorn again. But it was too late. Two people closest to her shoved her sideways, away from the station door, and the bullhorn fell from her hands.

She regained her balance, put her right hand near her hip to protect her weapon and tried to move backward. But someone else came in from the other side, blocking her way.

Then Jack's voice cut through the yelling. "Evelyn! Hey! Move away from her!" He started pushing toward her, leading with his shield, and knocked someone out of his way.

Suddenly everyone seemed to be moving at once, in different directions. The men on her left spun to face Jack, knocking her backward.

She stumbled, and righted herself just as a cloud of pepper spray dispersed into the air. It filled her lungs, making her cough with every breath. Her eyes burned, watering until it was hard to see.

The crowd moved fast to get away from it, shoving and pushing away from the station, and Evelyn went down hard on one knee.

She tried to get to her feet, but the crowd suddenly shifted again as a gunshot rang out. Someone slammed into her, and she fell to the ground. Then all she could do was curl up and try to protect her head, hoping she wasn't about to get trampled.

Five

Gabe slammed on the brakes, getting their rental car close to the rioting crowd in front of the Rose Bay PD, and wrenching Kyle against his seat belt. He'd unbuckled and opened his door before Gabe had the car in Park.

Kyle stepped outside and pepper spray stung his eyes, burned in his nose and throat. Instead of wading immediately into the crowd, he hopped on top of the rental car for a better view.

More reinforcements were right behind them. He'd heard the call come over the radios at the search party, drawing the cops and FBI agents back to the station. Since Gabe had spent extra time on the FBI's defensive driving course, he'd driven. At every turn, Kyle had urged him to go faster, so they'd beaten everyone else back to the station.

Whatever got them to Evelyn the fastest.

But where was she? Kyle peered through the crowd, assessing. Residents fleeing the pepper spray, fighting with the cops, pushing a handcuffed man toward a truck. Two cops down by a patrol car. Two more standing back-to-back, holding shields to protect themselves as the crowd jostled them. The police chief ducking as a resident threw a punch. And there, by the side of the station… Kyle squinted. Was that Evelyn?

The crowd shifted and, oh, shit, it was. She was down, and in real danger of being trampled.

He had to get to her *now*. Kyle jumped down next to Gabe and pointed. "She's over there."

"Let's go."

They'd been partners for three years, so he and Gabe didn't need to talk. They spent hundreds of hours each year training with live rounds, when knowing exactly where your partner was meant the difference between a successful training exercise and a real death.

They'd also been friends for three years, so Gabe knew how deep his feelings for Evelyn ran, how complicated they'd become. Gabe would understand that, right now, he was feeling pretty damn desperate.

Kyle waded into the crowd, sticking to the side, where he'd encounter less resistance. Gabe tracked along beside him, far enough away to allow room to maneuver, but close enough to provide assistance.

Kyle felt his eyelids swelling as he skirted the back of the cop car, close to where the pepper spray must have been dispersed. Residents—a few women but mostly men—rushed past him, heading in both directions, not seeming to know whether to flee or fight. Someone took a swing at him, and Kyle sidestepped it, twisting the man around and down onto the trunk of the squad car without breaking stride.

From the corner of his eye, he saw Gabe dodge a pair of men running full out for the street.

The crowd was dangerous, but it was relatively small. And he and Gabe had helped break up a prison riot last summer, so in comparison this was a piece of cake. At least here no one was trying to shank him.

As he closed in on Evelyn's position, he saw her roll away from a guy in a suit who'd stepped back to kick her.

Kyle put on a burst of speed and tackled the man before he could try again, throwing him off to the side.

Gabe came up beside him as Kyle yanked Evelyn up and over his shoulder. He felt a surge of relief the second he had her off the ground where he could protect her.

He heard more cars coming in, sirens blaring, as he rushed for the station door. The crowd scattered, moving faster; most of them had obviously abandoned thoughts of fighting.

But the man Kyle had tossed aside had gotten to his feet—Kyle hadn't thrown him hard enough to knock him out, hadn't wanted him to get trampled by the crowd. And instead of running away, he was coming back for more, fury on his face and a police baton in his hand, up and ready to swing.

Kyle just kept going, stepping over a bullhorn, and taking Evelyn farther away from the rushing man. Gabe moved in front of them fast, as Kyle had known he would, using the man's own momentum to push him against the brick of the station wall. Instead of forcing him onto the ground, Gabe twisted his arm behind his back, making him drop the baton, then pushed him inside the station alongside Kyle.

Kyle lowered Evelyn off his shoulder, steadying her as she swayed. He pushed her into a chair as she pressed a hand to a bump swelling her forehead. Tilting her head back to check her pupils, Kyle stared into her eyes. They were clear, the pupils normal-size and tracking. She looked a little dazed, but she was okay. Damn, when he'd seen her on the ground, he'd wanted to forget strategy and just plow straight through the center of the crowd.

He glanced back at Gabe. His partner had the man he'd brought inside cuffed to a metal bar on the station wall. When he caught Kyle's gaze, he nodded toward the door.

"Stay here," Kyle told Evelyn. "I'll be right back." Then he followed Gabe outside.

The mob was pretty much under control now. Most of the residents were long gone. A few were on the ground, being cuffed by the additional officers and FBI agents who'd arrived. The police chief was helping the cops near the squad car to their feet. A gruff-looking veteran officer set down his shield and grabbed a Glock from the ground, tucking it beside his own weapon.

"Where's the profiler?" the veteran cop asked, scanning the ground as if he'd seen her go down.

"She's in the station," Gabe said. "She's okay."

The cop scowled. "She shouldn't have been out here. She shouldn't be here at all." He spun away from them and handed the weapon he'd picked up to one of the newbies by the squad car.

Kyle looked at Gabe and pointed back to the station, and his partner followed him inside.

Evelyn got to her feet as they came in the door. The bump on her forehead was nasty and her eyelids were almost swollen shut from the pepper spray. Her suit was torn at the knee and shoulder, and from the way she hobbled when she walked toward them, he guessed a heel had come off her shoe.

But it could have been a hell of a lot worse.

"Is anyone hurt?" she asked. "I heard a gunshot."

"It didn't look like anyone was shot," Gabe said.

"Good." Evelyn bent down and took her shoes off, then peered up at them. "What are you guys doing here?"

"What do you think?" Kyle asked, a little more harshly than he'd intended. He took a deep breath. It wasn't Evelyn's fault things had gotten dangerous. And it wasn't her fault his emotions took over wherever she was concerned.

He didn't quite know how it had happened. But sometime between a year ago, when he'd first seen her in the BAU office, and now, everything had changed. She'd gone from the newbie agent he couldn't resist teasing to the woman he flat-out couldn't resist.

"We heard what went down. I was worried you were in the middle of it."

She frowned back at him, but then seemed to realize what she was doing, and said, "Thanks for the help. It got nasty out there fast."

"Is the station going to need reinforcements?" Gabe asked as cops streamed back inside, some hauling prisoners.

Evelyn shook her head, then put her fingers gingerly against the bump on her forehead. "I don't think so. They just didn't expect this reaction to bringing in Brittany's father."

"What a fucking mess," the veteran cop with the shield contributed as he came in the door hauling a cuffed and bleeding resident.

"Is anyone hurt, Jack?" Evelyn asked as Gabe signaled a free cop and swapped the cuffs on the prisoner he'd brought inside.

"Nothing serious." Jack pushed the resident into a chair. "Stay there," he told the man, then turned his gaze on Evelyn. "What the hell were you doing out there? Inciting them with the bullhorn? Are you crazy?"

Kyle forced back a response, because he knew it would piss Evelyn off to have anyone stand up for her. It always did.

"I was trying to calm them down, remind them what we all need to be focused on," Evelyn replied, a lot more calmly than Kyle had expected.

Jack snorted. "Yeah, that worked well."

Kyle couldn't stay silent any longer, but he tried to keep his tone nonconfrontational. "The problem wasn't trying to talk the crowd down. The problem was not planning better for that arrest." He should know. He'd helped execute arrests on enough high-profile targets.

Jack shot him a look, then turned pointedly to Evelyn. "How do you know those guys? Who are they? More feds?"

Instead of answering Jack, she asked Kyle, "Can you give me a ride back to the hotel?"

"You're just going to leave now?" Jack cut in.

What was this guy's problem? Kyle stepped closer, angling into Jack's line of sight with the kind of warning glare he liked to use on uncooperative targets.

"Let me grab a file, okay?" Evelyn raced off as though she hoped her disappearance would make Jack lose interest.

But Jack just moved forward, giving Kyle his own cop stare.

"You might want to watch your prisoner," Gabe said mildly as Jack got in Kyle's face.

"Shit!" Jack took after the bleeding resident he'd brought in a minute before, who was hobbling for the door.

Then Evelyn was back, and Kyle ushered her out the door toward Gabe's car. "What's with that guy?"

"Apparently he's held a grudge for eighteen years."

Kyle steered her around the broken glass from the patrol car headlights since she wasn't wearing shoes. "He had a grudge against a *twelve-year-old*?"

Gabe looked questioningly between them as Evelyn shrugged. Evelyn had told Kyle about her past, but Gabe didn't know what this case meant to her, or her history here.

Kyle had tried to respect her privacy and keep it to himself, but if she was in danger—and with a town that fast to mob, she definitely could be—he'd have to tell Gabe soon.

And he really didn't like the atmosphere in the police station, either. There was definitely something off about Jack.

To hell with sleep. When he got back to the hotel, he was going to check into the guy's history. "What's his full name?"

"Jack Bullock," Evelyn answered. Then she seemed to realize why he'd asked, and added, "I think it's just this case. He was on it eighteen years ago and couldn't solve it then. It's probably haunted him ever since."

Like it had haunted her.

She didn't have to say it; the words were written all over her face.

But considering why she was here, she was handling it a lot better than he'd expected. Maybe she was still too numb from learning that her best friend's abductor was back to really take in what was happening, or maybe she was just burying it all.

Either way, the calm wasn't likely to last long.

* * *

Evelyn sat on the edge of her bed in her hotel room, a police file on her lap. She needed to remove her dirty, torn clothes and take a shower. She needed some ice for her forehead. But she couldn't think about any of it until she looked in the file.

Inside was the original FBI profile of the Nursery Rhyme Killer.

She hadn't reviewed it when she wrote her own, because that could have subconsciously influenced her analysis. Now that she'd given her independent profile, it was time to look at everything else—from the original suspects to the original profile.

Since she'd profiled the abductor as being the same man from all those years ago and not a copycat, now was the moment of truth.

Did her profile match the one prepared eighteen years ago?

Back then, when Cassie had gone missing, an FBI profiler had come to Rose Bay. Evelyn had seen him at the police station once, confident and a head taller than most of the cops. She'd been leaving after another round of questioning from Jack Bullock. She'd seen the agent studying the volunteers as she'd walked at the rear of the search parties with her grandparents. When she'd spotted him leaving the Byerses' house, she'd run over and demanded to know who he was and when he was going to find Cassie.

He'd leaned down to her level and actually shook her hand. He'd been aware of who she was, of course, but back then she hadn't known why. Then he'd told her his name and explained what he did for the FBI.

And that conversation had changed the entire direction of her life.

She'd never seen Philip Havok again. But she could still remember the exact shade of his sharp blue eyes, the dark gray of his suit, the quiet confidence in his voice. He was the picture she'd had in her head all the years since, the idea of what she wanted to be. A profiler. Someone who could bring girls like Cassie back home.

She'd looked him up when she'd been accepted to the Academy, wondering if he was still in profiling, and discovered he'd retired the year before. He'd spent nearly twenty-five years in the Bureau—meaning, he'd been granted an exception to the FBI's mandatory retirement. More than half of that time had been spent profiling serial predators. Now it was her turn.

Evelyn opened the file. The basic description was right at the top: "white male, between the ages of twenty and thirty, works a job with flexible hours." Add eighteen years and that matched what she'd profiled.

She kept reading. "Unclear whether he is single, but if married, the relationship is controlling. Could have his own child, and if so, likely to be the same age as the victims."

Evelyn paused, realizing she hadn't considered every angle about kids. She'd thought about them as a reason the perp could have started the abductions—because he'd lost a child that age. And she'd thought of them as a reason he could have stopped the abductions—because he had an easy victim at home who had reached the age he wanted. But she hadn't considered the other possibility. That he might be abducting other children so he'd stay away from his own.

Evelyn closed her eyes, feeling gingerly around the

tender skin on her forehead where she'd bumped it. An image of Cassie filled her mind, vibrant, laughing and full of life. What had happened to her after he'd ripped Cassie away?

Evelyn pushed back the sleeves on her suit, opened her eyes and kept reading. When she finished, she closed the file and stared blankly at the bare hotel walls.

Philip had come to the same conclusions she had. Possible molester, possible delusions of being a "savior."

But how the hell did she figure out which one? And how the hell was she going to catch him before Brittany ran out of time?

There was just one man from the original list of suspects who hadn't been cleared or moved out of state in the past eighteen years. And he didn't match the profile in a very key way.

Still, with Walter Wiggins not talking, he was the best lead Evelyn had. She'd checked with Carly and discovered he was on their list for follow-up, but it hadn't happened yet, because he wasn't a high priority. Then she'd checked with Tomas and learned that the only officer not running down other leads was his head detective, Jack Bullock.

So, the two of them were driving to the nearby town of Treighton. They'd been on the road for fifteen minutes, but Jack had kept up a steady stream of questions that gave no sign of ending.

"If you think Darnell Conway is worth investigating, does that mean we should just disregard your entire profile?" Jack kept his tone casual, his hands loose on the wheel of his police vehicle. But the question fairly screamed his resentment.

Evelyn didn't even glance his way. "You read the Charlotte Novak file, right? You know why I want to talk to him."

"So, the profile…"

"Can have details that are off. The thing is to focus on the profile as a whole, not fixate on a particular point."

"That's a pretty huge point."

Evelyn shifted in her seat to face him. "The murder of his girlfriend's daughter was never solved. But after the investigation went cold, Darnell and his girlfriend left the state and came here. Do you know how old Charlotte would've been eighteen years ago, at the time of the first abduction, if she'd lived?"

Jack's mocking expression slipped off. "You're kidding."

"She would've been twelve that summer. Same as the Nursery Rhyme Killer's original three victims."

"So, then why the hell aren't those other FBI agents—the ones who *specialize* in this—chasing this guy down with everything they've got?"

Evelyn shrugged. "He was never arrested for that crime. He was a suspect, but obviously the cops didn't have enough on him to make a case. It's possible he didn't do it. He's got no other criminal history. And *that* case is the only reason he showed up on the list of suspects eighteen years ago. Which was probably a lucky fluke, since he was never charged."

"That's some fluke. How did they find out?"

"He was part of the search parties back then. The profiler had a weird feeling about him and did some digging. And I trust the profiler's gut on this. I just want to feel Darnell out, see how he responds to my questions."

"What if he's the perp? You said not to get too close

to Wiggins so we wouldn't scare him into killing Brittany if he's got her. Isn't the same true here?"

Evelyn leaned her head back against the headrest, still tired from the mob scene that afternoon. She glanced at her watch, realizing it had now been a full twenty-four hours since Brittany was grabbed.

She closed her eyes, trying not to dwell on something she couldn't change, but she could hear it in her voice when she told Jack, "If Darnell did kill his girlfriend's daughter, it was within a few hours. Walter is different. His MO was to get his victims comfortable with him first. He wanted to believe they were willing participants. That's part of his fantasy."

"Okay, but just like Wiggins..."

"I know. Darnell Conway would probably be noticed on High Street. But I need to check. And there's only so much I can tell from a copy of a cold case file. I need to see Darnell's face when I ask him about it."

Jack gave her a pensive glance as he drove over the bridge separating Rose Bay from Treighton. Fifty feet below them, the water looked calm in the fading light. Peaceful.

That instantly transported her back to when she was ten and she'd first come to live in Rose Bay. Her grandpa's car had been too warm as they drove over the bridge in the middle of the night. She'd kept quiet, knowing the heat was for her—wearing a pair of threadbare, tattered pajamas and no shoes. Her grandpa had tried so hard not to let her see his anger, his sadness, his guilt.

His weathered hand had folded around hers as they drove, as he'd promised her she'd never have to go back. She was going to live with him and Grandma from now on and they would take care of her. They would protect her.

She'd never been more sheltered than her first two years with her grandparents. But then Cassie had disappeared. And the world had seemed to slide out from under her again.

"...don't you think?"

"What?"

Jack sent her a perturbed look and she saw that he was on his cell phone.

"Well, maybe you should try to get the dad to let you in the house now." A pause. "He refused? You think he has something to hide?"

"What's going on?" Evelyn asked.

"Okay. Fine. Bye." When he hung up, Jack told her, "Wiggins woke up. He's in pretty bad shape, though, so they're keeping him in the hospital. Apparently he's not too happy about it, but he doesn't want to press charges against Brittany's dad. Which is good. Shit like that—protecting the perverts and criminals—is *not* why I became a cop."

"So Walter's dad won't let police search the house?"

"You got it. You think he knows the girl is there?"

Evelyn shook her head. "I doubt it. I know he wants to protect his son, but that's taking it pretty far. I've seen the families of pedophiles do their best to deny what their kid is, even when the proof is staring them in the face. But to be complicit in the abduction? You know his dad better than I do, but that seems like a stretch."

Jack nodded. "True. Though his dad's in bad health these days. I doubt he can walk down those basement stairs anymore. Maybe in his heart he knows she's there, but just doesn't want to believe it?"

Evelyn felt her lips twist downward. "Unfortunately, that's a real possibility."

When Jack's hands clutched the wheel so hard the muscles in his arms bunched, Evelyn added, "But honestly, I still have a real problem seeing Walter being able to stalk and abduct a girl here. He's got motive, sure, but means and opportunity?"

"Well, he's at the top of my list," Jack said as he pulled onto a dark street. "And frankly, a black guy like Darnell Conway on High Street would get noticed, too, especially eighteen years ago. Isn't that why you profiled the killer as white?"

Evelyn didn't answer as she gazed out the window at Darnell's neighborhood. The houses were small and close together, the yards overgrown; beware of dog signs were posted everywhere. Every house was in need of a coat of paint, most needed new roofs and every yard could have benefitted from an attempt to landscape. The sun was setting, making it hard to see, but Evelyn would bet there wasn't a single flower on the entire street. From the broken plastic kid's slide in the front yard of one house to the car without wheels up on cinder blocks in the next, the whole street was depressing.

The house Jack pulled up to was the best of the bunch by far. Darnell Conway might not have planted a garden, but he'd at least mowed his lawn. As they walked up to the front porch, they discovered he definitely believed in security. Next to Darnell's beware of dog sign was a security company sign; the lock on the door meant business, and all the shades were blackout-style.

Jack raised his eyebrows. "Seems like he's got something in here he wants to keep locked tight."

Evelyn nodded, frowning. "I noticed that."

"And judging by the lack of barking, I'm thinking most of those dog signs are for show."

"It is pretty silent," Evelyn agreed, glancing around. The kind of neighborhood where no one saw anything.

"Well, let's see what he has to say." Jack lifted his hand to knock on the door, but before he could, they heard bolts sliding back.

Three bolts slid free before the door swung open to reveal Darnell Conway. Evelyn knew he was in his late forties, but he looked younger, with smooth dark skin and close-cropped hair. It was only his deep brown eyes that showed his age. And something about the anger lurking in the depths of those eyes made the hair on the back of her neck stand straight up.

Was he the Nursery Rhyme Killer? Had he taken Cassie eighteen years ago? Had he stalked Evelyn, intending to grab her, too?

Did he recognize her now? It was hard to tell, because Jack reached in his pocket and held up his police shield, drawing Darnell's instant attention.

It had been twenty years since Darnell had first been investigated by police, when he found the body of his girlfriend's daughter. But as soon as he saw Jack's badge, hatred and fury raced across his features, so fast that if she'd blinked at the wrong time, she would have missed it.

Judging by the way Jack's eyes darted to hers, he hadn't blinked, either. "Mr. Conway, I'm Jack Bullock, Rose Bay PD."

"What are you doing in Treighton?" Darnell asked, his voice as smooth and even as his expression.

Jack motioned to her. "This is Evelyn Baine, FBI."

Darnell's eyebrows twitched, and then his lips did the same. "FBI, huh? Anything I can help you with?"

If her name meant anything to him, she couldn't tell. Damn it.

"Can we come in?" Jack asked.

From what little Evelyn could see of the house behind Darnell, she realized the inside was a hell of a lot nicer than the outside. Not just clean and tidy, but expensive furnishings. So, why live in this neighborhood?

Darnell's gaze flicked to Jack, then to her. "No."

"We're investigating the disappearance of Brittany Douglas," Evelyn told him.

"Never heard of her."

Jack scoffed. "Her abduction has been all over the news."

"I drove up the coast for a few days. Got back yesterday."

"She was abducted yesterday."

Darnell's eyes, hard and shuttered, settled on Jack. "Like I said, never heard of her."

"She's twelve years old," Evelyn said.

Darnell didn't blink, just stared at her.

"That's only two years older than your girlfriend's daughter was when she was killed."

Darnell's expression shifted into fury. "Are you implying something, *agent*?"

"You found her, didn't you?"

"So what? I wasn't arrested twenty years ago and there's a damn good reason. I didn't kill Kiki's kid. Leave me alone and get the hell off my property!"

He slammed the door so hard Evelyn took an instinctive step back.

"That went well," Jack said dryly. But as they got back into the car, he asked, "You think he did it?"

"I think we'd better take a close look at him. And fast."

Six

Tomas had never gone home last night, but he'd fallen asleep at his desk sometime after six. The call that had woken him less than two hours later had initially seemed like a crank call, a person who refused to give his name reporting "something suspicious" in the marsh. But when asked to explain the term *suspicious*, the person had said it looked like a body in a trash bag.

Brittany had been missing almost thirty-five hours now. The profiler had been on scene since yesterday and the CARD agents since the night before that. They'd given him the statistics, so he knew it was way too likely the caller was right.

The thought made him slow instinctively as he tracked through the marsh, and his foot sank into the goop at the bottom. Tomas yanked the top of his knee-high plastic boot until it popped free and pushed onward. Ahead of him, Jack Bullock moved forward with seeming ease.

And that was ironic. Except when taking a police call, Jack had probably never visited this part of Rose Bay. Tomas could actually see the house where he'd spent most of his formative years.

It was raised on wooden stilts at the back for when the marsh waters rose, and the exterior was stucco. When he was a boy, there had been a deck off the back, but it was gone now. His parents had finally moved once their last son left home, and since then, the house had gone through a series of owners. From this distance, it looked forlorn and neglected.

"Can you imagine?" Jack huffed, gesturing at a shack up ahead of them. "Who'd want to live there?"

Tomas kept quiet, deciding to assume Jack didn't know he'd grown up a hundred yards away. As for the shack, it was unoccupied and had been for more than a year. "It's empty. Let's check it out when we're finished here, make sure no one used it to hide Brittany." More likely, they'd just find someone's drug stash, but it was worth a shot.

Jack turned to say something else, then cursed as one of his feet slid out from underneath him. He caught himself before he was soaked, but still let out another stream of obscenities. "How far out into the marsh did the caller say it was?"

"It shouldn't be much farther."

"We should've taken the boat," Jack groused, breathing hard in the heavy humidity.

"The water level's too low." It only came up to their knees in the early-morning tide, and Tomas knew it wouldn't get much deeper where they had to search.

He'd spent enough time in the marshes as a child to know them. The spot he was now searching for a body had once been a favorite place for him and his brothers; it was where they'd row their dad's old canoe, race through the marshes and out into the ocean. Back then, the main thing they'd had to worry about was their drunken neighbor, who liked to shoot at anything that moved with his hunting rifle. Tomas longed for that kind of simplicity now.

Since Brittany had been abducted and Evelyn Baine had come to town, Jack had been a bigger pain in his ass than usual, Walter Wiggins was threatening to sue the police department for not protecting him after he'd been threatened and the whole town was in an uproar over yesterday's arrest of Brittany's father. To make matters worse, Evelyn had brought him a suspect.

Despite presenting a profile that pegged the abductor as white, late last night she'd returned to the station with Jack and named Darnell Conway as her key suspect. And if Rose Bay learned that a black man was the prime suspect in the abductions of young white girls, the riot at the station the other day was going to look like a peaceful gathering. And he'd be in for a shitstorm he wasn't sure his small police force could handle.

"How much farther?" Jack asked, sloshing ahead of him.

"We're close."

Being from the wrong side of the tracks wasn't something Tomas liked to advertise about himself. But it gave him an advantage in his job. He'd grown up seeing Rose Bay from the other side. Instead of the perfect, safe community where the rich could feel secure leaving their doors unlocked and their children with nannies, Tomas had seen the dangers.

He'd been raised to respect the natural perils, from the undertow in the ocean to the speed of high tide when it poured in over the sand bars. He'd known to avoid the neighbor who always smelled like sour whiskey and not to let the man who claimed he was from the energy company into the house when his father wasn't home.

Brittany's parents, on the other hand, had felt secure in allowing their daughter to play alone in the front yard, lulled into complacency by Rose Bay's seeming perfection. Nothing bad had ever touched them, so they thought nothing ever could. Until their daughter was taken from right under their noses.

"Over there," Jack called, pointing, and Tomas could see it, too, floating at the far end of the marsh. An industrial-size black garbage bag, with something heavy weighing it down. Had it not gotten tangled in the reeds, it probably would have sunk.

"Shit." The caller was right. It did look like it could be a body. A small body.

He'd come across enough dead bodies when he'd worked homicide in Atlanta—including a couple in the garbage. He'd taken the job in quiet Rose Bay, hoping to see fewer. And that was what had happened. But the child cases were always the hardest. If Brittany Douglas was in here, it would rank up there with the worse cases he'd handled.

Tomas wiped a hand across his forehead and it came back wet with perspiration from temperatures that were pushing ninety, at 8:00 a.m. He forced his feet to move faster, splashing through the murky water, until he reached the bag.

Jack got there ahead of him, but he waited, looking apprehensive. "Should we try dragging it out before we open it?"

In answer, Tomas pulled the switchblade from his pocket.

"What if it's just the air in the bag keeping it afloat?"

Jack asked, but it was too late, because Tomas had already run the knife through the top of the bag.

It deflated slightly, letting out a putrid smell. Jack adjusted his stance the way Tomas had seen him do dozens of times at crime scenes in preparation for something he didn't want to see.

Tomas folded the knife and stuffed it back in his pocket, then slipped on a pair of plastic gloves. He tore the bag open wider with his hands and things started spilling out. A perfectly good basketball. A filthy old pillow. Some green slimy substance he couldn't identify.

He braced his feet wide in the gunk on the marsh floor and stuck his gloved hand into the bag, feeling for anything that might have been a body. His fingers pushed through cans and tissue and a rubber ball, but nothing in the bag had ever been alive, other than the maggots feeding on old Chinese takeout.

"It's nothing," he told Jack, who rocked back on his heels with a relieved sigh.

"What a waste of time," Jack complained, pivoting gracelessly and plodding back toward shore.

Tomas sighed, shoved the spilled trash into the bag and hefted it over his shoulder. It weighed far less than a body, but it felt a thousand times heavier as he followed Jack back toward a town demanding answers he didn't have.

The tide raced greedily at Evelyn, soaking the bottom of her jeans as she walked toward the sand dunes shrouded by long grass. From the main part of the beach, the area was accessible only to the adventurous. To get here, Evelyn had clambered over an outcropping of rocks, fighting for purchase on the slick surface. Combined with the dunes to her right, this was an unlikely spot for beachcombers. For someone trying to hide a body, though, it might be appealing.

Evelyn pushed determinedly toward the dunes. The wind whipped sand around, like little needles dancing on her skin, and the waves crashed loudly into the rocks.

She'd chosen a spot away from the other searchers this morning, needing time alone to think. About Walter Wiggins and Darnell Conway. About the trickier aspects of her profile.

She hadn't been to this spot since before Cassie had gone missing. It had been Cassie's mom who'd shown them how to get here. Instead of risking the rocks, they'd come through the dunes. To a twelve-year-old, they'd seemed to go on forever, but then they'd arrived at this little stretch of beach, and it had been like their own private world.

She'd thought about it for the first time earlier today, and realized it had only been a month before Cassie's abduction that they'd come here. Maybe he'd followed them. Maybe he'd made it his private world, too.

A shiver raced through her, as hard as the wind ripping strands of hair from her bun.

"Hey!"

The unexpected voice made Evelyn's head snap up. Emerging from the dunes was Darnell Conway.

She felt a new sense of unease. Had he followed her out here?

Evelyn's hand grazed her hip, where her SIG Sauer rested reassuringly. Her holster had rubbed the skin underneath it raw in the South Carolina sun, but she never went anywhere without it.

After leaving Darnell's house yesterday, she'd done

some more digging and learned he'd kicked his girlfriend, Kiki, out of his house two years ago. It was possible he'd stopped the abductions after Cassie eighteen years ago because Kiki had started to suspect. Now, if he *had* decided to go back to his old ways, there'd be no one around to notice anything.

As Darnell walked toward her, an almost lazy swagger to his stride, Evelyn watched his hands for any sign of a weapon. But they swung loosely at his sides, empty.

"It's Evelyn Baine, from the FBI, right?" Darnell asked, an artfully blank expression on his face.

"What are you doing here?"

A hint of a smile curved one corner of his mouth, and a predatory gleam flickered in his eyes. "Well, after you and that officer told me about the missing girl, how could I not help with the search?"

"Don't you have to work?"

"I'm sure you know I work in sales. From home. I can set my own schedule."

He stepped closer and Evelyn continued walking, careful to keep him in her line of sight. "Why here?"

"The dunes?"

"Yeah. The cops were assigning searchers to groups."

"You're not in a group," Darnell said, lengthening his stride and moving close enough to give her a whiff of his aftershave. "Should you be out here all alone?"

His tone was neutral, but his words were calculated, intended to intimidate.

Evelyn felt her jaw tighten as she strode up the first sand dune instead of heading back toward the rocks. She'd need both hands for that climb, and with Darnell next to her, she was keeping her gun hand free.

Either he wanted to flaunt his guilt, thinking he'd

never be caught, or he was just one of those guys who got off on being aggressive, got power out of trying to bully others.

"Should *you*?" she tossed back, wanting him to know he didn't scare her.

Darnell kept pace with her, his expression shifting in a way that told her he liked the challenge. "What's the point of searching with the group? The more area we cover, the more likely someone is to find this little girl, right?"

Or the easier it would be to hide a body, with the convenient excuse of being out searching. Some killers liked to be the ones to "discover" their victims. And if Darnell had, in fact, killed his girlfriend's daughter twenty years ago, he was one of them.

A sick feeling roiled in her stomach. Was she going to find Brittany in these dunes? Was Cassie here somewhere, too?

She clenched her fists and intentionally slowed, so Darnell could pick the route. If he wanted to lead her to the bodies, pretend to find them, she'd go along with it.

His eyes narrowed slightly as she allowed him to get in front of her. It was as though he could read her. As though he knew exactly what she was doing.

She half expected him to call her on it, but instead he suggested, "Let's go this way," and led her deeper into the dunes.

Almost immediately, he started moving faster. He probably had ten inches on her, so his strides were much longer.

Was he trying to wear her out, make her easier to overpower once he got her deep into the dunes?

She kept a careful distance between them as they crested one dune after the next. Darnell was breathing heavily, his T-shirt soaked through and stuck to him, outlining biceps bigger than her thighs.

"Kinda sick, isn't it?" Darnell wheezed after ten minutes of silence.

"What?" Evelyn asked. She was sweating and thirsty, and the sun was beating down, no cloud cover in sight. The salty, humid air felt thick in her lungs. And the thought that Cassie could be buried under one of the dunes she was trudging over made chills dance across her sweat-drenched skin.

Because if Darnell was the Nursery Rhyme Killer, maybe she was right and he wanted to "discover" the bodies. Or maybe he was simply getting a thrill out of having her—an intended victim who was now investigating him—walk over them.

Of course, if he was worried that after eighteen years someone suspected him again, he could also be desperate. And desperate meant dangerous.

Darnell slowed down, eased in next to her. "Well, come on. No one wants to say it, but everyone knows. None of those girls were found eighteen years ago. The same guy is back now." He raised his eyebrows meaningfully.

When she didn't respond, he pressed, "They lure you into these search parties with the idea that you could help rescue this poor little girl. But let's be honest. We're looking for her body."

An image flashed through Evelyn's mind, and the shock made her slide partway down the dune. An image of a girl with blond ringlets bouncing in pigtails, sky-blue eyes dancing with happiness, a quick smile for everyone she met. Cassie.

The last time Evelyn had seen her, they'd played hide-

and-seek in Cassie's backyard. Evelyn had felt so free, felt she'd finally fit in somewhere, like she had a real home, a friendship that would last a lifetime. Instead, that day marked the last time she'd really been a child.

Anger swelled in her. Had this man taken that away from her? Taken Cassie?

The glare of the sun over the crystal-brown sand dimmed as Evelyn's hand instinctively jerked toward her weapon.

When she spun around, Darnell was right there, so close that if she breathed too deeply they'd be touching. She recognized the look in his eyes because she'd seen it before, usually in interrogation rooms. His words were meant to get a reaction.

His lips twitched, something wanting to break free. A snarl? A smile? But he held it back, staring her down, triumph in his eyes.

And she realized what she'd done. She'd gotten distracted, thinking of Cassie. She'd let him get too close.

She was armed, yes, but in the time it took to clear her weapon from its holster, he could take her down with sheer bulk. She could run, but which way? She was at the base of two dunes, with no idea how to get out.

Triumph showed on Darnell's face, telling her he could sense her fear.

And damn it, that infuriated her. It ignited all the anger she'd buried under mountains of survivor's guilt and mourning.

So, he had a hundred pounds on her, all of it muscle. She had hand-to-hand training from the FBI. And she wasn't going down without a fight.

She leaned her head back so he could see it in her eyes.

He was taken aback, like most bullies, when he realized sheer intimidation wouldn't do it. A flash of surprise, of panic, appeared in Darnell's eyes. He hid it fast and lifted his hand.

Evelyn instinctively jumped backward, her hands coming up fisted.

"Move back now!"

Evelyn identified the deep baritone instantly, and Darnell reacted to the order by calmly raking his hand through his hair. Then he took his time stepping away from her.

Finally Evelyn looked up, over the top of the dune, and right at Kyle, who was walking toward them, his weapon sighted on Darnell.

"Evelyn and I were just helping with the search," Darnell said, sounding way too calm for someone who had a weapon aimed at his head. "You always this trigger-happy, man?"

Not lowering his weapon or taking his gaze off Darnell, Kyle held his hand out for her.

Evelyn took it, and he tugged her up the dune next to him as if she weighed nothing, barely even adjusting his weight. Only then did Kyle holster his weapon.

But his hand still lingered close to it, and Evelyn recognized the battle-hardened look in Kyle's eyes as his "mission face." For someone who usually seemed laid-back and approachable, right now Kyle looked exactly like the trained operator he was.

Darnell clearly saw it, because he kept his movements slow and his hands away from his pockets as Kyle indicated that he should move in front of them.

"You need to sign in with the rest of the searchers," Kyle said as the three of them started walking out of the dunes.

"How do you know I didn't?" Darnell parried.

"Because when I asked around about where Evelyn was, I heard I wasn't the only one looking for her."

Darnell had told people he wanted to find her? That meant he probably hadn't intended to harm her, just to intimidate.

As her adrenaline level decreased, Evelyn cursed herself for screwing this up. If she'd stayed focused, she might have gotten him to slip up.

Darnell shrugged, glancing back at Kyle. "Evelyn was the one who told me about the girl's abduction. She mentioned the search, so I figured I'd join her."

As they stepped out of the dunes and onto the high grass alongside a parking lot full of beachgoers, Evelyn put her hand on Kyle's arm. When he turned to her, she gave a quick shake of her head. A silent request not to warn Darnell to stay away from her.

She'd trained in psychology for years before arriving at BAU, which was its own specialized course in how the most dangerous minds worked. And every bit of her training was telling her that Darnell would seek her out again.

Next time, she'd be prepared. She wouldn't let him catch her alone and off guard. Next time, he wouldn't be the only one playing mind games.

Because he might have spent his whole life fooling people, but her job was to get into his head and make him give her the truth. And her job was the biggest part of *her* life.

She knew Kyle didn't like it, but he kept quiet as Darnell glanced between them, obviously expecting a threat.

When none came, amusement glimmered in his eyes.

"I'll be back to help some more later. Can't let this guy get away with it."

He sauntered away, then called over his shoulder, "See you soon, Evelyn."

Seven

Kyle was pissed off.

Evelyn could see it in the set of his jaw, his white-knuckled grip on the steering wheel. He hadn't said a word as he'd hustled her into his car and started driving toward the church where the search parties met up. She'd parked her rental there early in the morning before heading off for the dunes alone.

She knew why he was upset. She'd taken a risk, gotten herself cornered by Darnell. And she hadn't let Kyle threaten the guy with bodily harm if he ever came near her again.

"He caught me off guard. It won't happen again."

Kyle nodded curtly, then seemed to forcibly pry his jaw open. "But you want him to seek you out, don't you?"

"He could be the Nursery Rhyme Killer. And if he is, he wants to brag about it. He wants to taunt me." She tried to shrug, tried to ignore the nausea rising up at even the thought of encouraging Darnell to brag about what he'd done to Cassie.

She'd used the same strategy dozens of times before in other cases, in interrogation rooms with suspects who thought they were smarter than her. She could do it for this case.

But judging by Kyle's frown, she knew he was remembering her last case, and what had happened when she'd tried to lure a killer to her. She'd almost died that day.

"This guy doesn't want to kill me. He wants to brag without actually admitting to anything."

Kyle's hands clenched the wheel. "What happens when you *get* him to admit to something?"

The way he said it, as if it was a foregone conclusion, filled her with warmth. "I'm not going to let him catch me alone again."

She heard Kyle sigh his acceptance, then one hand dropped off the steering wheel and his fingers wove through hers.

In the brief look he threw her before focusing back on the road, she knew he understood. She'd told him about Cassie's abduction. But she'd never told him the whole story.

Suddenly she wanted to. Wanted to really let him in and see where things went after that. "There were notes left behind at these abductions. In the note left at Cassie's house eighteen years ago, he said he'd taken me, too."

Kyle's fingers jerked in hers, then he pulled off to the side of the road. He faced her, sadness in his deep-blue eyes, and comprehension.

That little piece of information probably answered every question he'd ever had about why she put her job ahead of everything else, why she was always so serious, so secretive. Why she was alone.

She stared down at her lap, not quite able to hold his gaze.

"It's not your fault. You know that."

Trust Kyle to cut right to the heart of it, to understand exactly how she thought. For some reason, he always had.

"Yeah, I know. But that doesn't really change how I feel." She forced herself to meet his eyes. "I wanted to tell you, but I can't talk about this right now. I can't *think* about this right now. I have to focus."

She had to bury her emotions as deep as she could, numb herself as much as possible until she caught the Nursery Rhyme Killer. And then she'd allow herself the luxury of getting upset, of mourning Cassie. But not now. Not when it could throw her off track, could mean the difference between finding Brittany in time or leaving the Nursery Rhyme Killer file still unsolved.

"Just be careful, okay?"

Evelyn nodded, glancing down at his fingers still laced with hers, completely dwarfing them, his Irish skin pale next to hers. "I will."

Realizing there was only one person she'd told where she was going today, she asked, "How did you find me?"

"I asked around. Jack Bullock suggested I check these dunes."

"Did Darnell overhear you?"

"The guy we saw in the dunes? No. When no one at the search parties seemed to know where you were, I finally stopped at the police station."

"Huh."

Kyle's eyes narrowed. "You're wondering how Darnell found you?"

"Yeah. I only told Jack."

"Maybe Jack mentioned it to someone else and Darnell overheard that."

Evelyn nodded, skeptical. "Maybe."

"You think Jack told him?"

"No. We questioned Darnell together last night. He wouldn't have told Darnell where I was."

"Well, if it makes you feel any better, I did a little searching into Jack last night and nothing raised any flags."

Evelyn frowned. "Jack's not a suspect."

"Well, I didn't like his attitude the other day. But he's got a near-perfect track record as a cop. He's been married a long time. Overall, he seems solid. The Nursery Rhyme case eighteen years ago looks like one of the few he was on that didn't get solved."

"His attitude toward me is kind of weird." She suspected it had to do with the color of her skin, at least in part. But she didn't want to get into that now. "Whatever the reason for his resentment, I can handle it."

"I think he's pissed because you remind him of his one failure. And I think he's scared that now you're going to outshine him by solving the case he couldn't."

"Jack was a rookie back then. His dad was the police chief."

"All the more reason Jack can't let this case go," Kyle said. "Trust me. I know exactly what that's like."

He smiled at her, one of his knowing, dimpled smiles that made her feel like she was fifteen years old and just discovering boys. "Before I came to the Bureau, I was a cop, remember? Like my older brother. And my dad, the police chief."

"Really?" Kyle had told her he used to be a cop, that he'd come from a family of cops, but she hadn't realized his dad had been the chief of police. And for some reason, she'd assumed Kyle had made the transition to the FBI quickly.

She tried to imagine him wearing a police uniform,

but all she could picture him in was his bulletproof vest with FBI emblazoned across the front. "I guess I thought you'd come into the Bureau like I did."

"Always knowing I belonged here?" He shook his head. "Nope. It was a total fluke, me deciding to apply. One day on the job we had a situation that brought some agents from the local field office to town. I saved a kid that day. Caught their attention." He shrugged, fiddled with her fingers. "One of them suggested I apply."

"And it wasn't quite like you expected?"

He smiled, a soft, quiet smile so unlike his usual big grins. "Oh, in some ways it was better. But you know how HRT is."

She did. She knew he didn't just have memories of the people he'd saved, but of the ones he hadn't been in time to help.

Maybe they were more alike than she'd ever thought.

"Mac..."

A loud honk cut her off, turning Kyle's head, too. Pulled up beside their car was an old gray sedan. When the window rolled down, Evelyn went light-headed.

Kyle looked at her questioningly, but she was already opening her door to go talk to Cassie's parents.

By the time Julie Byers climbed out of her car, Kyle was standing beside Evelyn. He'd taken a protective stance, close enough to lend support without actually touching her. He'd obviously figured out who this was.

Julie Byers's blond hair was like Cassie's, although it was probably from a bottle now. Her blue eyes, too, were the same shade as her daughter's, but they seemed tired and sad, dragged down by dark, heavy moons. Lips that had once been so quick to smile were pressed together tightly.

"Mrs. Byers." Evelyn's voice cracked and she tried again. "I'm sorry I haven't come by…"

Julie's lips lifted into the facsimile of a smile, her eyes watering as she drew Evelyn into a tight hug. "Thank you for coming."

She smelled like lilac, a scent Evelyn had always hated, although she wasn't sure why. Julie was bigger than Evelyn, but she felt frail, like if Evelyn hugged her back too hard she'd break.

"Of course I'm here," Evelyn said, and even to her own ears, her voice didn't sound right.

Julie pulled back. "I knew if anyone could find Cassie…"

A heavy weight settled on Evelyn's chest, the knowledge of all the people counting on her. "I'm not leaving until I do."

Julie nodded sadly, as if she knew the only way Cassie was coming home was for a long-overdue funeral. As Evelyn tried to hold back her tears, Julie looked over at Kyle as though she'd suddenly noticed he was there.

Evelyn felt Kyle's hand low on her back and it evened out her breathing as he introduced himself to Julie's mom.

"Arthur's in the car," Julie said, looking back at Evelyn. "I'd better get him home, but do you want to come over and say hi? I'm sure he'd love to see you."

Cassie's dad. Evelyn nodded, feeling as though her feet were encased in concrete as she plodded toward their car, Kyle's hand at her back.

When she peered inside, she realized she wouldn't have recognized Cassie's dad. It had been thirteen years since she'd seen him, but he seemed to have aged more than twice that. His bony hand trembled as he held it out to her and his eyes were hazy and unfocused.

"Evelyn Baine," he said, taking her hand briefly. "Julie told me you were coming to find my Cassie."

"Yes," Evelyn choked out.

"And the other girl," he said, glancing off into the distance, where the search parties were barely visible. "It's just like eighteen years ago," he mused, apparently lost in a memory, not talking to her anymore.

Her own memories rushed forward like a blast of hot wind—the feel of her grandmother's wrinkled hand clutching hers, the adults in front of her walking a search pattern. Keeping her head up, eyes dry, trying to be brave as she searched for her best friend. The days stretching into weeks and then months, until finally the search parties dwindled down to nothing and her grandparents wouldn't let her go out looking anymore. The whispers she'd overheard, saying Cassie was never going to be found.

Then the present filtered back in. The smell of exhaust in the briny heat. The huge live oaks stretching across the road from either side to meet in the middle, creating a canopy of shade. The comfort of Kyle's hand at her back as he urged her away from the car. And the sound of Julie's voice…

"…heart attack," Julie was saying. She shook her head. "And he's had a couple more since then. He just never gave up on finding her. After eighteen years of hoping, it's taken its toll, a little more each year."

"I'm sorry," Evelyn whispered.

Cassie had been their only child. And she'd been missing for more years than she'd been with them.

Julie reached out to pat her hand. "We know how

much you loved her, Evelyn." She glanced back at the car where her husband stared blankly off at the search parties. "We're glad you're here. We need closure. I just don't know what he's going to do when we find out..."

Julie sobbed, then straightened her shoulders and said, "Well, I'd better get him home. I saw you through the windshield and it didn't matter how many years it's been." A real smile, tiny as it was, curved Julie's lips. "I knew it was you."

Evelyn tried to smile back, but she couldn't do it. How hard was it for Julie to see her daughter's best friend eighteen years later, when Cassie would never have the chance to grow up?

"Say hi to your grandma for me. She's still with you, right?"

Evelyn nodded.

"And say hi to your mom, too, if you see her, okay?" Julie said as she started walking back to her car.

"My mom?"

Julie paused, glancing back. "I ran into her upstate a few months ago. She'd moved in with a new boyfriend. So I thought..."

"Oh, okay."

"You still don't talk to her."

It was a statement, not a question, but Evelyn answered, anyway. "No."

When Evelyn was seventeen, her grandma had had a stroke, and Evelyn's mom had reappeared. Evelyn had graduated early so she could leave for college instead of living with her mother again.

"You might want to bury that hatchet while you still can," Julie suggested as she got back into her car.

She drove away and Evelyn just stood there until Kyle guided her back into his car.

Once he'd gotten in the seat beside her, he asked softly, "You okay?"

From the way he was looking at her, he knew she wasn't. But she could tell he assumed that she'd simply nod and get back to work. Just like she always did when emotions hit too hard.

She could feel his surprise when instead she launched herself across the seat and held on to him so tightly it hurt her arms. She buried her head in his neck as his arms wrapped around her, comforting and solid. She'd thought the tears building up in her eyes were going to burst free as soon as his arms closed around her, but they didn't.

Somehow it felt exactly like eighteen years ago, when she'd tried to hold back her fear. As though crying for Cassie meant she really wasn't ever coming home alive.

Intellectually, Evelyn had accepted it a long time ago. But damn, being back in Rose Bay, really being back here and searching for the truth, made the same stupid hope spring to life again. The hope that somehow, against all logic, Cassie was still alive.

That if only Evelyn could find her, she'd finally come home.

Her fingers felt clumsy as she held the tiny teapot and poured more pretend tea into her cup. The purple flowered tea set had been a present, but she hardly ever got to use it. Usually, tea party was her favorite game, but today, the little girl across from her refused to play.

The girl was crying again and she curled into herself, refusing to understand what she had to do. The dress she'd been wearing for two days was starting to smell and she wouldn't change into the new outfit spread out on the bed.

"I just want to go home," the girl whimpered.

"You are home."

The rough dirt walls and floor might not have been plush, but she'd worked hard to make it nice. To make it all a little less scary.

She'd started out small, asking for things she knew he wouldn't deny her. A pretty pink cover for the bed. Crayons to draw a picture she could hang on the wall.

He'd given in reluctantly, slowly, because decorating this place hadn't been his priority. It was eighteen years since she'd asked for those crayons, and the bedcover smelled musty. The drawing was yellowed, curling around the edges. But this felt like a place someone had once loved. It felt almost like a home.

"I'm going to take care of you. You weren't safe before." She repeated the words she'd heard him say so many times.

"I won't let anyone hurt you ever again."

"Who did you say you were again?" Kiki Novak, Darnell's ex-girlfriend, stared at Evelyn through a torn screen door and a haze of cigarette smoke.

Evelyn held her creds closer to the door. "Evelyn Baine, FBI. Can I come in and talk to you for a few minutes?"

She'd driven the half hour north from Rose Bay after Darnell had followed her into the dunes. He might not fit her profile in terms of race, but he was sneaky. And his behavior earlier had propelled him to the top of her suspect list. If anyone could give her more insight into him, it was his ex-girlfriend, mother of the girl whose murder twenty years ago had never been solved.

Kiki's stringy brown hair swung forward as she squinted at the credentials, then she looked up at Evelyn, suspicion in her muddy-brown eyes. "Okay. I guess so."

She held open the screen door and Evelyn walked into the house, almost a polar opposite of Darnell's. The street Kiki lived on was clean and the neighbors kept up their lawns and houses. Kiki, on the other hand, had a house with solid bones, but everything inside was dusted with a layer of neglect.

Empty cartons and stacks of magazines lay discarded on the dirty floors. The furniture was a nice quality, but stained and ripped, as though the occupant had once cared about it, but didn't any longer.

Evelyn followed Kiki through the entryway and into a living room, trying to lean away from the line of smoke that trailed from Kiki's cigarette.

Kiki gestured to a recliner in relatively good shape, then sank onto the stained couch with a sigh and a drag of her cigarette. "What do you want?"

Eyes itching from the smoke, Evelyn tried not to cough as she said, "I have a few questions about Charlotte's case."

Kiki's eyes went saucer-wide and clouded with tears. The hand holding her cigarette froze halfway to her mouth, and started visibly shaking. She held the position so long that a shower of ash fell onto the couch, but she didn't seem to notice.

Finally she brought her cigarette to her mouth, sucking on it until her pale face turned even whiter and her lips went bloodless. Then she stabbed it out in an overflowing ashtray. "My daughter was murdered twenty years ago," she whispered. "I thought there was no case anymore."

Sympathy rushed through Evelyn, and regret. She'd been thinking of Charlotte's death because it tied into the Nursery Rhyme case. And she'd been thinking of Kiki as Darnell's ex-girlfriend, a possible source of information.

But really, she was just like Cassie's parents. The difference was, Kiki had no more hope at all. She had gotten to bury her daughter, but she still didn't know why. Or who had killed her.

Evelyn leaned forward. "I'm sorry. I know this is difficult. But there's a possible connection between your daughter's case and an open investigation."

Kiki nodded, looking dazed. She blinked until her eyes were dry, then asked in a stronger voice, "What do you need to know?"

"Can you tell me about that day? The day you found her?"

Kiki tapped another cigarette from the package, but instead of lighting it, just clutched it in her hand. "August 6. Charlotte had turned ten a week earlier. I was working that day, and she was supposed to go to a friend's house after school. When I got home, she wasn't back. Darnell had been there all day and he said she never even called. I was mad. Like I said, she was supposed to be back by dinnertime."

"Where did the friend live?"

"Down the street. We were in an apartment then, back in Mississippi. So, I called the friend's house and it turned out she never showed up. I guess the girls argued at school and Charlotte told her she was going home instead."

Kiki's voice was monotone, and her eyes had gone

flat, like she was retelling something she'd recounted dozens of times, but trying not to think about it. A common reaction to talking to police repeatedly, especially for the loved ones of victims. But it could also mean she was retelling the version she'd gotten used to reciting instead of what she actually remembered.

To break Kiki out of anything rehearsed, Evelyn changed direction. "Was it just you and Charlotte living in your apartment?"

Kiki blinked, some animation coming back to her eyes. "No, my boyfriend, Darnell, he lived with us, too."

"How long had he lived with you at that point?"

"A year. Year and a half, maybe."

"How long had you known him when he moved in?"

Kiki's gaze darted upward, as if she was trying to remember. "About a year. We were together a long time."

Darnell and Kiki had only stopped living together two years ago. They'd made it through Charlotte's death with their relationship intact, which Evelyn knew from other child-killing cases was saying something.

"What ended the relationship?"

"With Darnell?" Kiki pursed her lips, then threw her hands up. "I don't really know. One day, he just asked me to move out. No warning, nothing."

"Okay…"

"Why? What does that have to do with Charlotte?"

Answering that question was probably a quick way to shut Kiki down, so Evelyn said, "Let's get back to the day you found your daughter. When you discovered that she wasn't at her friend's house, what happened?"

"We called the police. Then Darnell and I started looking for her. We walked down the street to the school bus stop, but nothing. I was ready to go back up to the apartment and wait for the cops, but Darnell said let's search the building. I don't know why Charlotte would have gone anywhere else in the apartment building, but we looked."

Her voice broke and she grabbed the edge of the couch, crushing her unlit cigarette. "We found her in the laundry room. It was down in the basement. Charlotte hated going down there. Gave her the creeps. But we walked in and there she was. We saw her feet sticking out from behind the machine."

Kiki closed her eyes and tiny tremors shook her whole body. "She was dead. Strangled. And her clothes..." She broke off on a sob.

Evelyn put a hand on her arm. "I know. It's okay. We don't need to talk about that." Charlotte Novak had been sexually abused before she was killed.

"I ran over there and tried to wake her up. Darnell, he pulled me away and checked for a pulse, but he couldn't find one. So he tried to resuscitate her, but it didn't work."

And in the process, Evelyn recalled from the case file, Darnell had made testing for his DNA instantly problematic. Since he'd tried to revive her, there was a legitimate reason to find his DNA on Charlotte.

"Did Darnell say anything when the two of you found her?"

"What?" Kiki raised tear-filled eyes to hers. "I don't remember. We were in shock, we were crying."

"Both of you were crying?"

"Of course! Darnell loved Charlotte like a daughter!"

"He'd only known her for a few years, right?"

"Why does that matter?" Kiki's teary voice got angry. "We were a family."

She shot to her feet and seized a framed photo hidden behind a stack of papers, turning it to face Evelyn. It was taken at the beach. Darnell and Kiki were on either side of Charlotte, grinning widely for the camera. Between them, Charlotte had been caught midlaugh. She seemed happy, not at all uncomfortable with her mother's boyfriend.

Evelyn tried to note the blond hair and dark brown eyes objectively, to focus on the confident posture and impish light in Charlotte's eyes that suggested she was outgoing. But all she could see was a different little blonde girl whose memory she carried around everywhere she went.

"Look at him!" Kiki pointed to Darnell. "He loved her."

"Okay. But you said he was home at the time Charlotte should have arrived from school, if she hadn't gone to her friend's house. Is it possible she did go up to your apartment that day?"

"No." Shock flashed across Kiki's face. "That's... She couldn't have made it up to the apartment. Someone must've taken her on her way home from the bus."

"But the police investigated Darnell..."

"Did they arrest him?" Kiki snapped. "No, they didn't. Because he didn't do it. He never would have hurt Charlotte. *Never.*"

Evelyn stared at the fierce light in Kiki's eyes, the hard angle of her jaw, the arms she'd crossed over her chest, and knew she'd never be able to consider the possibility that Darnell had killed Charlotte. Either she truly hadn't felt even a flicker of doubt, or she couldn't bear to believe it since she'd brought him into her home.

Evelyn suspected the latter, but either way, she wasn't going to get anywhere with it, so she changed tactics.

"Eighteen years ago, Darnell helped search for the victims of the Nursery Rhyme Killer." In fact, she had no idea if he really had, but she held her breath, hoping Kiki would confirm it. "Did you go with him?"

At the mention of the Nursery Rhyme Killer, Kiki's entire body shuddered, then she said, "No. I couldn't. But Darnell wanted to help."

Evelyn fought to keep her expression neutral. "He told you about it?"

Kiki narrowed her eyes. "Darnell would never hurt a child. And I don't want to talk about this anymore." Her voice dropped to a whisper. "I want you to leave."

Evelyn nodded, holding in her frustration. "I'm sorry to bring this up again. Thanks for talking to me."

Kiki scowled and led her to the door.

As Evelyn got back into her rental car, she considered what she'd learned. If Darnell *was* the Nursery Rhyme Killer, starting with someone familiar to him wouldn't be uncommon. Afterward, he might have realized that continuing to pick victims he knew could get him caught. Or he just hadn't had any more easy access to preferred victims, so he'd begun to troll for ones he didn't know.

Talking to Kiki hadn't diminished her suspicion of Darnell. But it hadn't given her much to work with, either. What she needed was a reason to get into Darnell's house. But she had no idea what pretext would actually succeed.

And Brittany Douglas—if she was still alive—was running out of time.

Eight

Mandy Toland bit down hard on her lip, glancing behind her as she eased the sliding glass door open. Slowly, slowly. She couldn't make any noise. Couldn't let anyone know she was going outside. She'd already been stuck inside all day long. She didn't want to get grounded, too.

When the door was open just enough to slip through, she went outside, a grin breaking free. She'd done it!

She figured she had fifteen minutes before her mom noticed she wasn't in her room. That would give her time to run down to the end of the yard and pick some flowers to put in her room. If she wasn't supposed to be outside, the flowers could come *inside*.

She understood why her parents were acting so crazy. Everyone at the park had been talking about it. She didn't really know Brittany—they'd been in different classes—but she knew Brittany was missing.

The parents had all been whispering about it when they thought the kids weren't listening. Mandy had heard little bits. Someone had stolen Brittany and no one had any idea where she was. She might even be dead.

Mandy shivered as she ran for the patch of daisies

that were her favorite. Her great-aunt had died last year, which meant they'd never see her again.

Mandy wondered if she'd ever see Brittany again. They were all supposed to start middle school next year.

A funny noise from the trees made Mandy slide to a stop. She didn't see anything, but it sounded like an awfully big animal.

Spooked, Mandy spun and ran back to the house as fast as she could, no longer caring if she got grounded.

Was Cassie's abduction—and Evelyn's intended abduction—the key to solving the case now?

Evelyn flopped in the uncomfortable chair in the corner of her hotel room, exhausted after giving Tomas suggestions for finding Brittany's abductor. She'd fought hard to get a pair of cops assigned to do surveillance on Darnell.

In case it was someone else, she'd also recommended they look into deaths of children around Brittany's age from prior to eighteen years ago. It was a long shot, but if the perpetrator was trying to make up for his own loss, the death might show up in a closed case file. And it would've happened a few years before the first abduction.

She knew that if she could figure out why the abductions had stopped, it would narrow down the potential suspects. And the more she thought about it, the more certain she was that she was the key. If he'd planned to take her but hadn't, what had gone wrong?

She didn't need the case file to remember the note that had been left in Cassie's bedroom. It had been burned into her brain a month and a half ago, when she'd requested the file.

The sick nursery rhyme had been based on "Georgy

Porgy." The notes found at the previous two abductions had been left outside, where the girls had been grabbed. But Cassie had been taken right out of her bedroom, his riskiest abduction. And the note had been on her bed.

> Cassie, Cassie, do you know why,
> They don't protect you, don't try.
> All alone, you and Ev play,
> But today is the last day.

Just thinking about it gave her chills. The profiler on the original case had interpreted the note to mean the abductor was coming after both of them, and she agreed. Cassie had almost always called her Evie. The one exception was when they were going somewhere together. Evelyn could hear Cassie's words in her mind as clearly as if she was speaking: "Let's go, Ev!"

The fact that the abductor knew this proved he'd been listening closely. And it didn't matter how often she tried to relive the days leading up to Cassie's abduction. She didn't remember feeling nervous, as though someone was stalking her, watching her every move.

All she'd felt was happy. She'd finally found her home, her life.

But he'd taken it from her. And now it was time for Evelyn to take his life away, too. It didn't matter what she had to do; she wasn't leaving Rose Bay until Cassie's abductor was in jail.

But she'd been struggling from the very beginning to stay objective, to think about this case like any other. So, she dialed her BAU partner, Greg.

"Evelyn. How are you holding up? How's the case going?" Greg answered.

"Hi, Greg. I wanted to run some theories by you."

"Did Dan put you up to this?"

A surprised laugh burst out at Greg's joke. She'd been at BAU just over a year, but her boss still babied her, suggested she get Greg's help on every case. And normally, as much as she liked and respected Greg, that made her resist asking for help at all. She didn't want to prove Dan right.

But on the cases where she really *did* want a second opinion, there was no one better than Greg. "No, I just need a little objectivity."

"Sure. Tell me about the case."

"Well, you know the basics." She took a deep breath. "But eighteen years ago, the note on Cassie's bed said he'd taken me, too."

Shock rang in Greg's brief silence. "I'm so sorry, Evelyn."

There was genuine sadness in Greg's voice, but Evelyn didn't want to get bogged down in the past. If she did that now, she might never get free of the quicksand.

"I only found out about that part recently, but here's what I need help with. Why *didn't* he grab me? He took Cassie at night, left the note on her bed that said he'd taken both of us. I lived next door. Mr. and Mrs. Byers discovered Cassie was missing that morning. They'd checked on her once, so there was a seven-hour window when she must've been taken. What happened? That's what I'm trying to work out."

"Because if you determine that, it could tell you who he is," Greg mused.

"Right. I gave the cops here a list of reasons this guy could have gone dormant for eighteen years—illness, jail, someone noticing him, victims in an easier capacity, trophies satisfying him." Her nails dug crescents in her palms. "I don't know why I didn't realize this earlier, but I was just thinking about the note in Cassie's room. And when I think *only* about that night..."

"Most of those reasons don't seem to explain why he didn't come back for you. If the trophies were going to satisfy him or he had easier victims, he wouldn't have taken Cassie or left the note at all. An illness probably wouldn't be that sudden. Jail is really unlikely, unless he took Cassie wherever he was keeping his victims and then got arrested between that time and as he was going back for you. It's possible."

"But, as you said, unlikely," Evelyn agreed, trying not to imagine Cassie stuck somewhere, all alone, with no way out. Trying not to imagine her locked up in some hole, slowly dying. Her voice cracked when she told Greg, "What if someone realized what was happening? Maybe someone noticed him that night."

"You think someone knows and is keeping this guy's secret?"

Evelyn closed her eyes, sickened by the idea that someone had just stood by while Cassie was hurt, perhaps killed. "That's why I want your opinion, Greg. Is there some other reason you can think of? Some reason he didn't come back?"

"Well, he could have *planned* to go back for you, but got delayed and then it was too late."

"Maybe, but it was the middle of the night. And he had a seven-hour window. He could've run into someone at home, but would he have gone home in between? Unless he lived *really* close? Since he left a note, every minute he waited meant Cassie's parents might have woken up and decided to look in on her."

"Could he have had a partner?" Greg asked. "Someone else who was supposed to grab you, but then changed his mind?"

"No." The reply came out before she'd even really thought about it, but his suggestion didn't make sense. The person who'd spent time stalking and studying his victims so closely, who left such personally motivated notes, worked alone.

"Okay," Greg said, not questioning that she was right. "Then your perp is probably married. Or living with someone."

"Damn it," Evelyn muttered.

"And you've got a point," Greg added. "That person must've noticed he was gone and either went looking for him or called him. Or he does live close by and went home and she kept him there."

"And she probably knows what he is."

"Or at least suspects."

Fury built up to suffocating levels, but she tried to force it down and just think about how she could use the information. "So, this woman might have died and can't hold anything over him anymore. Or they recently divorced or separated, freeing him up to start again." Like Kiki and Darnell.

"And we can use that." Greg said what Evelyn had been thinking.

"Involve the media. Put out a request for help." Evelyn sighed. "She's protected him this long. What are the chances she'll come forward now?"

"Maybe if it's anonymous," Greg suggested.

A tip line. They had one, of course, but they hadn't stressed that callers could contact them anonymously. If the woman was worried about being tied to the crime because she'd kept silent for eighteen years, maybe the promise of anonymity would work. Especially if Evelyn wrote a script for the police specifically targeted toward a woman like that.

"Thanks, Greg." Evelyn stood, filled with nerves and anger and a tiny flutter of hope that she had something new to offer Tomas. Now, she just had to pray that the person who'd kept this secret for eighteen years would finally break his or her silence.

Kyle should have been resting up for the night's surveillance. But whenever he'd tried, an image of Evelyn rose in his mind, the way she'd looked as she stared, dazed, at Cassie's parents. She'd had an expression on her face he'd never seen before—as if she was terrified and alone. As if her responsibilities were burying her.

So, he'd gotten up an hour early, leaving all his heavy gear behind, and gone to Evelyn's room. Which was stupid, because she might not even be here. Knowing her, she was skipping sleep and spending all her time at the Rose Bay police station.

But when he knocked, the door opened and she was standing there in capris and a T-shirt, her long, dark hair loose around her shoulders.

"Mac," she squeaked as he tried not to gawk.

"I had some time before my mission, so..."

"Come in." She cut him off, holding the door open.

He tried to hide his surprise as he walked inside, but she probably saw it. There wasn't a hell of a lot she missed—except perhaps the huge crush he'd had on her. That, she'd managed to miss for about a year, despite Gabe's constant and ridiculous hints.

Now, obviously, she knew. But what *he* still didn't

know was what she wanted to do about it. She was definitely interested, but he'd been called away too soon to figure out much beyond that.

Given the current circumstances, he'd expected her to be distracted and push him away. Instead, she was inviting him into her room.

It was tidy, with her travel bag tucked neatly in a corner and, surprisingly, no case files spread all over her bed. No notepads filled with profiling details on the table. Although, Evelyn being Evelyn, she'd likely memorized it all.

She perched on the edge of the bed, her feet jiggling as she looked up at him. The angle emphasized the circles under her eyes and the tension in her shoulders.

As he sat down beside her, the worn mattress sank, shifting her closer. "You doing okay, Evelyn?"

"I just got off the phone with the police chief."

Okay, not exactly an answer to his question, but Evelyn hiding behind her work was pretty typical. Maybe she was doing better than he'd thought.

"He's going to set up an anonymous tip line. I think someone knows who this guy is, Mac. Greg thinks so, too."

She turned a troubled gaze on him and he immediately revoked his last impression. She was sharing case details. She was definitely not okay. She was just hiding it better than he'd expected.

"You still think it's that guy from the dunes?"

"Darnell. Yeah, he's at the top of my suspect list. But if it's not..."

"What?"

She moved slightly to face him, her knee jammed

practically underneath his thigh. "If those notes are genuine, if this guy really believes he's saving these girls..."

She cut herself off, probably at the face he must've been making. The killer thought he was *saving* his victims? Damn. He saw a lot of screwed-up things in HRT, but at least he could go in fast and hard, and take down whoever was doing it.

Evelyn had to get inside these scumbags' heads. How did she get back out again, case after case, without all that evil leaving some horrible imprint behind?

He folded her hand in both of his as she continued softly. "Mac, maybe Cassie is still alive."

He'd gone on a raid in one of those cases—where a victim was still alive nine years after being abducted. A teammate had taken a bullet that day, so he'd been at the hospital when the girl's parents had shown up. He'd seen the disbelief, the joy, the fear, on their faces as a nurse led them toward their daughter's room. She'd been seven when she went missing and was sixteen when they'd found her.

They'd all known she had a long road back, but they'd thought she was one of the lucky ones. Later, they'd learned her Stockholm syndrome was far worse than anyone expected. Two years after her rescue, her captor had been killed in prison. Twenty minutes after the girl heard the news, she'd jumped off a freeway overpass.

Sadness flooded him and he tried to keep it off his face. But this was Evelyn, so of course she saw it and glanced away.

"Should I even want that? Eighteen years. I know what that means. I *know*."

Her gaze lifted to his again, hope brimming from her

eyes. “Maybe it’s better just to hope she’s gone, but I’ve never really been able to…”

He raised her hand, tugged her closer to wrap his arms around her, and she fell against him, twined her free hand around his neck and pressed her lips to his.

The first time she’d kissed him, a month ago, it had been tentative, questioning. There was nothing tentative about this. She actually got up on her knees to eliminate the height difference between them, practically in his lap as she crushed her lips against his.

God, was this her MO? To let him close only when she was an emotional wreck?

If that was hers, his MO was apparently to take what he could get. Because even as his mind warned this wouldn’t end well, his body didn’t seem to be getting the message.

One hand still clutching hers, he tightened his hold on her with the other, until she was plastered against him, his tongue in her mouth. Until she made a soft, utterly female noise that sounded like approval and she actually did climb in his lap.

And then anything resembling coherent thought fled. He had no idea how long he kissed her—seconds, minutes, hours —when her phone blared, loud and insistent.

She jerked backward so fast she would have fallen off the bed if he hadn’t grabbed her. Flushed and panting, she stared at him, eyes wide with pure shock.

Then she leaped off him and fumbled for her phone, answering it breathlessly.

He could immediately tell it was bad news, because all expression instantly fled. Her game face.

"Okay, I'm on my way," she said a minute later, then hung up.

"What happened?"

"Another girl was just abducted."

Nine

Evelyn entered the station's briefing room, overflowing with police officers and FBI agents. It was almost hard to breathe as she waded into too many opinions and too much emotion.

"Who did we have under surveillance when this happened?" Jack demanded.

"How close does this victim live to Brittany?" Carly called out.

"*How* did this happen?" a rookie officer boomed, his voice carrying above the fray. "How the hell did he grab her with the whole town out there looking for him? With all the cops on the streets? How could no one have seen anything?"

His loud, frustrated questions silenced the crowd and Tomas stepped behind the podium. The exhaustion that had been evident from the day she'd arrived had multiplied, leaving a grayish hue on his skin.

"We got the call one hour ago. Time is crucial," Tomas reminded them. "So, I'm going to brief you fast, and then everyone's going out. Four of the CARD agents are already at the victim's house, getting statements. But we've got the basics. There was a note."

At those words, the tension notched up. Evelyn looked around. Nothing but locked jaws and nervous eyes.

She felt as tense as everyone around her. Even though she'd expected the abductor not to stop—she'd tried to drive it home in her profile—she hadn't expected it to happen this fast. It meant the abductor was impatient. Which might make him more likely to mess up, but also more dangerous.

"We have a short window of opportunity for the abduction time. The victim's mom had seen her an hour before she found the note. The girl was grabbed from her own private, fenced backyard."

Cops shifted on their feet, visibly quivering with anxiety and anger. Someone muttered, "Parents are actually letting their kids outside alone?"

"She wasn't supposed to be outside," Tomas said. "She'd gone into the backyard when her mom thought she was in her bedroom."

"Are we sure she wasn't grabbed from her bedroom?" Evelyn spoke up, thinking of Cassie.

"Yes. The note was left in the backyard, taped to the girl's jump rope. Her mom said that's usually kept in their shed, so her daughter must have gone outside to play. She hadn't expressly told her not to go out alone." Tomas hunched lower over the podium. "The mom's beating herself up over that. But her daughter had said she was going to her room to read and the mom was running the vacuum, so she wouldn't have heard the door open."

Evelyn nodded. Of the original cases, only Cassie's had happened inside her house. It was logical that after eighteen years the abductor would be more cautious, not take that kind of risk again.

On the other hand, any grab in the middle of a multi-agency investigation of this magnitude was risky.

It was an odd combination—the careful abduction combined with the increased pace after eighteen years of silence. Her hopes for a mistake slipped away, and her worry over what he might do next increased.

"Any chance this isn't really the Nursery Rhyme Killer? Any chance it's a family thing?" Jack's partner asked.

"We're looking into that," Carly contributed from near the podium. "It's always possible someone is taking advantage of Brittany's abduction to make a grab. The girl's parents are divorced. We're trying to track down the dad, because he did fight hard for custody and lost. The stepfather is making a lot of noise, saying the note is just a way to get us to look in another direction, away from the girl's father."

The cops around her seemed to take a collective breath, until Carly added, "But the note was pretty similar, so our instinct is that this is connected."

"We'll have the profiler review it for her impressions," Tomas said, "but right now, we're putting most of our resources into the assumption that it's the same person."

"What does the note say?" someone asked.

Tomas looked down at the podium and flipped a few pages. "This time, he manipulated the nursery rhyme 'Humpty Dumpty.'" He picked up a remote, and the screen behind him flashed to life, showing the note blown up huge.

I can't believe you have the gall,
Not to watch 'cause the fence is tall.

She won't be safe until the moment when
I whisk her off to the warmth of my den.

"Sicko," a rookie spat, and around him officers nodded and clutched their batons.

Evelyn reread the note. The abductor was focused on the abduction stage and addressing the parents. His appetite for punishment was stronger now than it had been eighteen years ago. But he still seemed to think he was helping the girls he abducted.

Or at least that was the motivation he wanted them to see.

"Who's the victim?" Jack's voice, more timid than usual, seemed to echo in the room.

"Her name is Lauren Shay." Tomas flicked the remote and a picture replaced the note up on the screen.

Lauren was fair-skinned and freckled, her brown hair short and curly, her light brown eyes full of mischief. The picture had caught her midlaugh, looking like a twelve-year-old should. Happy. Carefree. Safe.

"Oh, God," the cop next to Evelyn whispered. "I've been friends with her stepdad for years. I can't believe it's Lauren."

"Where are we with the surveillance?" Evelyn asked. If the pair of cops had been watching Darnell, that would eliminate him as a suspect.

Tomas shook his head at her. "We'd just gotten that coordinated, Evelyn. We didn't have anyone on Darnell yet."

"At any rate, this knocks Wiggins off the list," Jack's partner said. "Since he's in the hospital."

"No, it doesn't." Tomas sighed. "He was released yesterday. We had officers on him for a few hours today, but he didn't leave his house, and we're stretched thin."

What he didn't say aloud, Evelyn knew, was that they'd been pulled to run some other leads she'd suggested instead.

Shit. What horrible timing. A coincidence? Or was Walter Wiggins more resourceful than she'd realized?

"I want to talk to Wiggins," Jack blurted, his tone indicating it wasn't a request.

Tomas looked pointedly at her and Evelyn nodded. "I'll go with him."

"Okay." Tomas glanced around the room. "We're also going to be reviewing the lists of search party volunteers. The search parties were out in force today, and Lauren's mom saw a lot of those volunteers searching the fields near her house. It was getting late by the time Lauren was taken, so the groups had thinned out. But it's possible the perp used the search parties as cover to grab Lauren."

Evelyn could sense disgust rolling through the room as she realized Tomas was right. She'd suspected all along that the abductor was joining the search parties. If he could use them to help him get a new victim, that would feed his fantasies even more.

"Noreen?" Tomas said, gesturing his administrative assistant forward.

Noreen walked toward the podium, wringing her hands. She was about twenty-five, with shoulder-length dark hair and perpetually downcast eyes. Every time Evelyn had seen her at the station, she'd been wearing a long skirt and blouse, and was almost painfully shy. She was clearly more comfortable working quietly behind a desk than talking to a room full of noisy cops.

But they must have respected her, because the cops quieted down as she reached Tomas's side.

"Noreen's in charge of taking the names of all volunteers. Anyone who joined the search parties is on her list."

"I'm doing background checks on everyone," Noreen told them. "We've got some volunteers with criminal histories, but nothing related to children so far." She looked over at Tomas, as if she didn't know whether she was supposed to say anything else.

Not surprising, Evelyn thought. Even though Walter was beginning to look like more of a possibility, her gut was still telling her the perp hadn't been caught before—at least not for any crime related to kids.

She'd also had Tomas check records for the night of Cassie's abduction, but there hadn't been any arrests. There *had* been a pileup that had sent several people to the hospital but none who fit the profile.

Tomas thanked Noreen, who scurried away from the podium. "Carly Sanchez, from the FBI's CARD team, will be giving out everyone's assignments," Tomas said. "Let's go now."

The cops around Evelyn sprang forward. They seemed encouraged by the fact that there'd been less time between Lauren's abduction and their notification. Which should mean a better chance of finding her.

But Evelyn knew what Tomas hadn't said. Since the Nursery Rhyme Killer had taken Lauren, Brittany's chances had just dropped to near zero.

"There it is!" Jack set his giant cup of take-out coffee in her drink holder and pointed.

Evelyn tried not to roll her eyes in response. Like she could possibly miss Walter Wiggins's house.

It was ten-thirty at night, but the street was well-lit, and all the houses had security lighting. West Shore Drive was lined with nicely manicured lawns and well-maintained middle-class homes. It practically screamed *respectability.*

And then there was the house at the end of the block. The house and yard were looked after, although lacking in personality or flowers. But someone had taken a sledgehammer to the white picket fence, spray painted the words *pervert* and *child killer* across the front door and driven a huge wooden sign into the ground. As they got closer, Evelyn saw the sign had Walter Wiggins's sex offender registry picture glued to it.

"Is anyone doing something about this?" Evelyn parked in the driveway, hoping no one would vandalize her rental while they were inside.

"Are you kidding me?" Jack demanded as he stepped out and stomped toward the front door. "We're a little preoccupied. Jeez."

Evelyn frowned. He was right. Brittany had been missing for forty-nine hours now, Lauren for an hour and a half. That was where her focus was, too.

But it made her sad to see the town she'd grown up in like this. As hard as it could sometimes be, she believed in equal application of the law; it had to protect criminals and innocents alike.

Will I feel that way if it turns out Walter is the culprit? a tiny voice whispered in her head. If she learned he'd abducted, molested and murdered Cassie? She hardened her heart, and pushed the thought aside, not wanting to answer that question, even to herself.

She tried to step in front of Jack as they went up the walkway, but he used his bulk to block her, and pounded on the door. “Wiggins! Open up! Police!”

“Jack. Low-key. Like we talked about in the car.” When he ignored her, she grabbed his sleeve and forced him to look at her. “I realize I’m not your favorite person here, but I know this kind of crime better than you ever will. You follow *my* lead here. Okay?”

When the door opened an inch—still chained from inside—Jack was staring at her in shock. Apparently, despite the past two days, he still expected her to act like the timid twelve-year-old he’d once brought to tears.

Well, he was in for a surprise. Because no way was she letting anyone screw this case up.

She peered through the crack in the doorway and into the well-lit house. “Walter Wiggins?” She held her FBI credentials up close to the sliver of face she could see—just a long, pale nose, blotched with purple from the recent beating, and nervous gray eyes. “I’m Evelyn Baine, FBI. I have a few questions.”

Walter squinted at her credentials. Then his gaze darted to Jack and a muscle near his eye started twitching. “What now?” he asked so quietly Evelyn had to lean closer to hear.

“This will only take a few minutes, Mr. Wiggins. Can we come inside?”

Walter’s prominent Adam’s apple bobbed, then the door closed and opened again, wider this time.

Evelyn tried not to reveal her shock. The vague memory she had of Walter from thirteen years ago—right before she’d left town for college—was still pretty accurate. Short brown hair was styled across his forehead in a schoolboy cut, big ears peeking out from the edges.

He couldn't maintain eye contact. He was thirty-eight, according to her records, but he could almost pass for eighteen.

Even the dark purple bruises beneath his eyes and the tape on his broken nose didn't make him look dangerous. To someone who didn't know him, Walter probably looked like a schoolkid who'd been bullied and beaten up. Not a convicted child molester who'd been on the losing side of an angry father's fists.

Discomfort squirmed through her. Walter's nonthreatening appearance would be an asset if he was still trying to charm children. Regardless of whether parents warned their kids to stay away from him, he just looked harmless. No outward sign of the monster within.

Behind her, Jack pushed his way into the house, aggressively enough to make Walter back up a few steps. "Wiggins. Can we take a seat somewhere?" Jack asked in a strained voice.

Walter blinked a few times, glancing from her to Jack, then straightened his spine. "Sure. Okay. Come on."

He led them down a short, dark hallway, walking on the balls of his feet, silently, and slightly hunched over.

As they reached the living room, a feeble voice called from the other end of the house, "Who's here?"

"It's okay, Dad!" Walter said. "Just a couple of guests!"

Jack snorted as he sat on a couch straight out of the fifties. He stretched his legs in front of him; he seemed to be settling in for the long haul.

Evelyn surveyed the room as Walter huddled in the recliner as far away from Jack as possible. The room had peeling wallpaper and doilies on every available surface, and Evelyn suspected it hadn't changed since Walter's mom had died. If there was any sign of Walter's personality here, she didn't see it.

It didn't give her much to go on. Usually, questioning people inside their houses gave her a starting point, some personality cues. With Walter, all she had was body language.

She sat on the third chair in the room, across from Jack and next to Walter. "Thirteen years ago, you were convicted of three counts of fourth-degree sexual assault and two counts of third-degree sexual assault. The victims were all girls around the ages of Brittany Douglas and Lauren Shay."

Walter's body seemed to go into spasms, and he ducked his head farther into his chest.

Jack turned toward her, and the smirk playing on his lips and his raised eyebrow seemed to ask, *This is low-key?*

Walter wrapped his arms around his stomach, folding further into himself. "I didn't—"

Jack's lips twisted in a snarl, and Evelyn interrupted before he could. "I don't want to argue about that. I just want to eliminate you as a suspect today. Can you help me?"

Walter's mouth dropped open, but just as quickly he snapped it shut and narrowed his eyes. He was clearly suspicious of what she'd said, but it was true. She had to consider him a suspect, but she didn't think he was sophisticated enough to pull off the recent abductions without being seen.

"How?" Walter asked. "The police already questioned me about Brittany. I was home, but they don't believe me."

"What about today? Where have you been the past three hours?"

"Home," Walter snapped, straightening up, his hands squeezing the chair arms.

"Can anyone corroborate that?"

"My father was home, but he's not well. His health… He was asleep and…"

"You want to prove you're innocent?" Jack broke in. "How about you walk us through your house, basement included?"

Walter squinted at Jack a long moment. "Like that would prove anything. Doesn't matter what I do, you're going to insist it's me."

Evelyn studied him as he glared at Jack. Was it pure resentment that made him refuse? Or fear of what they'd find?

Even if it was the latter, it didn't necessarily mean he was guilty of abducting Brittany and Lauren. The fact was, given his history, there was a strong likelihood he was hiding *something* in this house. Assuming he was innocent of these crimes, she guessed child pornography on his computer.

She tried to keep the disgust off her face. She needed him to see her as an ally—but how?

She knew he was intelligent; the degree from a top university and subsequent job with a high-powered lobbyist firm proved that. And judging from the way he was staring Jack down, he was less browbeaten than he'd originally appeared.

If he'd started abducting children when he was twenty, that meant he'd gotten away with it for a few years. Then he'd moved to DC and discovered he could find victims without having to kidnap them, which should've been less dangerous. But he'd been arrested, so maybe the brief stint in jail had scared him off. At least for a while.

Then, by the time he'd worked up the courage to try again, with his record, no one would let him near their kids. Maybe he'd once more resorted to abducting them.

But it still came back to whether or not he could get away with it without being noticed. He was a pariah in Rose Bay, his every move watched. Could he really have pulled it off?

As Evelyn pondered this, Jack raised his eyebrows at her, then finally let out an exaggerated sigh and stood. "I gotta use the bathroom, Wiggins."

Walter frowned. "Then go back to the station."

"Come on," Jack said. "Some reason you don't want me in there?"

Walter scowled and fidgeted, apparently trying to come up with a good answer, then finally stood up, too. He led Jack down the hall, glancing repeatedly back at her.

When he returned to the living room, his beaten-down mask was firmly back in place. "What's with all the harassment? You see what's happening in my dad's yard? Where are the police when I call?"

"You've called the police about this?"

"Yeah." Walter dropped back into his seat. "They took a statement. And they were sure to tell me how I was taking time away from searching for Brittany."

Evelyn leaned toward him. "Look, Walter, how about you walk us through the house? We're not interested in what's on your computer, okay?" Not now, anyway. But she was definitely going to be talking to Tomas about getting permission to check Walter's computer once Lauren and Brittany were found. "Just show us that no one's here."

He looked pensive and she thought he was ready to agree when Jack strolled back into the room.

Anger showed on Walter's face. "So you can find some way to set me up? I don't think so."

"I promise you, I don't care about any pictures you have down there," she lied, desperate for a chance to search his house. "Just let us take a quick look, verify the girls aren't there and we'll leave. Cross you off our list."

"Bullshit," Walter barked, straightening in his seat and folding his arms over his chest.

Okay, time for a new approach. "Have you seen the search parties around, Walter?"

"What? Yeah, I guess."

"How do you feel about them?"

"What are you talking about?"

"Do you think they'll find the missing girls?" she prodded. If she could get him to talk about the case, hopefully it would give her a sense of how much he was hiding.

Whoever had gotten away with the abductions for eighteen years was careful, resisted the natural urge to brag or talk excessively about the investigation. But he'd want to. And the abductions starting up again, with two so close together, meant he was less controlled this time around.

Walter glowered at her. "How should I know?"

Jack's annoyed gaze landed on her, too, and Evelyn tried not to squirm. She'd guided plenty of interrogations before, dealt with lots of uncooperative subjects. Was she approaching Walter wrong or was it the whole case?

Dan's voice rose in her mind, telling her she was too close to the case to be objective.

She vaulted to her feet and asked if she could use Walter's bathroom, too.

He threw her an incredulous look. "The police station have plumbing problems?" When she didn't answer, he pointed down the hall, apparently less willing to leave Jack alone.

This hallway resembled the one into the living room—poorly lit with bare walls. The bedroom doors she passed were closed, so finally she let herself into the small bathroom. Just like the living room, it was stuck in the past, with green trains on the walls and rubber ducky adhesive strips on the tub floor.

She assumed it was designed for Walter as a boy and had never been redecorated. But then, she didn't know how ill Walter's father was. Maybe he never left his bedroom and didn't know what was happening right down the hall.

After a brief internal argument, Evelyn eased open the medicine cabinet. Inside, everything had its place. Bottles of over-the-counter medicine were positioned just so, all the labels facing front. A manicure set was on the bottom shelf, Walter's name printed on it in black ink. A razor lay beside it.

Everything in the cabinet belonged to Walter. Nothing for a child. She frowned, closing the cabinet.

Unlike the living room, this was almost too orderly, even the soap dispenser at a perfect right angle to the sink. This was entirely Walter's space.

So, he was precise and careful, somewhat obsessive-compulsive. Not unexpected, really, given his personality. Though they were also traits the abductor shared.

She flushed the toilet and ran the sink tap for a minute. She was about to leave the room when she realized something was off. Glancing around, she noticed the tank on the toilet. The lid was slightly askew. Just a centimeter, but that was a lot for someone this neat.

She stared at it, debating. She shouldn't even have opened the medicine cabinet. But her feet were already moving and as she carefully lifted the lid and set it on the seat, her pulse picked up. Taped inside was a sealed plastic bag.

She pulled the edge of her T-shirt over her fingers as she took the bag out and removed the contents. And holy shit, Jack was right. Walter Wiggins could very possibly be the Nursery Rhyme Killer.

She flipped through the stack of pictures inside, carefully memorizing the faces of the young girls. And the backgrounds. Some of them had been shot at the park near where she'd once lived. And others had the elementary school in the background. How the hell had Walter gotten those shots?

And why was he taking them? Because he was a voyeur who couldn't get close enough to an actual child to go back to his criminal ways? Or because he'd been choosing new victims he planned to abduct?

She hadn't thought he was the Nursery Rhyme Killer, but that was partly because she hadn't thought he'd be able to get close enough to a child to grab one. She didn't know when these shots had been taken, but either he'd been using a damn good zoom lens or she was wrong on that second count.

Carefully resealing the bag, she taped it exactly where it had been. She debated whether to set the lid back straight, but decided to leave it slightly tilted, just as she'd found it.

Unease settled over her as she returned to the living

room where Jack and Walter were silently scowling at each other.

Had her insistence on putting surveillance on Darnell instead of Walter given him the opportunity he needed to grab Lauren?

They needed a real plan for Walter. And they needed it now.

"We should go," she blurted to Jack, then spun toward the door before he could respond.

"What?" he called after her. "If you don't have any more questions, I sure as hell do!"

"Let's go!" Evelyn shouted, replaying the pictures she'd seen in her head over and over again.

Neither Brittany nor Lauren had been in the shots. But maybe that was because he'd already grabbed them. For all she knew, Walter had a brand-new note waiting on his computer right now. Maybe one of the girls in the pictures was his next intended victim.

Ten

Nausea rose in Evelyn's throat as she replayed the girls' faces from Walter's pictures over and over in her head. Along with the images came memories she had pushed down for years. She gagged and tossed Jack her rental car keys.

"What the hell?" he demanded as he caught them. "We need to question him some more."

"I'll explain in the car. Just get in."

Scowling and swearing, he shoved the driver's seat backward so he could climb in and then they were speeding toward the police station.

When she stayed silent, Jack snapped, "So, explain."

"Inside the toilet tank in the bathroom, Walter had pictures of girls. Not Brittany or Lauren, but that age."

Jack glanced at her, looking unsurprised even as his hands tightened around the steering wheel. "I told you. He's a sick, slimy bastard. He did this."

"We need to talk to Tomas about trying to get a warrant."

"Yeah? How, exactly? Inside the toilet tank isn't in plain sight."

"I don't know." Evelyn sighed. "But you guys can get class pictures, right? I want to go through and identify them for you."

Jack punched down on the gas. "Yeah. How many were there?"

"About a dozen."

"A *dozen*?" Jack rubbed his forehead, swearing under his breath.

Evelyn turned her head and stared out the window into the darkness. It was past midnight, the streets empty, the search parties home in bed by now.

Had she made a mistake rushing out fast so she could try to identify all the girls she'd seen in case they were intended future victims? Should she have stayed, pressed harder to search the whole house?

Back in Walter Wiggins's basement, was Lauren locked up, unable to scream for help? Was Brittany there with her? If so, what hell were they living?

The nausea worsened until she knew she couldn't hold it back. "Jack, stop the car. Stop the car!"

He slammed on the brakes and she just managed to get her seat belt undone and heave herself outside before throwing up her dinner all over the curb. Her eyes watered, and the memories she'd suppressed for so many years raced through her, as vivid as if it had been yesterday.

The smell of cheap vodka seemed to fill her nostrils as an image of the old apartment she'd shared with her mom so long ago overwhelmed her. Evelyn's father had been dead four years by then, and his features had already started to blur in her memory.

Her mom had been trying to replace him ever since, with one man after the next. None of them lasted. Most ignored her, and she'd quickly learned how to hide from the ones with angry fists.

He'd been different. She'd never even known his name, but the guy before him had moved out and suddenly he was living with them. He'd looked normal. Not strung out or drunk like most of the others. But there'd been something predatory in his eyes that warned her to keep her distance.

For two weeks, he'd kept his distance, too. Until the night her mom passed out on the living room couch. Evelyn had been in her bedroom, using a reading lamp instead of her overhead light so they wouldn't realize she was still awake as she worked on her homework.

Slowly, the door had pushed open, and she'd seen his surprise that she wasn't sleeping. As he'd shut the door behind him, she'd instinctively scrambled off her bed. But he'd continued toward her, palms out as though he was trying to reassure her.

The bedroom seemed to shrink as she'd backed up until she hit the wall, with nowhere to run, no way to hide. She'd already been crying, silent tears dripping down her cheeks as she lifted her hands in front of her, expecting his palm to connect with her face.

Instead, he'd picked her up, lightning-fast, and tossed her on her bed. She'd landed on top of her spiral-edged notebook, the spine bruising her back. Then he'd been hovering over her, tearing at her pajamas, his rancid breath in her face mingling with the scent of her own fear.

She'd fought back, pummeling him with her small fists until he'd slapped her, so hard it bloodied her nose and halted her punching. Her right hand had landed on top of the pencil, and without thought, she'd clutched it.

Somehow, he'd already pushed his jeans down, so when she'd stabbed at him as hard as she could, the pencil had torn through the skin on his thigh, deep enough to embed in muscle. He'd yelped, stumbling on the jeans around his ankles, and falling backward.

And she'd run, screaming for help. But her mother hadn't moved on the couch, so she'd turned the other way, toward the bathroom, the only room in the apartment with a lock. She'd managed to latch it just in time and then he was there, pounding on the door until it shook and she knew it wasn't going to hold.

She'd curled up on the floor, huddled against the bathtub, sobbing. Then she'd heard banging at the front door, the police yelling at him to open up. She'd stood, held her ear to the bathroom door. Waited for the cops to take him away.

Then she'd heard her mom's voice, sounding only slightly drunk, telling the cops they'd had an argument and they'd quiet down. Evelyn shouldn't have been shocked, but she was.

As the police left, her tears had stopped. Strangely calm, she'd opened the bathroom window and climbed through it, then walked down the street in bare feet and ripped pajamas to the nearest pay phone. Thank God someone had left change in the return chute.

She'd called the only people who'd made her feel safe since her dad. Her grandpa had arrived so fast to pick her up he must have run every light for three towns. She'd gone to live with him and her grandma and never looked back.

It wasn't until later that she'd discovered how much her grandparents had agonized over what to do. They'd been afraid if they pressed charges, somehow they wouldn't stick—something Evelyn had seen too many times since, during her years in law enforcement. And they'd been afraid if they hadn't, her mom would have a kidnapping claim and still get her back.

Her mom had shown up again when Evelyn was seventeen and her grandma had her stroke. Evelyn had been shocked to learn her grandparents had threatened their daughter. They'd told her mom that if she ever tried to take Evelyn back, they'd do whatever it took to make sure she went to jail.

It was probably a threat they couldn't have fulfilled, but they must have convinced her mom, because she'd stayed away for seven long, blissful years.

Her grandparents had still kept in touch with their daughter, trying to get her clean, hoping one day she and Evelyn could have a relationship again. It had been Evelyn who'd cut off ties entirely. And she'd never really regretted it.

As the memories faded, Evelyn realized she was still hunched on the curb, her arms clutched around her stomach. Jack was crouched next to her, patting her back and muttering nonsense about everything being okay, they'd get Wiggins.

Her face heating, Evelyn got to her feet. "Sorry," she croaked.

Jack eyed her speculatively as he stood. "The cases with kids are always the worst. I get it. I go to domestic scenes, or these damn kidnappings, and I feel so helpless, so fucking useless." His voice gained volume. "Especially this kind of thing. You know someone's guilty, or you know someone is neglecting their kids, and you don't have the power to *do* anything. Makes me sick."

He blew out a huge breath, then got back into the car.

They drove the rest of the way to the station in silence and then Evelyn was telling Tomas what she'd seen at Walter's house.

Tomas glanced back and forth between her and Jack. "You put them back exactly where they were? He's not going to know you found them?"

"I put them back exactly where I found them." Evelyn frowned. "But he's obsessively organized. It's possible he'll move them, since both Jack and I were in there."

Jack nodded, scowling. "Yeah, and as soon as you left that bathroom, you practically dragged me out the door."

Tomas rubbed bloodshot eyes. "I'll talk to a judge, but it's not going to be easy. Just the fact that he's an offender isn't enough reason to get a search warrant. Shit!" He strode to his office door, then yelled, "T.J.!"

When he came running over, Tomas told him, "I need pictures from all the elementary school classes. Check with Ronald—I know we've got copies."

As T.J. ran back into the bull pen to talk to Ronald, the station's second administrative assistant, Evelyn gave Tomas a questioning look.

He sighed heavily. "Precautions. All these damn mass shootings over the past few years, we do drills at the mall and the schools. The school district went a step further and sends us information on personnel and students every year, just in case. I hoped like hell we'd never need any of it. Will you be able to pick the kids out?"

"I tried to memorize all the pictures, but there were twelve," Evelyn said.

T.J. hurried in with a small stack of pictures. "What's happening?"

"Get back out there," Tomas said. "And shut the door."

T.J. didn't look happy, but from the glance Jack shot him, Evelyn knew he'd get the scoop soon enough.

When he'd left the room, Tomas had her flip through the photos, and Evelyn identified nine of the girls, then shook her head. "I don't see any more."

Tomas turned to Jack. "What about you?"

"I never saw the photos."

"Damn it." Tomas slid behind his desk again, taking the class photos, now marked up with black circles around the girls featured in Walter's pictures. "I'm going to talk to these girls' parents."

"I don't think—" Evelyn began.

"I won't tell them you found the pictures illegally," Tomas interrupted. "I'm not going to tell them we found pictures at all. I'm just going to say we have reason to believe they should be particularly careful." He glanced at his watch, swore, then set down the phone he'd picked up. "I didn't realize it was already past midnight. I'll do it tomorrow."

When Evelyn got ready to argue about not saying anything to them, he asked, "Evelyn, do you have children?"

"No."

"Well, trust me, it's better I scare these parents than I stay silent and one of these girls is the next to go missing. I'll work on the warrant, but in the meantime, I've got to put those officers back on Wiggins and not Darnell."

Evelyn nodded, even though the idea of leaving Darnell without surveillance made her uneasy. "We've got to consider Walter a serious threat. But is there anyone you can spare for Darnell? He was with the search parties, his girlfriend's daughter's murder twenty years ago was never solved and he fits the profile in a lot of ways."

"Except race," Jack reminded her.

"Yeah, well, Walter was low on my suspect list for the same reason—not his race, but why I profiled the perp as white. That otherwise he'd get noticed on those streets. I just..."

"I know," Tomas said. "But I don't have the manpower. Talk to the CARD agents. Maybe they can spare someone."

Evelyn's shoulders dropped. She knew how these cases worked. The CARD agents couldn't sit on Darnell, either, not unless there was a much more compelling reason to suspect him than her gut.

But they could probably get the bloodhound close enough to Walter's house to do a perimeter sweep, if they hadn't already. She suggested it to Tomas and he picked up the phone again, waving her to the door.

Suddenly feeling every minute of the past eighteen hours since she'd woken and headed for the dunes, Evelyn stood. "Let me know about the search warrant."

Meanwhile, if the cops were covering Walter Wiggins, she'd have to figure out what to do about Darnell Conway.

Evelyn had intended to drive straight back to the hotel. But instead she found herself in Treighton, driving slowly onto Darnell's street.

The neighborhood was dark and silent, no streetlights and few porch lights lit up. Evelyn glanced at the dashboard clock as she pulled to a stop down the street from Darnell's house—2:00 a.m.

What had she expected? Darnell to be outside, with Lauren and Brittany in tow?

She rubbed her eyes, exhausted and frustrated, with her trip to Walter Wiggins's house too fresh in her mind.

Brittany had been missing more than two full days now. And since Evelyn had arrived, all she'd been able to give the cops were possibilities.

Maybe he's a molester. Maybe he thinks he's a savior. Maybe it's Walter Wiggins. Maybe it's Darnell Conway.

She needed something concrete. She needed to bring Lauren and Brittany home, and God, perhaps even Cassie.

Evelyn got out of her car. When she and Jack had visited Darnell earlier, she'd gotten the impression that in this neighborhood, no one saw anything. Hopefully she'd been right.

She walked slowly toward Darnell's house, blinking to adjust to the moonless night. She kept her steps measured, knowing that in the darkness movement might attract the attention of anyone who happened to be looking out the window.

She was at Darnell's house before she'd really thought it out—either what she could possibly hope to find or what she planned to do. But then she was slinking along the side of Darnell's house, toward his backyard.

The shades on the windows she passed were all drawn, no sign of light inside. The yard itself was darker than the street, lined entirely with thick arborvitae trees that provided a live fence. And a lot of privacy.

She moved carefully, her hands in front of her, because even with her eyes mostly adjusted, it was hard to see. But as far as she could tell, there was nothing in Darnell's yard. No patio furniture, no flowers, no sign of personality besides an obsessive neatness in the precision of the trees.

At the back of the house, too, the shades were completely lowered. Evelyn's steps slowed, even as her heart rate kept up its unnatural pace. There was nothing here.

And as a six-year law enforcement veteran, she knew how reckless her actions were. She was trespassing, and if she did find something, it would be tainted and useless. But as the best friend of a girl who'd had her whole life stolen from her, Evelyn couldn't bring herself to turn back.

Especially when she saw the shed at the corner of the property, nestled tight against the trees. Smaller evergreens had been placed in front of it, as though someone had planted those later to conceal the tiny structure.

There was a lock on the shed doors, but it was really basic. Evelyn glanced behind her. Seeing nothing, she reached into the messy bun she'd made after getting the call about Lauren and pulled out a bobby pin. Bending it straight, she shoved it into the lock and fiddled until the latch popped free.

She reminded herself that this was a bad idea, but opened the door, anyway, and stepped into the shed. Taking out her cell phone to use as a flashlight, she looked around the little structure.

It was the cleanest shed she'd ever seen. The floor was neatly swept, every tool in its place on shelving units. A wheelbarrow that looked brand-new stood against the back wall. Lined up next to it were a set of shovels that practically sparkled, although the worn handles showed they'd been used.

She angled her cell phone around, looking for anything that would tell her if Darnell stalked and abducted children. On the top shelf, she spotted three rolls of duct tape and several neatly coiled piles of rope. Some of the rope was of a size that might be handy for bundling yard debris; others were more suitable for something like restraining small victims.

But it was hardly unusual. Plenty of people used rope and duct tape, most of them for perfectly legitimate reasons.

The only thing she'd learned from Darnell's shed was that he was neat and orderly, very deliberate and careful. The fact that those were all qualities shared by the Nursery Rhyme Killer didn't mean they were the same person.

Hell, Walter Wiggins was neat and orderly to the point of obsession, too.

Just as she'd decided to give up and get out of Darnell's yard, the door to the shed was yanked open, and a light flashed in her eyes.

Evelyn instinctively went for her weapon, but froze as a harsh voice yelled, "Police! Hands up!"

She raised her hands toward the ceiling, dread squeezing her chest. What the hell had she done?

"I'm with the FBI. My creds are in my pocket."

The cop kept his weapon leveled on her, but lowered his light, and Evelyn blinked until the spots swarming in front of her eyes disappeared. In their place, a portly uniformed cop with a deep scowl filled her vision.

"Reach for your identification slowly."

Everything about his tone told her he wasn't inclined to give her any professional slack. As she handed over her creds, she hoped she hadn't just handed in her career.

He studied them, then raised his eyebrows. "What are you doing here, Agent Baine? We got a call about a trespasser."

Evelyn glanced past the cop, toward Darnell's house.

Did he have a sensor system in his yard? How had he known she was here? "Who called?"

He holstered his weapon, ignoring her question. "Let's go. You can ride with us to the station."

"I'm consulting on a case with the Rose Bay PD," Evelyn said quickly. "I was here to talk to this resident and I heard a..."

"You're really going to try the suspicious-noise bullshit on me?" the cop interrupted. "And I know exactly why you're here. That's the station you're supposed to report to, not Treighton. Someone from the Rose Bay PD called us, said they'd gotten the report of trespassing. The caller mentioned you by name, Agent Baine."

Then it was definitely Darnell. Evelyn felt her lips curl as she stepped out of the shed. "You knew I was with the Bureau when you pulled your weapon on me?"

"Hey, the report could've been wrong. Can't be too careful."

Biting back a sharp response, Evelyn said, "I'm parked just down the street. I can get myself to the station."

"Fine. But you'd better report there or it's my ass." He gave her a fake smile. "And if that happens, I won't be inclined to do you any favors when I write up my incident report."

"It won't be a problem," she told him as she headed for her car, cursing the entire way.

What was she going to find at the station? Tomas was already pissed about what she'd done at Walter Wiggins's house. She was in Rose Bay at their request. Would he send her home because of this?

And if he did, would her boss make sure this was her last case?

Eleven

"You came back."

The whispered words were so quiet Evelyn almost didn't turn around as she walked into the station. When she did, Noreen Abbott was standing by the door, looking like she was on her way out.

Her dark hair was wilted against her face, her bag tugged down her shoulder, a bag that was obviously full of work, and dark smudges lined her eyes.

"Yeah, just to talk to Tomas for a minute," Evelyn said, hoping Noreen didn't know the real reason she'd returned to the station at three-thirty in the morning.

"No, I mean, back in Rose Bay."

"Oh. Yes." Even though Noreen wasn't a police officer, she was so involved in the case she probably knew Evelyn had been an intended victim eighteen years ago.

"You don't remember me," Noreen said softly.

Did Noreen remember *her*? "Sorry. No. I think we were a few years apart in school."

"We were. I was just in kindergarten when your friend disappeared. But it's stamped on my memory."

"Oh." Of course it was. The child abductions had torn

apart all the illusions Rose Bay had about being a safe, close-knit community. And even though a kindergartner wouldn't have known any real details, Evelyn would've stood out, the only girl of mixed race in the entire elementary school.

She glanced toward Tomas's office, where the light was still on. "Tomas is waiting for me."

"Sure. No problem." Noreen nodded, looking at her feet. "Anyway, it sounds like you're really getting into this guy's head. We all appreciate it," she added as she turned and pushed open the door.

With a sigh, Evelyn headed in the other direction.

When she walked into Tomas's office, he lifted his head and glared at her with bloodshot eyes. "Sit."

"I'm sorry..."

"Just sit."

She did, her nerves jangling.

"Darnell Conway called me tonight, Evelyn. You're damn lucky I was still here when the call came in, because he demanded I get someone down there to escort you off his property or he was calling the Treighton cops and the FBI directly."

Pounding a fist on his desk, Tomas jumped to his feet. "I don't have the manpower to waste on this kind of shit! I should've let him make an official complaint to the FBI, but damn it, we need a profiler here."

He pointed at his door, toward the bull pen. "My veteran officers—the ones I *already* have problems with because they aren't thrilled to have me as their supervisor—are looking for any reason to get rid of you. And you just about handed it to them. When they hear about this, and believe me, they will, you're going to lose what little ground you've gained."

Losing steam all of a sudden, he sank back into his chair. "You want to explain what the hell you were thinking?"

"Darnell Conway is—"

"You know what?" Tomas held up a hand, shaking his head. "Never mind. I don't want to know. Just don't do this again, or I'll have to tell BAU we can't work with you. I won't have illegal searches on my watch, Evelyn."

She nodded, cringing a little as she met his furious and exhausted gaze. "I understand."

And she did. Normally, she was one hundred percent by-the-book. She liked having boundaries, knowing precisely what she could and couldn't do. She even liked the paperwork that came with her cases, assuring that every last detail was documented and the chain of evidence was always intact.

She'd screwed up, big-time. And the hell of it was, she couldn't be certain she wouldn't do it again if she thought it could lead her to Cassie. If there was any chance it might spare Brittany and Lauren whatever hell Cassie had gone through after she'd been stolen away.

"It took me twenty minutes to convince Darnell Conway not to press charges," Tomas said.

"It won't happen again," she promised, hoping that was the truth.

"Fine." Tomas waved his hand at the door, still looking disgusted with her. "Get out of here. I need you fresh tomorrow. What we're doing now isn't getting us anywhere. We need more from you."

Did she *have* more? Evelyn squared her shoulders, well aware that she'd have to come up with something. "Okay. I'll see you in the morning."

As she left his office and walked back through the quiet station, Jack Bullock stopped her, concern on his face.

Evelyn knew she looked like hell, but he looked even worse, as if he'd been up way longer than she had. He also stank, and she wondered if he'd been wading in the marsh waters.

She must've grimaced, because he said, "Sorry. We don't send civilians into the truly awful search areas. I haven't had time to change. But I'll tell you, late night in a sewer is a fucking sight better than talking to scum like Walter Wiggins."

Evelyn nodded, although she was surprised at just how deep his hatred of Walter went. It almost felt personal. "You didn't know any of Walter's victims, did you, Jack?"

"What? No." He cracked his neck, rubbed a hand over his eyes. "None in DC, anyway. But I have to wonder what he's done here in Rose Bay that we just haven't uncovered."

He started to walk past her, then stopped. "What are you doing here? I thought you went back to the hotel?"

Evelyn felt herself flush. "I'm going there now."

"Okay." Jack squinted at her. "You learn anything new on Wiggins?"

"No."

He scowled. "Is Noreen still here? I want to see if the search parties were ever near Wiggins's house. Maybe he found a way to use them as cover."

"She just left."

"Damn. I was hoping to catch her."

Evelyn glanced at her watch. "Jack, it's practically four in the morning. Why are *you* still here?"

"There are two kids missing, Evelyn. I'll sleep when

we find them. And Noreen may look like a little mouse, but she's tough as hell. If she's not here working, I'll bet she's at home going through the search party information."

Noreen *did* seem to be carrying a bag full of work as she'd left the station. "Did she know one of the original victims?"

"I doubt it. She was a baby back then. But her sister might have known Cassie. I think Margaret was in your grade."

"Really?" Evelyn shook her head. "I don't remember her."

"Oh, well, she was gone by then. But that's—"

"Gone?" Evelyn interrupted. Did Noreen Abbott have a sister who'd died? Could she have an older male figure in her life looking to save other girls that age?

Jack's lips twitched and he rolled his eyes. "Gone as in moved to Texas, Evelyn. Jeez. Noreen's parents got divorced. Her mom and sister moved away. Poor Noreen was stuck here with Earl."

"Earl? Is that her father?" Was a child leaving town enough of a trigger? Probably not, Evelyn thought.

Jack looked like he was working particularly hard not to show his exasperation in his voice, but it was written on his face as he said, "Yes, Earl Abbott, Noreen's father. Don't get all excited on me. Earl's dead. He's not out there abducting kids."

Evelyn's shoulders slumped. "Oh."

"Took forever, too."

"What?"

"For Earl to die. He was sick a long time. His brother, Frank, moved in with them, to help take care of him, but once Noreen hit eighteen, boom! Frank moved out, and it was all on Noreen. The girl is smart as hell, and she gave up college, gave up everything, to look after her father. So, my dad hired her. Last year, Earl died and poor Noreen was left with nothing. And yet, you'd never know it. She's a solid worker."

The annoyance on his face turned pensive. "Honestly, Evelyn, we've got all our officers, plus the CARD agents and you. But at the end of the day, it wouldn't surprise me if it's Noreen who identifies this asshole from the search parties. You should talk to her, too."

Evelyn tried not to be insulted by his unsolicited advice.

He let out a loud yawn, then told her, "Well, I'm heading home. You should get some rest, too. You look like you've been skulking around people's property without a warrant."

He pivoted and stalked toward the door before Evelyn could figure out if he'd been talking about Walter Wiggins or if he already knew about Darnell Conway.

And if Jack knew, the rest of the station wouldn't be far behind. Her credibility would be completely shot.

She followed slowly in Jack's wake. She'd come here so certain this was her chance to finally discover what had happened to Cassie. But with every day that passed, she felt that the truth was further and further out of her grasp.

Evelyn drove around to the back of the hotel and parked under one of the huge live oaks. As she turned off the engine, exhaustion hit so hard it felt like too much effort to get out of her car and walk to her room. The stress of looking for Cassie and the frustration of trying to lock in on one definite suspect were wearing her down.

She wished Kyle was here. He wouldn't care if she woke him in the middle of the night. But he was gone, off surveilling some group the FBI thought could be a threat. With his job, it would be anything. Possible terrorism, a cult with suspected rampant child abuse, a group who'd shown too much interest in bomb-making techniques.

Usually, Evelyn loved her job, so much that it had been her whole life for too long. Usually, she felt she was making a genuine difference, getting some of the most dangerous minds off the streets, saving untold numbers of future victims. Preventing others from going through the hell she'd felt when Cassie had gone missing. The hell she still felt.

But sometimes, like now, it was overwhelming. As if she wasn't stopping *enough* crimes.

At times like these, she needed her grandma's voice. Even locked in the throes of her worsening dementia, her grandma was her rock. Evelyn actually had the interior light on and her cell phone in hand before she remembered it was after four in the morning.

She was about to drop it back in her bag when she realized she'd missed a text message. From the time stamp, the call had come in while she was at the police briefing about Lauren's disappearance. The little girl had gone missing seven and a half hours ago, but it felt like much longer.

Her name had become part of a litany in Evelyn's head of the Nursery Rhyme Killer's victims. Penelope, Veronica and Cassie from eighteen years ago. Brittany and Lauren now. Would any of them ever come home?

Shaking aside the morose thoughts, Evelyn opened the text, and her heart rate kicked up. It was from one of the FBI's documents experts. Shortly after she'd arrived in Rose Bay, she'd convinced Tomas to send him the notes from eighteen years ago, along with the note left at Brittany's house.

The notes were typed on computer paper, but a documents expert could analyze a lot more than handwriting. They had specialized knowledge in deconstructing word usage and sentence structure that could tell them if the same person had written the notes.

Would he agree with her that this was no copycat?

She opened the text.

Word choices and structure are inconclusive. However, paper is the same type, from a brand that went out of business seventeen years ago. Strong likelihood this note was written on paper from the same ream—or at least the same batch—as paper from original notes.

The chances of a copycat having a ream of paper from the same batch as the original abductor were so slim they weren't worth calculating. Which meant she was right. It should have comforted her, but somehow it didn't.

Evelyn stared through the windshield into the darkness. With her interior car light on to read the note, she couldn't see very far. The low-hanging Spanish moss dangling off the live oak she'd parked under swayed lightly in the wind, casting bizarre shadows.

The way she was feeling, she expected the sky to suddenly open up, rain to drench her car and lightning to flash overhead. But everything stayed still and calm, except for her building frustration.

Trying to suppress it, Evelyn reached for her door handle just as her side window shattered, and specks of pain flared across her cheek. An instant later, a loud bang burst in her ear.

Instinct kicked in and Evelyn dove down sideways, one hand stretching up to switch off the interior light even as her other hand unhooked the seat belt and then grabbed for her gun.

Someone had just shot at her.

And if the shooter had better aim, he could have killed her. Bullets were supersonic, meaning that by the time she'd heard the crack, it was too late.

Her heart beating an erratic tempo, Evelyn wrenched her SIG Sauer awkwardly out of its holster. She tried to ignore the blood spattered on her hand, let her racing adrenaline block the pain in her face.

She had nothing to aim at as she slid lower in the car, trying to make herself a smaller target. Where the hell had the shot come from?

Her side window was spider-webbed with cracks, a big hole at the height of her head if the shooter had aimed a few inches over. It was too hard to tell the angle of the shot.

There were plenty of hotel windows with a line of sight down into her car. If the shooter was in one of those, could he still see her?

Evelyn tried to even out her breathing, to shrink lower against the floorboards, as people inside the hotel woke, opening windows and calling out.

Had someone called the cops, scaring off the shooter?

Or was he still there, waiting to get her back in his crosshairs?

Twelve

Sirens sounded off in the distance and a vehicle screeched to life, peeling out of the parking lot.

Evelyn slid up and peeked out the window, trying to get a look at the car, get a license number. But it was too late. If the shooter had been in the car, he was gone.

In case he wasn't, Evelyn slid low again, kept her SIG Sauer clenched tightly in her hand as she waited for the police to arrive.

It felt like hours, but was probably under a minute before the parking lot that had been bathed in darkness was flooded with flashing blue and red.

Still, she stayed crouched under the steering wheel until Tomas appeared at her window and opened her door. The force of his movement caused the rest of the window to crack apart, sending a shower of glass to the ground.

Tomas held his weapon, and the exhaustion she'd seen on his face back at the station was replaced by intense focus. "Evelyn, you hit?"

Stepping out of the car, legs shaking, Evelyn holstered

her own weapon and examined the blood sprayed across her left hand. The blood had come from somewhere else.

Carefully, Evelyn touched her head, but found nothing. Then she gently touched the side of her face, and winced as pain pricked her cheek.

"You probably need to go to the hospital and get that cleaned out," Tomas said. "Looks like the glass from the window got you. But I don't see any other blood. I don't think you were hit."

Tomas put his weapon away. Behind him, his officers fanned out, some checking nearby cars, and others heading inside the hotel. "What the hell happened?"

"I was sitting in my car. I'd just finished reading a text—the documents expert confirmed that the paper from Brittany's note matched the earlier ones."

"Shit." Tomas's face sagged.

"Yeah. Anyway, I was about to get out of my car when the bullet hit the window. I don't know..."

She cut herself off as a car squealed into the lot, going way too fast. She was reaching for her SIG when Tomas grabbed her hand.

"It's Jack. That's his personal vehicle. He's off the clock."

Sure enough, the big gray Buick came to a halt a few feet away and Jack hopped out, not bothering to properly park. He was in the same clothes he'd been wearing at the station. "Heard it on the scanner on my way home," he said, sounding winded, as if he'd run over instead of driving.

Tomas nodded. "Evelyn was just telling me she was sitting in her car. I think she was about to say she didn't get a look at the shooter."

"I didn't." Evelyn shook her head. "I can't even be

sure where the shot came from. I heard a car take off at the same time as I heard the police sirens, though, so he was probably shooting at me from his car."

"Did you see *anything*?" Jack asked, cringing as he studied her face.

"No."

"So, we have nothing," Tomas said. "I don't want you in danger by being here. I hate to say it, but maybe you should be consulting from Virginia."

"I'm not leaving," Evelyn snapped. Then, calming her tone, she added, "Actually, in some ways this is good."

"This guy turning your face into hamburger meat is good?" Jack asked, eyebrows raised.

How bad were her injuries? Evelyn resisted the urge to find a mirror. It didn't matter, and looking at it wouldn't change anything. "No. But the fact that someone shot at me means he's scared and I'm on the right track."

She glanced from Tomas to Jack, but neither seemed to have picked up on where she was going. "Think about it. Jack and I asked Walter Wiggins if we could search his house today. And I sure pissed off Darnell Conway."

Tomas nodded thoughtfully. "So you're saying the two of them just went even higher up the suspect list."

"Well, they were already at the top, but yeah…"

"Except how would either of them know where you were staying? Or that you were going to be in the parking lot at—" Tomas squinted at his watch "—almost 5:00 a.m.?"

"The perp obviously knows how to stalk someone," Jack said. "He must be damn good at it to have grabbed Lauren now, with the whole police force and a shitload of feds looking for him."

"That's an excellent point," Tomas agreed. "Okay, so Walter or Darnell—"

"Wait a second," Jack interrupted, glaring at Evelyn. "When did you piss off Darnell?" When neither she nor Tomas responded, he barked, "Did you question him again without me?"

"There was a little incident tonight," Tomas said, then turned to Evelyn. "He's going to find out eventually. She was looking around Darnell's yard."

Jack's eyes widened. "Are you fucking kidding me?"

Tomas put out his hands in a "calm down" gesture. "Listen, Jack, it was a bad move, but Darnell's not pressing charges, so there's no harm."

"No harm?" Jack stepped right up to her, raising his voice enough that other cops turned and stared. "You're destroying the chain of evidence everywhere you go, with every suspect! You're going to blow this case to hell! What happens if it *is* Darnell or Wiggins, huh? If we prove it's one of them, but we can't convict because you've screwed the legality of the whole investigation?"

"Jack—" Evelyn began.

"You get pissed at how *I* want to approach suspects, just because I think going in hard and aggressive works, and you pull this shit? At least I stick to the book, so that when I *do* get an arrest, it won't be thrown out!"

Tomas seemed about to speak, but Jack pivoted toward him. "My dad did things by the book, too. And you allow this? I told you she was a problem from day one. I want her out. And if you don't take care of it, I'm making a formal complaint myself, and I'm taking it straight to the FBI."

"Jack," Evelyn tried again as apprehension took hold.

But he ignored her, slamming the door as he got back into his vehicle, and peeled away as fast as he'd arrived.

"Shit," Tomas breathed.

Silently, Evelyn agreed. If Jack called her boss, he'd yank her out of Rose Bay in a second. And Evelyn knew if she refused to go, she might as well turn in her badge.

Evelyn's eyes opened slowly, her eyelids scraping against her eyes like sandpaper. There was an odd taste in her mouth and her head throbbed. Exhaustion kept her trapped on the bed.

It took too much effort to roll over, and when she did, pain exploded through her cheek. She groaned, blinking to bring the alarm clock next to her bed into focus. Nine-thirty. Judging from the sunlight streaming through the slats in her closed shades, it was morning.

That meant she'd gotten about two hours of sleep after she'd driven back to her hotel from the hospital. Apparently it was long enough for the painkillers they'd given her to wear off, because her cheek throbbed and felt swollen to double its size.

When she'd finally been able to check out the damage in a mirror, she'd discovered Jack was right. Her cheek was torn up, tiny bits of glass embedded all over it. The doctors had told her she'd been lucky no glass had made it into her eye. They'd debrided her cheek, put some liquid bandage on the worst of the cuts and sent her on her way. They'd also told her she wouldn't have any scars, but as she stumbled into the bathroom and glanced in the mirror, she found that hard to believe.

The injuries had swollen up while she'd slept, so if the police didn't kick her out of the station this morning just on principle, she could probably scare suspects with a glance. Cringing at her reflection, Evelyn prodded gently at the worst of the cuts, and pain burst in the left side of her face. She knew the doctor had gotten it all, but it felt as though there was still glass under her skin.

Trying to push back the pain, she splashed water on the right side of her face and downed two more painkillers. Then she threw on the clothes at the top of her suitcase as she tried to do the math in her head. Brittany: sixty hours missing. Lauren: twelve and a half hours missing. Which equaled no time to get any more sleep.

She needed to head to the station. Her plan was to continue as normal and pray that Jack hadn't followed through on his threat.

But the thought of arriving at the station and being ordered to pack up and return to Virginia made her nauseated.

Evelyn sank onto the edge of her bed and grabbed her phone with hands that shook—from lack of sleep, she told herself. It might even have been true.

What she should've done was called Dan at BAU and explained what had happened, then beg forgiveness before he heard anything from Jack. Instead, she found herself dialing the number for the nursing home where her grandma lived.

When the receptionist picked up, she said, "It's Evelyn Baine. How's my grandma today?"

"She's been missing you the past few days. Today she's not at her best, but she'll know you. You want to talk to her?"

"Yes, please put her on."

Her grandma's dementia had been worsening for more than a decade. Some days, she was sharp as ever, but more and more, she was losing memories. Her short-term memory was mostly gone and Evelyn knew her long-term memory was going, too. Evelyn wasn't religious, but in case there was a God, every day she prayed for more time.

"Evelyn," her grandma said a minute later when she came on the line.

Her voice was different, slightly uncertain, which Evelyn knew meant she was confused and didn't understand why. But at least today, she recognized Evelyn. In the past few years, she'd begun to have periods when she couldn't remember her granddaughter, didn't know her husband was long gone and her only daughter a drunk neither of them had seen since Evelyn was a teenager.

She wished, as she always did, that she could have the grandma who had raised her back. That she could've had more years with the woman who'd pulled Evelyn out of the hell of her childhood and made her who she was today.

"Hi, Grandma. How are you feeling?"

"Where are you, Evelyn?"

"I'm back in Rose Bay, Grandma."

She was about to add "for a case" when her grandma said, "You're over at Cassie's house again? Honey, you've got to tell me when you go over there to play."

It happened a lot, her grandma thinking it was some time in the past. But right now, when Evelyn needed her badly, it filled her with frustration. Guilt quickly followed. Her grandma had always been there for her. Now it was Evelyn's turn.

She tilted sideways until she lay curled up on the bed. "Sorry about that, Grandma."

"It's okay, sweetie. You've got to try to remember, though, or Grandpa and I will worry."

"I'll try," Evelyn whispered.

If you didn't count her mother—which Evelyn didn't—her grandma was the only family she had left in the world. Days like this made it hard for Evelyn to talk to her. Add searching for Cassie to the mix and she knew it was showing in her tone.

Evelyn pushed to her feet. "Sorry I forgot to tell you, Grandma," she said, trying to sound upbeat.

"Just be home for dinner, will you? Ask Mrs. Byers if Cassie can come with you. I'm making strawberry pie tonight. I know it's you girls' favorite."

A smile lifted the corners of Evelyn's lips as a memory surged forward, of her and Cassie racing to her house for her grandma's pie. She didn't remember what they'd been doing that day, but they were carrying their shoes and they were mud-covered from their feet to their knees. Her grandma had just laughed as they'd splattered mud all over her clean floors in their hurry to get the pie.

Warmth filled her, and a sadness she felt more and more often as she watched her grandma's decline. "I love you, Grandma."

"I love you, too, Evelyn. Don't forget to ask Cassie's mom before you bring her over."

"I promise."

"Okay. I'll see you in a few hours."

Evelyn ended the call, wishing that was true. Wishing she could turn back time, back to the day Cassie had disappeared, and somehow warn her.

But of course, she couldn't. All she could do now was help bring her home.

If ever there was a morning to start drinking coffee, it was now. Instead, Evelyn paid for her tea and raisin scone in the little coffee shop off the hotel lobby. Spinning for the door, she almost slammed into someone.

"Sorry!" she said, looking up to find it was Kyle. He was clad in camouflage pants and a dark T-shirt, a bag slung over his shoulder, probably stuffed with weaponry. It was 10:00 a.m., so he must've run late coming back from surveillance.

Heat rushed up her face as she remembered how she'd climbed onto his lap and fused herself to him a few hours earlier, then practically fallen off the bed when her phone rang.

He didn't seem to notice her embarrassment. As soon as he saw her injured cheek, the exhaustion on his face disappeared and his eyes widened. "Evelyn, oh, my God." He took her chin in his large palm. "What happened?"

Evelyn tried to shrug away from him. Beyond hoping it didn't leave scars, she hadn't really cared how her cheek looked until this second. "I think I'm getting close to one of my suspects. I scared someone yesterday. Now I just need to figure out who."

She tried to step around him, but he blocked her way, gripping her arms. "That's not an answer."

"Someone shot at me last night."

Fury lit his eyes and he studied her carefully. "You don't know who?"

His intense scrutiny made her fidget. "No."

"Where did it happen?" His forehead furrowed. "And what hit your face?"

"The hotel parking lot. I was in my car. It's from the window."

"*This* hotel?" Kyle asked, cursing when she nodded. "During the night last night?"

She could see him mentally berating himself for not

being there, but it wasn't his job to protect her. She was a federal agent. It was part of the job description that she might find herself on the receiving end of a bullet. At least this one had missed. "I'm fine."

"This time." Kyle spoke her fear. "What makes you think this person won't try again?"

Evelyn shrugged, hoping to seem unconcerned. "The cops got here pretty damn fast. He was almost caught. Hopefully that'll scare him off."

She started to move again, but Kyle got in her way. "What if it doesn't?"

"Well, there's not a whole lot I can do about that, is there?"

"You could go home," Kyle suggested softly. "Consult from the BAU office."

She glared at him. "I can't believe you'd even suggest that." She tried to get around him again, and when he stayed in front of her, she snapped, "I need to get to the station. You of all people should know what this case means to me!"

Moisture stung her eyes. Blaming it on her emotional talk with her grandma and barely any sleep in the past twenty-four hours, she ducked her head and walked past him.

"Evelyn," he called after her. "Be careful!"

"I'll try," she muttered as she pushed through the hotel door and out into the South Carolina sun.

The sunlight reflecting off the asphalt hurt her eyes, and she felt instantly overheated in the dress pants and short-sleeved button-up she had on. Putting on a pair of sunglasses, she tried to ignore the pounding in her head that told her she needed more sleep.

Her car had been towed last night for forensics, and

the rental place had dropped off a new one, same make and model. Glass remnants crunched underfoot as she unlocked the door and she hoped none were big enough to puncture her new car's tires. But she backed out of the spot without incident.

As she drove, she passed searchers out in force. Noreen waved as Evelyn drove by, giving her hope that Jack hadn't blabbed all over the station. When she'd made it halfway to the police station and the tires held, she thought her luck was changing. But then her phone rang and a glance at the caller display showed that it was her boss.

Cold shimmied across her skin, raising goose bumps. Jack must have followed through on his threat.

She considered ignoring the call, but that would only postpone Dan's wrath, so she picked up.

"Evelyn?" Dan barked before she'd even said hello. He managed to make her name sound like a contagious disease.

"Dan, I know why you're calling—"

"I would guess you do," Dan interrupted, his tone quietly furious. "You promised me you could handle this, but obviously we were both wrong. This is way beyond a conflict of interest. You've put yourself and the Bureau in a very bad position. And you've endangered the integrity of the case."

"He's not pressing charges," Evelyn said quickly. "I messed up. I know I did. But—"

"*But?* But nothing. I wouldn't care if you had a whole wall of silence around you—which you sure as hell don't, by the way. Your personal connection to this case has turned into a liability for everyone." When she started to interrupt, he added, "Including Cassie."

His words halted her argument. Forget the fact that somehow in the past few days Dan had managed to get up to speed on the case, when originally he hadn't even known about her personal connection. Forget that Jack had had it in for her since she'd arrived back in Rose Bay. They were both right.

Shame sprang to life. Obviously she hadn't expected to get caught, but besides the legal problems she'd created, she'd also tipped off Darnell. He'd known he was a suspect, but this must have driven it home fast—the fact that he was at the top of the list. It was probably too late for Cassie. But what if Brittany and Lauren were still alive?

Knowing she was closing in on him might have made him try to kill her in the hotel parking lot. It might also have made him kill his victims.

Guilt and self-disgust exploded inside her and she gagged. The street ahead dimmed and Dan's voice faded into the background until all she could hear was her own heartbeat, pounding in her ears. Yanking the steering wheel to the right, she pulled off onto the side of the road and tried to get her suddenly rapid breathing under control.

Slowly, Dan's voice penetrated. "Evelyn? Did you hear me? I said get back to Virginia. Now. You're off this case."

Thirteen

"What are you doing here?" Jack bellowed as soon as Evelyn walked through the station door.

Evelyn kept her head up and her jaw clamped and walked right past him, toward the CARD command post.

But he followed, practically stepping on her heels as he demanded, "I thought you were being sent back to Virginia?"

A pair of rookie officers stared curiously as they passed. Evelyn wasn't sure if it was Jack's fury or her swollen cheek drawing their attention.

She ducked her head and continued to ignore Jack as she walked into the room at the back of the station.

Carly looked up at them as Jack went on. "You're just a damn consultant! How come your office hasn't ordered you back home yet?"

She didn't tell him they already had. Staying when Dan had called her back to BAU meant she probably wouldn't have a job when she got home.

She couldn't dwell on that now, couldn't think about the empty days ahead of her without BAU. She'd been solely focused on the job for so long. In some ways, it had started before she'd declared her double major in college, planning for a future with the FBI. In some ways, it had started the day Cassie had gone missing.

She would fight for her job when she went home, but it wouldn't change anything. She'd disobeyed a direct order from her supervisor. There would be an investigation by the Office of Professional Responsibility and then she'd be kicked out of the Bureau, asked to hand over her gun and her badge. The very things that had defined her for most of her adulthood.

But Cassie had led her to the FBI. And Cassie still held too big a piece of her heart. Right or wrong, Evelyn had to see this through to the end. Unless Tomas threw her in jail, she wasn't going anywhere.

Jack gaped at her as she stood there silent. "You have nothing to say? *Nothing?*"

Evelyn finally found her voice. "I can't defend what I did. I screwed up. I know it. You know it."

Carly lowered her head, looking uncomfortable as Evelyn said, "My entire life—since I was twelve years old—has been leading to this point. To finding out what happened to my best friend."

She locked her gaze on Jack's. "This job is all I have. I know this kind of predator. Far better than anyone should. And I can find this guy. The fact that he shot at me proves I'm on the right track and he has something to lose. I can help you get him. And regardless of whether you want me here, I'm not leaving until I find Cassie. And Veronica. And Penelope. And Brittany and Lauren most of all, because there's still a chance we can bring them home alive."

As she fell silent, Jack was still scowling, but Carly stood up. "So, what you're saying is I need to get my agents zeroed in on Darnell Conway and Walter Wiggins exclusively. Am I right?"

Glad not everyone wanted to fry her for her mistake with Darnell, Evelyn turned to her. "Exclusively? No. Because there's always some small chance I got close to someone else's secret without realizing it. But putting *most* of your resources there? Yes. Definitely."

Jack looked back and forth between them, then dropped his arms to his sides. "I can't believe no one else thinks this is a big deal," he muttered, but then he added, "I want in on Wiggins. I've been saying it from the beginning. That guy is guilty."

Carly nodded. "He's at the top of my list, too. I'm going to call my agents back here and we'll get a new game plan together. Evelyn—"

"Evelyn." Tomas's voice, although quieter than Carly's, cut over her with its authority and fury. "Come to my office, would you?"

Jack's and Carly's curious gazes followed her out. When she was in Tomas's office, he shut the door behind them and nervousness bubbled up.

He didn't bother to sit at his desk, just told her, "I spoke to Dan Moore."

Oh, damn. That was a lot sooner than Evelyn had expected.

"He told me he's sending a different profiler out here to consult on the case."

Evelyn lifted her chin. "I'm staying on, even if it's unofficial."

Tomas's lips quivered. "Yeah, your boss told me you'd say that."

He had? Evelyn resisted the impulse to dart a glance behind her. What had Dan told Tomas to do about it?

"Apparently the new guy will be lead and you'll assist."

She would? Relief made her sway. Her job was definitely still in question, but she'd worry about that later; right now, all she could focus on was the fact that she was still on the case.

Tomas grabbed her elbow. "You okay?"

"Yes. Sorry. Hardly any sleep." She steadied herself. "Who's he sending?"

Tomas shrugged, dropped his hand from her arm. "I have no idea. Someone else from your office."

Damn. No one at BAU but Greg knew about her history here and she really wanted to keep it that way. She hoped Dan was sending him, but two miracles in one day was too much to hope for, especially from Dan Moore.

"Until then, Evelyn, I need you to stay in line. Understood?"

Evelyn nodded.

"Good. Now get back out there and help Carly figure out whether it's Darnell or Walter. We got a bloodhound as close to Wiggins's house as we could this morning, and nothing. But Carly told me he could've used countermeasures."

When Evelyn nodded again, Tomas said, "The two of you figure out if he did. I want someone in handcuffs by the end of the day."

"Here's all the information you asked for." Noreen Abbott held out a piece of paper covered in tiny, neat script. "I wrote down the dates and times Darnell Conway signed in for search parties. I can't verify that he stayed with the group, but I checked in with some of the other searchers, so they can vouch for part of it. Those times are marked, near as they could remember, on the sheet."

"Thanks." Evelyn looked at the paper, reading it quickly, then raised her eyebrows. "He showed up both yesterday and today, huh?" Even after she'd gone snooping at his house.

If he was flaunting something, he was pretty damn confident she wouldn't be able to prove it.

"What about Walter Wiggins?"

Noreen looked disgusted. "We wouldn't let him join a search party if he tried. I wouldn't have let him get past sign-up, and if I had, someone in one of the search parties probably would've gone after him."

"I didn't think he'd try. Just double-checking."

"Is this helpful?" Noreen asked. "And are you okay? Your cheek's pretty swollen."

Evelyn held in a sigh. "I'll be fine. Luckily the guy wasn't a great shot. But yes, this helps me see behavioral patterns. The fact that Darnell is joining the search parties, even when he knows he's a suspect, makes him look guilty."

"Really? I'd think it would make him look innocent. If he was guilty—if he knew where the girls were—why would he bother searching?"

"Because it's part of the sick thrill for him. He wants to see the faces of the community he's hurting." When Noreen didn't say anything, Evelyn asked, "Do we have the search party lists from eighteen years ago? I know lists were kept, because that's how the original profiler came up with Darnell as a suspect."

"There were?" Noreen sounded surprised. "Well, if we do have those lists, I've never seen them."

"They weren't in the evidence boxes, either."

"Maybe Jack Bullock would know," Noreen suggested. "He was on the original case."

"Right."

"Oh, you knew that, of course. Sorry."

"No problem. Hey, Noreen, Jack told me your sister was in my grade at school."

Shock flashed across Noreen's face.

"Is that wrong?"

"No, it's not."

"She lives in Texas now, he said. But what about anyone else from that class? Do you know?"

"From Cassie's class? Not that I'm aware of. And my sister, she's not in Texas."

"Is she close by? Do you know if she remembers anything about that time?"

Noreen looked at her shoes. "No, she passed away."

"I'm so sorry. Jack said… She died recently?"

Noreen met Evelyn's gaze. "She died a long time ago. Drunk driver. In Texas."

"I'm sorry, Noreen," Evelyn said, her mind racing. How long ago had it been? A drunk driver wasn't parental neglect—unless Noreen's mom had been driving when her daughter was killed. But who in Noreen's life might want to make up for that loss? Jack had mentioned an uncle, but was that close enough?

Noreen nodded jerkily. "Thanks. Look, Evelyn, I can see what you're thinking, but this has nothing to do with my sister. She wasn't even in Rose Bay then. And it's not like there was anyone in her life who could be doing this now."

"Of—"

"Anyway, could you keep this between us? No one here knows and I'd like to keep it that way."

"No one knows she's gone? Why not?"

Noreen frowned. "My dad…he couldn't bear the pity. My mom had already bailed on him, taken Margaret with her. To have to tell everyone his daughter was gone, too." She shook her head and tugged at her dowdy, shapeless skirt. "He made us promise."

"Us?"

"Me and my uncle Frank. No one else knows. Can you please keep it that way? Like I asked?"

"Sure, Noreen."

Noreen rolled her eyes. "I can tell from your face. You think my uncle could fit your profile."

"I need to look into it," Evelyn admitted.

"Fine. Do what you need to do. Just do it quietly, okay? You'll find out soon enough that he's no suspect."

Noreen seemed about to walk past, so Evelyn grasped her arm. "Your uncle moved in with you when your dad got sick, right?"

"Years ago," Noreen agreed.

"But your sister was gone by then?"

Noreen frowned. "Yeah."

"And once you turned eighteen…"

"He told me he'd wasted enough of his life being my father's caretaker. Not that he really did much of that, but he did pay my dad's bills, whatever disability insurance didn't cover. And there were a lot of them. He tried. He just couldn't deal with it."

"Can I ask what your father had?"

"CADASIL. It's kind of like MS. My dad had bad migraines, then strokes and pretty quickly his motor functions were in bad shape. And then came the dementia." She sniffed, wiped her eyes, shuffled her feet. "Look, I get it. You need to do your job. You want to talk to my uncle, go for it. I'll tell you right now that you're wasting your time, but do what you need to do. Please don't spread it around, okay? My uncle may not be the easiest person in the world to get along with, but he's the only family I've got left."

Evelyn nodded. "I can do that. As long as I can cross him off my list."

"That shouldn't be a problem," Noreen said, with such confidence in her voice it made Frank fall even lower on Evelyn's list. "Please keep quiet about Margaret, too, okay?"

"With your father gone…"

"I really don't want to have to explain to everyone why I kept it secret even after he died," Noreen cut in. "I grieved for her a long time ago. I don't want to have to do it all over again in public."

Like Evelyn would probably have to do once they found the Nursery Rhyme Killer. Because as much as she hoped to find Cassie alive, chances were close to zero.

Even the idea of having all those eyes on her, watching her mourn Cassie, made her uncomfortable. And she didn't have to live in Rose Bay, like Noreen did. "I promise."

Noreen's shoulders relaxed. "Thank you."

As Noreen continued through the police station, Evelyn stared after her, thinking. Regardless of Noreen's certainty and Evelyn's own feeling that she was probably right, her uncle had to be checked out. But since Evelyn had been shot at after she'd talked to Darnell and Walter, they were still her top suspects.

Evelyn rubbed at her eyes, which felt heavy and strained. She'd been at the station for five hours, giving Carly and her CARD agents as much information as she could on Walter and Darnell. Right now, the agents were digging deeper into both men's histories, to see if they could come up with anything new.

The second profiler was due to arrive soon. Evelyn should have been anticipating another set of eyes on the case, but instead she dreaded sharing her secrets with anyone from Aquia.

There wasn't anything she could do about it, so she went in search of Jack. She found him holed up alone in the break room, copies of the old case files spread out around him, crumpled chip bags, cans of energy drinks and half-empty coffee cups holding down the edges.

When she shut the door behind her, Jack looked up at her with red-rimmed eyes. The smell of coffee practically seeped from his pores. "What?"

"I want to ask you about Frank Abbott."

Jack rolled his eyes, picked up his pen and returned his attention to the case files. "Frowning Frank? Give me a break, Evelyn."

"Frowning Frank?"

"Noreen's nickname for him. But it fits. I somehow doubt kids would hop in his van."

Evelyn stepped closer. "He owns a van?"

Jack's pupils lifted. "It was a joke."

"Well, look, what can you tell me about him?"

Jack set his pen down with an exaggerated sigh. "You want to tell me what's put Frank on your radar?"

"How close was he to Noreen's sister?"

"How the hell should I know? She moved away—must've been twenty-odd years ago now."

"Think about it, okay? It seems like you and Noreen are friends. Besides, you know this town better than anyone."

Jack's eyebrows rose, his lips pressing together. She could tell he thought she was trying to flatter him for information, but what she'd said was true. His father had been the chief of police in Rose Bay for almost thirty years. Rose Bay had a lot of residents who liked to brag how many generations they could claim, but the Bullocks went further back than most.

"Yeah, I guess Frank and Margaret were close. He never married, never had any kids, and Earl was his only brother. Frank really resented him—and I think, by proxy, Noreen, too—after he had to move in with them. But Margaret was his first niece and I guess he did used to dote on her, way back before Earl and his wife divorced."

"So if Noreen's sister had died, he would've taken it hard?"

"Well, sure. Anyone would have." Jack crossed his arms over the papers in front of him, narrowing his eyes. "Why do you ask?"

Evelyn shook her head, planning to keep her promise to Noreen unless she had something real on Frank. "I might have a reason to suspect Frank. I need to check into some things first."

"What about Darnell and Walter?"

"They're still our focus."

Jack's shoulders slumped as he gestured at the case files on the table. "I've been going over this shit for two hours. I thought maybe looking through it again would tell me something new. You know, time and distance and all that."

He looked at his watch, then slumped even more. "But I'm not seeing anything I didn't see eighteen years ago. And Brittany's been gone for sixty-six hours, Evelyn."

"I know, Jack."

"What the hell can we do that we're not already doing?" When he gazed up at her, his eyes held dejection and exhaustion and just enough hope that she knew he'd never give up.

"We're doing everything right—"

"Bullshit. If that was true, we'd have brought Brittany and Lauren home by now."

He left unspoken that he thought it was her fault, but the words hung in the air, anyway. Or maybe that was just how she felt.

Evelyn tried to sound confident. "We have to keep at it until we find something that doesn't seem right and then dig and dig." Jack frowned and went back to his case files.

Evelyn took that as her cue to go call the field office in Houston, where she'd first been assigned out of the FBI Academy. Walking into the quiet of the parking lot, Evelyn phoned her old supervisor. He was still there, and luckily, he was fond of her since she'd practically lived at the office in her determination to fill her file with a record impressive enough to get into BAU. When she asked if he could look for a twenty-year-old accident report, he promised to get back to her within the hour.

Slapping her phone shut, she turned to go back inside when someone shouted, "Evelyn!"

She knew that voice. Evelyn felt herself grinning. "Greg?"

Dan had actually sent Greg? One part of her was shocked, but another part realized Dan probably knew Greg was his best chance of keeping her in line.

Greg Ibsen strode up to the station doors in dress pants and a short-sleeve button-up, no cartoon tie in sight.

A laptop case was slung over his shoulder and he clutched a coffee cup. "How are you holding up?"

As he reached her side and looked, horrified, at her cheek, Evelyn shrugged. "Getting close to something someone doesn't want me to know, obviously."

Greg studied her more closely. "Are you okay?"

"Yeah, I'm fine. How mad is Dan?"

"You're going to be in for it once you're home. There's no getting around that."

Nerves fluttered to life in her stomach. She'd hoped the fact that Dan was sending another profiler meant he'd forgiven her, but maybe it *was* as bad as she'd originally thought. Her voice was strangled when she asked, "Did I lose my spot in BAU?" She cringed. "In the Bureau?"

Greg shook his head and offered her a forced smile. "Are you kidding? The BAU's star profiler?"

She crossed her arms. "Give it to me straight."

"It'll be fine. Worry about it later, okay? Just focus on the case for now."

"Just tell me."

"You're really lucky the police chief here convinced the suspect not to press charges. And that Dan doesn't want it known someone would dare be insubordinate. I only know about it because I happened to be in his office when that police officer called. I don't think Dan's going to put it in your file—at least not the details."

"But?"

"Well, you're at the top of Dan's shit list."

Evelyn knew what that meant. She wasn't going to be asked to hand over her badge and gun and be physically escorted out of the BAU office when she returned. Instead, Dan would set her up to fail, meaning her days at BAU were numbered.

And without her job, what the hell would she do? Being a criminal investigative analyst for BAU had defined her for so long.

Without her job, maybe a better question was, who the hell would she be?

Fourteen

"She was playing at the park," Evelyn's former supervisor from the Houston field office said as soon as she picked up her phone.

"Wait," Evelyn said. "Noreen Abbott told me her sister was the victim of a drunk driver."

"She was. She was at the park with her mom and she ran into the street. Car came flying around the curb and hit her. The guy driving was way over the legal limit. He took off, too. But witnesses got a plate and the police grabbed him pretty quickly. The girl was dead on the scene."

"How long ago was it?"

"Nineteen years ago, almost to the day."

A year before the Nursery Rhyme abductions had started. A coincidence? Evelyn mulled it over. The timing was suspicious, but so was the murder of Darnell's ex's daughter. And since Noreen's sister had been hit by a drunk driver, could Frank Abbott really claim parental neglect?

"She ran into the street?" Evelyn asked. "Was her mom not watching her?"

"It sounds like it happened pretty damn fast and at exactly the wrong time. Girl was playing soccer. Chased a ball right into the street. There was never any question of blaming the mother. Witnesses said she yelled at her daughter to stop before she got to the street, even before that car came around the curb. It's definitely tragic, but it was one hundred percent the fault of the driver."

"Tell me about him." It was unlikely there was a connection, but it wouldn't be uncommon for someone like that to blame the parent instead of himself.

"He got fifteen years, but he only made it ten. Apparently he picked a lot of fights in prison and one of the other inmates took him out."

"Okay."

"Anything else you want to know?"

"No. Thanks."

"Hope it helps," he said, then hung up.

Evelyn closed her phone slowly as Greg raised his eyebrows at her. If Noreen's father was still alive, he might have been a good suspect, but an uncle?

If the Nursery Rhyme Killer was trying to make up for his own loss by blaming the parents of other young girls, it was more likely to be a father or significantly older brother. Someone who'd lived with the girl, who'd feel that void every day.

But she couldn't rule Frank out.

She pulled up his address on her laptop, jotted it down, then told Greg, "We need to take a drive."

Greg scooped up his own laptop from where he'd set it an hour ago as he'd made the rounds, being introduced to the agents and officers.

"Where are we going?" Greg asked.

Evelyn headed for the door. "I'll tell you on the way."

As she pushed the door open, someone pulled it from the other side, almost yanking her off her feet. Stumbling, she found herself staring at Brittany Douglas's father. His eyes were bloodshot, his skin sallow, and he seemed as though he'd lost twenty pounds since the mob scene two days ago.

He didn't appear to know her, because he just continued inside, but Evelyn followed and Greg trailed behind her. "Mr. Douglas?"

He spun back. "Yeah?"

"Can I ask you about what happened with Walter Wiggins?"

Before he could answer, Tomas came out of his office. "Mark," he said to Brittany's dad. "Figured you'd show up here at some point."

"Yeah, look, I'm sorry. I wasn't trying to get out of being arrested—"

"We know," Tomas cut in.

"But I'm turning myself in, okay? I don't want you guys wasting resources looking for me. I want you focused on my daughter." Mark Douglas let out a heavy sigh. "And Lauren."

Tomas nodded. "I appreciate that, Mark, but Wiggins isn't pressing charges. We're all focusing on your daughter here."

"Thank you," he choked out.

Tomas leveled a warning look at him. "You need to leave this to us to do the right way." His gaze moved to Evelyn. "Your actions could have compromised the whole investigation."

Brittany's dad went pale and he swayed. "I just wanted to find her," he said, his voice barely above a whisper. "I couldn't bear it if you all were wrapped in legal tape and my daughter was in that freak's house, being…being…"

"Mr. Douglas," Evelyn cut in. "Was there something specific that made you go after Walter? Something besides his history?"

Mark blinked. "Rose Bay has always been safe. Walter Wiggins is the only creep in these parts. It just makes sense."

Instead of correcting him on the number of convicted child molesters in and around Rose Bay, Evelyn asked, "Did you actually go inside his house?"

"You're damn right I did!" Mark said, and suddenly all the cops in the room stepped closer and went silent.

"Can you tell me exactly what happened?"

Mark glanced at Tomas. "Who is this?"

"She's with the FBI. So is the man standing next to her. They're both profilers, specially trained in cases like this one." Tomas stepped closer and put a hand on Mark's shoulder. "Tell them anything you remember, okay?"

"Sure." Mark looked at all the silent cops around him and frowned, his tone somber. "I caught him when he went to get his paper. It was afternoon, but he probably hadn't wanted to go outside earlier, because a crowd had been there yelling at him. I wasn't there then, but that's what his neighbor said. Anyway, I think he figured no one was watching anymore, the way he crept out the door. But I'd been waiting for a while."

When he stopped talking, Greg prompted, "Keep going."

"Well, I mean, you know I hit him." Mark straightened his shoulders. "I don't regret it, either. I don't see how it could possibly have compromised anything. But if she'd been in there…"

"Did you search his house?" Evelyn asked.

"No. He kept saying he didn't do it when I punched him, wouldn't admit a damn thing, so when he hit the ground, I ran inside." His eyes watery, Mark told them, "I called for my baby. Yelled and yelled, but the only person who answered was Walter's dad. I think he called the cops, too, but before they arrived, Walter was back up and swinging an aluminum bat at me."

"Where did you look in the house?"

"Part of the main floor. I was trying to get into the basement—the door was latched—when Walter ran in with that bat." Mark flushed and stared down at his shoes. "He's a small guy, but man, he wielded that bat like he knew how to use it. And he ran at me like a crazed man, swinging the bat around. I ran, tried to get away from him. And then I heard the sirens, and I took off."

Toward the back of the crowd, Jack's eyes locked on hers and she could read exactly what he was thinking. Mark hadn't gotten into the basement. The apparently locked basement.

And racing at someone with a baseball bat, someone who'd just beaten him badly enough to land him in the hospital, was a bold move. Especially from a convicted child molester facing an enraged father.

What the hell was in Walter Wiggins's basement?

Jack looked like he was going to jump in, but Tomas spoke first. "Is there anything else you can remember about the house, Mark?"

Mark watched the cops listening intently and shook his head. "It looked like it hadn't changed in decades, but I didn't see kids' toys lying around or anything, if that's what you mean."

"Okay. Thank you."

"That's it?" Mark asked as the cops returned to their tasks. "What are you going to do about it?"

"Mark, your daughter and Lauren are our only priorities right now," Tomas said.

Mark seemed ready to argue, so Evelyn turned to Greg and whispered, "Let's go."

As they got into Greg's rental car, he asked, "You want to tell me where we're headed?"

"I want to talk to a guy named Frank Abbott." Evelyn gave him the details as she directed him to the outskirts of town where Frank lived.

"Frank didn't move in with his brother until after his niece was already gone, right?" Greg asked.

"That's right."

"Well, he's worth investigating, but he'd be a more viable suspect if he'd ever lived with the girl."

"I agree. But the CARD agents are putting pretty much everything they've got on Darnell and Walter, so I want to check this out. Turn here." She pointed to a curving dirt road, overhung by hundred-year-old trees and lined with tall, overgrown grass. It wound lazily for a few miles until it finally dead-ended.

"This is still Rose Bay?"

"Yes. I know, it looks pretty different. This part is a lot more rural. Where I grew up had a suburban feel—lots of plantation-style houses, big manicured lawns. Very old-school South Carolina. This side of town is right on the edge of Rose Bay. Huge properties—they actually make the ones in town seem miniscule. We're talking hundreds of acres, but I think some are abandoned now. Mostly the people who own land here have had it in their families for generations. Eventually, I'm sure it'll all get developed."

"It's nice," Greg said. "Peaceful."

"Yeah." Evelyn looked at the field stretching out to her right, nothing but knee- and waist-high grasses, the occasional flower peeking out. Once the whole area had been working fields connected to plantations, and in this part of Rose Bay, farms had struggled on until only a few decades ago.

She hadn't spent any time here growing up, but seeing it now reminded her how segregated the town used to be. The town itself was for the wealthy white residents. Near the marshes were the poorer residents. Even though white people lived there, back then it had been thought of as the black part of town because of how completely white the main part had been. Except for her, of course.

And this little section where Frank lived had been a random assortment. There were a few recluses. Some of these places were second properties for families who lived in town; they'd had ancestors who'd owned so much of Rose Bay they still had bits and pieces of it all over the place. And there was the weird old guy who'd been one of the few Rose Bay residents who called her names.

"This it?" Greg asked as he pulled up a long, narrow dirt drive. A few birch trees dotted the property, but most of it was overgrown fields that extended for acres. The house at the end of the drive looked as if it had weathered a hundred years, and no one had bothered to give it a coat of paint in all that time. The dilapidated barn a hundred yards behind it didn't look much better.

Evelyn checked the address on her phone. "I guess so." *This* was the place Frank Abbott couldn't wait to get back to when he'd lived with Earl and Noreen? It made Evelyn wonder what kind of shape Earl's house had been in.

Greg turned off the engine and got out. "Let's go, then."

Evelyn followed more slowly. The barn was huge, the sort that might've existed on a working farm. But Frank Abbott was a handyman—he and his brother had been in business together for a long time and now he ran it himself. He'd never used this as a farm. Maybe the barn was for his work tools? It certainly wasn't filled with equipment to care for his property, because only the front yard around the drive was mowed. The rest of it was overgrown with waist-high grass, making it impossible to tell where his property ended and the neighboring yard began.

As they walked up the steps, Evelyn saw that the shades on Frank's house were all open, giving Evelyn a clear view inside. What she saw was clean and sparse, suggesting that Frank didn't spend a lot of time at home.

Greg pounded on the door, and when it opened a crack, steely gray eyes peered out at them.

"What?" Frank demanded.

Acting unaffected by the rude response, Greg said, "Hi, Mr. Abbott. I'm Greg Ibsen, with the FBI. This is my colleague Evelyn Baine. We just have a couple of questions, if you don't mind."

The door opened the rest of the way, revealing a man with hard living etched in the lines of his face, and hard work evident in the ropy muscles of his arms. "Figured you'd get here eventually." He turned and walked deeper into the house.

Evelyn and Greg glanced at each other, then went in behind him.

"Did Noreen call you?" Evelyn asked.

"Yep. Apologized for telling anyone about Margaret—

although it wasn't my choice to keep that secret—and said I fit some profile. That's it."

Evelyn tried not to grind her teeth. Noreen worked in a police station; she should've known better than to warn a potential suspect, even if he was family.

Frank kept walking, leading them past a small, bare kitchen that seemed rarely used, then into a den where he obviously spent most of his time. He settled down in a well-worn indentation on the couch. In front of the seat was a TV table, with a half-eaten sandwich and a drink on it.

Frank picked up his sandwich and took a bite, gesturing to the other chairs in the room, which looked practically new compared to the well-loved couch. "Sit."

Greg took the armchair on one side while Evelyn scanned the room. A pile of nonfiction books on an end table, a few dog-eared hunting magazines stacked beside them. Garage-sale quality artwork on one wall, as if Frank had started to make an effort with decorating, then given up. A TV directly across from the couch, set on mute to a news channel. Images of Lauren and Brittany were flashing across the screen, and Evelyn looked back at Frank to see his reaction.

But he was watching her, not the TV. "Stop staring at my stuff and sit down. You think I'm a suspect? Fine. Ask me whatever you want to ask. Hell, search my house if you need to. Rule me out and go find who really did this."

Evelyn sank into the other chair and exchanged a look with Greg. "Does that offer extend to your barn?"

Frank's flat gaze moved between them. "The offer to search? Sure."

Evelyn held in a sigh. If he was letting them check

the place out this easily, either he hadn't taken the girls or he was positive she and Greg would never find them.

Frank gestured toward the big picture window overlooking his backyard, which seemed to go on for miles, just overgrown fields. "A search party walked part of my property already, you know. Gave them permission to look wherever they wanted. There's a lot of unused land out here."

Greg leaned forward. "Are you saying someone might have been on your property, Mr. Abbott?"

"Hell, no, I'm not. I never saw anyone here. I'm just trying to cooperate." He turned back to Evelyn. "I've got nothing to hide."

"What do you think about all this, Mr. Abbott?" Evelyn asked.

He rolled his eyes. "Call me Frank. What do I think of this? That's the best question you have for me?" He locked his steely gaze on her. "Come on. You can do better than that. This is personal for you, right?"

"How about we keep things friendly?" Greg suggested, easygoing as always.

Frank didn't take his gaze off her. "It's not so friendly to suggest I'm abducting and killing young girls, now, is it?"

"We're not—" Greg started.

"Why do you say 'killing'?" Evelyn interrupted.

Frank finally lowered his eyes. "Eighteen years is a damn long time. *You* think they're still alive?" Not giving her a chance to answer, he said, "Just ask me what you want to ask me, Evelyn."

She didn't look Greg's way, but she could practically feel his increased interest. The way Frank had said her name sounded as if he knew her. She vaguely remembered him as part of the town, but she'd never spoken to him when she was a kid. Did he remember her because she'd stood out? Or because he'd once targeted her?

"Okay, Frank. Tell me about your niece."

"What's to tell? I'm sure you got the short and nasty version from Noreen. Earl's bitch of an ex-wife divorced him, took Margaret and moved away. Then she got careless and Margaret got killed."

Evelyn tried not to show any reaction to Frank's version of the story, but her heart rate picked up. He *did* blame his niece's mother for her death.

"It was years ago," Frank said, taking another bite of his sandwich. "What kind of profile says I mourn one little girl and then decide to kill others? How the hell does that make any sense?"

"Maybe these girls are replacements," Greg suggested carefully. "Rescued from parents who might also get careless."

Frank shot him a glance full of disdain. "Replacements? No one could replace Margaret."

"Not even Noreen?" Evelyn asked, curious about Frank's relationship with his only remaining niece.

"They're different people," he said.

"Have you been helping with the search parties?" Greg asked.

Frank kept his gaze on Evelyn, but something shifted in the depths of his eyes. "Yep. Just ask your friends."

"I'm sorry?"

"The ones pretending to be engineers? You're dating the dark-haired one, right? What's his name, Kyle?"

Evelyn felt heat rush to her face and looked over at Greg before she could stop herself. But like a good profiler, he kept his expression blank.

"Did you run into them at the search parties?" Greg asked smoothly. "Where were you exactly?"

"How did you know they were FBI? And why do you ask if I'm dating one of them?" Evelyn jumped in. Kyle would never have said that. She doubted he would've mentioned her at all. So how would Frank know they had any kind of connection? If it was purely speculation, he could just as easily have guessed Gabe. Or called them her colleagues. But he hadn't, which implied that he'd either seen or heard something by chance or he'd been watching her intentionally.

"People talk," Frank said, then looked at Greg. "Yes, I saw them at the search parties."

"What people?" Evelyn pressed as Greg lowered his eyebrows meaningfully, obviously wondering why she was so focused on the wrong thing.

But if Frank had been paying this much attention to her, could he have been the one who shot into her car?

Her gaze was drawn to the hunting magazines. "Do you own a gun, Frank?"

"Sure. Like a lot of people here." He gestured to her cheek. "I didn't do that."

"You heard about that, too, huh?" Evelyn asked. "People talking again?"

He snorted. "You getting shot at is pretty big gossip, Evelyn. That kind of shit doesn't happen every day." He got serious fast. "But if you're thinking I shot at you? Just because I know your little secret? No way. No damn way."

"What secret?"

"About that guy. Kyle whatever-his-name-is."

"Who told you that?"

"Black guy who shows up at all the search parties. You

want a suspect, look at him. No idea where he's from, but he doesn't live here."

"Darnell Conway?" That actually made sense. Kyle had pulled his gun on Darnell. "Have you talked to Darnell much?"

"No." Frank shoved the rest of his sandwich in his mouth. "There's something off about him."

Evelyn purposely didn't look at Greg, but he was probably thinking the same thing she was—that there was something off about Frank, too.

"So, he told you Kyle and Gabe are with the FBI and that he thinks I'm dating Kyle, then you two didn't talk anymore?" Evelyn made a point of letting him hear the skepticism in her tone.

"He's a talker," Frank said. "Mentioned that your boyfriend has a quick trigger finger, made some noise about complaining to the FBI about both of you. Then he went on and on about trying to find those poor girls. How he rearranged his whole work schedule to help. Blah blah blah. Like he wanted a medal for doing what everyone else was doing. But he struck me as weird, and like I told you, I know he doesn't belong here. I tuned him out after a while, tried not to get paired with him again."

"Okay," Evelyn said. "Were those his words or yours?"

"What?"

"Those poor girls."

Frank looked pointedly at his watch. "What do you want to know about my niece? Because I've got a job soon."

"You have your own handyman company, right?"

"Yeah. Used to own it with Earl. Now it's just me. You have questions or not?"

"How about you let us search and we'll talk some more when you get home?" Greg suggested.

Frank pushed to his feet. "Hell, no. You want to look around? Fine. But you do it while I'm here so I can be sure *you* don't pull any funny stuff. I'm not letting you set me up."

He raised his eyebrows pointedly until Evelyn and Greg got to their feet, then he led them to the door.

As they walked outside, he said, "You know, for FBI, you really seem to be missing the obvious."

"What's that?" Greg asked.

"The pervert."

"Walter Wiggins?" Evelyn asked.

"Yeah."

He started to slam the door, but Evelyn braced her hand against it.

He raised his eyebrows again, an impatient look on his face. "Something else?"

"Do you remember me, Frank? From eighteen years ago?"

"Of course I do. Your best friend was one of the victims. I saw you at the search parties. We all did." His expression softened. "Couldn't believe your grandparents let you go."

"So, you were at the search parties?"

He sighed. "Yeah. That make me more of a suspect in your mind? How exactly does that work? Stop wasting your time! I didn't do it. Come back when I finish my job. Search whatever the hell you want and get it over with. And then get back to looking for whoever did this!"

He knocked her hand off the door and slammed it shut.

Evelyn shrugged at Greg. "What do you think?"

He set off, returning to the car. "I don't know, but if he did it, I don't think those girls are here."

Evelyn nodded, getting into the rental. "Yeah, he was a little too fast to agree we could search."

Greg got in, too, and started the car, backing down the long driveway. "So, what was with all his questions about Kyle?"

The too-casual way he asked it told Evelyn he was suspicious. But not of Frank. Of her. Of her real relationship with Kyle.

Evelyn kept her tone neutral. "Darnell ran into me on purpose, tried to intimidate me, and Kyle showed up. So Frank could be telling the truth about getting that from Darnell. But why was he harping on it?"

Greg nodded, but the quick glance he sent her as he shifted into Drive said he didn't quite buy that there was nothing to it. "You're thinking he's been keeping some kind of tabs on you? That it could be because of eighteen years ago, if he's the perp?"

"Maybe. His reaction to being a possible suspect was odd. He should've been angry and offended. And he was. But not in the right way."

"No kidding," Greg agreed. "I think we'd better talk to the CARD agents. Have them add Frank Abbott to their suspect list."

Evelyn leaned against the headrest. She'd been exhausted for days, but it suddenly hit with the force of a sledgehammer. "We need to be narrowing down the suspect list, not adding to it."

Greg picked up speed on the road back to town. "There's a reason our perp, whoever he is, got away with it for eighteen years, Evelyn. If it was going to be easy, he would've been caught ages ago."

Would he be caught this time?

No matter how hard she tried to convince herself the answer was yes, a taunting voice in her head—a voice that sounded like Cassie—whispered, *You'll never know who took me.*

Fifteen

"Evelyn?"

Evelyn frowned as she placed one hand over her ear and listened to the voice at the other end of her cell phone. "Yes?"

"It's T.J."

"T.J.?" Evelyn stepped away from the table in the CARD command post where she and Greg had been digging through information on Noreen's uncle for the past few hours. So far, nothing had popped.

"Yeah, Jack's partner. Remember?"

"Sure. What's up?"

Greg glanced up at her, but she shook her head as she walked out a back door and into the quiet of the deserted parking lot. Most of the cops were out running down tips, helping with the search or following up on leads from the CARD agents.

"Jack and I are on our way back to the station, but we stopped in at the search parties first," T.J. said.

"Okay. Is something happening?"

"Darnell had just shown up again. I thought you might want to know."

"Oh, well, thanks." It definitely made her suspicious that Darnell kept showing up to search, but she already knew he'd been doing it.

"It's a little weird," T.J. continued. "He must've gone home for dinner and come right back, because Noreen said he was there earlier today."

Evelyn leaned against the brick wall of the station, the heat seeping through her shirt now that she was out of the air-conditioning. It was eight-thirty at night, but the temperature was still in the high eighties, the humidity making the air feel moist and heavy. Not all that different from Virginia, but somehow the air here seemed to weigh down on her. Or maybe it was just the memories.

"Is that unusual?"

"Well, not for family or close friends of the victims. But this guy has been here a lot for someone driving in from Treighton," T.J. explained, then said goodbye and hung up.

Evelyn stuck the phone in her pocket and stared into the distance. The police station was surrounded by other municipal buildings, most of which were closed for the night. In the quiet, empty parking lot, everything felt too still, the way the air sometimes did before a big storm.

Suddenly nervous—the last time she'd been alone in a parking lot, someone had taken a shot at her—Evelyn was about to go inside. Before she'd moved, a police car flew into the lot.

It parked right beside her, and T.J. and Jack stepped out. T.J. looked about the same, but Jack seemed even more worn down than earlier, with dark circles under his eyes, and wrinkles in his khakis and button-up shirt.

Jack ignored her, but T.J. said, "We figured you'd be

off running down some lead or we wouldn't have bothered calling."

As T.J. opened the station door, Evelyn grabbed Jack's arm. "Can I talk to you a second?"

He groaned. "Yeah, sure."

As soon as the door closed behind T.J., Evelyn said, "It's about Frank Abbott."

"You're still on that?"

"Yes."

"How could Frank Abbott possibly fit your profile? Are you leaving things out of this profile, or are you just picking suspects at random? Because Frank makes no sense as a suspect. And I've been working my ass off to find some way to get us into Walter's house."

"Did you come up with anything?" Evelyn asked hopefully.

Jack scowled and pulled out his key card. "Not yet."

Evelyn stepped in front of the door. "Do you remember how Frank acted at the search parties eighteen years ago?" Had Frank searched back then with the rabid devotion Darnell was showing now? Or had he just shown up once or twice for appearance's sake?

Jack propped his hand on his hip, next to his gun. "Yeah, I think I do. That was right around when Earl had his first stroke. It was maybe another year before he got really bad and Frank had to move in with him, but by then Frank was definitely helping out. And with everything going on, he still showed up as much as he could."

"So..."

"You're thinking that's suspicious? Because I've got to tell you, I've known Frank a long time. He's not my favorite person, but he's no child killer. I mean, he didn't exactly do right by Noreen, cutting out on her and Earl as soon as she hit eighteen. But hell, when Earl got really sick, he did take over the whole business, handle the bills, move in with them to help. It's more than some guys would've done."

"How old is Noreen now?" Evelyn asked, wondering how long Frank had been back on his own, with no one around to see what he was doing. Maybe he'd stopped the abductions because he was with his brother and niece. But as soon as he could get free of them, maybe he'd started up again.

"Twenty-four, I think."

Evelyn frowned. That meant Frank had been living by himself for the past six years. It was a long time to wait, if he was the perpetrator.

"What makes you suspect Frank, of all people? Just because his niece moved away…"

"She's dead, Jack."

"What?" Jack's hand fell off his hip and his eyebrows jerked up.

"Noreen made me promise not to say anything. But you know this town, know these people. So, I need you to tell me about Frank."

"Damn. Poor Noreen."

"Focus, Jack, okay? Just focus on Frank."

Jack looked bewildered and faintly hurt. "Why the hell would she have kept something like that secret?"

"Her dad didn't want anyone to know, didn't want the pity."

"Yeah, that sounds like Earl, to be honest. He was the same way with his illness." Jack closed his eyes. "Okay, Frank." He rubbed the back of his neck, staring past her at nothing.

Finally he shook his head, opening his eyes again.

"I don't remember him acting weird then. Bewildered, I guess, because of what was happening with Earl. At the time Cassie went missing, he was mostly worried. But then a year or so later, the shit really hit the fan. You could tell that Frank didn't want to move in with them, but he did it, didn't complain. Worked twice as hard to keep that business going, pay Earl's bills. He'd never had kids. I don't think he really knew what to do with Noreen, but he tried."

"Until she turned eighteen."

"Right," Jack agreed. "And then, hell, he probably just figured it was her turn. I always thought about it from her perspective, how unfair it was, but I guess it was pretty shitty for Frank, too."

"Noreen said her father had something called CADASIL?"

"I don't know what it was. All I know is, he went downhill real fast, but lingered forever. One day he seemed fine and then the next he could barely walk. Stroke, maybe? And a few months after that, he was in a wheelchair. I think he got back to using a cane for a while, but he never worked again. He sure wasn't in any shape to take care of himself or his kid."

"So, if Earl got sick close to when Cassie went missing and Frank was helping out, maybe that would account for the abductions stopping?"

"It's possible," Jack replied, "but like I said, it was a year later before he had to move in with Earl. And Frank's been back on his own a long time now. Why wait to start again, if it's him?"

"I have no idea." And it made him a less viable suspect—unless he'd had a recent trigger. "Anything major happen in Frank's life recently?"

"Not that I know of. He's typical Frank."

"His business is doing okay? No personal losses? Nothing?"

Jack shrugged. "His business is doing really well. It picked up recently since we've had some development in the area, so he's getting more work. And on the personal side? Well, Noreen is his only family. And she's obviously doing fine. Last year, she lost her dad's house—too many bills to keep up with after paying all of Earl's medical expenses. But she's got an apartment and a good job. She's probably doing the best she has in years, finally being free of all that baggage. She definitely seems happier."

Evelyn couldn't suppress a sigh. Learning that Frank's niece was dead—and that it was a secret—had seemed like such a good lead. But as much as she wanted him to, Frank didn't totally fit the profile.

"That it?" Jack asked.

"Yeah. Thanks." She stopped him as he opened the station door. "Keep this to yourself, okay?"

"No problem," Jack said, but he was obviously offended that Noreen hadn't told him herself.

His dad had given her a job, given her a place in the station. It seemed that Jack had taken on the role of Noreen's protector since his dad had died. It must hurt to know that Noreen had told an outsider her secret instead of him. Evelyn might have spent the most important seven years of her childhood here, but Jack still saw her as an outsider.

Evelyn trailed him into the station to see if Greg or the CARD agents had found anything on Frank that would make him a more likely suspect.

But when she walked into the CARD command post,

Greg looked up at her and shook his head. "I'm not seeing anything unusual in his history. On paper, this guy's pretty clean."

Evelyn had been a criminal investigative analyst long enough to know that didn't mean a damn thing. There were serial killers who spent their days handling the finances for their churches. Serial rapists could be well-liked volunteers at rape crisis centers. Child molesters could be community leaders. They all looked fine on paper, too.

Evelyn glanced at Carly. The lead CARD agent was still wearing a suit, possibly the same one she'd had on yesterday. Her hair was still tied on top of her head, her makeup still carefully applied. But underneath, lines of stress and exhaustion showed through, like a cracked foundation.

Carly met her gaze with bloodshot eyes. "Since you said Frank gave permission to search his house, we're sending some agents there tonight. Seems like a long shot, though."

"It is," Evelyn agreed. Damn, she felt useless. She'd gotten as deep into the abductor's head as she could, but there was only so far she could go without knowing the true motivation. She felt like a rat in a maze, stuck in a corner and banging her head against the wall.

"Why don't you go back to the hotel?" Greg suggested. "Take a break. You've had, what? Two hours of sleep in the past forty-eight?"

"That's what everyone else is running on, too. I'm fine."

"I'm not sure you…"

The ringing of Evelyn's phone cut Greg off. When she picked up, it was Noreen.

"Hey, Evelyn, I'm in my car heading home from the search parties—I handed it off to Ronald, our other administrative assistant. Anyway, Darnell just left."

"Just left?" Evelyn echoed. "T.J. told me he only arrived about twenty minutes ago."

"Weird, huh? Jack and T.J. said to keep an eye on him, which is why I'm calling. He jumped in his car as I was leaving, and he was in one hell of a hurry."

Evelyn frowned. "That could be anything. Maybe someone called with an emergency."

"Yeah, maybe," Noreen said. "Look, Evelyn, I know I'm not a cop or anything, but this guy is giving me a really bad feeling. I know there *were* cops on him. Are there still?"

"No." They'd been taken off and put back on Walter Wiggins. She couldn't seem to win on that front.

"Can you talk to Jack? Maybe he can check on Darnell. See what's going on. Or should I call him?"

"No, it's okay, Noreen. I'll handle it."

"Are you sure? After what happened before..."

Damn, did *everyone* know what she'd done? "I'm sure."

Greg thought she should get out of the station, anyway. And even though Frank was a possibility, her gut still insisted that Darnell was guilty of murder twenty years ago. And if he'd murdered once, he could do it again.

Noreen sounded relieved. "Thanks," she replied. "I asked him where he was going, tried to be all friendly. He gave me this weird look, like he'd figured out what I was doing, but he said he was headed home."

Which could have been a lie, but Evelyn didn't tell Noreen that. And it didn't really matter, because that was the only place Evelyn knew to look for him.

It was a bad idea, but she was going to do it, anyway.

"I'll fill you in on what happens," she promised Noreen, then hung up and met Greg's curious gaze.

"What are you going to handle?"

"Darnell took off unexpectedly from the search parties."

"Tell the cops," Greg said. "Let them deal with Darnell."

"I'm going to get a hold of Jack. I'll take him with me. But I want to go on this one."

"You think that's smart?" The tone of Greg's voice told her he didn't.

"I'll go back to the hotel afterward and get some rest."

"Just so long as you make sure you don't trespass while you're at Darnell's," Carly contributed, looking up from her computer search.

Evelyn flushed. "I already said I'm going to take Jack. I'll watch from a distance. I want to see what sent him off in such a rush."

Carly started to argue, but Greg broke in. "If you can't find Jack, come back and I'll go with you."

"Thanks," Evelyn said, then picked up her bag and hurried out the door and into the station's bull pen.

But as she walked through the station, she didn't come across Jack anywhere. Finally she asked one of the rookies where he was.

"We just heard from the 9-1-1 operators. Walter phoned in, said his dad needed an ambulance. Potential heart attack. The operators know what's going on, so they called us. We're sending a cop car along, on the premise that the Wigginses have faced threats. Jack's hoping it could be his ticket back into the house. He just left."

"Damn it." She glanced at the CARD command post,

but she really didn't want to take Greg with her. She wanted him here, going over all the evidence, in case he saw some fact, some hint, she'd missed.

"Where's T.J.?"

The rookie shrugged. "Saw him go outside earlier. Could've been for a smoke or he might have been heading out."

"Thanks." Evelyn hurried to the parking lot, hoping to find T.J. there, lighting up. She didn't; he'd obviously already left. And every second she wasted here was more time for Darnell to do something. Maybe she could catch him…

Maybe now, when she went to Darnell's house, he'd be the one facing criminal charges.

"Hey, Evelyn!" Kyle called.

He watched as she spun toward him in the Rose Bay police station parking lot, guilt on her face. Her hand froze on the door handle of her car. "Mac. What are you doing here?"

He changed direction, walking over to her instead of the station doors. He'd come to give her and Greg the news about his case, but that could wait. At the moment, Evelyn claimed his full attention. Wherever she was going, he knew he wasn't going to like it.

Rather than answering, he climbed into her passenger seat. "Going with you. Where are we headed?"

She stared at him blankly for a minute, then joined him in the car. "Actually, this is good," she surprised him by saying, apparently past her earlier embarrassment. "I need to see what Darnell's up to. I was planning to take Jack, but he's running down another lead, and I couldn't find T.J." She was talking at double speed as she put the car in gear and whipped out of the parking lot before he'd even buckled his seat belt.

"That asshole from the dunes?" The same guy who'd caused her to get a censure in her otherwise sparkling personnel file when she'd trespassed on his property?

What she'd done was wrong, but he understood. He didn't have a case like hers—he'd joined the FBI because it interested him, not because he had a driving need to solve some tragedy from his past. But plenty of agents had a painful incident in their histories that had pushed them to join the Bureau.

Still, he'd never met anyone so completely dedicated to the job as Evelyn. As much as he wanted to see her lay her demons to rest, he didn't want to watch her destroy her career in the process.

"Yes, Darnell Conway, from the dunes," Evelyn answered. "He left the search party in a hurry and I want to know why."

"You know where he's going?"

"No. I'll try his house." She hit the gas and sped around the car in front of her, getting honked at in the process, then raced onto the bridge that led out of Rose Bay.

"What could he have found out while he was with the search parties that would make him rush off?" It didn't seem like much of a lead to Kyle.

"I have no idea. Maybe nothing related. But maybe—I'm speculating—maybe he's got a sensor system set up wherever he's hidden the girls and it set off an alarm on his phone." He had sensors in his yard, so it was a possibility. "Or he heard that the search parties were going somewhere he didn't want them to look."

"What if he received a phone call?" Kyle asked. "Could he have a partner?"

Evelyn frowned as she increased her speed. "No."

She wove around traffic in the main part of Treighton, slowing down as she neared a residential area. Then she looked at him as if she'd suddenly realized something. "What are you doing here? Shouldn't you be leaving for your surveillance soon?"

"That's why I swung by the station. The official word came down today. We have what we need, and a tactical solution was ruled out, so we're getting out of here in the morning."

"Oh." He recognized disappointment on her face, but she hid it fast.

It wasn't as though they'd been able to talk except in passing, between his nighttime surveillance and her around-the-clock investigation. "You need my help with anything? The flight doesn't take off until 0700." He figured it was unnecessary to add that anything she needed, he'd do.

But the surprised way she shook her head told him that her disappointment was personal, not professional.

He tried not to grin too broadly. "You want to talk about earlier?" Earlier, when she'd kissed the hell out of him.

"Uh, well..." She slid her hand over the ever-present bun neatly wound on top of her head. "We're almost at Darnell's house."

He knew exactly what the problem was. The Bureau didn't care if its agents dated. But they couldn't be assigned to the same squad or work the same cases. And BAU and HRT worked a lot of the same cases.

Evelyn wasn't the kind of woman who would be interested in casual. And even if she was, the Bureau wouldn't care—to the bureaucracy, dating was dating and it meant reassignment.

There were no women on HRT, so he couldn't begin to guess how their situation would work. But he assumed it just meant that if his team got called out, they'd use a different profiler. And if she was already on a case that needed a tactical team, one of the other units would go out—that could get trickier because of their rotations, but the Bureau could worry about that. It didn't seem like a big deal to him; knowing Evelyn, it probably seemed insurmountable to her.

He'd spent the past year trying to get her attention. And he had a feeling it was going to be twice as hard to get anything more.

Now was without a doubt the worst time to push her on it, but he was sick of waiting. "You planning to take some vacation when you solve this case?"

He could tell she was about to answer no, but he cut her off. "Because I have the days off, if you want to go away somewhere." He threw it out there casually, in a tone she'd have trouble reading. For someone who understood the intricacies of every type of evil mind on the planet, she'd never been quick on the uptake with a joke.

She turned toward him again, such confusion and shock on her face that he had to laugh.

"Too soon for a weekend away? How about dinner, then? That's not much of a commitment, right?"

"Mac..."

"No? Lunch?"

She let out a surprised laugh.

"Lunch, it is," he said as she slowed the car and pulled onto a residential street, her face going serious.

"That Darnell's house?" he asked, gesturing to the house down the road with all its security lights on, although the sun was just starting its descent.

"Yeah."

"You think he's there?"

Before Evelyn could answer, Darnell's garage door lifted.

Evelyn sank lower in her seat, but they were in a running car parked on a residential street.

Instead of trying to duck under the dash, Kyle took off his hat and set it on her head, tilting the brim over her eyes. He popped open the glove compartment and removed a map, unfolding it and handing it to her to hold in front of her face.

Darnell was more likely to remember Evelyn's face than his, so Kyle just turned into the car, leaning close to her as though he was trying to look at the map, too. Darnell pulled out of the garage and onto the street, but now he'd only see the back of Kyle's head as he drove by.

Kyle heard the car slow down as it passed, but he kept his head carefully bent over the map. As soon as the car drove by theirs, the engine gunned.

"Shit," Evelyn said, shoving the map at him and shifting into Drive.

Kyle glanced over his shoulder as Darnell took a left out of the neighborhood.

Evelyn did a three-point turn and followed.

"Don't get too close," Kyle warned.

She sent him an irritable look. "I've done this before."

They had the same basic training, which included moving surveillance. But he'd had a lot more practice. They weren't in an ideal situation, with only one car and no GPS tracker. But the reality was, Darnell probably at least suspected he was being watched as soon as he'd seen the car on his street.

Kyle kept his mouth shut as Darnell darted around slower cars, getting honked at repeatedly, and making it impossible to follow stealthily. Evelyn did a decent job, trying to stay a few cars back. But with the shit Darnell was pulling, he was either a lunatic driver one ticket short of losing his license, or he suspected he had a tail and was trying to shake it.

"Damn it," Evelyn muttered as Darnell shot through a yellow light. She whipped around a few cars, checked traffic and sailed through the red.

"Might as well stay on his tail," Kyle said. "He knows you're there."

"He's going back to Rose Bay. He's on his way to the bridge. I just have to keep close enough that I won't lose him once we get over."

"You sure?"

"Yeah."

"You think he might be going back to the search parties?"

"No." Her hands gripped the wheel too tightly as she eased back, letting Darnell get out ahead of her again. "I don't know where he's going, but it's not the search parties."

She thought Darnell was going to his victims.

Kyle folded up the map and tossed it in the glove compartment. "Should we have Tomas put more cars on him?"

Evelyn shook her head as she continued to follow Darnell to the bridge separating Treighton from Rose Bay. "He knows we're here and he's attempting to get somewhere despite that. It means something's happening. I'm going to try and make him think he's lost me when we get into Rose Bay."

After they went over the bridge, Darnell stayed on the outskirts of town, where the roads weren't as populated, and Evelyn fell back. Darnell's driving became less erratic, so it looked as if Evelyn had succeeded and he thought he'd lost them.

"What the hell is he doing?" she grumbled as Darnell turned onto a long, winding dirt road with overgrown fields on either side.

She dropped way back, until Darnell was completely out of sight. "This is a dead end." She slowed even more as they drove for several miles, swiveling her head to peer down the few driveways they passed. Then she stopped and put the car in Park.

"What are you doing?" he asked as she got out.

"It dead-ends up ahead. Either he's parked there, just screwing with me, or he turned into one of those drives and I missed him."

Kyle stepped out of the car, crowding her to the side of the road as they walked forward. "He must've thought he lost your tail."

But Kyle wasn't taking chances. The last time he'd seen Darnell, the guy had been intentionally trying to intimidate Evelyn. And she'd been shot at the other day, possibly by him. If he was trying to lead Evelyn into a trap, Kyle didn't want her in the open.

There was a patch of dense trees as they neared the bend, blocking their view of whatever was ahead, and Kyle crowded her even farther to the side, pulling his weapon. Moving his finger inside the trigger guard would take under a second; clearing the Glock from his holster would have taken longer.

She didn't say a word, but from his peripheral vision, he saw her raise her own weapon.

Kyle scanned the cluster of trees, but saw no one. They rounded the bend, and found Darnell's parked car underneath a grove of oaks, no obvious sign of him inside. Beyond that was an empty field, filled with waist-high grass. An ideal location to lie down, hidden, and line up a long-distance shot.

Any of the snipers on his team would have loved this spot as a potential hide.

"Stay behind me," Kyle said as he carefully approached the car, checking inside. "Empty."

"Where the hell did he go?" Evelyn whispered as Kyle pushed her against the car.

"I don't know." He scanned the grass, looking for anything out of place, keeping Evelyn behind him.

Then a flash of movement off in the distance caught his eye. Darnell. He'd been crouched in the field, below the level of the grass, and he suddenly took off, away from them.

Evelyn holstered her weapon and raced after him, and Kyle cursed and followed.

Darnell was fast, and he kept looking frantically around, occasionally shifting direction. The field stretched out for miles, broken up by random clumps of trees.

"Where does this go?" Kyle called to Evelyn as he picked up speed, outpacing her.

"Just fields. Old farmland," Evelyn wheezed.

She'd broken ribs a month ago and he could tell that was slowing her down, but he didn't wait for her. Everything about this situation was bizarre, but if his suspicion that Darnell was trying to lead her into some kind of trap was correct, Kyle wanted to be between them.

Near the edge of the field, by a large live oak, Darnell came to a near stop. Kyle was too far behind to tell what he was doing, but he positioned his hand near his holster just in case.

Darnell glanced back at him, a panicked expression on his face, and took off again, darting sharply right, toward another patch of trees.

Kyle sped up, closing the distance. Another minute and he'd catch the guy, tackle him to the ground and get some answers out of him.

"Mac! Mac!"

He skidded to a stop at Evelyn's scream. He didn't see her.

Ahead of him, Darnell reached the trees and kept going.

Kyle spun and ran back toward where Evelyn must have fallen. "Evelyn! Where are you?"

Her head popped up above the grass in the middle of the field. She must've been running toward the spot where Darnell had paused. "Mac! Help me! I think I found something!"

When he got back to her, he realized the field wasn't as empty as it had appeared.

Evelyn was hunched on the ground, crouched on planks of rotting wood, obviously pieces of some structure that had fallen down years ago. She was tugging at something, and as he got closer he saw that not everything there was old.

Dread hit him hard and fast. Her hand clutched something amid what looked like planks of flooring. As he stepped closer, he saw her tugging at a shiny new metal latch.

The latch was attached to an old piece of wood, but a second glance showed him that it was hinged into the ground. She was trying to break the lock on the latch.

"Move," Kyle said. Instead of trying to open the lock, he kicked just behind the latch the way he would if he was breaking through a door. The wood splintered. Another kick snapped it free and Kyle grabbed the wood, yanking it up.

Below, the ground opened into a dark hole. Someone's man-made hiding place.

Kyle stared at Evelyn in the fading light. Her eyes were wide, broadcasting all her emotions. Disbelief, fear, hope.

Had they just found the Nursery Rhyme Killer's lair? If so, what the *hell* were they going to discover inside?

Sixteen

Paralyzed with the fear of finding out what was underneath her, Evelyn stayed rooted to the ground as Kyle shone a tiny flashlight into the dark cavern below them. It illuminated a ladder leading several feet to a dirt floor. The hole opened up at the bottom, extending under their feet, but she couldn't see what was down there.

Kyle held out the flashlight. "Hold this for me. I'll go in first."

"No," she said, finally recovering her voice. "Stay here. Keep an eye out for Darnell. You're more likely to spot him if he comes back."

Kyle looked unhappy, but she knew he couldn't argue. The sun was fading fast now, and if Darnell was any good, he might be able to sneak up on her. Kyle had a lot more experience watching perimeters. And Darnell probably wasn't gunning for Kyle specifically.

Besides, this was something she had to do herself. What if Cassie was down there?

What if she'd been stuck there for eighteen long years?

If she had, could she still be alive? Would she know

who Evelyn was? Would she even know who *she* was anymore?

Trying not to dwell on all the what-ifs, Evelyn strained to hear, but the pit was silent. If any girls were in there, they could have screamed themselves hoarse, but in the middle of an empty field on a dead-end road, miles from the nearest house, no one would ever hear. Especially with several feet of dirt above them to soundproof their prison.

Even if search parties had come through here, they could easily have missed this small spot. She'd run over it only because she'd detoured toward the tree where Darnell had paused, as though he was looking for something. And from the way the planks had been shifted alongside the door, revealing the latch, she suspected someone had moved them. Had it been Darnell—before they'd come around the corner?

If the searchers had happened to hit just this spot in the field, they might have mistaken it for exactly what it probably was. An old building that had fallen down decades ago. Grass was already growing through cracks in most of the boards.

It was pure luck that she'd seen the brand-new lock. Pure luck she'd realized the wood planks weren't lying on flat ground. Pure luck she'd run out here in the first place.

Gripping the rusty metal ladder with hands that trembled, Evelyn lowered herself carefully into the ground. When she got to the bottom, she had to crouch to enter the small cavern.

Someone might have originally built it as a root cellar. The ladder was old. But the lock proved it had become something else since then.

Evelyn took a quivering breath and reached for her

flashlight with one hand and her SIG Sauer with the other. She expected to find children inside—she prayed still alive—but the FBI had taught her never to enter an unknown situation unprepared.

With slow, careful steps, Evelyn eased inside, bent low so her head didn't bump the dirt ceiling. The scent of dirt and mold crawled into her nostrils.

And another scent. It took her a minute, then she recognized the acidic scent of urine, mixed with a smell she'd become too familiar with in her violent crimes days. It was the smell of sweat, when the person secreting it was terrified.

Someone was in here. Or at least, someone had been here.

Whose fear was she smelling? Brittany's? Lauren's? Or had it been trapped in an airless room for eighteen years?

She'd never been claustrophobic, but she suddenly felt closed in, trapped. Panic fluttered in her chest and she shoved it aside.

The cavern was completely dark. The beam of her flashlight illuminated sections at a time. A childish drawing hung on a dirt wall, the edges curled and yellowing. A plain white plate with a half-eaten sandwich on the floor, ants crawling all over it.

The beam of the flashlight shook as Evelyn shone it over the edge of a tiny bed, covered in a dirty, faded pink bedspread. And curled up at the farthest corner, a tiny figure, not moving.

"Evelyn," Kyle called. "You okay?"

"Yeah," she tried to shout back, but it came out too quiet. "I'm okay," she called again.

The child on the bed didn't move at her voice and Evelyn stepped closer, tears pricking her eyes as she touched the girl's shoulder. All the while, her mind was taunting, *Only one. There's only one.*

Who was it? Brittany or Lauren? And was she still alive?

As she gripped the child's shoulder to turn her, the girl flipped toward her. Terrified brown eyes brimming with tears latched on to hers. Evelyn recognized her instantly from the police photos.

She sucked in a breath and her own eyes clouded with tears, but she blinked them away fast. "It's okay, Lauren. You're okay. I'm with the FBI."

Quickly, she shone the flashlight around the rest of the room, looking for Brittany, but there was no one else in the cramped cavern.

"Mac!" she yelled, her voice sounding distant and weak. "Call for an ambulance!"

Putting her weapon away, Evelyn tried to smile reassuringly at Lauren, but her lips shook. "I'm with the FBI," she said again.

Trembling, Lauren pushed to her knees, then launched herself at Evelyn, wrapping thin arms around her so tightly Evelyn had trouble breathing.

"It's okay," Evelyn repeated, over and over, as she lifted the girl up and walked back to the ladder. "We're coming up," she told Kyle, keeping one hand on Lauren and using the other to pull herself up and out of the cellar.

"Ambulance is on the way," Kyle said, his profile tense as he continued to survey the area, watching for threats. "We need to meet them back on the road. Police are coming, too."

As if on cue, Evelyn heard sirens approaching.

"You got her?" Kyle asked.

Evelyn nodded, and he let her take the lead as they headed back through the field toward the road, Lauren's silent tears running down Evelyn's neck. Every step she took away from the cellar made Evelyn long to run back, to search the whole area. What if Brittany was still somewhere out there? What if they all were?

Could there be other holes dug into that seemingly deserted field? Other children buried deep in the ground?

Could any of them still be alive?

The ambulance tore down the street, whisking Lauren away from the pit where she'd been held captive for twenty-six hours. Evelyn stared after it until well past the time she could no longer see the taillights, until she couldn't even hear the siren.

Lauren's parents were on their way to the hospital to meet her. Evelyn had seen enough of these cases to know how they'd react. Initially, nothing but pure relief and joy that their daughter was coming home to them alive.

Then they'd start to wonder exactly what had happened to Lauren during those twenty-six hours. When the ambulance had taken her away, Lauren had still been wide-eyed, unresponsive except for clinging to Evelyn and crying silently. She hadn't said a word about who had taken her or what she'd endured.

Evelyn had worked her way into the minds of too many child abductors and their victims in her year at BAU. The possibilities were endless, every one more horrifying than the last. Her limbs felt heavy with the knowledge that no matter how many of those predators she helped put behind bars, there'd always be more.

"Evelyn."

The soft voice at her ear slowly registered and Evelyn

realized Kyle had been repeating her name. She turned, blinking him into focus, and discovering he had an arm wrapped around her waist, almost holding her up.

She straightened, trying to get her feet to work normally. Behind Kyle, police cars dotted the edge of the empty field, all their headlights on and pointing toward the cellar. Cops were everywhere, walking in specified patterns through the field, collecting evidence from the cellar, setting up a perimeter.

They'd only been on scene a few minutes, but they'd gone to work fast. Rose Bay was a small town. The news that Lauren had been found would get out soon and residents would start showing up. Among them were bound to be Brittany's parents.

By the time they got there, would the police be able to hand them their daughter the way she'd handed Lauren to the paramedics? Or would they still be searching? Or worse, calling for a coroner?

Tremors shook her so hard there was no way Kyle wouldn't have felt them. She tensed, trying to will them away, and locked her gaze on his. "Come with me?"

Her voice was weak, barely more than a whisper. What the hell was she going to find back in that field?

"Let the cops handle it, Evelyn. You don't need to be here."

She shook her head, pulled free of his supporting arm. Time to turn on the analytical side of her brain and shut down the emotional, the way she always tried to do with this kind of case. When she spoke again, her voice was steady, stronger. "I'll see things they won't."

The Rose Bay officers and CARD agents would be in charge of collecting any physical evidence that might indisputably confirm the abductor. But until Greg arrived, she was the only one with the training to look for clues that had nothing to do with DNA or trace evidence. Clues that might be the key to putting the Nursery Rhyme Killer behind bars for good.

And even after Greg showed up, she was the only one who had the added advantage of knowing the town, having a history here.

She had to go back into that cellar and analyze the personality of the man who'd turned it into his own personal hiding place. She had to stand in the same cramped room where Lauren had been imprisoned. The same room where she'd been locked in the dark, not knowing if anyone would ever return for her. Evelyn had to look around that room and try to get into the head of the person who'd enjoyed putting Lauren through this torture.

Nausea welled up her throat. Had Cassie been in that same dark hole? Had she died there?

"I'll come with you," Kyle said, walking beside her, somehow lending her strength as they went back to the cellar.

Night had settled fully all around them, and the beams of light cutting through the field from the police cars, various stationary lights and cops' flashlights lent an eerie glow to the scene.

"You were good with that little girl," Kyle said softly, probably trying to keep her mind off what they might find.

"Thanks." Her mind flashed back to Lauren, the way the child had clung to her, not saying a word.

"…can't believe she was on the Bullock property this whole time," someone said.

Evelyn whipped around to face the cops behind her. "What did you say?"

"This is the old Bullock property," Stan Kovak, an RBPD veteran, answered.

"This is *Jack's* property?"

"Well, it belonged to the old chief. But now that he's gone, Jack owns it, yeah."

The Nursery Rhyme Killer had hidden his victims on the old police chief's property? Could he possibly have done that eighteen years ago, without Jack's father noticing? Or was this a brand-new spot, just for these victims?

"Did Jack's father use the property?" Evelyn asked.

Stan nodded. "Yeah. You said there was part of an old cabin or something that fell down where you found Lauren, right? I'll bet the old chief built it. That was a real joke back then."

"What was?" Kyle asked.

"Jack's dad was a great chief, but he couldn't build for shit. He sure thought he could, though. He lived in town, but you know how long the Bullocks have been here." He looked at Evelyn, who nodded. "So, he had all this land out here, this old farmland, and he always talked about how he was going to build a house out here in the middle of nowhere and retire in peace."

The rookie beside him smiled, as though he'd heard the story before, and his partner continued. "But every house he tried to build just fell down. There are probably a whole bunch of fallen-down structures on this property."

"Does Jack ever come here?" Evelyn asked.

The rookie shrugged, looking pale and nervous as he stared in the direction of the cellar. "I doubt it. Why would anyone come here?"

Evelyn considered the little she knew about Jack Bullock. Back when Cassie had gone missing, Jack had been a rookie, married with a new baby. As far as she knew, he was still married, his son now grown. "Does his son live around here?" The officers glanced at each other, then back at her.

"What?" Evelyn pressed.

"His son died as an infant, Evelyn," Stan said quietly. "He and his wife could never have any more kids. They tried for years—Miranda really wanted a daughter—but it never happened for them."

Next to her, Evelyn could sense Kyle getting ready to ask more, but Evelyn cut him off. "Where's Jack?"

"Right here," Jack's voice boomed.

Evelyn jerked around and there was Jack, running to catch up to them.

His skin was tinged with green. "You found Lauren under my dad's property?"

"Yes," Evelyn said. "Did you know about the cellar?"

Jack shook his head. "It's possible my dad dug it out, but I have no idea. Equally likely someone else did it later. Everyone knew he was building out here."

"Was he building around the time Cassie went missing? Could someone have used this property back then without his noticing?"

Jack scowled and cracked his neck. "Probably. He only came out here on random weekends. And you remember how small towns are. Everyone knows what everyone else is doing. If this spot was an early place my dad started to build…" Jack shrugged.

"What?" Kyle prompted.

"If this one fell down, he wouldn't have tried to rebuild it. He'd move somewhere else, start all over." Jack's steps slowed as they neared the cellar, where officers were already working. "He didn't like to see evidence of his failures. He'd just call it a trial, pick a new spot and try again."

Evelyn slowed beside him as she watched a pair of FBI CARD agents who also worked as evidence response technicians descend into the cellar with their equipment.

The scene would be processed before anyone else—including her—could go back in.

Standing near the cellar, wearing his shirt inside out, his uncombed hair sticking up and every minute of his fifty-odd years showing, Tomas glanced over at her. "We've got an APB out on Darnell. Without his car, he shouldn't get far. But most everyone is here. Once we process the scene, Evelyn, you can go in and see if it tells you anything. Your partner's on his way, too."

"Good."

Tomas looked at Kyle, standing silently beside Evelyn, then back at her. "The FBI is bringing some more bloodhounds from the closest field office." He sighed, rubbing a beard that had come in during the few days she'd been in Rose Bay. "Different from the dog they sent before."

"These are Victim Recovery Team dogs?" Kyle guessed.

Tomas nodded somberly. "In case there are bodies."

In the distance, Evelyn heard vehicles coming closer. The Rose Bay residents were arriving.

"Damn it," Jack muttered.

Then a car door slammed in the distance and a hysterical woman's voice carried over to the officers and agents. "Where is she? Where's my daughter?"

Brittany's mom.

Evelyn cringed as an officer physically restrained her as she broke down sobbing in his arms. His partner was holding Brittany's father back, but he yelled, "Did you find her? Did you find my baby?"

"Chief."

The quiet, sad voice of the officer startled Evelyn; she turned and found him standing behind her.

His skin was ashen, and tears shimmered in his eyes. "I think we found Brittany Douglas."

Seventeen

Evelyn felt Kyle's hand on her back, steadying her, ready to catch her if she faltered. She walked numbly, her feet somehow moving even as her brain tried to shut down, following the rookie officer who'd told them they'd found Brittany.

A hundred feet past the cellar opening, a group of cops stood in a circle. Had they discovered another cellar?

As she neared, a rookie officer darted away, stooped over and threw up violently.

Beside her, Tomas swore and Kyle clenched his jaw and Evelyn just kept putting one foot in front of the other.

She suddenly couldn't stop picturing the images of Brittany Douglas from the photographs her parents had provided. Her long, dark brown hair flung out behind her as she ran through a field not unlike this one, spirit in her hazel eyes and pure joy in her grin.

But she would never smile at anything again, Evelyn saw as they finally reached the cops.

Jack turned toward them, his eyes glistening with unshed tears as he shook his head.

Behind him, the cops had dug a hole, approximately

three feet deep. "We saw evidence of a disturbance here," Jack said in a shaky voice. "It's her."

She didn't want to look, but she couldn't stop herself. In the hole was a wooden box, with flowers painted on it in a child's hand. The cops had pulled off the top and inside, wrapped in a soft blue blanket, was Brittany.

Spinning away, Evelyn took a few steps back, her gaze going to Brittany's parents, way off by the road. Their images wavered through her watery eyes.

It didn't help that she knew the statistics. Brittany's chances had been slim before Evelyn had even arrived on the scene. She should be happy that they'd even brought one little girl home today.

But all Evelyn could see was Brittany, so small in that blanket someone had tucked carefully around her.

Something niggled in her mind, telling her she was missing an important piece of information, but all she could focus on was Brittany's parents, yelling and crying, asking what was happening.

"Evelyn," Kyle said, and she realized she'd sunk against him.

She righted herself and trod back toward the cellar where the CARD agents were climbing up, heading over to Brittany. Carly nodded solemnly as she passed, a hardness to her profile that told Evelyn she'd been at scenes like this one too many times.

It was the cops' job to dig Brittany out, to deal with her parents. It was the CARD agents' job to analyze the scene and advise in the manhunt for Darnell Conway. It was her job to descend into the killer's hideaway and dissect his sick personality, and use that to catch him before he went after anyone else.

"Evelyn," Kyle said again, sticking so close to her

there was practically no space between them. "Greg is here."

He pointed into the distance and Evelyn saw her partner coming toward them.

Evelyn nodded and kept walking, but Kyle took hold of her arm.

"Let *him* go down there," Kyle said.

"No." Evelyn shook her head. "I need to do this."

But Kyle didn't release her. "At least wait and let Greg go with you."

She looked up at his face, the deep-blue eyes staring at her with such concern, and some of her numbness lifted. The world around her sharpened again and, with it, pain rushed in, stabbing through her with a physical intensity.

How many more graves would they uncover today?

She pushed the thought aside and nodded. She couldn't leave this to anyone else, not even Greg. But he would be an impartial second opinion.

"Evelyn." Greg strode up beside them, his worried gaze moving to Kyle.

They seemed to share some silent communication Evelyn couldn't focus on and then Greg's attention was back on her. "You ready?"

Evelyn nodded, suddenly feeling incapable of speech. She forced her feet to trudge toward the cellar and the world around her seemed to dim again, the cellar entrance, bathed in portable light, filling her vision like the destination at the end of a tunnel.

"Can you stick around?" she heard Greg ask Kyle behind her. Kyle must have nodded, because Greg replied, "Good."

Then she was snapping on the gloves Greg handed

her, slipping booties over her shoes and climbing back down into the dank cellar.

This time, instead of being pitch-black, it was lit with small portable lights the cops had set up. The bedspread was gone, bagged as evidence and already taken away. The sandwich was also missing, probably in its own bag, on the off chance that Lauren hadn't been the only one to eat from it. A yellow evidence marker with black numbers stood where the plate had been.

Evelyn looked around the space, taking in new details in the bright light. She bent over and stepped closer to the picture stuck to the wall. It was drawn in crayon, clearly by a child, and covered in a layer of dirt and dust. There was a yellow sun in the top corner, a layer of grass and purple flowers dotting the bottom and, in the center, two stick-figure girls holding hands.

Who were they supposed to be? One girl had brown hair. Like Brittany or Lauren. Veronica had also been a brunette. Penelope had been a redhead, so neither girl was meant to be her. The other girl in the drawing was blonde. Like Cassie.

Evelyn continued to stare at it, contemplating. There were no crayons in the cellar, no paper. The picture was obviously old. Had it been drawn by one of the victims? Did it mean he'd kept more than one at a time?

A lot of abductors only chose, stalked and abducted the next victim after they'd killed the previous one. But some started a collection, keeping multiple victims alive at once.

She sensed Greg moving around behind her, taking in other details. The setup of the space, what the abductor had provided the girls—a bucket for a toilet in the corner, a bed and food. What he hadn't given them—light or toys. Or if he had, he'd taken them when he'd left.

Evelyn turned in a slow circle, studying every detail, trying to see the meaning behind everything in the room. She and Greg didn't speak for a long time. Finally, once she'd committed the space to memory, she looked at her partner.

Greg was kneeling down, staring intently at something, and Evelyn stepped closer.

"They found blood here when they sprayed Luminol," he said, pointing to the sharp corner of the bed frame.

A sick feeling swirled in Evelyn's stomach. She couldn't see anything, which meant the killer had cleaned the blood. But Luminol applied in a darkened space would make any organic remnants glow blue.

"How much?" Evelyn asked. "And did they find it anywhere else?"

Greg's face was grim. "They just found it on the bed frame corner, not on the bed itself. We should talk to the CARD agents and the cops. See what they know about this blood and how Brittany died."

Evelyn nodded and walked to the ladder. It was only a few feet to the surface, but she couldn't seem to climb it fast enough. Even with the light filling the tiny room, she didn't feel as if she could breathe until she was back on the surface.

Evelyn grabbed at the ground outside the pit, stumbling as she pulled herself out of the cellar.

Kyle steadied her, helped her to her feet, and then Evelyn made her way over to the cluster of cops standing by Brittany's grave. While she and Greg had been down in the cellar, someone must have told Brittany's parents, because they were gone, and a coroner's van was driving away.

How long had they been down there? Evelyn wondered, peeling off her gloves and rubbing her eyes, which felt as rough as sandpaper.

"What do we know so far?" Greg asked when they reached the cops and CARD agents.

Carly sent Kyle a brief, perplexed look, then focused on Greg. In a calm, professional voice, she said, "Initial assessment—unofficial, of course, until the medical examiner does the autopsy—is that Brittany's cause of death was blunt force trauma to the head."

Evelyn felt her throat constrict and she braced her feet a little farther apart, trying to steady herself as Carly continued.

"We found blood at the corner of the bed frame, and the shape looks consistent with the damage to her head. There's a strong chance she hit the corner of that bed frame, likely from a fall."

Surprised, Evelyn asked, "There's a chance her death was accidental?"

Carly nodded. "Could be. It's very possible the assailant pushed her or threw her and she hit the edge of the bed. I think there's actually a pretty good chance that Brittany's abductor didn't intend to kill her."

That meant there was a much stronger possibility that Cassie was still alive somewhere.

She looked out across the vast field where cops were walking strip patterns, searching for any evidence—or additional cellars. A flicker of hope burst inside of her, and no matter how Evelyn tried to force it down, it kept growing.

"Evelyn?"

Evelyn realized Carly had been talking to her. "I'm sorry. Can you repeat that?"

"I said that our ERT agents went over the whole cellar for fingerprints and we've only got one set. We matched them to the ones from the elementary school safety program. They're Lauren's."

"What?" Evelyn gaped at her. "How can that be?"

Carly gave a humorless laugh. "You forgot to mention that this guy is completely paranoid. Either he always wears gloves, or he regularly wipes everything down."

"Maybe he suspected you were getting too close," Kyle spoke up. "He did take a shot at Evelyn last night."

If he'd planned this carefully in case his hiding spot was found, did he have backup plans? Evelyn glanced at Greg and knew he was thinking the same thing.

"He's meticulous," Greg said. "We knew that from the crime scenes, but this guy is a planner to the extreme. Wiping down a hiding spot that he obviously returns to on a regular basis means he's very conscious of forensic countermeasures."

Carly frowned, looking around at the cops and agents watching her somberly. "It means he could already be gone."

"How far could he get without his car?" Tomas asked, gesturing to Darnell's sedan, still sitting at the end of the road where he'd left it.

Carly shrugged. "If he's this careful? Who knows what kind of preparations he's made? But let's not rule out anyone else until we can tie Darnell to this location with DNA."

"That doesn't look like it's going to be easy," a CARD agent said. "I'd be surprised if we get anything."

"The bed sheets?" Evelyn asked, dreading the answer.

Darnell Conway—if he'd murdered Charlotte Novak as she suspected—was a sexual predator.

Carly shook her head. "We got a hit, but from the smell, it's urine. We'll test, but I don't think his DNA is there."

"Sheets were new, though," another agent said. "Not like that disgusting bedspread. It's possible he changes them every day, just like he wipes the place down."

"You taking the mattress?" Greg asked.

The agent nodded. "We will, but the mattress pad was waterproof."

Evelyn glanced back at the entrance of the cellar, lit up like a landing pad. She thought about Darnell Conway's house, the sliver of it she'd seen when he'd opened the door. Expensive, everything in its place, obsessively clean. It matched what she saw here.

But why the dirty pink bedspread? It was clearly old. Maybe he'd picked it for the first girl, eighteen years ago, and kept it for sentimental reasons. Just like the drawing on the wall.

When she turned back to the group, they were all staring at her. "What?"

"We're wondering what you think about the other girls," Tomas said. "What's your professional opinion? Were they kept here, too, or are we looking for more cellars? Is there any chance the others could be somewhere under this field, like Lauren?" Tomas's voice broke when he added, "Alive?"

Evelyn's eyes instantly met Greg's. She tried to push all emotion out of her analysis, but it was impossible. The desire to find Cassie alive had been whispering inside her for eighteen years. She knew it was clouding her profile, but she had to tell them. "It's possible. If Brittany's death was an accident..."

Greg nodded. "I agree. There is a chance. There's also a chance that there are more girls than we know about."

Evelyn dropped her eyes.

"Looking at Darnell Conway's timeline, we can't completely rule that out."

Evelyn gave a shaky nod when Tomas turned to her for confirmation. If it *was* him, Darnell had waited two years between Charlotte Novak's murder and his first abduction. But that was only what they knew about. It was possible he'd waited to let the heat from Charlotte's murder fade, but it was also possible that he'd been working his way toward this pattern. He could have started with lower-risk victims, not left the notes initially. And since he'd moved out of Kiki's house a year ago, the same was true now.

"How likely is this?" Carly sounded unhappy that the idea hadn't been explored before.

"Percentage-wise? Low," Greg said. "But it's something we need to consider. Darnell—"

"Hey!" one of the cops in the field yelled. "Chief! Get out here!"

Everyone's heads swiveled toward him. He was standing a few hundred feet behind where they'd found Brittany's body, surrounded by several other cops, in a small copse of trees.

He waved the shovel in his hand, adding, "I think we have another body!"

Eighteen

Four hours later, Evelyn shivered in the balmy night air as she stared down into the hole the cops had dug. It was about five feet deep. Beside her, when she could focus enough to take it in, she realized Kyle hadn't left her side. Greg stood across from her, beside Carly. Both of them looked grim.

Down in that hole was an open coffin. ERT agents had carefully put some of the dirt from immediately around the coffin into a vial for testing. Then they'd sifted meticulously through more of it for any item that might have been left behind by killer or victim until Evelyn had wanted to scream at them to hurry.

Now the coffin lay open, revealing little more than bones. Evelyn didn't have the expertise to be able to tell anything about them other than that they'd been there a long time. No clothing remained except a zipper and a metal button someone had photographed and bagged. The body itself had no soft tissue at all anymore, although there were teeth, which might provide an identity. The bones were small, definitely belonging to a child, but Evelyn couldn't tell the gender.

The button and zipper kept flashing through Evelyn's mind, telling her even if the skeleton was eighteen years old, it couldn't be Cassie. Cassie had gone missing in her pajamas during the night. No zipper. No button. It wasn't her.

She looked at the coroner, who'd just gotten Brittany's body back to his office when they'd called him and asked him to turn around. Her voice came out barely above a whisper as she asked, "What can you tell us about the body?"

He frowned at her from where he'd been perched at the edge of the hole, his knees not touching the ground. Standing, he dusted off spotless pant legs and pulled off his glasses with long, bony fingers. "It's old."

He gestured to his assistants, who'd been patiently waiting for the past half hour. The coroner moved away from the grave and they stepped forward, beginning the meticulous process of removing the body from the ground for transportation to the coroner's office for autopsy.

The coroner strode over to where Tomas had been talking to a pair of cops, and Greg and Carly followed.

Feeling as if her feet were encased in lead, Evelyn trailed after them. Kyle stuck to her side, obviously afraid she might faint and he'd need to catch her at any instant.

It occurred to her that he'd probably have to leave soon—it was three in the morning and he'd said he was flying out today—but she didn't have the energy to ask. Instead, she kept walking, letting herself lean on the arm he'd wrapped around her waist. She had no idea when he'd done that.

Tomas stepped away from his officers and met them

midway. "What can you tell me, Owen?" he asked the coroner.

Owen shoved his glasses into his pocket, his lips pursing. He seemed to be collecting his thoughts for a frustratingly long time. Evelyn had the impression he spent more hours trying to get dead people to tell him things than relating to live ones.

Even in the middle of the night, the tall, gaunt coroner wore a dark suit and dress shoes. Blue eyes, so pale they appeared almost white, squinted in his pale, droopy face.

"I'm taking the body back to my office, but you'll need a forensic anthropologist to look at the skeleton. From the teeth and pelvic area, I can tell you the victim was prepubescent. That means I can't make a good guess at the sex."

Tomas nodded. He looked like he'd aged in the past few hours, and every new piece of bad news made his shoulders sink even lower. "What else?"

"Cause of death is also a problem to determine. I see no fractures at this point that speak to a violent death, although the manner of burial certainly doesn't suggest death was natural." He tapped two pale fingers against an equally pale cheek. "With no soft tissue to work with, it's possible we may never know cause of death."

Tomas rubbed bloodshot eyes. "Can you give me an estimate on how long the body's been here, Doctor?"

"Years." Owen's eyes flicked upward as he nodded thoughtfully. "Many years. All indications are that the tissue decayed naturally. In this climate, that would only take a few years. Accounting for the moisture level, I wouldn't expect to see any soft tissue at all after five years. I can't tell you anything more specific, but my guess is that the body's been here longer than that."

With a loud exhalation, Tomas demanded, "How long? Are we talking fifty years here or eighteen?"

"You'd need a forensic anthropologist to say for sure, but my guess—and that's all it is, an educated guess—would be closer to eighteen."

Evelyn closed her eyes to hold in the sudden tears. The image of a young blonde girl rose in her mind, an uninhibited laugh she hadn't heard in eighteen years ringing in her ears.

Before she could will that image away, the frantic voice of a cop shouted from somewhere behind her, "Chief! I think we have another one!"

She didn't want to, but she pried her eyes open and turned toward the cop waving his arms frantically at them. Owen's face wavered in her peripheral vision, a frown on his lips but curiosity in his eyes.

The cop hurrying toward them was carrying a shovel and behind him were three more cops, digging fifty feet away from where they'd found the last victim.

"Make that two more!" one of those cops yelled.

The violent pain in her stomach caught Evelyn off guard. Before she could move away, she was hunched over, spilling the meager contents of her stomach all over Owen's shiny dress shoes.

Three, she thought mindlessly. Besides Brittany, that made three more victims. Veronica, Penelope and Cassie.

Her vision blurred, Owen's ruined shoes swimming in front of her eyes. Then she became aware of Kyle's steadying hand on her arm, and Evelyn straightened, wiping a hand across her mouth and muttering an incoherent apology to Owen.

"Mac?" she heard Greg say from what sounded like a great distance.

"I've got her," Kyle responded, and then, somehow, instead of moving toward the graves like she'd planned, Kyle was leading her back to the street, back to her car.

"I need to go..." Evelyn started.

"There's nothing you can do here just now. Greg will call with an update."

He was right, but it didn't stop her from feeling she was somehow betraying Cassie all over again by walking away. Even though she tried to make herself turn around, her feet kept plodding beside Kyle's as he propelled her toward the street.

The next thing she knew, she was in the passenger seat of her rental car, heat blasting out of the vents onto her chilled skin. As Kyle drove, Evelyn shut her eyes, willed the tears not to fall.

And they didn't. There was just a strange mixture of numbness and this unending cold in the still-warm night, as if her body temperature had plummeted like Cassie's all those years ago. Pinpricks danced along her nerve endings, and it hurt to breathe, but there was a layer of numbness over everything. It felt as if she were watching someone else's pain.

She'd known how slim the chances were, of course. She'd known it even when she was twelve, when too many months had gone by and the number of searchers had dwindled. She'd known it when her grandma had gotten sick and she'd moved to a new state to start college early so she wouldn't have to move back in with her mother. She'd felt so lost then, like she was losing her last connection to Rose Bay, like she was truly leaving Cassie behind.

She believed she'd genuinely accepted it once she'd begun working for BAU, thought then that she'd made the transition from hoping Cassie would return one day to planning simply to find the truth. After spending more of her life with Cassie gone than she'd spent knowing her, Evelyn had thought that if she hadn't moved past it, she'd at least turned it into a kind of fuel—a determination to save other victims.

But she'd been wrong. The knowledge that Cassie was probably in the ground back in that field made pain, anger and frustration swirl inside her until she felt it would burst through her skin.

It would take time to identify the bodies, but what was the likelihood one of them *wasn't* Cassie? Three known victims from eighteen years ago and three bodies.

It felt so terribly wrong that Cassie had been here, not ten miles from where she'd grown up, for the past eighteen years.

The search parties could've been here back then, could have walked right over Cassie's grave and never been aware of it. Had her abductor taken joy in that, in denying them more than just Cassie, but closure, as well?

"Evelyn. We're here."

It took her a minute to hear Kyle's voice, and then she realized the car was parked at the hotel and he was holding her door.

Evelyn stared up at him blankly, still seeing the open grave back in that field as she climbed out and followed him inside.

She tried to remember the day Cassie had gone missing, the day she'd spent eighteen years wishing she could forget. The details came back with surprisingly ease—the yellow dress covered with white flowers Cassie had worn, the too-long laces on her own red tennis shoes, the tang of Mrs. Byers's lemonade on her tongue. The scent of lilac in their backyard, a scent that made her anxious even now, although she couldn't say exactly why.

Eighteen years ago, had she had any sense that she and Cassie were being watched, being stalked, being scrutinized for the right moment to steal them away? As hard as she tried, she didn't remember anything but happiness in the days leading up to Cassie's disappearance. Those details, the ones that might have mattered, still eluded her.

She could feel Cassie's hand in her own as if it were yesterday, but she couldn't remember ever feeling vulnerable in Rose Bay. An outcast, sure. But never unsafe. Not with her grandparents looking after her and Cassie by her side. It had been the first place she'd ever felt safe, those precious two years between the time her grandfather had picked her up and Cassie had disappeared.

The memories from those years had all been good, filled with the sound of Cassie's laughter, the brand-new sense of belonging and a friendship she was sure would last the rest of her life. Instead, it had only lasted the rest of Cassie's.

A sob that Evelyn couldn't suppress welled up as Kyle pushed her silently along, opening the door to a room and ushering her inside. It wasn't until she was sitting curled up on the chair in the corner, staring sightlessly ahead of her, that she realized it wasn't her room.

"My plane goes wheels-up in a few hours," Kyle said. He sounded far away, even though he was kneeling directly in front of her. "Give me ten minutes to take care of it and I'll be right back."

She must have responded in some way, because he promised again, "Okay. I'll see you in a little while."

And then she was alone in the room, with Kyle's open

bag of HRT gear. Fifty-plus pounds of equipment, guns, flash bangs and anything else he might need to take down a violent threat. If only her job came with such simple solutions.

The whole room wavered as she forced herself to think back eighteen years, to search desperately for any memory that could make a difference now. To search desperately for any hint of Darnell Conway skulking at the edges of those memories, waiting for an opportunity to snatch her and Cassie away to his underground dungeon.

Eighteen years ago, if she'd done some small thing differently, would Cassie still be here? Or would Evelyn be lying alongside her in that field, in a fourth grave?

"Why would he do that?" Evelyn asked as Kyle came back in the room.

She didn't know how long he'd been gone, but she'd slowly come out of her stupor and started thinking again. Mostly about Darnell.

She was still curled up on the chair in the corner of Kyle's hotel room. She was still ice cold, despite the fact that the temperatures were in the upper seventies outside.

Kyle closed the door behind him and turned off his air conditioner, then yanked the comforter off the bed and settled it over her, tucking it around her shoulders. "Why would who do what?" Kyle asked, sitting on the ottoman in front of her.

"Darnell Conway. Why would he run through that field, knowing we were following him?"

"Well, he did try to lose us," Kyle replied. "And when we first spotted the empty car, he was hiding in that field."

"Yeah, but then he got up and ran. We never would've found that cellar if he hadn't run into the field."

Kyle shrugged, studying her too closely. He was probably looking for signs that she was going to collapse under the strain of knowing one of those old graves likely belonged to Cassie.

She shivered, drew the comforter more tightly around her and pushed the thought out of her mind. She needed to distract herself with Darnell, with her job. Like she always did.

"Maybe he wanted us to find her?" Kyle suggested. "Brittany's death might have been an accident, right? Maybe it freaked him out and he didn't want Lauren anymore. That could be why the whole place was wiped down—because he planned to lead us straight to her."

Evelyn nodded slowly. That actually made perfect sense in a way. "But why would he leave the search parties so abruptly? And why would he decide to give her up?"

The last questions weren't really for Kyle, but he said, "Maybe he knew you'd get a call about his strange behavior at the search parties. Maybe that was his plan. Meeting him in the dunes that day, I got the impression he's crafty as hell."

"Yeah, he is." Evelyn's mind still felt fuzzy, from lack of sleep and from being too preoccupied with Cassie. "But I'm pretty sure he's killed before, to cover up sexually assaulting a girl. So, why the hesitation now?" She shook her head, trying to clear it. "None of it fits."

"Could the last time have been an accident, too?" Kyle asked.

"No. But I guess there's a good chance it wasn't premeditated. It was probably a gut reaction—needing to stop the girl from telling anyone what he'd done." She tried to grasp the psychology that would mesh Darnell's actions twenty years ago with now.

That was particularly hard because she couldn't *prove* he was guilty of any of it. The reality was, he might be innocent of Charlotte Novak's murder. But finding her body could've been the impetus for him to take action on his own fantasies.

Her struggle must have been evident, because Kyle said, "Get some sleep and figure it out in the morning. Lauren is safe. The clock's stopped ticking."

She looked up into the sky-before-a-storm blue of Kyle's eyes and felt her own eyes fill with water. The clock had stopped ticking for Brittany, too—and probably for Cassie.

Even though that clock had likely stopped years and years ago, to Evelyn it felt as if it had just come to a violent end a few minutes ago in that field.

If she slept now, what demons would visit her dreams?

Getting to her feet, Evelyn shook her head. She struggled with the comforter, trying to keep it wrapped around herself as she started pacing Kyle's room. She needed to think. About anything but Cassie and that big, seemingly empty field.

"There was no kind of sensor system in the cellar. It didn't seem that the search parties were heading there, but I should call Noreen and ask."

"Evelyn." Kyle tugged her down beside him on the ottoman. "It's four in the morning."

"She'll be up. Everyone in town's probably heard by now," Evelyn said, then felt herself pale. Had Cassie's parents heard? Were they already driving out to that field? "I should go back."

Somehow, Kyle knew exactly what direction her thoughts had taken because he said softly, "The cops are just going to say there's no information yet. You won't be able to tell Cassie's parents any more than that. There's nothing for you to do there."

Was she doing anything by being here, in Rose Bay, at all?

When she'd gotten the call from Cassie's mom, she'd been filled with such dread, but it had finally been her chance, too. She'd been so certain she could make a difference here. And yet there was nothing around her but pain. And she didn't even have a suspect in custody to show for it.

She didn't even have the answer to the question she needed most to answer. Cassie had been wearing pajamas all those years ago, no metal button or zipper. So the first set of bones they'd uncovered probably wasn't her. What had the cops found in the other graves? More bones of young girls? Or had the other two been older?

Cassie could have died the very night she'd been taken out of Evelyn's life. Or she could've been alive until just a few days ago, when the new abductions began.

She could have faced every night locked in that pitch-black dungeon, only to see light when her abductor came in to assault her in some heinous way. Or she might have been locked down there, forgotten or abandoned, left alone until she starved to death, while her best friend went about her life a few miles away.

The tears rushed forward unexpectedly, blinding her. Sobs racked her so violently they hurt her chest and made it hard to draw air.

She fell forward against Kyle's chest and his arms went around her, pulling her closer. He held on until the tears eventually slowed and then finally, finally, Evelyn closed her eyes and just stopped thinking entirely.

Mandy Toland wheeled her scooter down the drive. She'd finally convinced her babysitter to let her play in the front yard. When she glanced back, Amber was staring at her through the window, looking equal parts bored and sick.

When she'd gotten up this morning, her mom had said she was going back to work. She'd stayed home since Brittany had gone missing, afraid to let Mandy out of her sight.

Mandy had heard her mom answer the phone this morning. They'd found Brittany and Lauren. The person who'd taken them was still out there, but everyone knew who it was now, and her mom said they'd catch him soon. She said everything would go back to normal.

Still, her mom had spent twenty minutes telling Amber not to let Mandy out of her sight, while poor Amber sneezed and coughed. There wasn't anything to do outside, but Mandy didn't want to be anywhere near all that snot.

Reaching the end of the drive, Mandy set her scooter on the grass and bent down to pick some of her mom's pink flowers. She could try weaving them into a crown, like Amber had shown her last week, when everything had been normal. Back before Brittany had gone missing and her mom had stopped going to work, afraid to leave her.

Her mom had cried after she'd gotten the phone call, but she wouldn't tell Mandy why. All she'd say was they knew who the bad guy was and they were chasing him now. She said Chief Lamar would get him.

Mandy was sure her mom was right. Chief Lamar had come to their school last year and talked about safety. He'd told them all about chasing down bad guys and even shown them his handcuffs. She wondered if he'd come back and talk to them again now that she was going to start middle school.

Clutching an armful of her mom's prettiest flowers, Mandy stood and promptly jumped backward, dropping them all. Someone was standing behind her.

Mandy whipped around, ready to scream for Amber, but relaxed as soon as she saw who it was. "You scared me."

"Sorry, Mandy. You need to come with me, honey. Your mom was in an accident."

Tears rushed down her face. "Is she okay?"

"She's okay. I'll take you to her now."

"Good." Mandy wiped her face and took the offered hand, not at all worried. Chief Lamar had told her back on safety day never to let a stranger take her anywhere. But she was sure it was okay if the person was with the police.

Nineteen

A persistent ringing blared in Evelyn's ears, distracting her from the vision of Cassie running through her backyard in a yellow flowered dress. Evelyn tried to ignore the sound, but it buzzed over Cassie's voice, suggesting they go play hide-and-seek.

Evelyn fought to pull her hands from the cocoon of warm blankets and clasped them over her ears. In her memory, she was running her hands over a huge lilac bush, trying to decide if it was a good hiding spot. Purple pollen had fluttered over her clothes as she'd peered into the bush, seeing…seeing…

"Evelyn."

Evelyn blinked her burning eyes, moving her hands away from her ears. She was lying on a bed, wrapped in a comforter and tucked close against Kyle. She blinked some more and realized she was still in his room, though she had no recollection of moving from the ottoman, of falling asleep. She had no idea how long she'd been out.

"What?" she asked, her voice scratchy, her throat sore from crying.

He held out her phone. "You just missed a call."

It took her a minute to disentangle herself from the covers, to pull away from Kyle's warmth. The room was boiling hot, but there was a feeling of safety in being pressed up against Kyle. As soon as she moved away from him, all the fear and anger and grief that had temporarily left her during sleep came flooding back.

She took the phone, looking at the clock. Ten-thirty. She'd slept about six hours. It felt like way more and way less at the same time.

With shaky hands, she accessed her voice mail. She'd missed a call from Tomas.

"Evelyn," he said, and she immediately knew from his tone that something horrible had happened.

She pushed herself to a sitting position, wrapped her arms around her knees and waited for him to tell her. Was it about Cassie? Could they have learned more about the skeletons this quickly?

"Evelyn," he finally said again, "another girl went missing this morning. Please get to the station."

Her voice mail system asked her three times if she wanted to keep or delete the message, then hung up on her when she did neither. Evelyn set the phone down and looked at Kyle, suddenly realizing his fingers were threaded through her free hand.

"What happened?"

"He got someone else."

The words were hard to form on her tongue and she stared up at him in disbelief. Darnell should've been on the run, getting as far away from Rose Bay as possible. Hell, even on the off chance it wasn't Darnell, the culprit should still have been running scared.

But instead, he'd gone back into town and grabbed another victim. And she'd been here, sound asleep, dreaming of Cassie in better days.

Evelyn frowned, trying to remember what exactly she'd been dreaming. She'd been playing hide-and-seek with Cassie. It had been the day Cassie went missing. And she'd sensed something was wrong.

Evelyn sank back against the headboard. She'd gone over that day so many times. First for the cops, when Jack Bullock had made her recount it again and again. Then for herself, trying to piece together anything she might have missed.

And now she knew she'd missed the most important part. She'd *known*. She'd sensed something wasn't right, sensed that someone was watching. It had taken her dream—a dream based on a memory—to tell her that. If she'd warned Cassie, would it have made a difference?

A sob inched up her throat, but Evelyn held it in and clutched Kyle's hand when he reached for her. She couldn't get buried in past mistakes. Not now.

Shoving back the covers Kyle had piled over her last night, Evelyn staggered to her feet. She was shaky, and it occurred to her that it wasn't all from emotion. She couldn't remember the last time she'd eaten.

As she found her shoes by the ottoman and put them on, she tried to think back through yesterday, tried to recall when she might have had anything to eat. A quick glance in the mirror told her she'd better run to her room and change before going to the station. Her clothes were rumpled and dirty from being in the cellar, her bun half-pulled out from sleep.

She stumbled for the door, but before she reached it, Kyle was in front of her. She looked up into his worried eyes and it suddenly occurred to her. "Didn't you have to fly home this morning? Did you miss your flight?"

"No, Evelyn," he said patiently, as if he'd already explained once. "The rest of my team left a few hours ago. I got permission to stay behind with you. I took some of that personal time I told you about. My boss is taking care of the paperwork."

Time off wasn't always easy to come by, and time off with no notice was unheard of except in a true emergency. It occurred to her that Kyle had probably just put a great big dent in his personnel file. And he'd done it for her.

Thank you seemed inadequate, but she didn't have the energy for anything else.

"Go shower and change. I'll meet you at your room in twenty minutes or so with some food and then we'll go to the station. Okay?"

She nodded and made her way out the door on feet that didn't seem to work right. When she followed him down to her rental car almost half an hour later, biting into a sandwich he'd bought in the coffee shop downstairs, she felt marginally functional.

Kyle hopped into the driver's seat, looking wide-awake despite having been on surveillance the whole night before and then chasing Darnell and standing around a field of graves all day and into the next night. Evelyn sipped the strong tea Kyle had gotten her, pressing a hand to her stomach as it rebelled against everything she forced down. But the food was clearing her head, and as Kyle started the car, she called her partner.

"It's Evelyn," she said when Greg picked up. "Give me the details."

The noise in the background almost drowned Greg

out as he told her, "I hope you're close to the station. You know the players better than I do. And we've got to take a second look at everyone."

"I'm on my way now, with Kyle. Who was the victim?"

"Girl's name is Mandy Toland. Twelve years old, just like the others. Grabbed right from her front yard. Very, very small time frame—about an hour and a half ago. First daytime abduction. The babysitter says she was watching Mandy pick flowers through the window when she had to go get a tissue. She blew her nose, came back to the window and Mandy was gone. She ran out there and found a nursery rhyme."

Evelyn clutched her tea too tightly and the cap popped off. Ignoring it, she said, "That's his riskiest abduction yet, if he grabbed her in the time it took the babysitter to get a tissue. What, a minute? Less?"

"Especially since all the cops in town now have a picture of Darnell on their dash."

"Why does the victim's name sound familiar?" Evelyn asked.

Greg sighed. "That's part of why you need to get back here, Evelyn. Mandy is one of the girls you identified from the pictures in Walter Wiggins's bathroom."

"Oh, shit, that's right."

"There's more." Greg's voice was weary when he added, "The coroner completed Brittany's autopsy. There was no evidence of sexual assault."

"What?" But Darnell Conway was a sexually motivated offender. Wasn't he?

"Yeah. Hurry up and get here, okay? We need you."

"I'm almost there," she told Greg as Kyle glanced at her and punched the gas.

"What's Lauren saying?" Evelyn asked. "Did she identify Darnell?"

"Lauren hasn't said a word since you got her out of that cellar. The girl is badly traumatized."

Greg hung up before she could ask anything else and Evelyn stared out the windshield, the food on her lap forgotten.

How had Darnell—or anyone else—grabbed another victim *now*? And if there was no sexual assault, why had Darnell grabbed her? Could it have been Walter? He'd had Mandy's picture. But his motive would have been the same. What about Frank Abbott? The field was close to his house. But how would Darnell know where the cellar was if it wasn't his?

What the hell was she missing?

And after failing Brittany so completely, did she have any hope of bringing Mandy home alive?

"Where is she? Where's my daughter?"

Mandy Toland's mom had gone into the CARD command post an hour ago to give them information, but Tomas could still hear her voice ringing in his ears. It sounded too much like the voices of Lauren's parents, of Brittany's parents.

Last night, he'd been the one to tell Mark and Heather Douglas that their daughter was never coming home. Jack had stood next to him, lending support as Heather Douglas pounded her fists against Tomas, crying and screaming.

He'd let her do it, until finally she'd run out of energy had and one of his veteran officers had driven them to the coroner's office. Tomas knew he deserved worse. He'd failed them. He'd failed all of them.

And the hell of it was, it looked as if Evelyn had been right from the beginning. The mistakes rolled through his mind now—the way he'd resisted her suggestion that Darnell was a suspect because he didn't match the profile. The way he'd taken surveillance off Darnell at exactly the wrong time. And the guy was still out there, had somehow managed to grab yet another girl.

How the hell was he doing it?

Tomas scrubbed a hand over eyes that burned from too many hours without rest. Around him, the station was loud. Officers and FBI agents rushed around, playing catch-up with a predator who'd been too far ahead of them for eighteen years.

Tomas glanced at the open conference room, where the new profiler—Greg something—was advising a handful of CARD agents on strategies for interrogating their most likely suspects. The CARD agents would be the lead on that. It was his job to get the suspects to the station.

The Amber Alert had gone out, and he had most of his officers out in cars already, searching for Darnell. While they did that, he had to focus on the other prospects.

It wasn't too likely that Darnell Conway had just come across that cellar and it really belonged to someone else, but it was possible. Or maybe Evelyn was wrong and Darnell had a partner. And it was damn suspicious that Walter Wiggins had Mandy's picture in his house.

Not that he could use it as a reason to bring Walter in for questioning, since Evelyn had found it illegally.

Tomas heaved out a sigh and called into the bull pen, "Where's Jack?"

There were only a few officers at the station, and most of them were on their way out. One rookie looked up at him and shrugged. "He said he was going to go run a lead early this morning, before we heard about Mandy."

"What lead?" Tomas demanded. "Does this have anything to do with Wiggins?"

The rookie shrugged. "He just said it was a long shot and he'd be back in a bit."

Damn Jack. He'd expected to follow in his father's footsteps and take over as chief. When it hadn't happened, he'd been bitter as hell. On a good day, Jack was a pain in his ass. On a bad day, he was downright belligerent, acting as if he were in charge, chasing leads without telling anyone.

Today, of all days, he didn't need that.

"Where's Evelyn?" he asked Greg.

"I'm here," she said.

Tomas turned around and there she was, flanked by that other FBI agent—the one who looked as though he had a past as a special-operations soldier and now worked as Evelyn's personal bodyguard.

Tomas nodded at Kyle—no reason to piss that guy off—and told Evelyn, "I've got two of my officers picking Walter up now. Greg is advising the CARD agents on interrogation strategies, but I want you there."

"Get Frank Abbott in here, too."

"What?"

"Noreen's sister died nineteen years ago."

Tomas frowned, trying to absorb that news. Noreen still talked about her sister occasionally, and it always sounded as if she were alive. So had Earl, back before he passed. Why would they have kept something like that a secret?

"Frank isn't my top suspect, but we need to check him out. His house is closest to that field."

"No," Tomas argued. "There's an empty house between Frank's and the old Bullock property where you found the cellar."

"I mean, it's closer than any of the other suspects."

Tomas unlocked his jaw. "I didn't know Frank *was* a suspect."

"The CARD agents were looking into it. It's a remote possibility, but…"

She didn't even look sorry for not telling him about that. Tomas just prayed they'd find Mandy soon—alive—and that all the feds would leave Rose Bay for good.

"T.J.!" Tomas called. "Go pick up Frank Abbott, would you?"

"On what pretext?" T.J. asked, just as Noreen rounded the corner, her face ashen.

"I'll go get him," Noreen whispered.

"No." Tomas shook his head. "You can go with T.J. if you can get him to come in voluntarily, but you're not going by yourself."

"He didn't do this, Tomas."

She looked so horrified, so small and vulnerable. It reminded him of the day he'd been hired as chief, when she'd introduced herself and then asked if he was going to fire her. He'd understood in that second exactly why Jack's dad had hired a girl with no experience.

But it hadn't taken long to understand why he'd kept her on, why he'd given her more and more responsibility. She worked hard. And she was dedicated to the police officers she supported and the town of Rose Bay. She was smart, and as far as he could tell, she didn't have much of a life outside the station.

"Why didn't you tell me, Noreen?" he asked quietly.

She stared down at her shoes. "My dad didn't want

anyone to know. After he died…" She looked up at him and cringed. "I didn't know how to say it had all been a lie."

"I realize he's your uncle, Noreen, but I need you to try and be impartial here. Is there any chance he could have done this? To make up for Margaret?"

Noreen shook her head, but she waited a beat too long, and Tomas knew she wasn't sure.

"I need you to go with T.J. Get your uncle to come here voluntarily and answer some questions, okay? Get him to give us permission to search his house again, too."

Noreen nodded shakily, and then followed T.J. out the door.

"Is that a good idea?" Evelyn asked. "Sending her, I mean?"

"She'll get him here," Tomas replied. He pointed to the conference room. "You should be in there now. Give those agents whatever they need so they ask the right questions, because Wiggins is on his way. But I have to ask…"

"What?"

"Greg told you about Brittany's autopsy?" When she nodded, Tomas said, "Lauren was checked out at the hospital. She's still not saying a thing, but the doctors have confirmed it. No sexual assault. Are we even looking in the right direction?"

Evelyn took a sip of her tea, shifting her weight as if she were exhausted.

She looked like hell. She had for more than a day, but she looked almost worse than she had last night. He hoped to God she wasn't going to fall apart on him now, because he needed her.

He'd run some nasty investigations in his days as a

detective, before he'd come back to Rose Bay and been hired as chief. But this, he couldn't begin to understand.

"Wiggins's MO was to lure kids to him slowly, earn their trust first. In the cases in DC, he did it over a period of months."

"I read the case files," Tomas said impatiently.

"So, here, even though the girls were immobilized, he might have been doing the same thing. Trying to win them over."

"Win them over?" Tomas asked incredulously. "He locked them up under the ground!"

"I know. It's not logical. But in his own mind, Walter needs an excuse for what he's doing. He tells himself they were willing."

Tomas swore. "That's—"

"Disgusting, I know. But it's how he worked before. So, like I said, it's possible that he was trying to do the same thing here, only in a controlled environment. It's possible he was waiting until he felt they trusted him."

"And Brittany?"

"The evidence suggests her death was an accident. Maybe Walter didn't have long enough to win her trust before that happened."

Tomas closed his eyes briefly. "What about Darnell?"

Evelyn shifted her weight again. "Well, I suspected him because I believe there's a good chance he sexually assaulted and then murdered his ex-girlfriend's daughter twenty years ago."

Tomas nodded.

"Which would imply he wouldn't wait. If I'm right about what happened back then, he'd most likely assault the girls as soon as he had them in his control. Since they weren't assaulted, there are two options."

"Which are?" Tomas prompted when she paused.

"Either I'm wrong and it's not him at all."

"He ran straight to that field," Tomas pointed out.

"Yeah, and I find it hard to believe that was a coincidence. Very hard to believe. The other possibility is that twenty years ago he was innocent."

Tomas shook his head, not understanding. "If he was innocent, what motive would he—"

"It's possible Charlotte Novak wasn't his victim but his trigger."

When Tomas seemed confused, she clarified. "He didn't do it, but finding his girlfriend's daughter, seeing what was done to her, was the trigger that made him decide to act on his own fantasies. And if that's the case..." She shrugged. "He could actually have an MO similar to Walter's, which would explain the lack of sexual assault."

"Damn it," Tomas groaned. "How many of these people are out there?"

"Too many," Kyle said from where he'd been standing silently behind Evelyn.

Tomas glanced at him, wondering what his job really was, then back at Evelyn. "There's an APB out on Darnell across the whole county. Most of my officers are looking for him."

"I think I know where he could be hiding."

"Where?" Tomas scanned the station, which had mostly cleared out, except for the CARD agents talking to Mandy's parents or waiting to question Walter and Frank.

"I'll go," Evelyn said.

"Are you kidding me?" Tomas demanded, but he didn't have a whole lot of other options.

"I'll take Mac with me."

He frowned at her, but the reality was that it would be faster to let her go than to call back one of his officers. "Fine. Go. But don't do anything that'll trash whatever evidence you find when this thing goes to court. If he did it, I want the bastard to fry."

"Believe me, so do I."

Evelyn turned toward the door, but not before Tomas saw the expression on her face, the burning desire for revenge.

He said a quick prayer that she wouldn't kill the bastard if she found him, then hurried into the CARD command post to help ready the room for the rest of their suspects.

"I've got the master key," Kyle said, deadpan, when they arrived at Kiki Novak's house.

"Would that be your foot?"

"Pretty much."

"Kiki probably won't answer if I knock on the door. But she might for you." Evelyn studied him. He was in civilian clothes, but what had seemed funny when she'd run into him posing as an engineer was now just frustrating. Kyle might have an easygoing expression on his face, but there was no hiding his physique or the intensity in his eyes. And those things couldn't say *law enforcement* any more clearly.

He gave her a wide grin, showing his dimples, and winked.

It made Evelyn's blood pressure spike, but she grinned back, her first real smile in days. "Okay. Do that, and she'll definitely open the door."

"What are you going to do?"

Evelyn instinctively patted the holster at her hip. "Cover the back of the house."

"You really think she's harboring him?"

"I think there's a better-than-average chance. She doesn't believe he killed her daughter."

Kyle nodded soberly, took out his cell phone and called her as he opened his car door. "So you can hear what's happening."

"Good idea." Evelyn answered her phone, then stuck it back in her pocket with the line open. She followed Kyle until they got closer. Then she darted out of sight, slipping around the house next door to get to the back of Kiki's house so no one from inside would see her.

It was noon, so most of Kiki's neighbors were probably at work. But on the drive over, Evelyn had checked Kiki's schedule at the restaurant where she was a server. Kiki had taken the day off work. Hopefully, she was home and not on the run with Darnell.

Kyle gave her time to get in position, then she heard him knocking on Kiki's door.

There was silence through the phone line for so long that Evelyn's shoulders slumped. If Darnell was inside, maybe he'd looked through the window, recognized Kyle and told Kiki not to answer.

Evelyn stared up at Kiki's house. There were two doors, one at the front and one at the back, so if Darnell was in there, his options were to hide or jump out a window. Surveying the back of the house, Evelyn saw that shades were drawn over all the windows.

If Kiki didn't answer voluntarily and let Kyle in, the next option was to use the bullhorn in her car and identify themselves as FBI. She didn't have the time to wait Kiki out, but often sheer embarrassment would do it.

The dread that anyone close enough to overhear would learn that the FBI were camped out at her house. Just as she was resigning herself to that option, Evelyn heard, "Can I help you?" through her phone.

Evelyn pressed herself up against the brick wall, out of sight of the back windows, and waited.

"Kiki Novak?"

"Yeah." Kiki's voice came back, sounding suspicious.

"My name is Kyle McKenzie, with the FBI."

There was a bang that Evelyn realized must have been Kyle bracing his hand on the door as Kiki tried to slam it shut.

"I need to know if Darnell Conway is here."

Evelyn tensed, straining to listen.

The door next to her burst open, catching her off guard. She pushed away from the brick, and Darnell spotted her.

Instead of running in the other direction, he dove off the steps straight at her.

He hit like a football player, diving low and catching her hard enough to wrench the air from her lungs. She crashed to the ground in a V, the center of her body landing first, then her head bouncing off the dirt.

Darnell landed on top of her, then quickly levered himself halfway, his snarling face staring down at her. Evelyn shifted for leverage but, too fast, Darnell raised his fist.

It never connected.

She didn't know where he'd come from, but suddenly Kyle was there, tackling Darnell from the side, and throwing him off her. He flipped Darnell onto his back with ease and was already cuffing him when Evelyn got to her feet.

"Darnell Conway, you're under arrest." Kyle pulled him into a standing position. "And you'd better have a damn good explanation for how you knew where that cellar was."

Twenty

"You found him."

The whole room grew silent as Evelyn and Kyle walked in with Darnell Conway cuffed, head down, between them. The few cops seemed frozen in shock, until Tomas came forward.

"Nice job," he told her, taking Darnell by the elbow. "I'll put him in a room and be right back."

Evelyn nodded as Carly and Greg stepped out of another interrogation room. Greg was nodding, looking unsurprised, and Carly gaped at her.

"The ex-girlfriend was harboring him?" Greg guessed.

"Yep."

"What's the strategy?"

"Strategy?" Carly broke in. "We go at him hard. Mandy's been missing three and a half hours. We bring her home so that number never hits four."

She turned toward the room where Tomas had disappeared and Evelyn seized her arm.

Carly whirled around, yanking her arm free. "What? You disagree? You may know all about how these sickos think." She glanced at Greg. "No offense. But

I've worked a hell of a lot more child abductions than either of you."

"BAU gets a lot of those cases, too," Greg, who'd been at BAU for eight years, replied neutrally.

"This guy is crafty," Evelyn said. "Whatever he is or isn't guilty of, he likes to taunt. He walked that line really well during the search parties. He knows exactly how much to say. And we don't want him lawyering up, which is probably the first thing he'll do. Unless..."

"Unless you go in there?" Carly asked.

"Unless we make him want to keep taunting us. Unless we make him think he's so much smarter than us that he doesn't need a lawyer."

Carly put her hands on her hips. "And he'll think he's that much smarter than you?"

"If he is the killer," Greg said softly, "he's been waiting to taunt Evelyn for eighteen years."

Carly's hands fell off her hips as she looked between them. "Can you handle being in there with him? If you're right, that means he's going to taunt you about what he did to your friend."

Evelyn took a deep breath. "I know. I want you in there, Carly. But I'm taking lead."

Sensing Greg's gaze on her, Evelyn glanced in his direction.

"Can you do this?" he asked.

She clenched her jaw. "Of course," she answered, even though she knew he was really asking, *Should you do this?*

Kyle spoke up. "What about the other suspects?"

Greg shook his head. "We've got both Walter and Frank here. Carly and Tomas have been talking to them and I've been advising. So far, nothing."

"What do you think?" Evelyn asked.

Greg pursed his lips. "Honestly? We can't rule either of them out, but my gut says neither one did this."

Carly stared at Greg, then turned toward Evelyn. "If it's not Darnell," she said, "then Frank is my next guess."

"Why?"

"There's something wonky with this guy. Pretending his niece is still alive for nineteen years? No matter what his brother wanted, that's just plain weird. He lives close to that cellar and he sure as hell knows the area. He's got a business that lets him set his own hours and you said he blamed his sister-in-law for what happened to his niece. Not to mention that unlike Wiggins or Darnell, he *wouldn't* stand out in the areas these girls were abducted."

Evelyn nodded, looking at Greg.

"The timing makes me hesitate," he said. "Six years is a long time to wait if he's been desperate to start abducting girls again. That's how long it's been since Noreen turned eighteen and he moved out, right?" When Evelyn nodded again, Greg continued, "Considering how quickly the perp grabbed three girls, that reeks of desperation."

"But he's not so desperate he's making mistakes," Evelyn reminded him.

"That's true. Like I said, both of these guys are possibilities, but I'm not convinced about either one. The timing isn't quite right with Frank, and Walter is extremely timid around adults. I'm not sure he has the nerve to pull off these abductions. If someone even saw him near a kid, he would've been in for another beating like the one Brittany's dad gave him."

"Well, he obviously got close enough to take those pictures Evelyn saw," Kyle contributed.

Damn, did everyone know about that? Evelyn tried not to cringe.

"Which is why we can't rule him out," Greg said. He turned to Evelyn. "But Darnell running into that field, right past that cellar? You know how I feel about coincidences."

"Yeah. Me, too." They happened, but more often, if there seemed to be a connection, there *was* a connection.

"Okay. Let's do it. Follow my lead," she told Carly. "This guy likes to be physically intimidating and right now, he's got to be feeling pretty panicked. We want to relieve some of that tension, make him feel he's got some power."

"This is the plan for interrogating Darnell?" Tomas asked as he rejoined them.

"Yes. Carly and I will go in there. Darnell enjoys bullying others and he'll be less threatened by two women."

Carly scowled at that, but the truth was, sometimes being underestimated because of her gender could be a benefit in this job.

"You should sit at the table across from him," Evelyn instructed Carly. "You're tall, so I want you to hunch a bit—not like you're bored, but as though he makes you a little uncomfortable. Just don't overplay it or he'll see through it. Take in a folder with Darnell's name on it, but don't open it."

"What about you?" Tomas asked.

"I'm hoping he'll look at me and see the girl he missed grabbing eighteen years ago. If he's our killer, seeing me should make him equal parts frustrated and smug. Frustrated because I got away and smug because he thinks

I'm still afraid of him." Something she'd let him believe as he'd left those dunes two days ago.

"He'll want to say just enough so that I know he could have grabbed me any time he wanted—whether it's true or not. And if it's him, he'll flaunt the power he's got by having Mandy. The trick is to get him to go just a little too far and actually admit it."

"And you think you can get him to do that?" Tomas asked skeptically.

Evelyn nodded at Carly. "Let's go find out."

"This is bullshit," Darnell said as soon as Evelyn and Carly walked into the room.

He was putting on a good front, his expression angry and indignant. But his gaze was a little too shifty, his whole body a little too tense.

Carly sat across from him, setting the folder with Darnell's name on it in full view. Then she glanced at Evelyn and stooped her shoulders.

Evelyn remained standing at the edge of the room, as if she didn't want to get too close to Darnell. The truth was, her head throbbed from hitting the ground, and she was pretty sure when she got back to the hotel room tonight she'd discover her whole back was bruised.

"Mr. Conway, Chief Lamar read you your rights, correct? You waived your right to an attorney and you're aware we're recording this conversation. Do you have any questions—"

"I know my rights," Darnell barked at Carly, then looked over at Evelyn. "You really think you can get away with targeting me like this? You trespass at my house, then trespass at Kiki's house..." He crossed shaky arms over his chest, leaning back in his seat.

"Do you have an explanation for running through that field?"

"Of course I do! You and your boyfriend were chasing me."

"So, you're telling me it was a coincidence that you ran directly over the spot where the kidnap victims were found?" Before he could answer, Evelyn added, "The one who's still alive, that is."

Darnell swallowed visibly, fidgeting in his seat. "This is a frame-up, okay? You really think if I did it, I'd lead you right to them? That would be stupid!"

He leaned forward again, glanced briefly at Carly, then back at her. "I know you don't have anything on me, because I didn't do it! And even a public defender could get this thrown out. I happened to run across a field. Big fucking deal."

"You went through the field while trying to outrun two FBI agents," Carly said.

"They. Were. Chasing. Me," Darnell enunciated slowly. "And that one—" he pointed at her "—had already trespassed at my house, making all kinds of accusations. Her boyfriend pulled his gun on me for no reason when I was helping with the volunteers." He sat back, a smirk playing on his lips, but fear in his eyes. "What would a jury say about that?"

"What jury?" Carly asked.

"Well, you arrested me, didn't you? You think you have enough to make these kidnapping—" he frowned "—and murder charges stick."

Darnell squirmed in his chair and Evelyn broke in before he went too far with that line of thinking and decided to get himself a lawyer. "Why did you join the search parties?"

He stared at her for a minute, pensive, then finally said, "Why wouldn't I? You told me a girl had been abducted. Of course I wanted to help bring her home."

"Didn't you tell me in the dunes that Brittany was dead?"

Carly jerked in her seat and Darnell's gaze moved over her slowly, as if trying to decide what her role was. Then he dismissed her, looking back at Evelyn.

"Logical assumption. Everyone knows it's the same guy from eighteen years ago. Does anyone really believe those girls are still alive after eighteen years?" He shrugged. "I just figured if he was killing them then, he'd be killing them now."

When Carly leaned closer, interest on her face, he added quickly, "Obviously I hoped I was wrong. That's why I joined the search parties."

"Did you know any of the girls who went missing eighteen years ago?"

He snorted. "No. Why would I have known twelve-year-olds from other cities?"

Making a mental note that Darnell had referred to the exact age of the victims, Evelyn continued smoothly, "But you helped with the search parties back then, too, didn't you?"

Darnell scowled. "Yeah. And back then, I assumed we'd find them alive. At least that last girl. Your friend."

It was the opening she'd been waiting for, but hearing him say it felt like a fist to the stomach. She cursed herself, knowing she'd visibly reacted, but when she saw the light come into Darnell's eyes, she realized it was actually a good thing.

Keep him off balance, she reminded herself. *Make him believe he's winning.* She tried to keep her tone unaffected, but her voice cracked, anyway, when she said, "Cassie. You thought they'd find Cassie alive?"

"Cassie," Darnell repeated, drawing out her name. "Yes, I thought they'd find her alive and bring her home."

"But they didn't."

Darnell lifted his shoulders, his nervous tics fading. "Guess not."

"Maybe this guy was never a killer," Evelyn said.

Carly shot her a glance that demanded, *What the hell are you doing?* But she kept silent.

Darnell looked suspicious, too. "Maybe," he said slowly.

"It appears that Brittany's death was an accident. In that case the person who did it should probably get out in front of it. Before he gets arrested for straight-up murder."

Darnell raised his eyebrows, his lips curling up as he let out a forced laugh. "That's your pitch? Really? You think I did this and I'm going to admit it in hopes of getting, what? Some kind of lesser charge? You're talking about kidnapping kids! And doing horrible things to them. I didn't do that and I'm sure as hell not going to let you pin anything on me!"

"What do you think was done to them?"

"How should I know? I heard they were kept in a pit under the ground! That can't be good."

"You ran right over that pit."

Darnell huffed out a put-upon sigh. "You *chased* me there."

"I followed you to there," Evelyn countered. "And you seemed to think you'd lost me when you drove down a dead-end road."

"I'm not from here..."

"You obviously know the town well after helping with all those searches over eighteen years. And you found me in the dunes easily enough."

"I asked where you were," he snarled. "You were the one who told me about the search parties. Someone else pointed the way. Told me where to find you."

"Who?"

Carly straightened in her seat, as though she were anxious to get to the questions about Mandy, but Evelyn wanted to keep changing directions, not allow Darnell to get too comfortable with his story.

Darnell gave a tight smile. "A cop."

"Which cop?"

"Bullock, I think his name was." He paused meaningfully. "You know, the guy whose property that pit was on?"

"How do *you* know that? If you're not familiar with the town and all?"

Darnell scowled. "I...heard it on the news."

Evelyn nodded, although she had no idea if that had been in the news or not. "Okay. Why did you run through the field, Darnell? You were already out there when I drove around the corner."

Darnell stared down at the table, then finally looked back up at her, his expression thoughtful. "I was framed," he said. "Someone texted me, okay? To meet there."

Carly all but rolled her eyes as she asked, "Who texted you?"

Darnell rubbed his chin. "Not sure. It was a—a business thing."

"That's pretty convenient," Carly scoffed.

"It's not convenient for me! I mean, look what happened! He was trying to set me up! And look, I didn't mention it at first because I know it sounds kind of stupid. But it's true."

"What kind of business did you have in a deserted field?" Evelyn broke in.

"It's a sales thing. Confidential."

"And you're telling us whoever texted you right before you went into that field is the kidnapper?" Carly asked scornfully.

"Well, yeah. Must be, right?"

"And you thought it made sense to conduct business with someone you didn't know in a deserted field?" Carly pressed. "You said earlier that Evelyn chased you there."

"Well, hell, I didn't think she was going to catch up to me, okay? And I wanted to do this, uh, deal, before I lost my chance. So I tried to lose her, so she wouldn't screw it up for me. She was hounding me. She wouldn't leave me alone!"

"What were you afraid I was going to find?" Evelyn asked.

"Nothing! There's nothing to find. But you were trying to pin Charlotte on me. And now you're trying to pin this on me! I didn't do any of it!"

"That's quite a coincidence, don't you think?" Evelyn asked. "Murdered little girls keep showing up wherever you are."

"Hey, now." Darnell lifted his hands in front of him. "Charlotte—that was horrible, horrible, to see what had been done to her. But I don't have anything to do with these other girls. Just because they're in a nearby town. I don't know them. I *didn't* know them."

"Is that what Lauren's going to tell us?" Carly asked. "Police are talking to her right now."

"Hell, yes, that's what she'll tell you!"

Evelyn frowned at the confidence in his voice. Then again, if the killer was Walter or Frank, neither had even bothered to run. If the killer had expected Lauren to be found, did he also have some reason to expect she'd keep quiet?

Evelyn stepped closer to Darnell, drawing his attention. "Are you sure?"

"Yes, I'm sure," Darnell said, but sudden doubt flickered in his eyes.

Evelyn pounced on it, taking a step closer to him. "Whatever you might have threatened her with to keep her from talking, it won't work. Lauren is surrounded by cops. They're going to convince her that you can't do whatever you threatened her with."

Evelyn could guess what it was. Pedophiles were predictable. Threaten the people around the child with harm if the child tells anyone. Tell the child she'll be blamed or get into trouble. The younger or more naive the victim, or the more control the predator had in her day-to-day life, the easier it was to pull off.

But the child's silence would only last so long. Eventually, she'd start talking—especially if she learned the person who'd made the threats was locked up himself.

Darnell glanced back and forth between them. "*I* didn't threaten her with anything."

"The cops will tell her—"

"They're telling her to name me?" Darnell burst out. He jumped to his feet, which made Carly get warily to hers.

"I didn't do this!" He looked frantic, the gravity of his situation clearly setting in. "This— I was framed! Fuck! The text was a lure—a...a lie."

"If there's really a text, let us see it," Carly insisted.

"I…" Darnell turned from one to the other, a trapped expression on his face. "If that girl says it was me, someone told her to do it!"

"Give me a break," Carly snapped.

"He's setting me up because *she* thinks it's me!" Darnell pointed at Evelyn again, his finger shaking. "I didn't do this! Damn it! I didn't make that cellar!"

Evelyn placed her hands on her hips, wearing a disbelieving glower. From the corner of her eye, she saw Carly follow her lead, although Carly had already been looking skeptical.

"I didn't do it!" Darnell backed away from the table, knocking his chair over and not seeming to notice as he kept backing toward the far wall.

"If your story is true, then show us this text," Evelyn demanded, stepping closer.

"I can't. I, uh, erased it. But you can check my cell provider! The number will show up, anyway, right?"

Carly frowned. "We can probably retrieve a text message," she said slowly.

"I got a message. I got a message to meet there. Just by that big tree off to the side." Darnell's voice was getting higher and higher pitched. "You can check the call records for the number, but not the text. It's, uh, trade secret stuff—I'd lose my job."

"You *knew* where that cellar was when you ran into that field!" Evelyn raised her own voice with every word. "You said yourself that you didn't think I would catch up to you. You went there to go into that cellar, to your victims!"

"No!" Darnell shook his head frantically. "No, I didn't—"

"You went straight there!"

"I didn't know there was a cellar there! I was going to the tree, for my hook… For the sales meeting."

"And it's a total coincidence that exactly the same thing was done to these girls that was done to Charlotte?" Evelyn kept her tone and posture unchanged as she laid the bait.

"Oh, God. Oh, God." Darnell's eyes went saucer-wide. "He's framing me. Charlotte—that was an accident. But I didn't—I didn't…"

Evelyn faltered in her movement toward Darnell and she realized he saw it. She'd expected him to smirk at her again, knowing they wouldn't find evidence of sexual assault on Brittany or Lauren.

"I… That's not what I meant. I didn't…" Darnell closed his eyes and sank to the ground. "I want a lawyer."

"You're going to need one," Carly said, pulling him to his feet and leading him out of the room to take him back to a holding cell.

Evelyn stayed rooted to the same spot she'd stopped when Darnell had blurted out the truth.

He'd killed Charlotte Novak.

But he wasn't the Nursery Rhyme Killer.

So who was?

Twenty-One

"You believe him?" Tomas asked Evelyn. He sat slumped in a chair in the CARD command post.

Around him, Carly, Greg and Kyle all stared back at her. The other agents and cops who'd been out searching for Darnell had been reassigned to chase down other leads, mostly from tips that had come in regarding Mandy and where she might be. So far, none of them had panned out.

"About not being the Nursery Rhyme Killer?" Evelyn nodded. "I do. You watched the interview. He didn't know what condition Lauren and Brittany were in."

"Any chance he could be lying?" Tomas asked next.

"I doubt it. He thought he was going down for everything, and that made him confess to killing Charlotte. If he really was guilty of all of it, I don't think he would've done that. At least not this way, not this fast."

"I agree," Greg said. "He panicked over Charlotte. He's not the one."

"He said her death was an accident," Tomas reminded him.

"No way!" Greg said. "He killed her so she wouldn't

be able to tell that he'd sexually assaulted her. And his confession may have been unusual, but it'll stick. Especially because I think I know why he was so cagey about that text message."

"Why?" Tomas pressed.

"Before he cut himself off the last time he mentioned it, didn't it sound like he'd started to say he was going to that spot for his *hook-up*?"

"That could be it," Evelyn said. "That's what had him so nervous. He was so busy trying to hide what he'd been doing in that field, he wasn't watching the rest of what he said carefully enough."

Carly swept back curls that had gone wild in the humidity. "Why the hell would he be hiding a *hook-up*?"

"If this person set him up, what would lure Darnell Conway to a deserted location?" Greg prompted. "What would that text message say?"

Carly leaned back in her chair. "Of course. I should have known."

Tomas glanced at both of them. "What?"

"I bet if we look at Darnell's computer, we're going to find a series of chats between him and someone claiming to be a twelve-year-old girl," Greg said.

Tomas rubbed his eyes. "He would do that in the middle of this kind of investigation?"

"Pedophiles are determined SOBs."

"And he didn't suspect he was being set up?"

"I'm sure he did. But either this guy was very convincing or Darnell couldn't resist checking it out once he thought he'd slipped away from Evelyn."

"Well, maybe we can track Darnell's message to the real Nursery Rhyme Killer," Tomas said.

"We're going to try," Carly told him. "But I've got to

say, anyone smart enough to do what this perp's done probably didn't send these texts from his own phone." She stood up and began to pace. "At least Kiki Novak will finally know the truth. At least she'll finally have closure."

"I think this is actually going to make it worse," Evelyn said sadly.

"Why?" Carly asked. "After twenty years, her daughter's killer will be going to jail, probably for the rest of his life."

"Yeah, but she believed him. She harbored him when we thought he was the Nursery Rhyme Killer. She lived with him for another nineteen years after her daughter's death. She brought him into her house, treated him as a surrogate dad for Charlotte. If we never found Charlotte's killer, she could've gone on believing it was a fluke, a stranger who spotted Charlotte on her way home from school. Now, she has to live with knowing it was her boyfriend. Now, she has to live with the guilt of not just giving him access to Charlotte, but standing by him all those years since."

"You can't tell me you're sorry we closed that case?" Carly demanded.

"Of course not." But it made her sad, and as she met Kyle's gaze across the table, she could see that he knew she was thinking of more than just Kiki Novak. Had her mother ever felt any guilt? In the years Evelyn had been gone, living with her grandparents, her grandparents had made sure her mom stayed away. And in the thirteen years since her grandma had gotten sick, her mom had tried calling, but Evelyn had refused to talk to her. Refused to forgive her.

She had no idea what her mom believed about that

night twenty years ago. Did she tell herself Evelyn had lied, unable to accept that she'd brought home someone who would hurt her daughter? Or did she know what she'd almost allowed to happen? Did she live with that guilt? Or was she still burying it in a haze of alcohol?

Trying to tell herself she didn't care either way, Evelyn sat straighter, ready to get back on topic.

Carly beat her to it. "If it's not Darnell Conway—and I agree with you, it's not—then why did he draw so much attention to himself, following you in the dunes and showing up at the search parties?"

"Charlotte," Greg said simply.

"He knew I suspected him because Jack Bullock and I went to question him at his house. And he'd gotten away with this for twenty years. He wanted to flaunt it. He figured after this long, he was in the clear. The forensic evidence couldn't convict him, so he was feeling smug about it. He didn't plan to ever admit anything, so he just wanted to taunt me."

"Really?" Carly's eyebrows went up. "That seems pretty ballsy. And risky. Especially if he was still trolling for girls on the internet."

"Well, the other side of it is his compulsion," Greg put in. "He thinks like a pedophile first, with his specific compulsions. He wanted to be part of the search parties when we found the girls. He wanted to be there. He wanted to see."

"Gross," Tomas muttered.

Carly closed her eyes, looking worn out. "Yeah, that makes sense—in a totally sick way."

"So, if it's not Darnell," Kyle said, "who's the next best bet?"

"Frank?" Carly suggested.

Greg nodded slowly.

"What about Walter Wiggins?" Tomas asked.

"He's still a possibility," Evelyn agreed.

Tomas looked around the room at the somber-faced agents. "You don't sound convinced about either one."

That was because if she'd been laying bets, she would've placed everything on Darnell Conway.

Evelyn gave it to Tomas straight. "Or it's someone we haven't even considered yet."

Mandy's tears subsided as she looked up and saw a tiny sliver of light. She'd never been afraid of the dark before, but then she'd never seen such pitch-black as the darkness that enclosed her here. She was under the ground, huddled on a blanket that didn't disguise how hard the floor was.

The whole place was made of dirt. The floor, the ceiling, the walls. And she was going to live here! That was what she'd been told.

Mandy clutched a teddy bear to her chest. It wasn't her teddy bear. It was old and it smelled like it had been stuck in someone's attic for too many years. But at least it was something to hold on to. Otherwise, it would just be her and the darkness.

Fear crept in again, a fear Mandy had never experienced before. She didn't know where she was. She didn't know how long she'd been down here. But it felt like a long, long time.

Her heart was pounding, and her mouth was dry and her eyes ached from crying. She wanted to scream, to tell people where she was, but she knew she couldn't. She knew what would happen if she said a word. And she didn't want anyone to hurt her mom and dad. So she stayed silent.

But that sliver of light beckoned.

There hadn't been any light before. Slowly, slowly, Mandy got to her feet. One hand clutching tight to the teddy bear, Mandy held her other hand out in front of her and took a step forward, then another, until her fingers closed around the bottom of a ladder.

It was difficult to climb holding the teddy bear, but Mandy didn't want to let it go. She pulled herself up, her hands slippery with sweat, terrified she'd get to the top and that door would open again and…

Mandy closed her eyes. *Don't think about it!*

She lifted a shaking hand up to the door and pushed. It moved!

Mandy gasped, then quickly slapped her hand over her mouth, almost falling down the short ladder. She tried again. The door hadn't been latched right.

Mandy tried pushing harder, but she wasn't strong enough to open it. She started to sob at the thought of never seeing her mom and dad again. But she fought her tears, tucked the teddy bear under her armpit and used both hands to shove the door as hard as she could.

It popped back, letting in sunshine so bright that even after Mandy squeezed her eyes shut, white light still flashed over her eyeballs. Her breath coming in short, panicked gasps, she pushed herself up, and fell into the dirt.

She was surrounded by high grass. She scampered to her feet, crouching down, looking around for anyone. But she saw nothing except empty land.

Her gaze darting around her, she stood there, unmoving. Which way? Which way?

The huge shadow of an ibis flying overhead drifted past her and Mandy scampered forward, following his flight path, praying he'd lead her home. Clutching the teddy bear close, she ran as fast as she could.

Her feet tangled and she hit the ground, bumping her chin and scraping skin off her knees. But she ignored it, pushed herself back to her feet and kept running.

"We found Mandy Toland."

Tomas's announcement echoed off the walls in the near-empty CARD command post as Evelyn leaped to her feet.

Beside her, Kyle stood more slowly. "Alive?"

"Yes." Tomas turned back the way he'd come. "She escaped. I'm going to the hospital to talk to her now. I want you to come, Evelyn."

Leaving her briefcase, Evelyn yanked photos out of the file Carly had begun, then hurried toward the door.

"I'll stay here and keep going through this," Kyle said. "I'll call you if I come up with anything."

For the past hour, they'd been reviewing the coroner's reports on Brittany Douglas, along with everything that had come back on the cellar. Kyle was HRT now, but just like her, he'd started in a regular FBI unit. She'd started in violent crime; he'd cut his teeth working terrorism cases. He knew his way around evidence and coroners' reports.

Evelyn nodded at him gratefully as she followed Tomas. She still couldn't believe he'd taken time off work to stay here for her.

As soon as she had a minute that wasn't taken up by this case, she had to figure out what was happening between them. And what it might mean for her career—if she still had one.

"Where's Carly?" Tomas asked, striding through the near-empty station.

"Talking to Frank again. She took her partner in with her. Greg is advising."

Tomas glanced over at her as he held open the front door. "Why Greg? Why not you? And is that going anywhere?"

"Greg was advising on Frank's and Walter's interviews from the beginning. He knows what's been going on. We talked about it beforehand, but it seemed like a better idea for me to look through the information from the crime scene. And no, we don't have anything from either interview. What do we know so far about Mandy?"

They rushed to Tomas's car and climbed in, then Tomas peeled out of the parking lot, sirens blaring.

"We got a call from a guy on the outskirts of Rose Bay. He found Mandy wandering on his property, dirty, bleeding, confused. The ambulance already picked her up. We're meeting them at the hospital."

"Do Mandy's parents know?"

"They're on their way, too."

"She escaped?"

Tomas nodded, his jaw a hard line as he raced through the streets of Rose Bay. "As far as we can tell. The guy who called said she wasn't talking. She actually ran from him at first, so he yelled for his wife, and between the two of them, they convinced her they were going to help her. She refused to go in their house, so they waited outside with her for the ambulance."

"Where exactly was she found?" Evelyn asked as Tomas swung into the hospital parking lot.

"Way out on the edge of Rose Bay. The couple whose property she showed up on live on a hundred or so acres. They spotted her in their field and went running out there. They said she came from the west, which means the same direction as the place we found Brittany and Lauren."

Evelyn stepped out of the car, slamming the door shut. "How close?"

"Maybe a mile."

"Could there be more cellars dug behind where we found Brittany and Lauren?"

Tomas raked a hand through his hair as he hurried toward the hospital entrance. "You know how much empty land is out there, Evelyn. Obviously we were searching the whole area, but the priority was to excavate the cellar and those older bodies."

He held open the door and Evelyn half ran to catch up. The smell of antiseptic and sickness crept into her nostrils, reminding her of all the times she'd visited her grandma in the hospital after she'd first had her stroke. She couldn't go into a hospital without the memories rushing back. The fear of losing her grandma, only two years after her grandpa. The fear of being all alone in the world.

"We thought we had everything we were looking for," Tomas continued, bringing her attention back where it needed to be. "I mean, we have three older bodies and we found Lauren and Brittany. Last night, that was the right number. Our focus wasn't on searching for more cellars."

"But we still have a presence out there, don't we?"

"Of course. There were cops out in that field, still working the scene this morning when Mandy went missing. There's no way Mandy was brought there, not to that particular location." He shook his head as he approached the front desk. "But that field stretches for hundreds of acres. Could she have been somewhere else on that land? Yeah, it's possible."

A nurse stepped toward them. "Come with me, Chief Lamar."

"How is she?" Evelyn asked.

"She just got here. Her parents, too. You'll have to wait until the doctor sees her, but I can tell you she's pretty traumatized."

Tomas sighed. "Shit, she's not talking, either?"

"Not yet," the nurse replied, leading them down a long, sterile white hallway to a different waiting room. She left them there, promising to return with the doctor soon.

"What about Lauren?" Evelyn asked, settling into the closest chair.

Tomas sat down next to her. "Not a single word," he said. "We've gotten her to nod, or shake her head a few times, but that's it."

"Has she looked at suspect pictures?"

"Damn it, Evelyn, the girl's still terrified. Completely terrified. Honestly, I don't think she's in any shape to look at pictures and I don't think her parents would have allowed us to try."

He sighed again, and Evelyn's gaze was drawn to the stress lines on his forehead she didn't remember being there when she'd arrived four days ago.

"I don't know what this guy did to Lauren, but like I told you, she won't say a word. She's still here, and not because she's got any obvious medical needs. She's just afraid to go home. We've got cops posted outside her door at all times and until we find this guy, we'll put them at her house, too. The hospital will probably only keep her for another twenty-four hours."

He braced his elbows on his knees, set his chin in his hands. "I thought the APB would get Darnell in and this would be over." He shifted to face her. "Are you *positive* it's not him?"

"Ninety-nine percent."

"Damn it." He dropped his face into his hands, then sat back up. "Okay. So now Frank's our strongest possibility? You think Mandy had the chance to escape because we had him at the station?"

Evelyn shrugged. "Maybe."

Tomas's whole body tensed. "You're the one who knows how these bastards operate. What's he going to do next? Now that we have Mandy? Because unless you or Greg or Carly come up with something soon, I'll have to cut both Frank and Wiggins loose. We don't have anything but your gut—and their histories—on either one of them. The second I release them, is another girl going to go missing?"

The words hung in the air until the nurse came back into the room, trailed by a doctor who looked weary and jaded.

Both Evelyn and Tomas jumped to their feet. "Well?" Tomas asked.

"No obvious sexual trauma," the doctor said steadily. "She has some superficial injuries—consistent with falling down, probably when she was running away—but that's it." The doctor lowered Mandy's patient chart to her side. "She is traumatized, though. She hasn't spoken at all since she came in. Not even to her parents."

"Can we talk to her?" Tomas asked.

The doctor nodded. "She's a strong kid. But go easy."

"Come on, Evelyn." Tomas headed down the hall, then glanced back.

The doctor pointed at a nearby door and Tomas knocked.

"Come in," a teary voice answered.

Tomas pushed the door open, and once Evelyn stepped inside, she closed it behind her.

The room was too small for her, Tomas and Mandy's parents to all stand around. It felt overcrowded and stuffy, and Mandy looked petrified, tiny in the adult-size hospital bed. She wore a hospital gown and held a blue teddy bear that had obviously come from the hospital gift shop because its shirt read Feel Better Soon.

Following Evelyn's gaze, Mandy's father, a tall, broad man with bags under his eyes and stoicism in his face, turned his head away from his daughter. "She didn't want to hand over the one she had with her," he whispered, "so we got that from the gift shop."

Evelyn glanced from him to Mandy's mom, a tiny blonde with red-rimmed eyes who was clinging to Mandy as if she'd never let go. "She had a teddy bear with her?"

Mandy's dad nodded. "The doctors have it, along with her clothes." He looked at Tomas, frowning. "They said you'd want it all for evidence."

Tomas clapped Mandy's dad on the shoulder. "Yes, for fibers or anything we might find. Jim, we'd like to show Mandy a few pictures. Is that all right?"

Jim turned to his wife, whose lips trembled as she nodded. "Okay. But we stay in the room."

"Of course."

Evelyn knelt next to Mandy's bed. The child was pale against the stark white of the hospital, her skin blending too easily with the sheets. She looked frail, her eyes huge and lighting nervously on anything that moved. She'd been missing for seven and a half hours, but she looked like she'd been gone for months.

A weight settled in Evelyn's chest. Of all the girls, Mandy had been luckiest, probably suffered the least trauma.

Trying to put her emotions aside, Evelyn gave Mandy what she hoped was a reassuring smile. "Hi, Mandy. My name is Evelyn. I'm with the FBI. Do you know what that is?"

The girl didn't nod, didn't react at all, just stared at Evelyn with her too-wide, too-wary eyes.

"She does," her mom said from behind them.

"I'm here to find the person who did this, Mandy. He can't hurt you now. We're going to put police officers right outside your door and they won't leave until we've got him, okay?"

Mandy clutched her bear tighter and clamped her lips together.

Evelyn resisted the urge to glance back at Tomas. Talking to victims wasn't her strong suit, but her words should have reassured Mandy. Instead, she seemed more nervous.

"I want to show you some pictures," she went on. "If one of these people is the man we should arrest for taking you, Mandy, you can just nod, okay?"

Mandy didn't respond, so Evelyn took the first picture from her stack. Darnell Conway.

Mandy's eyes flickered to her mom, back to Evelyn, then down to the picture, but otherwise, she had no reaction.

"Does he look familiar?" Evelyn pressed.

When Mandy did nothing but stare, Evelyn swallowed

her frustration and flipped to the next picture. Frank Abbott.

Again, Mandy's eyes dipped down to the picture, then back up to Evelyn, but nothing else changed.

"Okay, how about him?" Evelyn asked, turning to the shot of Walter Wiggins.

Mandy glanced down and unease shifted across her face. It was so subtle Evelyn probably would have missed it if she hadn't been watching so carefully.

"Is this the man who took you?" Evelyn asked.

She asked twice more, but Mandy didn't answer, and her expression didn't change.

Finally Evelyn stood and nodded at Tomas.

"Thanks for letting us talk to her," Tomas told her parents. "We'll have officers stationed outside the door within the hour. Please call us if Mandy starts talking."

"Did she identify someone?" Mandy's mom asked quietly.

"I don't know," Evelyn said truthfully. Mandy had recognized Walter, but he lived here in town and he'd taken pictures of her. Did that flicker of fear mean he'd abducted her? Or did it just mean she'd seen him watching and known she should stay away?

Unless she started talking, there was no way to be sure.

Evelyn turned to go, but Mandy's dad grabbed her arm, his hold strong.

"Who was in that picture?"

"Sir, we don't know—"

"Who was it?" he boomed.

"Jim," his wife said, pulling his hand off Evelyn. "We need to focus on Mandy. Let the police worry about who did it."

As Jim scowled, his wife added, "But if you don't arrest someone by the end of the day, we're getting our lawyer involved. She was supposed to be safe. You were supposed to have someone in custody!"

"We're working—"

"She was supposed to be safe," Mandy's mom repeated.

"I'm so sorry," Tomas said.

"Just go. Just go arrest whoever did this," Jim said tiredly, then he and his wife turned back to their daughter.

Evelyn nodded and opened the door. Once it was closed behind her, she said, "Let's go pick up the items the hospital collected from Mandy. I want to see this teddy bear."

"A toy," Tomas mused as they walked down the hall, back toward the nurse who'd helped them before. "There were no toys in the cellar with Lauren."

"No, just that child's drawing."

"You think one of the girls from eighteen years ago drew it?" Tomas asked. It was obviously old, so it wasn't made by Lauren or Brittany.

"Probably. Which means the abductor provided them with crayons and paper. It's possible he left toys during the day and took them away in the evening. Or, since he'd wiped the place down, probably intending for us to find it, maybe that's why everything else was removed."

"So why leave that picture?"

Evelyn shook her head. "Maybe he wanted us to know he took care of them?"

Tomas stopped abruptly. "Evelyn, he *killed* Brittany. And, as far as we can tell, the three girls eighteen years ago."

Evelyn's heart lurched at the one thing she was trying desperately not to think about. The forensic anthropologist had arrived, and the dental records were being checked, but it could still be a while before they knew whose bodies they were. "I'm not talking about reality. I'm talking about his perception. If we're back to his motive being the idea that he was 'saving' these girls, then he believes he's caring for them. And like I said from the beginning, even if it is really about molestation, with someone like Walter, he'd want an excuse. He could be telling himself he's helping them. He might actually believe it."

"Damn," Tomas muttered, just as the nurse met them with a bag of Mandy's belongings. Tomas took the bag and they continued outside.

The sun was bright, a slight breeze blowing across the parking lot, preventing the day from being too hot. Evelyn looked up at the cloudless blue sky, so perfect—and so deceptive when a child predator was at large.

"Do we buy Darnell's assertion that someone texted him and told him to meet in that field?" Tomas asked as they got into his car and he blasted the air-conditioning.

"Carly is trying to get someone from the phone company to confirm."

Tomas snapped on a pair of latex gloves and opened the bag the nurse had given him. He showed her the teddy bear, wrinkling his nose. "Old."

Evelyn stared at it. She knew it wasn't Cassie's, but she tried to mentally review the case files from eighteen years ago. "Does this look like something that belonged to one of the original victims?"

"I don't think so."

"So, he probably bought it for them."

"You think he's held on to it for eighteen years?"

"Smells like it," Evelyn said. "We should run it. See if we get any DNA hits for the original victims."

Tomas nodded, shoving it back in the bag and sifting through the rest of the items. "A pair of underwear, tennis shoes, a dress. Wait, there's something in the dress pocket." His face went ashen and he took out a small pin. "What the hell?"

"What is it?"

Tomas's hand trembled as he held it out toward her. "This pin belonged to Jack's father."

"Well, it was his land where we found Lauren and—"

"No, Evelyn. The office gave this to him the day he retired. It says RBPD Chief on it. When he died, it went to Jack. He always wears this. Every day. On his lapel."

A bad feeling settled in Evelyn's stomach. "Where is Jack?"

Tomas shook his head. "He went out to run a lead hours ago. I haven't seen him since early this morning."

"Since before Mandy went missing?"

Tomas swore. "Yeah."

"Let's get back to the station."

Tomas pulled out of the hospital parking lot. "There's no way it's Jack Bullock. No way."

Evelyn wanted to agree. But too many things piled up in her mind. The way he'd wanted her gone from the second she'd arrived. The weird impression Kyle had gotten from him, enough to run a background check. The fact that the cellar had been on his property.

As Evelyn leaned against the headrest, a memory rose up—Jack questioning her eighteen years ago. The way he'd gotten right in her face, his eyes hard and angry.

The way he'd demanded she give him details she didn't have until she'd broken down and cried.

The whole time, had he been holding Cassie down in that cellar?

Twenty-Two

She crouched inside the cellar, tears tracking down her face. Beside her were pieces of the tea set she'd loved for so long, shattered on the ground.

The girl was gone. She'd known, of course, since she'd been the one to wrench the latch open. She'd known the girl would run. She'd wanted her to run, because that way she'd live.

The girl hadn't been the right one. Nothing was right.

Nothing had been right for eighteen years. For so long, he'd brought her sisters and then taken them away.

And for so long, she'd been so lonely.

Every time, when she could tell he was really mad, when she knew another girl was going away, she'd tried so hard to get him to change his mind. But no matter how much she begged him not to take them away, he always had. Leaving her all by herself.

It wasn't going to be like that anymore.

She hadn't wanted the little girl to die. Mandy was her real name. Mandy had cried, too, at first. Then Mandy had just gone silent.

And she'd known Mandy wasn't going to work, either.

That was why she'd made it so Mandy could escape. It was better this way. At least Mandy would live.

But it meant she was alone again. Always alone.

She closed her eyes and breathed in the scent of the familiar cellar. Just breathed it in, one last time. As the years passed, she'd begun to feel more at home under the ground than anywhere else.

She opened her eyes, dried her tears and picked up the shattered pieces of the tea set. He'd never liked it when she made a mess. And she couldn't leave anything behind.

Because she knew what was coming. It would be time to move on soon.

"We put out an APB on Jack," T. J. Sutton, Jack's partner, announced grimly as he entered the CARD command post.

"Good," Evelyn said, before Tomas could respond.

"There's no way—" T.J. started.

"The APB just lists him as missing," Tomas said calmly. "Let's not blow things out of proportion."

"Blow things out of proportion?" T.J. snapped back. "You think he's the Nursery Rhyme Killer!"

"All we know right now is that Mandy had his pin in her pocket," Evelyn said. "We have to consider all the options."

"You've hated Jack since you were a kid!" T.J. shouted.

"No, I—"

"I want you out there, T.J.," Tomas interrupted. "You know Jack best. Go talk to his wife. He's one of us, so until we learn differently, we assume he's doing exactly what he said."

"Maybe he ran into trouble," T.J. persisted, but doubt crept into his words.

"Just get out there," Tomas repeated. "And keep me updated."

When T.J. closed the door behind him, Tomas heaved out a sigh. "Could it really be *Jack*?"

"He did have access to the investigation the whole time, which would put him a step ahead of everyone else," Kyle said. "And as a cop, he's not going to seem out of place in any neighborhood. Plus, he wouldn't even need to snatch them. Kids would probably go with a police officer voluntarily."

Tomas looked queasy and Evelyn knew why. If Jack Bullock had been abducting young girls while working as a Rose Bay police officer, that was a public relations nightmare that could destroy the station and cost Tomas his job.

"It is suspicious that the cellar was on empty land he owned," Greg said.

"Everyone around here knows that land is vacant," Tomas argued. "Jack and Miranda live right in town. Jack's never been interested in building out there. He only kept the land because he's sentimental when it comes to his father."

"I was thinking more about eighteen years ago," Greg said. "Jack had a handy excuse for being on that property. And would search parties have bothered to look on the police chief's land? Especially if everyone in town knew he spent time out there, trying to build a house?"

"Okay." Tomas straightened, turning to Evelyn. "So, are you suggesting that Jack has some tragedy in his past involving a young girl that none of us know about? Or that he's a pedophile?"

Evelyn cringed at the ugly question. But being a cop didn't absolve Jack of all sins. She'd solidified her spot in BAU, back when she worked violent crimes in Houston, by picking a rapist out of the police force.

"Given the autopsy results, the more likely option is that the killer is trying to make up for a loss in his own life," Evelyn finally said.

"Well, Jack doesn't have anything like that," Tomas said stubbornly.

"That we know of," Greg inserted.

"I looked into his background when I first met him," Kyle said.

"Why?" Tomas burst out.

"I got a weird feeling from him," Kyle replied unapologetically. "It was just a cursory check, but nothing like that came up. He did lose a son, though, when the boy was an infant. He and his wife never had any other kids."

"They couldn't." Tomas paused for a moment. "Could this have something to do with losing their son?" he asked, sounding reluctant.

"Probably not," Greg answered. "The abductor's specifically grabbing twelve-year-old girls, which strongly suggests that's who he lost."

Tomas shook his head. "Well, then, it can't be Jack. He never had a daughter."

"That we know of," Evelyn interjected, echoing Greg's earlier comment. "There's always a possibility he had an affair. Or it could just be a girl he was close to. What about Noreen's sister?"

"What about her?" Tomas asked.

"Jack and Noreen seem to be pretty close. Was he close to her sister before she died?"

"I doubt it. I don't think Jack was close to Earl or his

wife. And he's close to Noreen now, but that happened when his father hired her. Besides, you said Jack didn't even know Noreen's sister was dead until you told him?"

Evelyn frowned. "That's true. Or at least, he claimed not to know."

"I honestly think you're looking in the wrong direction here, Evelyn," Tomas said. "Jack and I don't always see eye to eye, but he's a decent person. I can't imagine him doing this. There has to be some other explanation."

"He was intensely involved in the original investigation," Evelyn said.

"So was everyone who worked here then," Tomas countered.

"He seemed to have a lot of resentment toward Evelyn," Kyle said. "Considering he hadn't seen her in more than a decade and his only real interaction with her back then was to interrogate her about her friend's disappearance."

Greg nodded slowly. "Jack's behavior around Evelyn is odd. And that's something we'd expect from this perp, since he originally targeted her and failed to carry out that abduction."

"Well, why is that?" Tomas asked. "Why didn't he carry it out?"

"He could've been called into work for some reason," Kyle suggested.

"Cassie's parents didn't realize she was missing until the next morning," Evelyn said.

"Yeah, but Jack's a cop. Even if he was off duty, his father was the chief. If something happened that night, he could've gotten called back to work."

"Can we check that?" Greg asked.

"Ah, shit," Tomas said.

"What?"

"We don't need to check. It's mentioned in one of the old reports. When the notice came in about Cassie's abduction, they had to pull a bunch of cops off another scene they'd been working half the night. Bad car accident by the bridge."

"Was Jack there?" Kyle asked urgently.

"I don't know." Tomas shrugged. "But there's a damn good chance he was. This has always been a small force. Even the off-duty cops got called in for that one. I know, because the report says officers were pulled in from the accident and from regular duty."

"Okay, then we have an explanation for what could've stopped him from grabbing Evelyn back then. Plus probable opportunity and means with the other abductions," Greg said. "But do we have motive? And what about the eighteen-year gap?"

Evelyn spoke up. "Could a case he worked have been his trigger?"

"What do you mean? What kind of case?" Tomas asked.

"After Jack and I talked to Walter Wiggins at his house..."

"What?" Tomas demanded when she trailed off.

"I just realized. Those pictures I saw at Wiggins's house? Jack used the bathroom first."

Tomas closed his eyes briefly. "You're suggesting he planted them?"

"I don't know, Tomas. But the reason I looked is that the tank was off-kilter and everything else in that room was so precise." She sighed. "We all know how much Jack wanted to nail Walter for something. Maybe it was an attempt at a frame-up."

"That's a risky frame-up, Evelyn." Greg's tone was skeptical. "He'd have to assume you'd look at those pictures illegally."

Evelyn felt her face grow hot, but she nodded. "Maybe that wasn't the original intent. Maybe he planned to leave them there, set Walter up some other way that would give us probable cause for a warrant and then we'd find them later, legally."

"Damn it," Tomas muttered.

The room was silent for a moment, then Greg asked, "What were you going to say about Jack and a case?"

"What? Oh, right. Possible motive. When Jack and I were driving back from Wiggins's house, Jack talked about cases with kids being the worst. He talked about being called in on domestic abuse or neglect cases and feeling helpless when he couldn't do anything."

"Come on," Tomas said. "We all feel that way. Every good cop feels like that."

"Maybe Jack decided to do something about it," Greg suggested. "Did he investigate a case that involved the death of a twelve-year-old girl due to parental neglect?"

"I have no idea," Tomas replied. "You'd have to check the files. Or T.J. might know."

"So, it's possible," Greg said. "But then we're back to the eighteen-year gap."

"Maybe the stress of grabbing someone in his own hometown, with his father leading the investigation, was too much," Evelyn suggested. "Maybe he's one of the few who can just control his impulses that well. We've seen that before."

"It does happen," Greg agreed.

Evelyn knew he was recalling a case in which a serial killer had been dormant for decades before suddenly deciding to taunt the press with his trophies. He'd stopped killing for twenty years, then for some reason the need to brag had overcome him. In the end, he'd brought himself down. If he hadn't, that case would likely never have been solved.

Were they looking at a similar situation here? Jack had controlled his urges for eighteen years and then something in his life—maybe the acceptance that he was never going to reach his goal of taking his father's place as police chief—had prompted him to start again?

Evelyn looked around the room at Greg, Tomas and Kyle. "I think we need to consider Jack Bullock our new prime suspect."

"Miranda hasn't seen Jack since he left for work this morning," T.J. said as he entered the CARD command post.

Evelyn looked up at him, her eyes bleary. She'd spent another hour watching Greg and Carly talk to Frank and Walter one last time, then both had been allowed to go home.

"You check any other typical haunts?" Tomas asked.

"Yeah. Nothing. None of the other officers have heard from him since he took off this morning, either."

"Shit." Tomas sighed.

"Maybe he's in trouble," T.J. insisted.

"Yeah, Rose Bay is such a hotbed of crime," Tomas blurted sarcastically. Then he pinched the bridge of his nose. "Sorry. Look, T.J., do you know if Jack ever pulled a domestic with a twelve-year-old female victim?"

T.J. scowled. "Not with me, he didn't."

"It would've been a long time ago," Greg said. "Did he ever mention anything like that?"

"No."

"Okay," Greg said. "Then we'll start with the cases from eighteen years ago and work backward."

"This is bullshit," T.J. insisted, but his voice lacked conviction.

"What about doing another run at the field where Lauren was found?" Kyle asked.

"We've got officers there now," Tomas replied.

"What about a helicopter?"

"Grounded." T.J. sighed. "Our pilot got food poisoning this morning."

"I can take it."

"Really?" Tomas squinted at Kyle. "The FBI teaches you that?"

"Not exactly. I had my pilot's license before I joined the FBI. I come from kind of a small town. Not a lot to do besides football and barbecues. But we had a little private airstrip one town over. I learned to fly before I learned to drive."

Evelyn stared at him, surprised. When she'd met him a year ago, she'd seen a cocky, can't-take-anything-seriously adrenaline junkie who wore a ton of the FBI's best ass-kicking gear. Slowly, they'd gotten to be friends. And even more slowly, something else was developing, something stronger. But the more she learned, the more she felt like she'd barely scratched the surface with him.

Kyle stared back at her a little too long, then winked, and looked back at Tomas. "I can take it up. T.J., you want to ride with me?"

T.J. raised his eyebrows at Tomas. "We covered for that?"

"Let me worry about the approval," Tomas said. "You just get up there and check it out again. I want to know where the hell Jack is. And if he's somewhere in those fields—unless he's already underground—it'll be a hell of a lot faster to find him from the air."

"Fine," T.J. said. "But when we do find Jack and there's a logical explanation, I want you to remember that I knew it all along."

"Let's go," Kyle said, heading for the door.

T.J. trailed behind him.

"How should we divide this up?" Tomas asked.

Evelyn studied the eighteen-year-old files spread out in front of them. It could take them all night to get through the huge stack, plus the boxes waiting under the table. And although uncovering a case that matched would go a long way toward establishing motive, right now they needed to locate Jack.

It wasn't her role anymore. As a profiler, she knew she belonged in this stuffy room, looking through the files to find one that might have turned a cop into a child abductor.

But the longer she was stuck in here, the harder it felt to breathe. It felt as if the past was creeping back up on her, and she still couldn't make any sense of it, still couldn't fix it.

"Can you two handle this? Carly should be back soon to help, right?" Not waiting for an answer, Evelyn started backing toward the door, desperate to get outside, where she could breathe. "I want to take a ride."

"You want to go with Kyle and T.J.?" Greg asked, worry in his eyes.

"No. Just go for a drive."

"Okay," Tomas said, already focused on the files. "We'll call you if we find anything."

Greg watched her as she continued to back out of the room. "You okay, Evelyn?"

"Fine. I'll take a drive down the road that goes out to where we found Lauren."

"There are cops out there right now," Greg reminded her.

"I know. I'm not going to join them. I just need to see the area again."

Greg's eyes narrowed. "Why?"

They'd worked together long enough for him to see something was bothering her. Instead of telling him that if she stayed and flipped through folders looking for twelve-year-old girls who'd died, all she'd be able to see was Cassie, she told him the other part. "I feel like I'm missing something that should be obvious. I need to see the scene again."

"Call us if you have any new ideas," Tomas said, then shoved a teetering pile of folders at Greg. "You take this stack."

Before Greg could ask anything else, Evelyn hurried out to her rental. She rolled down the windows, needing more air, and wind whipped inside. Rain was coming.

She'd planned to head directly toward the dead-end road where she'd followed Darnell Conway yesterday. But instead of driving toward the outskirts of town, she found herself turning the other way, toward Magnolia Street.

She hadn't been back there in thirteen years. But it looked exactly the same—a winding road, lined with perfectly manicured magnolia trees, bursting with huge white blooms. The houses set way back off the road looked the same, too—big and private. Classic South

Carolina–style, with columns out front and big hedges to separate them from prying neighbor eyes.

In the cul-de-sac at the end of the road, the Byers house looked forlorn, all the yard and porch lights out. Were Mr. and Mrs. Byers inside, sitting in the fading evening light, waiting to hear if one of the skeletons found in a field across town was their daughter's?

Evelyn knew she should stop, pull into the drive and talk to them. She owed them that much. But she couldn't do it.

Instead, she drove slowly past, gazing at the gnarly branched live oak out front that she and Cassie had liked to climb. They'd get up high, sit together where the branches started to sway just a little from their combined weight and giggle about things Evelyn couldn't remember.

Next door, her grandparents' old house looked pretty much as it always had. The new owners had painted the doors and shutters a new color, added some more flowers. Otherwise, if Evelyn squinted, she could almost see her grandpa rocking on the chair on the covered porch, her grandma standing beside him, shading her eyes and watching Evelyn and Cassie play.

A sad smile quivered on her lips at the memory. Those days were long gone. Her grandpa was long gone. Cassie was long gone. And her grandma was still with her in body, but less and less in spirit every year.

There was no time to linger in the memories. It was time to find closure, time to move on.

With one last look at the place that had made her who she was today—probably the last look she'd ever have—Evelyn put her foot on the gas and set out for the other side of town.

She was back at the long, dead-end road before she expected, and then she put everything out of her mind except the day she'd followed Darnell out here and found the cellar. Something about that day was niggling in her mind, some small piece of it refusing to surface. Maybe being here would coax it out, whatever was bothering her subconscious.

She drove slowly, surveying the overgrown fields on either side of her. Houses and trees dotted the landscape at random, mostly set far back. She recalled following Darnell down this road, wondering what the hell he was doing. She passed Frank Abbott's house now, as she'd done on that day, then another house, boarded up. Then she rounded a bend with the copse of trees, where she and Kyle had originally stopped.

The field came into view, edged with police cars. The field itself was still bright with portable police lights, crime scene tape strung around several sections. The cellar. And the graves.

The graves. Evelyn put the car in Park, staring out at the officers still searching for evidence in the huge field. Overhead, in the distance, she heard the approaching buzz of a helicopter.

There was something about the graves. Evelyn struggled to get her mind to latch on to whatever it was that had struck her as odd. And then suddenly, as vividly as if she was looking into the little coffin, Evelyn saw it.

Brittany's body, wrapped in a soft blue blanket.

Evelyn's heart started a slow crescendo. Someone had carefully folded that warm blanket around Brittany before tucking her into the ground. Someone had wanted to protect her from the elements, care for her even in death.

It was a big behavioral cue and she'd totally missed it.

Evelyn flashed back to the day she'd called Greg and talked about reasons the killer might not have come back for her. During that phone call, they'd come to the conclusion that he lived with someone who'd noticed him missing. Someone who might not have suspected then, but surely suspected now. Someone who'd known what was happening.

A woman who'd known what was happening.

Evelyn slammed her hand against the steering wheel, furious at herself for not realizing sooner. Wrapping the body so carefully was a sign of remorse. It was often seen in cases where a parent killed his or her child, but almost always it was a woman. In this case, a woman who'd tried to protect both the victim and the predator?

Whoever had prevented the Nursery Rhyme Killer from taking Evelyn eighteen years ago still knew what was happening. Because she'd been the one to wrap Brittany gently in that blanket before placing her in the ground.

That meant the killer wasn't the only one who knew where his new hiding spot was. There was a woman involved, too. A woman who knew everything.

Twenty-Three

Evelyn sat at the end of Jack Bullock's driveway, studying the small, tidy house. The porch lights were on, and so were lights in the front room. Miranda Bullock was probably inside, waiting for Jack to come home.

Was she waiting for the police to find him? Or did she know exactly where he was?

The mother of an infant who had died within his first two months of life would have reason to gently wrap a dead twelve-year-old in a blanket before allowing her husband to bury her. The stay-at-home wife of an overbearing and obsessive policeman could also have reason to fear turning that man in if she knew he was also a child abductor.

Especially if she understood his reasoning. If Jack had resorted to the abductions because of something he'd seen on the job, his wife might even agree. A neglected or abused child the law couldn't protect? Maybe that child was better off with them. They couldn't have any more of their own children, so they had room to take one in.

And one of the veteran cops had told her Jack's wife had always wanted a daughter.

But of course, no one could know. And what better way to hide them than on land they owned but no one used? Land that had once belonged to a police chief and was now owned by an officer. Why would anyone suspect that?

Evelyn nodded to herself as she went over the reasoning Miranda might have used. It was too easy to imagine her rationalizing the abductions over the years.

Evelyn reached for her cell phone to call Greg and let him know she was going to question Jack's wife and realized she'd left it in the station.

"Shit," she muttered, but stepped out of the car and strode up to the house, anyway. Her car was parked right outside, something the neighbors would certainly notice, and she was armed. And T.J. had been by earlier. Jack wasn't home.

Even if he'd come home since T.J.'s visit, his smartest move was to claim he'd been off doing exactly what he'd said he was: running down a long-shot lead that had gone nowhere. No one could disprove that, and although at this point Jack probably knew they suspected him, all they had was his father's pin. Stacked against a lifelong career and family legacy in law enforcement, it wouldn't hold up.

Evelyn knocked on the door and it opened fast, as though the person inside had been watching her approach.

Miranda Bullock was frail-looking. She was even shorter than Evelyn's five foot two, with wary brown eyes and brown hair streaked with gray knotted severely on her head.

"How *dare* you treat my husband like some common criminal?" she snarled with a lot more aggression than Evelyn had expected from someone who seemed so beaten down.

"I'm Evelyn Baine," she replied evenly, ignoring the question. "I just want to ask you a few things."

"T.J. was already here," Miranda snapped. "Jack isn't home. He's working."

"Well, the station doesn't know where your husband is," Evelyn said.

"It's not their business. Jack's been on the force for twenty-one years. Before he was an officer, he worked for his father, doing odd jobs at the station. He started that as a teenager. He knows what he's doing, more than anyone else at that station, including the new *chief*." She spat the last word.

"Well, whatever leads he's running, I'd like to assist," Evelyn said smoothly, changing the tactic she'd planned to take with this woman. It was obvious that she'd never get her to turn on her husband. Which made Evelyn's suspicion ratchet higher. How far *would* Miranda go to protect Jack?

"Bullshit," Miranda said, looking Evelyn up and down with a disapproving sneer on her face.

Evelyn recognized that look instantly, but she forced herself not to react. She knew Jack held at least some animosity toward her because of her skin color; it shouldn't surprise her that Jack's wife would, too.

"Ma'am, I'd just like to know—"

"Get off my property," the woman snapped as she started to slam the door.

Evelyn braced her hand on the door before it could close and Miranda seemed surprised by her strength. Evelyn locked a steely, determined gaze on her, a gaze she'd perfected in her years at the FBI, one that said, *Don't underestimate me.*

"It won't take long."

Miranda chewed her lip, squinting from Evelyn's hand braced on the door back to her face. Her own hand, still pushing the other side of the door, trembled. "Fine." She let go and walked inside.

Evelyn closed the door behind her, checking warily around her as she followed Miranda into a small sitting room. Just because Miranda said Jack wasn't home didn't mean it was true.

But the house felt empty and no one jumped out of the shadows.

"Someone stole Jack's pin yesterday," Miranda announced as soon as Evelyn sat down.

Damn it. "Did T.J. tell you we'd found it?" Evelyn asked, although inside she was seething. She couldn't believe T.J. had told Jack's wife what they had on him.

"Yeah. Said it was on that girl who went missing this morning. But Jack lost it yesterday."

"He lost it or someone stole it?"

"Well, who knows? But it wasn't on his lapel when he got home last night."

Evelyn didn't push. Instead, she asked, "When did you last see Jack?"

"This morning."

"What time?"

Miranda shrugged. "Don't remember. Before he went to work."

"His shift would be over now, wouldn't it?"

"Not when there's a kid missing."

"We found her," Evelyn said. "So, shouldn't he be home by now?"

Miranda crossed her arms over her chest. "No. He takes these cases seriously. He won't slow down until this guy is caught."

"Has he always been this dedicated?"

"Yes," she insisted. "Jack is a good cop."

"Do you know if there's a case in particular that really drives him?" Before Miranda could say no, Evelyn added conversationally, "We all have one, of course."

Her eyes narrowed even more. "Sure, he's got some of those. But he takes every case seriously. He's very dedicated to his job."

"So much so that he doesn't have time for a home life?" Evelyn wondered.

"He has plenty of time for me. But his job is very important. It has to come first." She said it as though it was something she'd been told repeatedly.

Evelyn nodded. "Of course. What about kids?"

Miranda's hands jerked in her lap. "What about them?" she asked faintly.

"You don't have any?" It was a cruel question to ask a woman who'd lost her only child, especially if Jack was innocent or she knew nothing about what he was doing. But if he was guilty and she was complicit, her reaction would tell Evelyn a lot.

Miranda wouldn't meet Evelyn's eyes. She didn't answer, just got stiffly to her feet. "I want you to leave. And I'll be telling my husband about your visit."

She said the last part as if it were a threat.

Evelyn stood, too, studying Miranda for any sign of guilt.

But the woman had stiffened her shoulders and locked her jaw, only anger showing on her face.

When Evelyn didn't immediately move, Miranda

stepped forward aggressively and screamed, “Get out! Get out now!”

Evelyn held up her hands and backed toward the door. “Okay. Please ask Jack to call me when he gets home.”

“You bet I will,” Miranda yelled as Evelyn reached the door. “You can bet he’ll have something to say about it, too.”

As soon as Evelyn stepped outside, Miranda slammed the door, hard enough that a blast of angry wind smacked Evelyn’s back.

Walking slowly toward her car, Evelyn glanced back at the house. A curtain moved in the front window; Miranda was still watching. Or could it possibly be Jack in there?

Evelyn couldn’t tell, and the curtain fluttered back into place.

So much for getting anything out of Jack’s wife.

Evelyn climbed into her car and sank down in the seat without starting the engine. Where the hell was she going to look next?

Had Greg and Tomas come up with a case in Jack’s past that would motivate him to abduct young girls? Evelyn didn’t have her phone and she didn’t want to drive back to the station. Instead, her mind wandered over all the information she’d learned about Jack in the past four days.

As she ran through everything, she jolted forward in her seat. Noreen. Jack had been close to her, so she’d wondered if he’d known her sister before she died, that Margaret was the trigger. It had seemed like a long shot.

But what about Noreen? Frank Abbott was still a suspect. He wasn’t as high on her list as Jack Bullock, but she didn’t know where else to look for information on

Jack. And if Frank was the killer, maybe Noreen was the woman in his life afraid to turn him in.

Eighteen years ago, Earl's declining health could have stopped Frank's abductions. Back then, Noreen would've been too young to know anything. But now, especially working at the police station, maybe she'd begun to suspect. Maybe she'd figured it out too late to save Brittany, but had carefully wrapped the child in a blanket before her uncle buried her.

Was it possible?

Evelyn leaned back in her seat, the engine running but her rental car still outside Jack Bullock's house. The world outside was getting dark, and Jack wasn't home yet.

There was nothing she could do about that, so she turned her mind back to Frank and Noreen. With her father and sister dead and her mom seemingly out of the picture, all Noreen had was the station and her uncle Frank.

Both Jack and Tomas had said Noreen was incredibly smart. If she'd realized it was her uncle, would she be able to turn him in?

She clearly had mixed feelings about him. Resentment at the way he'd left her on her own to look after her father as soon as she hit eighteen. Gratitude that he'd stuck around that long. Loyalty and love because he was the only family she had.

Evelyn knew what it was like to have too few people in her life, too few family members, too few friends. She knew exactly what it was like to want to hold on as tight as she could to what she still had.

It was probably the same for Noreen. Evelyn found

it easy to imagine her love and loyalty to her uncle extending too far.

Evelyn shifted out of Park and pulled away from the Bullock house, the idea gaining momentum in her mind. Noreen was only twenty-four. Naive and socially awkward. Not much of a life outside the police station. If she'd turned her uncle in, it would've destroyed everything she had in one swoop.

Evelyn tried to put herself in Noreen's shoes, imagined discovering that the only family she still had was a killer. Having worked in the police station for years, she'd know that the death penalty was a real possibility for this kind of crime. And if he was the killer, what would the officers she worked with have thought of her? Would they want the niece of the worst criminal in Rose Bay's history working in their station? Probably not.

So if Frank Abbott *was* the killer and Noreen turned him in, she'd be left with nothing at all.

Evelyn sped up as she headed toward Noreen's apartment. The girl had mentioned she lived in a walk-up a few blocks from the station. When Evelyn got there, she'd find out which unit.

Because no matter what Noreen's motive might have been for keeping her uncle's secret, Noreen believed in her job. Evelyn was sure of it.

She remembered the long hours Noreen had put in coordinating the search parties, the work she'd taken home with her, the way she'd called Evelyn with information. When Evelyn had first suspected her uncle, she'd seemed to genuinely believe he wasn't guilty.

Which meant that if Frank *was* guilty, she'd probably uncovered something along the way. She'd probably only learned her uncle's horrible secret recently, likely after Brittany was already dead.

Evelyn could imagine the horror she must have felt when she learned what he'd done. Had Noreen confronted her uncle? Was that how she'd found out about Brittany? Or had she known of his hiding spot and discovered Brittany already dead, too late to save? Either way, if this theory had merit, if Noreen had been the one to wrap that blanket around Brittany, it was because she felt guilty.

Guilty for not realizing sooner. Guilty for being related to the killer. Guilty for loving him—and her own life in Rose Bay—too much to turn him in.

But if she felt guilt, it also meant that if Evelyn handled things right, she could talk Noreen into giving her uncle up.

Assuming her burgeoning theory was correct.

The truth was, she had too many theories and too few facts. Profiling wasn't an exact science.

In some ways, that was better. It took her places that physical evidence alone couldn't.

But in other ways, it was frustrating as hell. Because there would always be elements of profiling that were conjecture. The right conjecture could connect dots that a regular investigation would never find. The wrong conjecture could waste time, manpower and resources, and lead everyone off track.

And right now, Evelyn felt as uncertain about her profile as she'd ever felt about anything.

Was it Jack? Was it Frank? Hell, was it Walter Wiggins or some other resident of Rose Bay Evelyn had never even considered?

The only way she'd know was by taking her theories as far as she could and seeing what she found.

Evelyn gritted her teeth and parked in the only apartment complex within walking distance of the police station. A quick stop in the manager's office told her that Noreen Abbott did live here, but she'd gone out an hour ago and hadn't yet returned.

Borrowing the manager's phone, Evelyn called the station and got Greg. "How's the search going?"

"Nothing yet. Jack pulled a few nasty domestics as a rookie, but none that involved a twelve-year-old girl." Greg sounded dejected. "How about you?"

"I stopped by Jack's house. His wife was not happy to see me. And T.J. gave her a head's-up on the pin."

"Shit."

"Yeah. Hey, is Noreen there?"

"Nope. Carly's back, though."

"Okay."

"You coming back now?"

"Soon. Thanks, Greg." Hanging up, Evelyn handed the phone back to the apartment manager and returned to her car.

The station was right down the street. Time to go back.

But when she started the car, she turned it in the other direction. Back to the same dead-end road where she'd followed Darnell Conway to Jack Bullock's property. The same dead-end road where Frank Abbott lived.

Frank already knew he was a suspect. He wouldn't be surprised by another visit.

But Noreen might be there. If she could just find Noreen alone, maybe she could get her to admit whatever she'd learned about her uncle. Maybe the whole thing would finally unravel.

The dirt road felt different as the darkness settled

around her and thunder cracked the air, more ominous somehow. Maybe it was because she knew what was at the end of the road, in that field.

The cops working that scene were surely calling it a night by now, especially if a storm was coming.

As if to confirm her thought, Evelyn heard the hum of a low-flying helicopter. It kept going, back toward the runway at the other end of town.

Evelyn continued driving, and pulled into Frank Abbott's drive. At the top of the drive was an old beater that hadn't been there last time she'd visited Frank's house. Noreen's car?

She parked and stepped out of the car, glancing around at Frank's property. The huge, overgrown field behind his decrepit house. High grasses similar to the field at the end of the road, going on for miles, broken up only by the occasional copse of trees. The barn at the very end of the drive, half-hidden behind the house, that agents had searched the other day with Frank's permission.

They'd found nothing there. Nothing in his house, either. But that was to be expected, since Frank had invited them to search. If he was the killer, he'd make sure he had nothing incriminating in his house or barn.

She didn't really want to talk to Frank. He knew she suspected him and he'd never tell her anything. But she wasn't worried about it, either. Frank had already been released from the police station; they didn't have anything on him that would stick. And Rose Bay was the kind of small town where news like whose pin Mandy Toland had when she'd escaped would already have made the rounds.

Frank must know that Jack was the primary suspect now. If Frank was the killer, he'd want to throw that in her face. They'd been looking at him, at Darnell, at Walter, and all along Jack Bullock had been working the case.

Hoping Noreen was here and she wouldn't have to talk to Frank at all, Evelyn strode up the long walkway to the house. If Noreen was inside, Evelyn decided she'd play the Jack card. Tell Noreen they needed her back at the station for her theories on Jack, since the two of them had known each other so long. Then, once she got Noreen alone in her car, she'd ask the real questions.

But the closer she got to the house, the more her hopes dropped. Despite the car in the drive, the house looked dark and empty. The porch lights were off, and there were no lights on in the front of the house, either.

Unlike the last time she'd visited, all the shades were tightly drawn. Evelyn rang the bell, anyway.

When no one came to the door, she rang it again, watching the windows for any sign that someone was checking to see who was there. But everything remained still.

Evelyn sighed, ready to give up, when lightning cracked across the sky and rain pelted her head, the kind of fast storm South Carolina often got in the summer. It showed up fast and hard and moved through the same way.

She was drenched in seconds, but she turned to sprint back to her car. Lightning flashed through the sky again, and all the hair on Evelyn's neck shot to attention.

She reached for her weapon as she spun back around, but her SIG never cleared her holster. The front door of Frank Abbott's house was standing open and a gun was pressed against her forehead, the barrel cold and hard.

Holding the gun was Noreen Abbott.

Twenty-Four

"Noreen." Evelyn gulped, her eyes darting up to where the gun pressed against her forehead.

She could just see the barrel at the edge of her vision. A Glock pistol. It was what most law enforcement officers carried. A solid, capable weapon with no external safety. One that required a mere three and a half pounds of pressure to pull the trigger and fire a bullet.

She knew what a gunshot from that close would do. She'd seen it at crime scenes. It would make a mess. It would blow out a chunk of her head, splatter blood and brain and tissue on the ground somewhere behind her. It would leave a circle of black powder around the spot where most of her forehead used to be, telling the agents who investigated her murder just how close she'd allowed her killer to get.

How the hell had she let Noreen sneak up on her?

It was a rookie mistake. A potentially fatal mistake.

Evelyn lifted her hands slowly, away from her weapon, trying to reassure Noreen that she wasn't a threat.

Noreen's eyes darted around wildly, and her skin was abnormally pale. Her long hair was sopping wet and plastered against her, wind whipping it in her face. Her gun hand trembled just slightly, making the barrel dance against Evelyn's forehead.

She looked terrified, like a woman who'd never held a gun before. Which actually made her more dangerous, because she probably had her finger inside the trigger guard, more likely to shoot accidentally. And judging by the anger that locked her jaw, more likely to shoot at any provocation.

"Noreen, it's me, Evelyn Baine." Obviously Noreen knew it, but maybe Evelyn could convince her she'd come here to talk about Jack. That she had no idea about Noreen's uncle. If she played dumb, as if she thought Noreen hadn't realized it was her when she'd pulled the gun, maybe Noreen would play along.

"I know who you are, Evelyn," Noreen said in a voice that quavered as much as her gun. "And I know why you're here."

"It's about Jack—"

"You think you can fool me?" Noreen demanded.

"No, of course not," Evelyn said evenly, though her heart was slamming against her chest with rib-cracking power. She'd lifted her hands in a surrender gesture less than a minute ago, but they felt numb, as if all the blood had drained out of them. "We found a pin on Mandy Toland. I didn't know if you'd heard. It was Jack's pin. I came by to tell you. And ask for your help."

Noreen bent her head and her voice was suddenly calm as she asked, "You want to try that again?"

Shit, why hadn't she tried to learn more about Noreen when she'd had the chance? Noreen was young; she would've been only a few years out of college if she'd had the chance to go. She was shy, socially awkward, from a broken family. She'd grown up isolated, with too much responsibility and not much of a childhood. She'd grown up and dedicated herself to another purpose—a purpose in law enforcement.

So many of those things Evelyn could say about herself. In a lot of ways, she understood where Noreen had come from, how she felt about herself and the world around her. But did Evelyn dare to say why she was here? Could she talk Noreen into seeing those similarities and accepting another path for herself, a path that didn't involve cleaning up her uncle's mistakes?

The hard barrel of the gun trembled against Evelyn's forehead and rain poured over her, making her cold. Her body wanted to shiver, but she fought it. Any movement could set Noreen off.

"Noreen, I know what a difference you've made at the police station, for Rose Bay, for so many years." It was easy to sound genuine, because Evelyn knew it was the truth. And somehow, she managed not to sound terrified.

Noreen's elbow dropped, the weapon pointing briefly upward, before she locked it again, and the barrel was sealed against Evelyn's forehead. "That doesn't matter now."

Panic raced through her. *Please don't let Noreen be suicidal.* If she thought she was past the point of no return—if she felt that by failing to prevent Brittany's death she was also responsible for it—would one more death on her conscience matter? Would taking Evelyn's life matter to her at all?

Or would she see it as a final chance to protect her uncle? After all, Frank had been released from the station. The cops were chasing down Jack Bullock. Only Evelyn had come back to Frank's house.

So Noreen might be thinking she could get rid of Evelyn and everyone would continue to blame Jack.

Evelyn silently cursed herself. She'd thought Jack's being the prime suspect made her safe here. It hadn't occurred to her that it could actually put her in more danger.

"Noreen, please put down the gun. Let's talk, okay?"

Noreen scowled, backed up just enough to pull the gun slightly away from Evelyn's damp skin. Bracketing the weapon with both hands and keeping it steady on her, Noreen ordered, "Walk."

"Noreen, there's still time to stop this. Right now, you don't have any culpability in what happened."

It wasn't entirely true, if she'd helped bury Brittany and could have prevented Lauren's or Mandy's abductions, but it was close. She'd hidden evidence of a crime, but she hadn't abducted those children herself; she hadn't been the one to kill Brittany. "You can still help yourself here."

"You really think that?" Noreen asked, but there wasn't hope in her voice, just disdain and a hint of smugness Evelyn didn't understand.

"I really do," Evelyn insisted.

Disgust curled Noreen's lips. "You're a fool. Now walk."

The gun shook and now that Noreen had backed up a step, Evelyn could see she'd guessed right; Noreen did have her finger inside the trigger guard.

"Okay," Evelyn said, keeping her hands up. "Can you just take your finger off the trigger?" She gave a little smile, as if this was all a misunderstanding between friends. "You're making me a little nervous."

Noreen's jaw jutted out. "You *should* be a little nervous." She shook her head, her voice turning sad. "You shouldn't have come here, Evelyn. Now toss your weapon over there. Do it slowly. I've worked at a police station for six years now, since I was eighteen. So I know the right way to do it. You try anything stupid and…" She smiled. "Well, like you said, my finger's on the trigger."

Evelyn nodded slowly. "Okay. Sure." Damn it. Noreen was a hell of a lot more committed to protecting her uncle than Evelyn had expected. If she wanted any hope of talking Noreen down, she had to remind her of her equal dedication to the police station.

But just now, even though it went against every self-protective instinct and every FBI mandate, Evelyn carefully pulled her gun from her holster using two fingers and tossed it, low and slow, over to Noreen.

The gun landed in the grass alongside the walkway, slightly behind Noreen.

But instead of bending to pick it up and giving Evelyn the opening she'd been hoping for, Noreen gestured down the walkway with her gun. "Walk."

Evelyn turned, every movement measured, keeping her hands up, until her back was to Noreen. She felt her shoulder blades tense, knowing Noreen was directly behind her, that Glock aimed at the back of her head. She moved one foot, then the other, until they were back on the driveway.

The rain was still coming down hard, rushing into Evelyn's eyes, and she longed to wipe it off her face, but all she could do was try to blink it away. "Where are we going?"

"Toward the field," Noreen said, turning on a flashlight. Dread tightened Evelyn's chest.

She didn't argue. She just stepped off the walkway and into the soggy field. She followed the path Noreen lit up with her flashlight, as everything else got darker and darker. Wispy grass got higher with every step, until it was brushing the tops of her thighs, but Evelyn didn't look back.

Her car was still in the driveway. She didn't want Noreen to notice it, because maybe someone would see it and know she'd come out here.

But as Noreen kept directing her farther and farther into the field, Evelyn realized it wouldn't matter. This field was too much like the one at the end of the road. It extended too far, nothing but waist-high grass that looked like it concealed nothing, but in reality could hide too much.

And damn it, Frank had said searchers had already walked through it, searching for Lauren and Brittany. There'd be no reason for them to come back here for her.

She'd only told Greg that she was going to the crime scene. She hadn't told him about her suspicions of Frank. He would have no reason to think she'd come back here, either.

She tried to strategize, wanting to glance back at Noreen, but she didn't need to. She could sense the gun steady on the back of her head, could hear Noreen sloshing along close behind her as the rain went from a downpour to a drizzle.

"Stop here," Noreen finally said and, as though it was synchronized, the rain stopped, too.

Evelyn halted, slowly turning to face Noreen, her hands still up. Dread pooled in her stomach as she took in the field around her. Grass this high would easily hide a body. At least until the buzzards caught the scent. Certainly long enough for Noreen and Frank to get out of town and disappear.

Was Noreen going to execute her out in this field?

* * *

"How's the search going?" Kyle asked as he strode back into the CARD command post, T.J. on his heels.

Greg and Tomas were right where he'd left them, only the stacks of files looked bigger. They were now surrounded by Carly and her team, each of them running through police files and checking their own resources.

Greg blinked and rubbed his eyes. "Slow. We have a possibility, but it's not as close as I'd like for a solid motivator, so we're still looking."

"I sent the officers who'd finished their shifts home," Tomas said. "Just about everyone else is out running down possible locations for Jack. So far, no one's found him."

"That doesn't mean anything," T.J. said, but his denial was quieter now.

"How did the helicopter flight go?" Greg asked.

"We spotted three additional locations where the old chief might've been building houses." Kyle gestured to T.J., who spread out an aerial map they'd marked. "I'd recommend sending some officers out to those sites in the morning and see what's out there, just in case the chief dug out a root cellar at every one of those locations."

"Or Jack did," Greg said.

"Yeah. Where's Evelyn?"

Greg checked his watch and frowned. "She left right after you did, around eight." He looked over at Tomas. "What time did she call?"

Tomas shrugged, flipping through files again. "Nine-thirty?"

"That was an hour ago." Worry lined Greg's forehead. "She said she was on her way back. Damn it."

"What?" Kyle asked, his own worry surfacing.

"She wanted to see the crime scene again. When she called, she'd also gone to see Jack's wife. What do you want to bet she went back there?" Greg smiled ruefully. "Answering to anyone—and checking in—isn't exactly Evelyn's strong suit."

"You think she's at Jack's house?" T.J. asked. "Why?"

"Evelyn is persistent," Greg replied. "It's possible she took another run at the crime scene, but I doubt it. The officers have all come back from there. It's too dark to do much, especially in the rain. And when I talked to Evelyn, she asked me who was back here. I told her Carly was on her way. Evelyn knew we'd be getting extra help and we didn't really need her on this." Greg glanced at T.J. "Why did you tell Jack's wife about the pin?"

"What?" Tomas blurted out. "Damn it, T.J.!"

T.J. rubbed the back of his neck, looking rueful. "I'm sorry. Jack's been my partner for almost a decade. I just couldn't believe..."

When he trailed off, Kyle got them back on the subject that mattered most to him right now. And that wasn't Jack. "We saw Evelyn's car on that dead-end road by the crime scene as we were bringing the bird back in. Why was she going there at all?"

And why hadn't Greg stopped her? The last time she'd been there, they'd found Brittany's body. And they'd dug up skeletons of older victims, one of whom was almost certainly her childhood friend.

Kyle really didn't like the idea of her going back there by herself. What good would that do?

He knew Evelyn well enough to suspect she'd be drawn back there by guilt. She and Cassie had both been targeted and only Cassie had been taken. Evelyn had lived with that survivor's guilt—hell, she'd *defined* herself by that survivor's guilt—ever since.

Revisiting the scene where Cassie had probably died wasn't going to give her closure. It would only make her feel worse.

Kyle pulled out his phone. "I'm going to see where she is and join her."

Greg shook his head and picked up a cell phone beside him. "She forgot her phone."

Kyle frowned and put his cell back in his pocket, then held his hand out for hers. "All right. I'm going to take a drive. See if I can find her."

Across the table, Greg stood. "Are you getting a bad feeling here, Mac?"

Kyle shook his head. "No, just a sad one."

"Shit." Greg rubbed his eyes. "She said she felt like she was missing something, wanted to take another look at the scene. I wasn't thinking..." He shrugged. "You want me to come?"

"No. Keep on this. I'll call you when I find her."

"Please, Noreen," Evelyn begged. "Don't do this."

In the darkness, Evelyn could barely see Noreen holding the gun straight out, supporting it with both hands. Hands that no longer trembled. She didn't look terrified anymore, either, just resigned.

She clutched the flashlight, underneath her weapon, lighting a circle below Evelyn's eyes. Right where the bullet would hit if she fired.

"Who did you talk to about my uncle?" Noreen demanded.

"My partner," Evelyn said quickly, forcing confidence into her tone. If Noreen thought others knew, thought that killing Evelyn wouldn't really help her, maybe she'd reconsider.

"Your boyfriend or the other profiler?"

"My boyfriend?" Frank had called Kyle her boyfriend, had claimed Darnell had told him that. But had Frank actually been watching her all along?

The idea sent shivers up her arms. She didn't know how long she'd been out here, but everything around her had gone dark. Was Frank watching from the house? Could he see her in the light from Noreen's flashlight?

Had he sent Noreen out here to shoot her? To make her an accomplice in all he'd done, secure her loyalty even more?

Did he plan to observe while Noreen killed her, eighteen years after he'd planned to do it himself?

Fury rushed through her, warming her chilled skin. Evelyn blinked, squinting at Noreen, trying to see her better, to gauge her reaction to what she was about to say. "Are you really going to let your uncle destroy your life the way he destroyed all those little girls' lives?"

The stoicism in Noreen's face cracked, and the Glock trembled, the flashlight drawing a crooked circle around Evelyn's face.

Hoping she was on the right track, Evelyn pressed on. "You can't keep covering for him, protecting him. It's going to come out. All you can do now is pick which side you end up on. And there's only one good choice, Noreen. You know that."

Noreen's lip trembled, and Evelyn hurried to add, "Everyone at the Rose Bay PD cares about you like family. They took you in, gave you a place where you belong."

Noreen frowned, and opened her mouth as if she were about to argue.

Evelyn cut her off. “I understand. I understand what it’s like to grow up without much family. I understand what it’s like to have to turn on family, Noreen. And I understand what it’s like to choose new family, to choose it in a group of law enforcement officers. You did that, Noreen, just like me. You belong there.”

“Not anymore,” Noreen whispered, her voice timid and almost childlike.

“Yes, you do,” Evelyn insisted. “You need to make a choi—”

“No!” Noreen snapped. “Take out your handcuffs, Evelyn, and cuff yourself.”

Evelyn shifted her feet, nervous energy burning through her. She’d been handcuffed by someone who meant her harm once before. Everything in her rebelled against the idea of letting it happen again.

But the fact that Noreen wanted her cuffed gave her hope. Why cuff her if Noreen planned to kill her?

“Now!” Noreen took a fast step closer, lining the weapon up against Evelyn’s forehead. “Don’t make me ask you again.”

The way she said the words was awkward. And ominous. As though they’d been said to her and she was just repeating them.

Was part of Noreen’s determination to protect her uncle because he’d physically or mentally abused her as a child? Her father had gotten sick around the time Cassie had gone missing, which would have made Noreen six years old. Frank had lived with them until Noreen was eighteen. That was a long time for Frank to work on making Noreen dependent on him, through love, loyalty and fear.

Evelyn pulled out her handcuffs. She told herself not

to do it, that Noreen could be immobilizing her for Frank to come and finish what he'd started eighteen years ago.

But if her choices were to have Noreen shoot her now or to put the handcuffs on and live a little longer—long enough to get out of this—there was really no choice.

She snapped the cuffs on first one wrist, then got them around the other, closing them as loosely as possible. She still couldn't get free, but every bit of maneuverability could help.

"Good," Noreen said, relaxing a fraction, lowering the Glock slightly. "Now, open it."

She aimed the flashlight at the ground to the left of Evelyn. Panic fluttered up again. Beside her, flush with the ground, a shiny new wooden board was latched down. Another cellar.

Evelyn lifted her gaze back to Noreen. She tried to keep her face blank, but she didn't need to see Noreen's reaction to know she'd failed.

Was this where Mandy had been kept? What about the other girls? Had they always been in the other cellar or had any of them been here? Had Cassie been here?

Pain burst in her chest, powerful and unexpected. How long had Cassie been locked in one of these cellars?

Had she spent a few days in terror, like Brittany, before her life had been cruelly, unfairly snuffed out? Or had she been trapped under the ground for years, wondering why no one had come for her?

Had Frank visited her every day? Had he hurt her? Or had he left her alone for days at a time, locked in the darkness, not knowing if she was slowly going to starve to death or if he'd come and keep her alive a little longer?

God, which was worse? Having the pain end fast, or living in hope for too many years, until it was finally taken away? And when that day came, would she have welcomed death?

Evelyn didn't realize she was crying until the tears splashed her cuffed hands.

"You're thinking about Cassie," Noreen said softly, sadly.

Evelyn lifted her head, and she swiped at her tears with cuffed hands. "Your uncle killed her! He killed my best friend!" Evelyn raised her hands, toward the cellar door, and Noreen's gun snapped up at the fast movement. "After locking her down there, in the dark! How can you protect him? How could you do that?"

Noreen shook her head. "It wasn't like that. She was supposed to be happy. They were all supposed to be happy."

She sounded so earnest. How long had Frank been brainwashing her with this?

Evelyn had assumed she'd only found out after Brittany died and he'd taken Lauren. But maybe she'd learned much earlier. It seemed unlikely she'd have any clue about what her uncle had been doing before he lived with them, when she was just in kindergarten.

But afterward? Maybe he'd told her a few years after he'd moved in, after she'd learned to depend on him. Then his presence was probably the one thing keeping her home with her father. If Frank had decided to leave, what would have happened to Noreen? Her mother hadn't shown any interest obviously. The relationship with Frank was a powerful bond based on need, and cultivated when she was at an extremely impressionable point in her life.

If that was the case, did Evelyn have any chance of breaking that twisted bond?

Noreen shook her head, as if she could read Evelyn's thoughts. "You don't believe me. But it was only..." She shrugged. "You won't understand."

She pointed the gun at the cellar again, and her voice shifted from the almost childlike plaintive tone it had taken on to a hard, cold demand. "Open it." She pointed the gun at Evelyn again, staying too far away for Evelyn to even consider rushing her. "Do it now."

Evelyn's wet clothes abraded her skin as she leaned down and unlatched the cellar door, pulling hard to open it. There was a metal ladder leading down, just like the last cellar. But this ladder didn't go down as far, and the installation looked sloppier, less sturdy.

It was too dark down in the ground to see anything, but the second she opened the door, a rush of unease prickled Evelyn's skin. Someone was down there. She would've bet her badge on it.

Frank? A new victim?

"Start climbing," Noreen said when she got up again.

"Noreen..."

"Now! Get down there now!" Noreen screeched.

If Frank hadn't owned so much land, if there'd been neighbors anywhere near, they would have heard. But the house next to Frank's on the one side was too far, and on the other side, Evelyn remembered seeing foreclosure signs.

"Noreen," she tried again.

Noreen's whole face hardened, her eyes going flat as she leveled the gun on Evelyn, this time center mass.

Sucking in a breath and praying it wasn't the last one she'd take aboveground, Evelyn grabbed the ladder with her cuffed hands. It was awkward to swing herself down, but she made it, then carefully lowered herself into the cellar. It was tiny, the ceiling so low that if she moved into the main part of the cellar, away from the space taken by the ladder, she'd have to bend down.

Standing on the dirt ground, she blinked, trying to adjust her eyes. It had been dark outside, but here the darkness seemed so much more complete.

Then, in the corner, she sensed something. Someone.

Evelyn squinted, moving a little closer, but not wanting to get too close.

When she realized who it was, she gasped. It was Jack.

He was curled up in the corner, his hands awkwardly in front of him, probably cuffed, as well. He was bleeding from the head and unconscious. At least she hoped he was unconscious and not dead.

She began to move toward him to check his pulse, but something made her turn back and look up at Noreen. Outside, Noreen stood above the cellar, her weapon pointed down, the flashlight shining in Evelyn's eyes.

But then she shifted, and the little bit of light started to disappear. She was closing the door, Evelyn knew, and panic burst out.

"Noreen, please! Noreen, I can help you! Please don't do this!"

The door stopped moving and Evelyn felt a moment's relief, but a moment later the flashlight lit up Noreen's face. On it, Evelyn saw determination, commitment and a hint of sadness.

A slow smile crept across Noreen's face and the door slammed down, plunging Evelyn into total darkness.

Twenty-Five

"Wait!" Evelyn screamed as loudly as she could, not even sure if Noreen would be able to hear her above the ground.

Bits of dirt rained down on her head when the door was slammed, indicating that the cellar wasn't as stable as it should have been. There was plenty of air, but Evelyn's lungs tightened, as though she was in danger of suffocating. The smell of dirt filled her nostrils, along with the tangy, metallic scent of blood. Panic threatened as she imagined being trapped down here.

Would Noreen and Frank cover the door with dirt, leave her and Jack down here to starve? And that was assuming Jack was still alive.

Would her grandma wonder what had happened to her? Just like Cassie's parents had been left to wonder when she'd vanished one night, never to return?

Evelyn choked on a breath that sounded like a sob, then closed her eyes and told herself to calm down.

Screaming at Noreen to open up, Evelyn fumbled to shove her hand in her pocket. Noreen hadn't taken her cuff key. Carefully, Evelyn pulled the key out and shifted it in the palm of her hand until it faced the proper way.

Awkwardly, she fit the key into the lock by feel. The cuff on her right hand clicked open.

Evelyn left the key in the lock. Not bothering to unhook the other cuff, she debated. Check on Jack or try to call Noreen back?

Evelyn made her decision fast. If Noreen intended to leave them down here and never come back, there wouldn't be anything she could do for either of them.

Rushing forward, she grabbed the ladder, yanking herself up. It was only a step until she could pound on the wooden door above her head. She banged her fists against it over and over, leaning on the ladder to maintain her balance.

Hitting the wood until splinters wedged under her skin and her hands felt swollen and raw, Evelyn screamed, "Noreen! This isn't the legacy your sister would have wanted!"

The door swung back so fast and so unexpectedly that Evelyn slipped. She tried to grab the ladder and steady herself, but missed, and fell backward. The tunnel up to the door was narrow, so her head hit the dirt wall behind her. Then she fell straight down to the ground, her legs buckling.

The flashlight bounced over her face, blinding her, and Evelyn squinted. The light continued to dance over her face, in her eyes, and she realized Noreen was descending into the cellar.

Evelyn stayed on the ground, finding her balance, ready to spring upward at Noreen as soon as she had the chance. Hope and fear mingled as Noreen came closer.

The light changed and Evelyn saw the gun pointed at

her again, but Noreen was closer this time. There wasn't much room in this part of the cellar. Not much room for Noreen to keep a safe distance. Not much room for Evelyn to maneuver, either.

She stayed low, waiting for an opening, and did what she did best. She tried to profile Noreen, so she could talk her into making an error.

Noreen had, in fact, made a mistake by moving so close. If Evelyn could get within arm's reach of Noreen, she could disarm her. She just had to time it exactly right, because at this distance, if Noreen got a shot off, there was no way she'd miss.

Adrenaline rocketed through Evelyn's veins. She kept her hands close together, hoping Noreen wouldn't notice they were no longer cuffed. Blinking rapidly, she tried to adjust her eyes, to see past the light shining on her and bathing Noreen in darkness.

"My sister was killed by my mom's neglect," Noreen said, her voice quavering with emotion.

Evelyn didn't have to see her to know there were tears running down Noreen's face. She had to tread carefully here. She kept her voice soft and steady as she said, "Your uncle killed girls, too, Noreen. Girls your sister's age. Some of them left behind siblings, too. Siblings who miss them. Friends who miss them, even now."

The flashlight shook in Noreen's hand, and Evelyn could finally see her face. She was crying. Slow, silent tears that tracked down a face already drenched from the rain. There was sadness in her eyes, but something else, too. Something that made warning bells jingle in Evelyn's head. Something that looked a little too much like madness.

How had she missed this all those times she'd talked to Noreen at the station? And when Noreen had called her?

Noreen had called her from the search parties. Noreen had been the one to put her on to Darnell. And Darnell had said he'd received a text sending him to the field where Lauren was found.

"It was you who texted Darnell, wasn't it?" It made sense; Noreen worked with police officers. She'd probably known how to play it, and there was already a naive, almost childish quality about her. Evelyn could see her convincing Darnell she was a twelve-year-old, foolish enough to meet a stranger in a deserted area.

"You texted him just before you called me. You wanted Lauren to be found." Hope shot forward again, the hope that Noreen really did want a way out of this. "You were trying to prevent the same thing from happening to Lauren that happened to Brittany. You were trying to save her, weren't you, Noreen?"

Noreen shuffled her feet, her shoulders stooped, her gaze dropping. "She wasn't right. But I didn't want her to have to die."

Evelyn tried to keep all reaction off her face, as if she'd known that from the moment she'd come to Frank's house to talk to Noreen.

As Noreen frowned at the ground, Evelyn moved a fraction. She angled slowly, carefully, into a better position to use her calf muscles to push herself up and out at Noreen like a sprinter taking off for a big race. She just needed to keep Noreen talking, get her to move the gun off to the side a little more in the tight space.

"You did a good thing, Noreen," Evelyn said, still in the same soft, reassuring tone. "You saved that little girl's life."

Noreen's gaze drifted past her, into the darkness of the cellar. Her body language seemed to change as she collapsed into herself, her chin lowering submissively. Her voice seemed to change, too, into something higher-pitched and childish as she said, "They always went away. He always made them go away."

Evelyn's heartbeat seemed to slow to a stop, then continued at double speed. *Always?* Had she seen the girls Frank had abducted, back when she was six years old?

What a horrible thing for a child to witness, she thought sadly. Had she even known what was going on back then? Maybe her father had actually been sick earlier than anyone had realized. Maybe Frank had been involved sooner than anyone had known.

Had Noreen been in the cellar eighteen years ago? A wrenching pain joined the sadness. Had she met Cassie down in a cellar?

The pain spread, immobilizing her. Had she seen Cassie die?

She needed to keep talking, to keep Noreen talking, but Evelyn's mouth felt glued shut as memories of Cassie filled her mind. Then the images fled and all she could see was a small, bare skeleton in a box in the ground.

Evelyn gagged, losing her equilibrium. She braced one hand on the ground and then looked up at Noreen.

Her distraction had cost her. Noreen seemed confused, but she'd squared the gun on Evelyn again.

Then Noreen's chin jutted out and her gaze focused on Evelyn's hand. Her uncuffed hand.

Noreen lifted an eyebrow. "I forgot to take your handcuff key." Noreen nodded to herself, as though she were making a mental note for the future—in case she needed to abduct some other law enforcement officer.

"He never should've taken them away." Evelyn forced out the words, her voice strangled as she tried to get Noreen to focus elsewhere. With the gun pointed at her, if Noreen told her to recuff herself and toss over the key, she'd have to do it.

But her plan seemed to work, because sadness overtook Noreen's face again at her words.

"They were supposed to be my new sister," Noreen said. "Each one he brought, he told me she'd be my big sister now that Peggy was gone." She shook her head, her hair dancing around her shoulders, her soggy clothes making her look smaller and younger than her twenty-four years.

This girl had never had a chance.

The thought went through Evelyn's head, but she ruthlessly pushed it out. Eighteen years ago, Noreen might not have had a choice, but she did now. She could have turned in her uncle as soon as he started abducting children again. She could have refused to help him.

"Your uncle was wrong—"

"No, not Uncle Frank."

"What?"

"It was my father. It was my father who brought them to me."

She wasn't here.

Kyle idled at the edge of the field where they'd found the cellar. His headlights cut a path through the tall grass, mingling with the large portable lights the police had left up at the crime scene. The yellow crime scene tape fluttered in the wind, and fog lifted off the ground.

This was the last place he'd seen Evelyn's car, when

he'd been flying over this road. But it wasn't at the crime scene.

He'd swung by Jack's house on his way over, just in case Evelyn was there and needed backup, but he'd only found Jack's wife, angry and uncooperative.

Where the hell was Evelyn?

The worry over her emotional well-being changed to a deeper concern. Was she in danger?

Kyle swung his car around, heading back the way he'd come, down the long, winding dirt road. The house closest to Jack's father's property had boarded-up windows and a for sale by bank sign in the front yard. The house one door down looked familiar.

Kyle slowed to a stop, trying to figure out why. Then he recognized it. He'd seen it in a picture at the police station. Greg had flipped past the picture, saying officers had walked through the house and barn on his and Evelyn's recommendation. Frank Abbott's house.

They'd let Frank go, but hadn't one hundred percent ruled him out.

He'd seemed gruff but otherwise normal when Kyle had met him the first day he'd helped with the search parties. But the very fact that he'd been at those search parties could be a sign of guilt.

Had Evelyn reconsidered his status as a suspect while she was out here?

Kyle turned into the drive, coasting slowly toward the house. The porch lights were out and the house was dark. An old beater vehicle sat at the top of the drive.

He sighed and put the car in reverse when he noticed the tire tracks in the mud skirting around the beater toward the barn. It was probably nothing, but his investigative instincts were humming just enough to make him put the car in Park and get out.

Everything was dark and silent, but Kyle pulled out his flashlight and headed for the house. He walked up the long drive and knocked on the door, but there was no answer.

With one last pounding for good measure, Kyle turned back the way he'd come. He'd go take a peek in the barn. If he saw nothing, he'd call Greg and the Rose Bay PD for backup.

Evelyn stared stupidly at Noreen. "Your father? But he's dead." Wasn't he?

"He was alive eighteen years ago," Noreen said, squaring her shoulders, looking more like the young woman Evelyn was used to seeing at the police station.

She was taller than Evelyn, and standing in the opening of the cellar, her head was only a few inches below the open door. She was also bigger than Evelyn, and there wasn't a lot of room in the tunnel area.

It meant Evelyn was close. Just not close enough.

"My mom let Peggy die," Noreen insisted. "She took Peggy away from my dad and then let her die. He said thank goodness he'd gotten to at least keep me safe." A fierceness entered her tone when she added, "And he said he wasn't going to let other parents do that to their kids."

The space beside the ladder was cramped, and Evelyn was hunched partially underneath, where the ceiling lowered. Behind her, she sensed Jack, but he wasn't making a sound. He might already be dead.

"Noreen, you know that wasn't his only motivation," Evelyn said, trying to shift her weight into position to strike.

Noreen steadied her gun, stepping back against the ladder, which made a chunk of dirt break off the wall and fall at her feet. "Don't do it, Evelyn."

"My feet fell asleep." It was partially true.

"Too bad," Noreen said nervously as she tightened her hold on the gun.

Evelyn went still, her legs bunched awkwardly underneath her. "Your father was looking for a replacement back then. And now your uncle is doing the same thing."

Was he, though? Or did Frank have a different motive? She and Greg had been hesitant to name Frank as a suspect, since he hadn't grown up with Noreen's sister. But maybe Frank was after something different than his brother, just using the same methods because Earl had never been caught.

She'd dismissed the copycat theory so completely and she cursed herself for it now. And yet everything about the crimes had been so similar, down to the notes written on the very same paper. "Did your uncle help with the original abductions?"

She'd been so sure there was only one person orchestrating the abductions, but it would explain how Frank was doing everything so similarly now.

Noreen shook her head and answered, almost conversationally, "Uncle Frank didn't know anything about them. Eighteen years ago, he spent almost every day with my dad. They even had a business together. Hell, my dad used the work van for the abductions and Frank didn't have a clue."

"After all that time, what made him decide to pick up where your dad left off?"

Doubt whirled through her as she asked the question. How was she going to talk Noreen into letting her go if she'd been so far off in her profile? If she hadn't figured out Frank's true motivation?

And how had she been so wrong? Going over the behavioral evidence in her head, it still didn't quite stack up. Was Noreen lying to her? Blaming a dead man instead of admitting her uncle had been the killer all along?

But how could Noreen possibly think that would help her? Even if she hadn't decided to lock Evelyn underground to keep her silent, Earl Abbott was dead. If Noreen was telling the truth about her father—and Evelyn suspected she was—that still left Frank on the hook for the recent abductions.

"Uncle Frank is an idiot," Noreen spat.

Unease filled Evelyn. Noreen's statement should have been a sign that she was finally seeing Evelyn's side, that she'd turn on her uncle. But she was leaning against the ladder, seeming completely unconcerned about being underground. In fact, she looked almost comfortable. And the hand pointing the gun at Evelyn was steady.

"My dad was an idiot, too," Noreen said quietly, as if she was afraid someone would hear her say it. "He shouldn't have done what he did. He shouldn't have made them leave. If he'd given them more time..."

"What, Noreen?"

"If he'd given them more time, it would have worked."

"What would have worked?"

Noreen's gaze locked on hers, her eyes distant and unfocused. "They would have adjusted. They would have believed they were whoever he said they were—and he said they were Peggy. I told them. I told them it would be better for them to just say what he wanted."

She frowned down at the ground. "They were older than me and I knew it." With a sudden burst of anger, she swung the gun up and down wildly. "Why didn't they just do what he wanted?"

Evelyn tried to harden herself against the pain. *Ah, Cassie. You resisted, didn't you? Held on to your identity no matter what. And it got you killed.*

The thought made tears sting her eyes, but gladness swelled in her heart. She was proud of the little girl she'd known so long ago.

"That's called courage," Evelyn said firmly, even though she knew she shouldn't.

Noreen scowled at her. "If he'd been able to wait longer, they would've come around. They all would have eventually. He got rid of them because they weren't Peggy. But if they'd *tried* to be Peggy, like he'd wanted, maybe he would've let them stay." Her voice turned plaintive, wistful. "So he wouldn't have to try again with someone else."

"What about me?" Evelyn asked, because she suddenly had to know.

"Why did he want two?" Noreen shrugged. "Maybe to double his chances of finding a sister for me. He'd never tried to take two before."

"No. Why didn't your dad come back for me? What happened that night?" Was that when Frank had discovered the truth?

"He got sick." Noreen's gun hand lowered, her expression sad. "He had his first stroke that night. He recovered mostly from that one, but with the CADASIL, he knew he was on a downward slide. His doctor had told him years ago, with all his awful migraines. The doctor hadn't expected him to function so well as long as he did."

She sighed. "Then, suddenly, he couldn't do it anymore. He needed help with even everyday things. And that night, he definitely couldn't make it up that tree to get you. He barely made it back home with your friend."

Shivers slid along Evelyn's skin as she realized how much Earl Abbott had told his six-year-old daughter. So much that he'd actually told her he'd planned to scale the live oak tree right outside Evelyn's room to abduct her.

What about Cassie? What happened to Cassie? sat on Evelyn's tongue, but she couldn't seem to form the words. In her heart, she knew. But she was afraid to hear it confirmed.

Maybe that was when Frank had gotten involved. Evelyn knew he'd had to change his whole life to look after his brother, even moved in with them a few years later. But maybe that night, when Earl had barely managed to get Cassie to the house, maybe he'd called Frank.

And Frank, instead of calling the police, had taken her down to the cellar like his brother had asked.

Could it be? Then Frank had become occupied with running his and Earl's business all by himself, caring for his brother, paying his bills.

Perhaps that day with Cassie had awakened something buried in him, the way she'd thought finding Charlotte Novak might have awakened something in Darnell if he wasn't her actual killer. What if Frank had resisted for a while? Once free of his responsibilities to his brother, maybe he'd started feeling the lure, the desire, to take over where Earl had left off.

He'd moved out of his brother's house six years earlier, but Earl had died only last year. That certainly could have been the trigger that set Frank off. Maybe that was when he'd started planning, studying what his brother had done and preparing to resume Earl's activities.

The nerves on the back of Evelyn's neck tingled, telling her she was on the right track.

"My dad would bring them to the house," Noreen continued, seeming almost relieved to have someone to finally share it with. "He'd let me play with them. Each time, he'd tell me this one would be my big sister. He'd let me get to know them. They couldn't stay at the house all the time, of course. Only when he was there. When he had to work, and at night, they had to go in the cellar."

A light came into Noreen's eyes, a flicker of happiness. "Sometimes, he'd let me go down there with them so they wouldn't be lonely."

A feeling of disgust overwhelmed Evelyn. Earl Abbott had abducted girls to make up for one daughter dying, then locked his remaining daughter down in the ground along with his victims?

No wonder Noreen was so damaged. It was astonishing that she'd managed to lead any kind of normal life, hold down a job at the police station.

She compartmentalized, Evelyn realized. It worked for many children who grew up with domestic abuse. Hell, Evelyn knew she did it herself. Why not Noreen, too? The people around her would see a socially awkward woman who didn't allow anyone to get too close, and they'd see the hard worker. But they wouldn't see beneath that…

They wouldn't see that under the timid, awkward administrative assistant was someone who'd never fully grown up. Part of her was still a small child, still hoping for a sister.

That was why she was so determined to protect Frank.

It wasn't really about love or loyalty, or even fear, as Evelyn had assumed. It was because this was what Noreen had always known with her father. But also because she still wanted what her father had promised her all those years ago—a replacement for the big sister she'd lost.

"Did you draw the picture we found in the cellar at the old Bullock property?" Evelyn asked.

Noreen grinned. "Yes! I did it for Peggy. So she'd like her room better. So she'd do what he asked and want to stay. It took me weeks to convince my dad to let me draw it for her. He didn't like the cellar. For him, it was just..."

Noreen frowned, shaking her head as though she was having an internal fight about which reality to believe. "The cellar was just because of the police. And that's where he took the girls later, when he decided he didn't want them."

Evelyn hesitated, trying to figure out the best direction to follow. Whichever victim Noreen had made the picture for originally, she was so invested in her fantasy she'd called the girl by her sister's name, and called the cellar her bedroom.

Evelyn could try to force her to see reality, hoping she'd choose the path of law enforcement she'd grown up to embrace. Or she could let her continue with her fantasy, and try to make her understand that letting Frank escape would mean he was taking Peggy away from her, over and over.

It was clear that Frank had come to the same conclusion Evelyn had. That Noreen was still part child, still longing for a big sister. And he'd seen how he could use that longing. He could use Noreen, use her connections at the police station to get away with it, and to cover it up if anyone got too close.

But how did Evelyn get Noreen to break free now?

Should she force her to break with the fantasy she'd lived most of her life? Or push her deeper into that fantasy?

Either approach was a risk. For now, Evelyn decided to put off the decision, see if she could get Noreen to relax her white-knuckled grip on the Glock another way.

"Why did he put the cellar on the police chief's property?"

Noreen laughed, a high-pitched giggle that sounded like a child's laughter. "Jack's father built it! Isn't that great? He was going to use it as a root cellar. My dad just found it. He knew the chief would never go back there after that house fell down. So it was perfect! What better place to hide them? No one would ever look on the chief's property."

She leaned toward Evelyn. Another chunk of wet dirt fell from the wall behind her as Noreen added in a stage whisper, "If he thought the police were getting too close, he was going to frame Chief Bullock."

Evelyn tried to keep the skepticism off her face. Did Earl Abbott really think that would've worked?

"You thought it was Jack," Noreen said petulantly, as though she could read Evelyn's mind.

They'd all believed it was Jack. A well-placed pin, a cellar on Jack's land. And then Jack going missing at exactly the right time. "Did you steal Jack's pin?"

"That was pretty easy," Noreen said, sounding proud of herself, and sounding more like the adult Evelyn was used to hearing at the police station.

It made her nervous how fluidly Noreen was shifting between the two. The adult who worked with the cops and the child who'd watched first her dad and then her uncle abduct young girls.

"Did you lure him out here, too, so your uncle could

knock him out and drag him down here?" At least she hoped he was only unconscious. The longer she talked without hearing any movement at all, the more concerned she became that Jack would never move again.

Noreen rolled her eyes. "Jeez, Evelyn. Here I am, doing all this work to make sure everything doesn't come out. And I shouldn't even have bothered. You're just like Jack. You don't have a clue, do you?"

Dread rose up in Evelyn's chest. "You led the police to Lauren. You probably arranged it so Mandy could escape, didn't you? To protect them?"

Noreen nodded somberly. "I did. They knew what would happen if they told on me, but I didn't want either of them to get hurt. When Brittany didn't work out…" She shuddered.

"Brittany's death was an accident, right?"

Tears welled up in Noreen's eyes. "Yes. And then with Lauren and Mandy, I just knew. I knew they weren't going to work, either. They wouldn't play along. And I didn't want anything to happen to them."

"What would have happened to them?" Evelyn pressed.

"I might have hurt them," Noreen said, her voice hardly more than a whisper. She met Evelyn's gaze, her eyes huge and regretful. "The way I hurt Brittany. I didn't mean for her to die."

Noreen hung her head. "I just wanted my sister."

Understanding and a brand-new fear darted through Evelyn. "You're the one who took over where your dad left off. You're the Nursery Rhyme Killer now, aren't you, Noreen?"

Twenty-Six

The barn had no windows.

Kyle frowned as he finished walking around it. There was no way to see inside. As he started to head back to the drive, a squishing sound caught his attention. Footsteps in the mud.

Kyle pulled his weapon, simultaneously lifting his flashlight, revealing Frank Abbott's face. Kyle quickly ran the flashlight down Frank's button-up, worn loosely over a T-shirt, to his hands. Empty.

"What are you doing here?" Frank asked.

Kyle strode closer, until he was a foot away from Frank. Something about Frank's tone set off Kyle's internal warning system, so he didn't holster his weapon.

"Can you put that away?" Frank asked, and Kyle realized what was making him suspicious.

Frank seemed too unconcerned. Too unsurprised.

"Why are you here, anyway?"

"I'm looking for Evelyn Baine," Kyle replied, still holding his Glock loosely at his side. He kept his tone conversational, too, but looked at him in a way he'd perfected before HRT, when he'd worked counterterror. A warning that Frank didn't want to find out what would happen if he lied. "Do we need to have a conversation about the penalties for harming a federal agent?"

Frank scowled, pasting an unimpressed expression on his face. But the eyes gave him away. They widened, then darted nervously to the gun before squinting back at Kyle.

"Haven't seen her," Frank said.

Kyle took a step closer, studying Frank intently. "You sure about that?"

Frank nodded, held his hands up. "Yeah, positive. I haven't seen her since I left the station."

He was hiding something, Kyle could tell, but he was pretty sure it wasn't about Evelyn. He was a dead end.

Just to be sure, Kyle asked, "Whose car is in your drive?"

Frank shuffled his feet. "My niece. She stopped by to check on me. She was exhausted, so I told her to sleep in the guest room and go home tomorrow."

"Where's your car?"

"In the barn."

Kyle studied him, waiting for Frank to shuffle nervously again, but he didn't. "I want to talk to your niece."

"She worked forty hours straight! She's sleeping and I'm not waking her," Frank said.

"She might know where Evelyn is."

"She's been here for hours. After everything that girl's been through, she deserves a little peace."

"What has she been through?"

Frank folded his arms over his chest. "She's worked this case harder than anyone, that's what I mean."

"No, it isn't."

"You're a fed. You must have heard the story. You

know why she got a job at the police station. How the old police chief felt sorry for her, taking care of her dad for so many years. Last year, she had to foreclose on his house, and now she's got to work a case like this!"

Kyle pictured the for sale by bank sign on the house next to the Bullock field. "She lived next door to you?"

Frank looked at his feet. "Yes, until she got buried in his debt and had to get an apartment. Now, she lives right by the police station, as if she doesn't take work home often enough. Listen, I don't know where Evelyn is. But she's not here."

"Can I search the house?"

"Fine, you can go in," Frank ground out. "But you're staying out of my spare bedroom. You can't wake my niece."

Kyle nodded. He'd heard from Greg how Frank had let officers search his home and barn before. His acceptance was too immediate, his expression too nonchalant. Evelyn wasn't in there.

"Cops will be here in five minutes," he told Frank, then holstered his Glock and started to turn toward his car. He'd call them on the road and have them search the house, just in case.

Frank also started to turn. As he did, the button-up shirt caught in a gust of wind and blew open, uncovering a weapon tucked in his waistband. A SIG.

Kyle began to pivot back, but Frank moved fast, leaping toward him. He had twenty years on Kyle, but plenty of upper-body muscle, and he hit like a pro football player.

The tackle put Kyle on the ground and Frank reached for the SIG.

That was his second mistake. His first mistake was tackling an HRT agent.

Kyle shifted his weight fast, knocking Frank off him and off balance. Quickly, he grabbed Frank's gun hand, twisting hard.

Frank yelped and the gun dropped from his hand.

Keeping the pressure on Frank's wrist—obviously broken—Kyle got a knee underneath him and turned Frank until the man was lying on his back.

Then Kyle stood, twisting Frank's arm the other way and flipping him onto his stomach. "Where the hell is Evelyn?"

"I don't know." Frank swore into the mud.

Kyle got his handcuffs out of their case and snapped them on Frank's broken wrist, then onto the other one. "You had her weapon."

"No, I didn't," Frank said, but his voice shook. From pain or because he was lying, Kyle couldn't tell. But as Kyle tucked the weapon into his waistband, he knew he was right. The weapon was a SIG Sauer P228. Most FBI agents carried Glocks, but not Evelyn. She liked the SIG.

Sure, Frank could own one, too. However, he was a big guy and the P228 was a weapon preferred by female agents because it was smaller than the normal P226.

"Where is she?"

"I don't know," Frank insisted again.

So, Kyle levered Frank to his feet, pulling him up by his arms, which would be horribly painful on his newly broken wrist.

"I don't know," Frank said a third time, his voice high-pitched with pain.

Kyle spun the man around.

There were tears shimmering in Frank's eyes, but Kyle could see honesty there, too. He truly didn't know where she was.

"I don't like that name," Noreen pouted. "My father didn't like it, either. The nursery rhymes were supposed to explain everything. He always told me they should've called him the Nursery Rhyme Savior."

Panic fluttered in Evelyn's stomach, mingled with anger. Anger at herself for having profiled the case so incorrectly. Of every case she'd ever had, this was the one that had defined her whole life. And she'd screwed it up!

If she died down here, would Noreen get away? Would anyone ever really know what had happened to Cassie and all the other girls?

The anger tightened all her muscles. Her hands shook with the sudden, overpowering need to rush Noreen.

It was one thing when she'd thought of Noreen as a manipulated, unwilling accomplice. A damaged girl who'd been under the thumb of first her psychotic father and then, later, her equally criminal uncle.

But that wasn't the truth at all. The truth was, Noreen was as culpable as her father. She'd known what he was doing eighteen years ago. And instead of telling anyone, she'd stayed silent. Then she'd done exactly the same thing to three other girls once she grew up.

The fury spread, until her chest hurt and she felt sick. Until she knew her hatred blasted from her eyes.

"Don't look at me like that, Evelyn," Noreen said softly, her little-girl voice back. "If their parents had been watching like they should have, I never could've taken any of them. It's their fault, those awful parents! Not mine. They deserved to be punished."

Anger flashed across Noreen's face. "None of them deserved their daughters back. But maybe now, they'll learn. Maybe they'll take care of those girls like they should."

How delusional was Noreen? Evelyn bit her tongue to keep the question in. It didn't matter what Noreen really believed and what she was just saying to rationalize her crimes. All that mattered was getting out of this cellar so Evelyn could make sure Noreen was locked up for the rest of her life.

It wouldn't be down in a pitch-black cellar, never knowing if anyone would return for her or if she'd slowly starve to death in the dark. Never knowing what would happen when that cellar door opened, what pain or torture was coming. Never knowing if she'd ever see her family again—or knowing if she'd live to see another day.

That was what Noreen deserved, but Evelyn would have to settle for behind bars or, more likely, a psychiatric facility. Her gaze locked on Noreen's gun and she started breathing faster, her hands twitching with the desire to lunge for it. To use it.

"Don't even think about it," Noreen snarled. It was as if a switch had flipped and she was back in the persona she usually showed the world, only less timid, less tentative. "You try to take this gun and I'll pull the trigger." She gestured vaguely toward the back of the cellar. "Jack taught me how to shoot. I'm good."

"Then how can you do this to him?" Evelyn asked, willing her heart rate back to normal, trying to ease the pain and anger eating at her.

Noreen shrugged. "He came here looking for Frank. I could see it in his eyes when he showed up this morning. He knew he'd missed something. He just couldn't put his finger on what it was. I had to take care of him before he figured it out and realized it wasn't my uncle."

"How did you get him down here?" Had Frank known? Had Frank helped? How had Noreen lugged Jack down here? He was much bigger than she was. There was no way she'd dragged him down that ladder.

Noreen giggled again. "I played all innocent, started crying. I told him I'd found something on my uncle's property. I took him out here to see and acted scared to go down. He went in first, gun out, looking for anyone inside. I hit him over the head." Regret appeared briefly on Noreen's face, then she blinked it away. "I had to do it."

"That's when you decided to frame him?"

"No. I decided that a while ago." She scowled at Evelyn. "That was *your* fault. You were getting too close. I tried to get rid of you."

"*You* shot at me?"

"Yeah. I missed, but don't let that fool you. The window messed me up, threw off my shot. At the range, I hit the bull's-eye every time."

Better get off the topic of guns. Evelyn asked quickly, "What does that have to do with Jack?"

"I was just going to try to get rid of you again, because no one else was getting close. No one else had a clue. But Jack called me that night as I was driving home, with questions about the case, and he said you two had talked about my sister. I was worried that if you kept digging, eventually you'd see the truth. Or at least I thought you would. Guess I overestimated you."

Evelyn gritted her teeth, forced herself not to snap back. It was true. She *had* missed this. If Noreen hadn't held a gun on her, would she ever have realized the truth?

She felt sick with doubt. Doubt at the one thing in her life she was most certain of—her ability as a profiler.

Maybe she wasn't the profiler she'd believed she was. Maybe Dan had been right from the beginning and a more experienced profiler had been needed here. Had her insistence on coming to Rose Bay destroyed the case? If Noreen got away with everything, it would be all her fault.

"I was going to try again," Noreen repeated. "But I knew I had to wait until dark. So, in the meantime, I had to stay a step ahead of you. I didn't want to tell you my sister was dead, but I sure as hell didn't want you figuring it out on your own. And I knew I could make you think it was my uncle." She smiled. "Which you did."

The smile fell. "I thought that would buy me time and I could follow you back to the hotel again, wait until you got out of your car. Then that other profiler showed up, and I realized I had to come up with a new plan. Jack was the obvious choice. My dad was going to frame his dad. So I picked Jack. It just made sense, since the cellar was on his land now."

Noreen sighed. "It's too bad, really, because Jack's always been nice to me. But I have to protect the secret. There are still girls to save." Her tone grew wistful. "I'll have to look for Peggy somewhere else now."

"That'll draw attention to you, leaving as soon as the abductions stop," Evelyn said.

Noreen smiled, a tight, disturbing smile. "Oh, I'll wait until Jack is found. Everyone knew we were friends. I'll claim it's too much for me to stay now. I'll go somewhere else. I'll have to stop leaving the notes, though." She glanced up. "Sorry, Dad."

Evelyn got ready to lunge, but Noreen's gaze was back on her too fast.

Keep her talking, Evelyn told herself as suspicion started to show in Noreen's eyes.

Evelyn asked the first question she could think of. "Did your dad train you for this?"

Noreen stared at her, lips stretching in a flat smile. "I know what you're doing, Evelyn." She waved the gun in a circle. "But I haven't been able to talk about this, and it's nice to finally tell someone. It seems right that it's you."

Evelyn felt herself gape at Noreen.

"It does," Noreen said. "You searched so hard for Cassie. It only seems fair that you should know before… Well, anyway, no, my dad didn't train me. After he got sick, he didn't talk about it at all. I knew he was secretly hoping he'd get better and be able to bring me another sister, but he never did."

She gave a heavy sigh. "He died feeling like he'd failed me. And I was mad at him for years, for not letting me keep one of the girls he'd brought me before. For leaving me all alone. And when I lost his house…"

She broke off on a sob, her gun hand shaking, then stiffened and continued. "But it turned out to be okay, because when I was cleaning out the house, it just hit me what I needed to do. I realized it didn't have to be over, especially when I packed up his old paper and his computer. And a couple of months ago, when you called and requested the case file, I was the one who dug it out."

Evelyn felt the blood drain from her face. Had *she* pushed Noreen into taking that final step?

"I'd been trying to find a legitimate way to go through the notes again. I have access to the evidence, of course, but we do keep logs. And I didn't want my name on them without a reason." She smiled wistfully. "But that gave me the time to really memorize them all, make sure I could imitate everything, make sure I remembered it all." Noreen's eyes grew unfocused, as if she were looking into the past.

Trying to push back the guilt, Evelyn moved subtly, trying to work out the kinks in her legs, which had started to tingle from being awkwardly folded for so long.

"Not having the house was a challenge, though. Especially after I decided to give up the Bullock cellar." She frowned, focusing on Evelyn again too soon. "I couldn't bring the girls to my apartment, obviously. And then when I led Darnell to the Bullock cellar, I had to dig this one out."

As she spoke, a sprinkle of wet dirt fell from the ceiling. Noreen frowned. "I'm not as good at this. I need practice. And this one's not ideal, since it's on Uncle Frank's land."

"He knows, doesn't he?"

"No. He's so busy lately, he's hardly home. And by the time I had to come over here, the police had ruled out his property, since they'd searched it." She smiled, calculation in her eyes. "Thanks for that."

"You don't actually think you're going to get away with this?"

"Of course I am. Jack will take the fall. And if not, well, you and the other profiler already suspected my uncle..."

"You're going to frame your own uncle?"

"It's not my first choice," Noreen whined.

"And that's it?" Evelyn demanded. "You work in a police station! You never even considered how wrong this was?"

Noreen shook her head, looking sad. "You still don't understand. Cassie was better off with us."

Fury overtook Evelyn so fast she didn't realize her hands were clenched and she was standing up until she hit her head on the low ceiling. A big chunk of dirt broke off and covered her hair.

Noreen pulled her gun closer to her chest, keeping the aim steady on Evelyn. "I've made you mad. But it's true. If you thought about it, you'd see. But we don't have time for that."

Evelyn felt a spurt of panic. She was in a horrible position to rush Noreen. There was zero chance she wouldn't get killed if she did it now.

Still, if Noreen was about to shoot, there was no other option. She tensed her calf muscles, ready to leap forward and to the side.

"I guess I should thank you," Noreen said. Her finger was still against the trigger, but it wasn't moving. "I was originally going to have Jack simply disappear, so everyone would assume he'd gone to ground. But that would keep you looking. I needed you, too. You coming here made my plan so much easier. I thought I was going to have to call you again, try to get you out here by yourself."

"If you're planning to make it look like I shot Jack and then got hit myself, you should have kept my gun," Evelyn said, sounding way more calm than she'd expected.

But Noreen just smiled. "That's not the plan." Noreen gestured to the back of the cellar, still eerily silent. "This is Jack's weapon. It's going to be a murder-suicide, Evelyn. Jack knew he was about to get caught, so he killed you, and then he killed himself."

Noreen straightened her arms, lifting the gun into position.

"Jack's injured!" Evelyn burst out.

Noreen rolled her eyes. "You seem like the type to fight back, Evelyn. You attacked him before he shot you." She sighed. "It's too bad my dad got sick when he did."

Her finger started to move on the trigger as she added, "I think you and I could have been good sisters."

Kyle shifted his weight, lifting Frank's cuffed hands higher in the air behind him.

Frank shrieked. His broken wrist had to be hurting like hell.

Normally, Kyle wouldn't resort to this kind of tactic, although technically he wasn't doing anything wrong. But even if Frank didn't know precisely where Evelyn was, he knew something.

"Where is she?" Kyle growled.

Frank shook his head.

Kyle yanked on Frank's arms so his left one was lifted higher, making the handcuffs pull downward on his broken wrist.

"Fuck!" Frank shouted. "I don't know where she is!"

"What *do* you know?" Kyle demanded, dropping Frank's arms so the man fell back on his heels.

"You going to beat me to death if I don't tell you?" Frank sneered at Kyle even as a stream of water made a path from his eyes to his chin.

Kyle took an aggressive step forward. He put as much intensity into his gaze and his voice as he could. "You have no idea what I'll do for this woman."

Frank jerked backward. He blinked the tears away,

and Kyle saw sadness in his eyes. "I swear, I didn't know anything about it," he whispered.

"*What* didn't you know about?" Kyle pressed, impatient. Where the *hell* was Evelyn?

Frank sighed, his head dropping. "I never suspected either of them until recently. I didn't want to believe it, but..."

"Damn it, Frank! Spit it out."

"She was visiting so much lately. I fell asleep on the couch tonight, and when I woke up I looked outside and saw a flashlight." He cringed as he finally met Kyle's gaze. "She's my only family."

Noreen Abbott.

"Damn it," Kyle muttered again. He'd seen the case notes when he'd helped out earlier today. No one had ever suspected a woman. "Where were they going? Where was Noreen taking Evelyn?"

Frank shook his head. "I honestly couldn't tell you. I saw Evelyn's car in the drive and I suddenly knew." He squeezed his eyes shut. "Those crap rental cars. I can hot-wire anything older like that. I put it in the barn. I was just... I didn't know what else to do but try to protect her." His eyes opened and the tears started flowing fast. "She's all I have left. I just couldn't turn her in."

Kyle reached for his phone. He needed to get officers back to the Bullock property now. Those other collapsed structures he'd seen from the air were all potential spots Noreen could have taken Evelyn.

They couldn't wait for morning.

"Don't move," Kyle warned Frank, and called Greg. As soon as his friend answered, Kyle told him, "I'm at Frank Abbott's house and I need backup right now. Noreen Abbott is the killer. And she's got Evelyn."

* * *

This was it.

Noreen was smiling her creepy, weirdly childish smile as her finger moved against the trigger.

Evelyn didn't hesitate. She leaped toward Noreen, shifting to the right as much as possible. Her goal was to throw Noreen off balance, to get alongside her fast, so the gun wouldn't be pointing at her.

They were so close it was difficult to get any momentum, but she hit Noreen as hard as she could, slamming her into the ladder. Dirt crumbled around them, falling off the wall.

Noreen grunted as her right elbow buckled and the gun angled down and left. It went off, the sound deafening in the small space.

Ears ringing, Evelyn swung a fist up toward Noreen's rib cage.

But Noreen recovered a lot faster than she'd expected, twisting sideways, and Evelyn's fist smashed into the metal ladder instead. Pain darted from her knuckles up to her elbow.

And then Noreen was swinging the gun back toward her.

Evelyn twisted, too, grabbing Noreen's right hand at the elbow and pinching hard, trying to make her nerves fail and her fingers open.

But the gun didn't drop. Jack must have taught Noreen defensive techniques, because she stepped backward and tried to jab her fingers into Evelyn's eye. When Evelyn jerked away, Noreen raked her hand across Evelyn's damaged cheek instead, drawing blood.

Her face stinging, Evelyn pounded her fist into the junction between Noreen's shoulder and her chest. She hit as hard as she could with her limited momentum. The strike made her sore hand throb with pain, and Noreen still held the gun.

And then somehow Noreen's free hand was in her hair, yanking on it hard. She wrenched Evelyn's head sideways, smacking it into the ladder.

She was pretty sure she was screaming as she hit back, although she couldn't hear it, couldn't hear anything over the ringing in her ears from the gun going off. She punched up and out, striking Noreen under the chin, the handcuffs attached to her wrist whipping up and slapping Noreen in the throat.

Noreen's head snapped back, but she still had a tight grip on Evelyn's hair. She yanked Evelyn toward her, pulling Evelyn off balance until she pitched into Noreen, her feet twisting under her.

She still had Noreen's right elbow gripped in her left hand, forcing the gun to point out and away from her. But her hold started to slip as she threw her hand out to stop herself from falling.

Noreen took a step backward, bumping the other dirt wall behind her, and Evelyn went with her.

She managed to get her feet under her as a shower of dirt fell on her head, getting into her eyes and mouth. Sputtering, she grappled for a better hold on Noreen's elbow as Noreen wrenched it straight out, away from her.

For a quiet, dowdy administrative assistant, Noreen was surprisingly strong.

Evelyn whirled around, trying to grab Noreen's arm again with both hands, to keep the gun pointed away from her. As she turned, Noreen shoved against her chest, hard enough to make her fall backward.

Her head slammed the low ceiling at the edge of the

tunnel. She bounced off it, stumbling forward as Noreen's gun swung around.

Shooting her hand out fast, Evelyn slapped the gun away from her.

It went off again, and this time, the bullet hit the low ceiling right beside Evelyn's head. Another huge chunk of dirt broke off and fell between them, and then something hit the back of Evelyn's legs, bringing her to her knees.

As she crashed to the ground, the ceiling caved in. Dirt dropped on top of her, completely flattening her, and knocked all the air from her lungs.

Evelyn flailed her hands, trying to push the dirt off her, trying to catch her breath, but the weight on top of her was too much. The entire cellar had collapsed. And she couldn't move.

She gasped for air and inhaled dirt. Her body went into spasms, and she coughed, her lungs trying to suck in more air.

Desperately, she pressed her arms into the ground, trying to thrust herself up. But nothing happened.

Pain and panic burst inside her as her lungs kept instinctively gasping for air, choking her. They started to burn and spots formed in front of her closed eyes. She was going to suffocate here.

Noreen's father had killed Cassie. And Noreen had just killed her.

Twenty-Seven

"I've got Frank Abbott in cuffs," Kyle was telling Greg as a gunshot split the air. The sound was muffled, but he shot hundreds of rounds each week at practice, wearing ear protection. He'd recognize it anywhere.

"Hurry," he told Greg, then began to run. "Don't move," he yelled back at Frank.

The shot had come from somewhere behind the house, but as Kyle rounded the side wall and passed the barn, all he saw was a wide, empty field, with waist-high grass. A field way too similar to the one at the end of the road where Lauren was found.

He swung his flashlight across the field, searching for any sign of life, but didn't see a damn thing. "Evelyn!" he yelled, but the only response was an owl hooting back at him.

"Damn it." The moon was just a sliver, providing almost no light, and fog was still lifting off the ground, reducing visibility even more. The field stretched a long way, but the sound could have come from a distant house. Or from underground—although firing a gun inside a cellar like the one he'd seen at the crime scene would be incredibly stupid.

Kyle stepped farther into the field, shining his flashlight from left to right. But he still saw nothing.

Then a second gunshot went off, and a plume of dust rose from the ground directly ahead of him, maybe two hundred feet away.

Kyle started running. When he was still a hundred feet from the spot, someone seemed to materialize out of the tall grasses and took off across the field.

Kyle couldn't tell for sure who it was, but he knew it wasn't Evelyn, so he didn't change direction. Putting on another burst of speed, he ran full out for the settling cloud of dirt.

When he finally got there, he fell to his knees.

There was a hole in the ground going down maybe six feet, a busted metal ladder dangling from one side into the hole. At the bottom, dirt was piled up, filling most of what must once have been the entrance.

He shone the flashlight into the tiny hole between the tunnel and the main cavern. Another cellar. "Evelyn!"

No one answered, and Kyle couldn't see anything inside. It was impossible to tell from this angle if the whole cellar had collapsed, or only the entrance.

So he dropped to his stomach, leaning over the hole, and frantically scooped up dirt with his hands and tossed it out of the tunnel. If Evelyn was trapped under the dirt, every second counted.

He worked toward the cavern, widening the tiny hole, assuming that if Evelyn was down there, she'd be in the back. As the space grew wider and Kyle aimed the flashlight inside, he spotted a bound, motionless figure way in the back. But it wasn't Evelyn.

"Shit!" Kyle scooped the dirt directly below, throwing handfuls of it behind him.

He wanted to jump into the narrow space beside the ladder, but he was too afraid of landing on her if she *was* there, under the dirt piled at the junction between the tunnel and the cavern. So he just kept leaning farther and farther in, scooping out as much dirt as he could.

His heart thudded at an unnatural tempo as he prayed that if she was down there she had a pocket of air. Because if she didn't, too much time had probably passed.

He worked faster, dangling halfway into the tunnel as he scooped, raising his torso as he threw aside handfuls of dirt. More and more dirt, until he was covered in it and the tunnel was half-empty.

And then, suddenly, something moved in the earth below him.

Instead of gathering up any more dirt, Kyle grabbed the sides of the tunnel and pushed himself backward. Then he flipped around and lowered himself carefully into the tunnel, staying as close to the ladder as possible.

When he reached the bottom, his feet braced at the very edges, he shoveled dirt off to the smaller part of the tunnel until he saw skin. Shoving his hand back into the dirt, he took hold of the exposed arm and pulled.

Evelyn slid forward an inch and then she flailed her arm, and her head popped out of the dirt.

Relief rushed over him as she gasped in huge breaths of air, then coughed, spitting dirt on him.

He heard someone repeating, "Thank God," over and over and realized it was him as he skimmed his hands down her back, pushing more dirt off her so she could wriggle free. Then he dragged her up and crushed her in his arms as she continued wheezing in air.

"Jack," she finally croaked.

"The cellar didn't collapse on him," Kyle told her. "I'll lift you out and then I'll get him."

"Not…sure…he's…alive," Evelyn managed.

Kyle nodded grimly, loosening his grip so he could look at her. She was so covered in dirt and mud that her features were pretty much indistinct except the whites of her eyes and her mouth.

"Nor…" Evelyn tried, choking again.

"I know it's Noreen," Kyle said. "Frank Abbott is cuffed out front. Backup is on the way. You ready?"

"Yes," she managed.

He tucked her SIG in her filthy holster, then hoisted her up and out of the tunnel.

After that, he turned back and focused on the opening into the cellar's cavern again. The collapse seemed to have been centered over Evelyn, so it took less time than he expected to clear a hole he could climb through.

As he pushed his way into the back of the tunnel, leading by feel since he'd left his flashlight outside, he heard a low moan. "Jack? It's Kyle McKenzie. I'm getting you out of here, man. Just relax."

Finally he found Jack. His hands were cuffed in front of him and he was bleeding, but he was alive. Kyle hooked an arm over Jack's chest, under his armpits, and hauled him backward through the cellar cavern, back to the tunnel.

Jack was a lot heavier than Evelyn, so it was awkward to lift him up until he could gain purchase on the ground outside the tunnel. Evelyn grabbed him from the top and Kyle pushed him out, then pulled himself up and out of the tunnel.

His discarded flashlight shone an eerie circle of light

over the top of the cellar, illuminating the pile of dirt he'd thrown out and a brand-new wood door pushed open. Evelyn sat on the ground beside Jack, looking dazed but breathing normally.

Kyle picked up the flashlight and directed it at Jack. He had a nasty gash on his head, but it looked like it had stopped bleeding. Otherwise, he didn't seem to be in bad shape.

Jack looked up at Kyle. "Noreen Abbott. Did she get away?"

Evelyn turned to him.

Kyle pointed the flashlight to his right, off into the distance. "She ran that way."

"Back to my land? Or next door, to her dad's old place?" Jack asked, closing his eyes. "I can't believe it was her. I can't believe it was Noreen. She was the one who took my pin. I realized after she lured me down there, right before she cold-cocked me. It all came together, but too late to do anything."

He opened his eyes again, looking at Evelyn. "I owe you an apology. I never thought Noreen..." He sighed heavily, putting a hand to his head. "And I didn't trust your judgment on this case, because of your history, and..."

Evelyn nodded, reaching out briefly to squeeze his hand. "What matters is that it ends here. That we get her."

"Still," Jack insisted. "I want you to know that I was wrong. Now, and eighteen years ago. I shouldn't have pushed so hard. It was never about you. I just wanted to solve it, to end the case my dad never could. It haunted him until he died."

"Thanks, Jack. I'm sorry, too." She got shakily to her feet as the sound of police sirens got louder. The dazed expression faded behind the serious profiler face he knew so well. "It's all fallen apart for Noreen. First, her plan to take over where her father left off, because she ran into the same problem he did. She just couldn't replace Peggy. Then her whole murder-suicide setup to get away with it. Now, reality is staring back at her and she can't accept it. She's probably decompensating."

"What does that mean?" Jack asked, just sounding weary. And betrayed.

From the other side of the house, the police sirens got louder and then stopped. Backup had arrived.

Evelyn's hand slid to her holster, where her SIG now rested again. "It means she's deteriorating mentally. It means the idea of getting caught is now a real possibility, so she's destabilizing. It's the most dangerous time when you're dealing with this kind of personality—both for her and for us."

Jack glanced around. "How?"

"We know who she is. Which means she's out of options. And she'll make mistakes. But she's also more likely to take desperate actions." Evelyn gestured to the cellar. "Like try to kill a cop and a federal agent. Or herself."

"Well, how does that help us? She took off."

Evelyn nodded, but she wasn't even looking at Jack anymore. She seemed to be talking to herself. "Yes, but we know where. She'll go back to the place she feels safest, happiest."

"Next door?" Kyle asked. "Where she grew up?"

Evelyn shook her head, looking up at him, a glint in her eyes Kyle didn't like. "Back to the original cellar."

Before he could tell her to wait for backup, she clamped her jaw and took off running for the Bullock land.

"Evelyn, wait!" Kyle called after her, but of course, she didn't.

"Damn it." Backup hadn't rounded the house yet. "Wait for the cops," he told Jack. "Tell them to get Frank into custody, then meet us at the cellar."

Without waiting for a reply, Kyle raced after Evelyn.

"Don't try to stop me," Evelyn warned as Kyle caught up to her.

She didn't slow down, as he'd probably hoped. Instead, the light from his flashlight let her move faster through the wide, open field. She should've been tired and sore from being flattened by three feet of dirt. Instead, all she could feel was a burning anger that propelled her forward.

She didn't see Noreen anywhere, but there was only one place she'd go.

"You know where she's headed," Kyle said. "We could join the cops in front of Frank's house and drive over."

"And tip her off? No way."

"Evelyn." Kyle grabbed her arm, pulled her to a stop.

She tried to yank free. "I'm not letting her get away!"

"Of course not. Let's do this rationally, okay?"

There was concern in his eyes. It didn't make any difference. She yanked her arm hard enough that Kyle would have to release her or risk hurting her. She knew he'd drop her arm. And he did.

"Don't you dare try to stop me."

Not giving him a chance to respond, she took off again, running as fast as she could. She heard him curse behind her as she ran, straining to see.

She passed Earl Abbott's house, slowing only slightly. That wasn't where Noreen felt safest. She liked to be underground. Up ahead, Evelyn finally spotted the portable lights from the crime scene.

The whole field had a haze of fog over it, obscuring her view, but she didn't see Noreen anywhere. Was she wrong? Had Noreen picked her father's old house instead? Or did she have a backup plan? Did she think she'd still somehow get away with it? That she could skip town and start up again somewhere else?

All of Evelyn's profiling instincts told her that Noreen would be at the original cellar, where this had all started for her. But her profiling instincts had been wrong too many times in this investigation.

Panic mingled with her anger, and she increased her pace until her feet felt as if they were barely touching the ground. She sensed Kyle beside her, even though her vision seemed to have shrunk to the yellow crime scene tape fluttering in the breeze.

As she finally reached it, Evelyn stopped, and her gaze followed the arc of Kyle's flashlight as he did a sweep.

She glanced at him, then nodded toward the open cellar entrance and pulled her SIG from its holster.

"I'll go in," Kyle whispered.

She shook her head and stepped closer, careful not to get too close as Kyle angled the flashlight down into the tunnel. She saw nothing, but if Noreen was down there, she'd be in the cavern, by the back. Where the girls she and her father abducted had been trapped.

"Cover me," she whispered to Kyle, but she kept her weapon in hand as she moved slowly closer.

She didn't know if Noreen had lost her gun when the cellar collapsed or if she'd managed to hold on to it. And she hadn't forgotten Noreen's words before—that if it hadn't been for the car window between Evelyn and Noreen's bullet, she would have hit her.

"I'm going in," Evelyn said in a low voice. There was no movement from below, no sound. But she was suddenly overcome with certainty that Noreen was below her.

She didn't have her flashlight, so she held her hand out for Kyle's, without looking back, and he silently handed it over. Pointing it into the tunnel, Evelyn stepped slowly closer, ducking her head to see as far into the cavern as she could. Nothing.

Which meant there was no choice but to go in.

She took a breath and turned around, crouching so she could lower herself down the ladder. Before she could climb in, something—someone—flew toward her.

Evelyn whipped her flashlight up, but had hardly focused on the figure leaping at her before Kyle slammed into him from the side.

The two of them landed hard as Evelyn scrambled to her feet. She lifted her weapon alongside the flashlight, but Kyle had Frank flattened beneath him.

"How the hell…"

Then she sensed movement behind her and whirled around, aiming the flashlight and the gun into the cellar, just as a figure darted back into the cavern. Her heart rate jumped. She'd been right. Noreen was down there.

"You have Frank?" Evelyn asked without turning.

"Yeah." Kyle sounded pissed. "He should already have been in custody. He's still cuffed."

"Leave her alone!" Frank barked.

Evelyn spun back, raising her weapon. "You know what she did!"

"Don't hurt her," Frank begged. "Earl made her like this. Please. She's a victim, too."

Evelyn ground her teeth and lowered her gun, turning back to the cellar and once more pointing the flashlight down. "I'm going in," she told Kyle.

"Cuff her and bring her back up," Kyle said, his tone implying that he thought she'd take another action.

"Cover Frank," she responded, and put her foot on the ladder facing into the cellar instead of toward the wall. It was awkward, but safer.

Her heartbeat drumming in her ears and Cassie's image in her mind, Evelyn reached the bottom. The same claustrophobia she'd felt the first time she'd come down here, the same panicky trapped feeling, settled inside her. The smell of dirt, mold and death filled her nose, even though she knew the last one was just in her head.

Gripping her gun too tightly, she crouched low and stepped into the cavern.

In the corner, hunched beside the child's bed where Cassie had probably once slept, was Noreen. She had her knees drawn up to her chest, her arms wrapped tightly around them. She was filthy, streaked with almost as much dirt as Evelyn. But clean tracks ran down her cheeks. She'd been crying.

She looked up as Evelyn entered, her eyes brimming with tears. "I begged him so much to let me keep Cassie," she cried. "She was the right one. My dad didn't see it, but I knew. *Cassie* was meant to be my sister. And I tried so hard to find one just like her, but I couldn't do it."

"Keep your mouth shut," Evelyn croaked. "Put your hands over your head and stand up slowly."

Noreen didn't move, but she blinked back the tears, her gaze seeking Evelyn's, pleading. "If only he hadn't gotten sick… He told me about you, how you and Cassie were like sisters. That's what I wanted."

"Get. Up." Evelyn's hands clutched her weapon so tightly they hurt.

"I just want you to understand," Noreen whispered.

Evelyn willed herself to relax, but her arms started to shake with anger, and she couldn't keep the words inside. "You let her die! You let Cassie *die*!" She choked on the last word and felt her own eyes well with tears.

Noreen shook her head. "I didn't want him to do it. But I was six. I couldn't stop him. He took her down into that cellar and…"

Evelyn's ears started ringing and her vision seemed to dim, Noreen's words fading out. Some part of her had hoped, prayed, that there was still a chance. But Cassie really was gone. And Noreen had *known*.

Evelyn's breath came way too fast as she centered her SIG on Noreen's forehead. A memory of the very first time she'd seen Cassie ran through her mind. Cassie had come to the door and asked if Evelyn wanted to play. She'd said they were going to be best friends. And they were.

Noreen and her father had stolen that from her. They'd stolen Cassie and they'd stolen any chance Evelyn had of a normal life.

The gun shook in her hands, her finger tense as it slipped inside the trigger guard.

"Evelyn." Kyle's calm voice penetrated the fury fueling her. "I have extra cuffs."

Hers were dangling from her wrist. Not that she was sure she needed them. Maybe Noreen still had her weapon. Something inside her wished Noreen would pull it now, to give Evelyn a defensible reason to fire hers.

She'd seen horrible, horrible things as a profiler. Never in her life had she actually wanted to shoot anyone.

"Bring her up," Kyle called, his voice so calm, even though he had to know what was running through her head. "Let's get her into custody. Give Cassie the justice she deserves. Do it the right way."

Evelyn loosened her painful grip on the weapon, moved her finger outside the trigger guard where it belonged.

She wanted to shoot so desperately that it scared her. She'd never been that person. She didn't want to become that person. Not even to avenge Cassie.

A sob escaped and she swallowed, tried to rein in her emotions. "Go up now, Noreen."

"Just do it," Noreen whispered back. "I'd rather die down here like my sisters. This is where I belong."

"Walk out of here yourself," Evelyn ordered, "or I'll knock you out and bring you up. Your choice."

For a minute, Noreen looked as though she were going to resist, but then defeat settled over her features. She stood slowly and climbed out of the cellar.

A moment later, Kyle called down, "She's unarmed. And cuffed."

Evelyn looked around the cellar one last time, feeling a deep sadness she wasn't sure would ever leave. Then she holstered her SIG and started climbing up.

Noreen was kneeling on the ground beside her uncle, both of them cuffed. On the road that dead-ended at the field, police cars approached, sirens wailing. Kyle held out his hand.

Evelyn turned and stared into the depths of the cellar,

then raised her head and put her hand in Kyle's, holding on tight.

She'd found the truth she'd searched for, for eighteen years. Now she just had to find a way to live with it.

Epilogue

"You can do this."

Evelyn looked at Kyle as her rental car idled in the Byerses' driveway. She'd been watching the house for five minutes, trying to work up the courage to go inside.

Last night, after Noreen and Frank had been booked down at the station, and Jack was stitched up at the hospital, Evelyn had returned to the hotel with Kyle. She'd awakened to the sound of her cell phone. The forensic anthropologist had conclusively identified the skeletons from the field. They were the three original Nursery Rhyme Killer victims.

Cassie's parents had already gotten the news, but Evelyn couldn't leave town without talking to them personally.

Kyle's fingers wove through hers. "You gave them the closure they needed, Evelyn."

She nodded and turned off the engine. "Yeah, I just wanted to have different news." It was ridiculous, because Cassie had died when she was twelve years old, but some irrational part of her felt as if it was her fault for not being able to give the case a different ending.

"You want me to wait here?" Kyle asked, obviously expecting her to say yes.

She shook her head. "Come with me?"

"Of course."

He stepped out of the car and walked beside her up to the big wraparound porch, so much like her grandparents'. So much like the porch on the house she'd bought in Virginia, because it had reminded her of the good days here.

This wasn't the outcome she'd hoped for when she'd flown out here five days ago, but despite everything, there was a sense of peace inside her that she hadn't felt in a long, long time.

Evelyn reached for the bell, but Julie Byers opened the door before she rang it. Evelyn didn't say a word before Julie stepped forward and wrapped her in a hug.

The arms around her felt stronger today than they had a few days ago. "Thank you, Evelyn," Julie whispered. "Thank you for bringing her home."

When she stepped back, there were tears in her eyes, and Evelyn could tell she'd cried this morning when she'd gotten the news. But there was something else on Julie's face, too.

It took Evelyn a minute to figure out what was different and then she realized. The lines of strain that had dominated Julie's face the last time she'd seen her had eased.

Evelyn gestured to Kyle. "This is Kyle McKenzie. He works with me."

"I remember." She took Evelyn's hand and pulled her into the house. "Come in." She nodded at Kyle, who followed silently.

Julie led them into the living room Evelyn remembered from her childhood. It had new furniture, but the big bay window at the back was exactly the same. Evelyn could picture Cassie sitting there, smiling.

Cassie's father sat in a chair in the corner. He seemed as frail as he had when Evelyn had seen him earlier and she felt her heart seize, knowing how much hope he'd pinned on finding his daughter alive.

He held out his hand and Evelyn came closer, Julie still clutching her other hand. "Thank you," he croaked. Unshed tears hazed his eyes as he looked up at her. "The coroner told us she didn't suffer."

Evelyn gave him a trembling smile and nodded. There was no way to truly know that, but they'd been able to determine she'd died not long after she'd been abducted. Noreen had patterned her actions after her father's, so chances were Cassie hadn't been harmed until then, and she hadn't rotted away in the cellar, hungry and alone.

They didn't know for sure how Earl had killed his victims, and the skeletons only told so much. Noreen didn't know, either, just that her father had taken them away when he decided they weren't "right," didn't fit the mold of his dead daughter.

But Evelyn did know one thing for certain.

"She was brave," Evelyn told them, remembering what Noreen had said about Cassie refusing to pretend to be someone else. "She never gave up. And she never gave in."

Her own tears slipped free as she added, "I'm so proud to have called her my best friend. She's one of the best people I ever knew."

Cassie's parents smiled back at her, real smiles, and Evelyn knew they were going to be okay.

"We're going to get her a stone tomorrow," Julie said.

"It will be good to have her close to us, where we can go and talk to her."

Cassie's dad squeezed her hand, tighter than she'd thought he could. "I hope you'll come back and visit us sometime, Evelyn."

She nodded. She'd thought this would be her last visit to Rose Bay, but suddenly she realized that she wanted to return some day. To see Cassie's parents again. To see Cassie's gravestone, the rightful tribute to her life. It might have been short, but it had been special.

As she and Kyle went back to the car a few minutes later, Evelyn asked, "Do we have time to go to the beach before our flight? I want to show you something."

He lifted her hand to his lips and grinned. "If we miss it, I'll commandeer something and fly you home myself."

"Good." She didn't actually think he could do that, but with Kyle, who knew?

As she drove toward the beach where Darnell had caught up to her days ago, Evelyn considered how much the town had changed since she'd arrived. Noreen and Frank were in custody. Frank probably wasn't looking at much time, but Noreen would never get out.

Neither would Darnell Conway. The murder charge alone would put him away for good, but cops were already looking through his computer history and putting together additional charges. Because of his confession about Charlotte, Kiki was doing everything she could to help. Evelyn hoped Walter Wiggins would be joining him in prison soon. Evelyn had talked to Jack at the hospital and he'd denied having anything to do with the pictures in Wiggins's house. She still had some niggling doubt there, but not about the likelihood that Wiggins was a potential reoffender. Tomas had put officers on him around-the-clock, determined to make sure he never got near another child.

Rose Bay had a lot of healing to do, but people here were finally getting the chance to move on. And the same was true for her.

Evelyn parked and led Kyle down the long path to the beach. Then she clambered over the outcropping of rocks that took them to the spot Cassie's mom had shown her and Cassie eighteen years ago. Kyle followed without question, and minutes later they were alone on the small stretch of beach.

The dunes lay behind them, the pristine white sand sparkling in the sun. In front of them, the ocean lapped at the shore, the color of the water almost the same shade as Kyle's eyes.

Evelyn slipped off her shoes, felt the sand between her toes as she took Kyle's hand and stared out at the expanse of the ocean. "This was our spot. Cassie and I thought this was our own private island."

She closed her eyes and breathed in the salty ocean air, throwing her head back to feel the breeze across her face.

She had no idea what was waiting for her back in Aquia. Her place with BAU was in trouble. She'd have to fight like hell if she wanted to keep it. But more than that, her whole life's mission—to find out what'd happened to Cassie—had concluded.

Evelyn couldn't remember the last time she'd thought about what she wanted and it didn't have anything to do with Cassie. But now the whole world had opened up to her in a different way, possibilities she'd never allowed herself to even contemplate. She was going to be able to figure out what it was *she* wanted.

In some ways, that was terrifying. In some ways, she

wasn't sure *what* she wanted. But in others, it was suddenly very, very simple.

Evelyn opened her eyes and looked at Kyle, waiting patiently beside her, and suddenly all the reasons she'd had to resist dating someone in the Bureau seemed unimportant. "What is it you always say about having no censures in your personnel file?"

He grinned at her, showing the dimples that made her heart flutter like a teenager's. "If you don't have any, it means you're either an ass-kisser or just sitting on your ass."

He tugged on her hand, pulling her into the edge of the water. "So don't worry about the procedural stuff. You're too good. Dan's not going to let you go."

She grinned back at him, a lightness in her heart she couldn't remember feeling since she was twelve years old. "Good. Now what was it you said about taking some time off?" He'd been joking about going away somewhere, but she knew that underneath the joke was hope. "Can you still get the time?"

Surprise widened his eyes, but he nodded. "Hell, yes."

"Good." She yanked the hand still wrapped around hers, diving into the water, drawing him with her, heedless of ruining their clothes or what they'd wear on the plane. It was time she started living her life.

She was pretty sure Cassie would have approved.

* * * * *

Acknowledgments

I'd like to give my sincere thanks to the people who shared their knowledge, including the Special Agents at the FBI Academy at Quantico, and from the Washington Field Office. I'd also like to offer a special thank-you to Ian Anderson and Chris Kobet for helping me figure out key details and always answering my tough questions. Any mistakes or liberties are mine alone.

Thank you to my critique partner, Robbie Terman, who is always willing to brainstorm, critique or just talk me off ledges. And to my mom, Chris Heiter, who reads every book, in every short time frame I request. Thank you to my Aunt Andy Hammond and my Uncle Tom Dunikowski, for giving me feedback and for being so excited about each novel—hearing from you always makes me want to write more. Thank you to my sisters, Kathryn Merhar and Caroline Heiter, for your support and love through the nerve-wracking process of seeing my first book out in the wild. Thank you to my friends Charlie Schaldenbrand and Kristen Kobet, for wanting the next book before I've even written it. To Mark Nalbach, for making my video trailer, fixing my website and jumping in whenever I have graphics needs—thank you for making it all look so good. And to my mystery writers' group: Ann Forsaith, Charles Shipps, Sasha Orr and Nora Smith—thank you for pushing me to make every scene better.

Thank you to my agent, Kevan Lyon, for believing in me for so long, and for your unwavering support through every step of the process. Thank you to my editor, Paula Eykelhof—I don't know how I got so lucky, but I do know that working with you has impacted my writing and my life in huge, incredible ways. And to the entire team at Harlequin—thank you for all your hard work on my novels, from cover to marketing to sales and everything in between.

Finally, a huge thank-you to my family and friends, for the love, support and encouragement you've given me over the years.